DREAM WALKER

EPISODE 1 OF THE WALKER SAGA

SHANNAN SINCLAIR

For Dream Walkers everywhere

ONE

SHE KNEW before she opened her eyes. Something was different. The faintest hum of static electricity tickled across the hairs on her arms as if there were a breeze. But there wasn't any breeze. The windless air was leaden, pressing heavily upon her. She began to feel claustrophobic and opened her eyes.

Rusty dirt. Gray shrub. An infinite landscape, the same in every direction. She turned a full circle—nothing broke the monotony. She scanned for the skyline of a city, the outcropping of an oasis—anything by which she could orient herself. Nothing. Not even one anemic shrub was taller, wider, or of a different shape than any other.

The sky shared the same palette as the earth—ochre, sulfur, smoke. It looked acrid, poisonous. She inhaled hesitantly, but found that the air was crisp and tasted sweet.

Where am I?

With that thought came another; not only did she not know where she was, but she also didn't know where she came from or where she should be. Panicking, she rummaged through her mind, closing her eyes and squeezing her head in her hands, hoping to wring just one memory from it to pin herself to reality. Thinking, thinking—but the topography of her brain was as desolate as the landscape she stood in.

A slight trembling tickled across the soles of her feet. The ground beneath her was moving. The vibrations grew into a rumbling that worked its way through her body and into the marrow of her bones. The surrounding atmosphere morphed; the sky warped like the heat of a mirage.

The space around her began to spin, and she found herself in the center of a centrifuge. Particles came together, then pulled apart, dancing wildly in waves of energy.

The earthquake intensified, shuddering and roaring. The earth belched open and one edifice after another birthed itself into reality. Structures manifested across the open plain in short, quick bursts, like popcorn in a Pop-O-Matic. There was a loud crack, and she no longer stood in an empty red desert but in the decrepit ruins of a city—or what was once a city—a city after a cataclysmic end.

She stood, stunned, in the middle of the empty street, feeling more alone here than she had in the previous forsaken landscape. Although she could orient herself, she was immobilized by fear, confused by the sudden eruption of this new world.

She picked a direction—moving anywhere was better than lingering nowhere—and began to walk.

A thick layer of ash encrusted everything, giving way beneath her, her feet sinking into the soft silt beneath. She made her way down the lonely street, leaving a trail of imprints in the gray snow that would never melt.

Skeletons of skyscrapers towered above her, their cement melted and peeling like charred skin. Their twisted metal bones protruded at odd angles against the backdrop of a sky that still sizzled. Burnt carcasses of parked cars lined the street, neat and aligned. As she passed them, she noticed a dark silhouette skipping from shard to shard across the smoke-stained and spider-webbed windows. She moved toward it and gazed at a reflection that could only be her own.

She had auburn hair that was pulled back into a slick ponytail. Her skin was pale, naturally so, not because of the petrification that ran rampant within her. Her nose was sprinkled with faded flecks of cinnamon, remnants of a sun-dappled youth. Yes, she was remembering now.

"Aislen," she sighed with relief. And she hated those freckles.

She settled into the small comfort of finally remembering her name. It could keep her from slipping into the madness. She repeated her name over and over, fixing on the image of herself in the glass. She wore no makeup, her face fresh and bright. Her lips were lush and perfectly defined.

"My name is Aislen Walker." Another wave of relief washed through her as she pulled the nugget of her last name out of the blank recesses of her memory.

She leaned closer to her reflection, hoping it would tell her more. There was an indent in the center of her chin. It was so slight and shallow; she did not recognize it as a part of her own face. Another memory blossomed, of someone placing their finger into that shallow groove and gently caressing her chin.

"I love your little butt-chin, Buttercup."

She caught her breath. It was a voice that wasn't her own—a male voice. Her heart stuttered, and her limbs went weak from an overwhelming grief that flooded her veins.

Who was that? Whose voice did I hear?

She racked her brain, but could not recall a face that went with the voice. She tried repeating it.

"I love your little butt-chin, Buttercup."

But the memory was already gone, reabsorbed into the abyss of amnesia as quickly as it had come.

What was going on?

She heard footsteps fast approaching from around one of the many street corners. The crunch of feet in the crusty ash echoed off the walls, through shattered glass, into the empty shells of buildings, and back out into the street. It sounded as if there was more than one pair of them.

Fully alert, Aislen hid. There was no telling what was walking around here, and she definitely knew she didn't want to be found. She moved behind the flattened tire of the remains of a car and peeked up through the windshield.

Two figures came stomping around a corner. Thunderheads of fine dust exploded at their feet and columned up around their legs. They marched with the confidence that they were alone, acting like they owned the place. Two more massive figures followed close behind the first pair, but there was something flat and robotic about them, and despite their enormity, their footfall made no sound. No clouds of ash billowed at their feet.

The soldiers moved with an air of absolute authority, their boots crunching through the ashen streets. Aislen shrank behind the rusted-out car, barely daring to breathe.

She stole a glance at them. Military. That much was obvious. The pixelated pattern of their uniforms—slate, desert, and drab green—was unmistakable. But something about the fabric was *wrong*.

The material seemed to shift in the dim light, tiny mirrored squares glinting like fractured glass. Aislen frowned. Was the uniform... moving? No, not moving—*pulsing*. Electricity flickered through the pixels, an eerie shimmer running over their bodies like ripples in water.

She swallowed hard, shifting her focus. Each soldier had a patch on their shoulder, but instead of an embroidered insignia, there was a screen—a tiny, flickering television.

A swirling spiral of color radiated outward from the center in a wave—up, then down to the left, then up and down to the right. The pattern looped again and again before forming a glowing infinity symbol. Gold and hypnotic. Aislen couldn't tear her eyes away.

What kind of military used living uniforms?

A sharp movement yanked her attention upward. Their faces were hidden. The visors they wore reflected nothing but the fiery sky above, erasing their eyes, their expressions. Only the tight, emotionless set of their mouths remained visible. The only sign they were even human.

Aislen's stomach twisted. They carried weapons. Big, sleek, unfamiliar. Unlike any gun she had ever seen before.

Her breath hitched as the leader stopped. He turned his head—just slightly.

He was looking for something.

No. He was looking for someone.

And Aislen had left tracks.

The man who led the way raised his fist in a motion that halted the group's forward march. He was tall, and Aislen could see the etching of muscle definition bulging through the busy array of his coarse uniform.

The squad stopped, took a defensive posture, and scoped out the area carefully.

The leader moved forward, crouching down to investigate the tracks Aislen had left in her wake. He rose, flipped up his visor, and followed the trail with his eyes as it led straight for the car she was trying to hide behind.

He's going to find me! The thought screamed in her head.

She shushed it, held her breath, and lowered herself further from the leader's line of sight, hoping he would move on. Wishful thinking. The leader immediately started walking toward the car—toward *her!*

A sound interrupted him, and he turned toward it. Another figure was approaching quickly from the opposite end of the street. The leader flipped his visor back down, raised his weapon, and took aim. The other three soldiers scuttled into formation beside him, dropped to their knees, and aimed their sights as if ready for a showdown.

Aislen dared not turn her head for fear the motion would alert the group back toward her presence. She kept her eyes fixed upon the foursome.

The lone person continued to advance toward the squad. Aislen could see the newcomer at the periphery of her vision. If the others moved like predators, this one moved like an intruder —confident, but out of place.

He was wearing the same type of uniform; the helmet, vest, visor, and weapon looked exactly like the other four, but there was no animated patch on his shoulder. He had no patch at all.

He ignored the threatening stance of the group and the imposing presence of their leader and marched directly up to the soldier standing off to the right. Aislen noticed that this soldier was smaller than the others. He lacked the muscular build of the other three and appeared frail and slight.

"Blake!" The newcomer's shout made Aislen jump. It had the same effect on the small soldier. "You have been forbidden to come here!"

Blake lowered his weapon and looked as if he were about to stammer something when his leader interrupted.

"Blake. Carry on," the leader commanded in calm monotone.

The newcomer turned toward the leader. "I don't know who you think you are to assume you have more power over Blake than I do. You have some fucking nerve! I demand that you let him leave here with me and never contact him again."

"That isn't going to happen," the leader replied in a steely tone.

"Then I will be forced to report you to the authorities!"

The firm line of the leader's mouth turned up ever so slightly. "Blake. Carry on." His voice was firmer, but still unemotional.

The small soldier named Blake pulled a handgun from out of a vest holster, raised it at the newcomer in front of him, and aimed it square between the lone soldier's eyes. There wasn't a hint of a tremor in his hand.

"Blake," the solo soldier shouted again, this time with a bit of hysteria. "I demand that you put that gun down right now!"

But Blake did not lower his weapon, and his aim did not waver. The leader looked back at the newcomer, his smirk now more a snarl. Then he turned back to Blake.

"Blake. Kill."

And with that, a single gunshot ripped through the city and into the soldier's head. His body enfolded upon itself like an accordion, dissolving from the uniform, evaporating into thin air, before it even hit the ground.

Blake lowered his weapon and looked up at the leader.

"At ease," the leader said as he kicked the lump of uniform at his feet. "He definitely won't be a problem anymore."

He turned back to Blake. "Now you."

Without hesitation, Blake turned his weapon around and placed the muzzle into his mouth.

An involuntary gasp escaped from Aislen.

The whole group jerked their heads her direction. The

leader strode toward the car she was hiding behind; the two lumbering soldiers followed him. Instinct took over, and Aislen made a run for it. She lurched out from behind the car, but the thick ash encased her feet and she stumbled forward, falling face-first onto the charcoal crust.

It was too late. The leader was already upon her. He raised his rifle. The other two monster soldiers mimicked the leader's movement and raised theirs as well. She could never outrun them or their bullets.

"Get up," the soldier demanded.

Aislen, covered in soot, got to her knees and raised her arms in a gesture of surrender. She hoped he would see she was an unarmed, harmless woman and would spare her life.

"How did you get here?"

"I don't know," she whispered. "I don't know where I am."

The leader paused for a second, analyzing her, his rifle still on target for her brain. "Blake! Come here."

Blake shuffled over beside the leader, gun still in hand, but he seemed confused and lethargic now.

"Blake," the leader told him. "Carry on."

Blake raised his gun. The muzzle leveled at Aislen's head.

She held her breath, her heart hammering.

His stance was steady. His hands didn't shake. There was no hesitation in the way he pointed the weapon at her, just like there hadn't been when he shot the other man between the eyes.

Aislen swallowed hard. She could barely see his features behind the mirrored visor, just the faintest reflection of the burning sky. His body was leaner than the others, smaller, but the way he carried himself was all soldier. All machine.

Then—something shifted.

His grip faltered.

Something in the set of his shoulders... not quite grown.

Her mind snagged on the thought before she could shove it away.

Blake lowered the gun slightly, his breathing suddenly ragged, uneven.

The leader's voice cut through the moment like a knife.

"Blake. Carry on."

Blake tensed. His shoulders stiffened, his posture snapping back into place. He raised the gun again—this time with a flicker of hesitation.

Aislen could barely choke out a whisper. *Please, don't.*

Blake's breath hitched. His fingers trembled.

And then, slowly, he reached up and unlatched his visor.

The moment stretched into eternity as he pulled it away from his face.

Aislen's stomach dropped.

He wasn't a hardened killer. He wasn't a man.

He was a boy.

Maybe thirteen. Fourteen, at most.

His eyes were wide and unfocused, his expression blank with something that wasn't quite fear—but wasn't quite *anything*. His features were caught in that awkward stage between childhood and adulthood, his jaw too sharp for his round cheeks, his limbs too long for his frame.

A choked sound escaped him. He dropped the gun.

Then, in a single broken sob, he collapsed to his knees.

Aislen barely had time to process when the leader took off his visor and stormed toward the boy.

His voice, once cold and emotionless, dripped with pure fury.

"Blake! Attention!"

But the command elicited no response. Blake was done, slumped and broken, staring blankly down at the gray particles of ash. The leader grabbed the boy by the hair, pulled his head back, and looked into his eyes. The glassy, vacant orbs must have said it all. Blake was lost. The leader kicked the gun from Blake's hand, then turned to face Aislen.

Time stopped. With his visor removed, the intensity of the soldier's face blazed. His sculpted features looked as if they had been carved from marble reserved only for a mythological god. The glacier-blue of his eyes bored into hers, chilling her bones yet burning her with terror.

He took several deliberate steps toward Aislen, his eyes unwavering from hers. She could find no sign of warmth, but she felt held by them, cradled and calm. She was his prey, hypnotized and entirely at his mercy. He stopped in front of her, bringing the barrel of his weapon up underneath her chin, lifting it to get a better look at her face. He surveyed her for a moment, then cocked his head to the side.

"Do I know you?" His voice almost soothing despite his demeanor.

"No," Aislen managed to say.

"Good." He took a step backward and aimed the muzzle at the center of her forehead.

Aislen squeezed her eyes shut, bracing herself for the impact. A cracking sound split through her skull, jarring her brain, taking her breath away. A loud tinnitus burned her eardrums and reverberated throughout her body. She felt a chill wash over her flesh and then felt a breeze caress her skin.

She lay breathless. Was she crumpled up like an accordion now, too? No. She felt stretched out and flat on her back. She felt a lifting sensation, her body moving up, up, and further up like she was being raised into the sky. The piercing ringing in her ears faded away, replaced by a hushed, whirring sound.

Is this what it is like to die?

Pale light glimmered through her eyelids. Aislen took a

breath and opened her eyes to a blur of dark and gray, shades of amorphous shadow.

Where am I?

She blinked a few times and rolled her head to the side. Neon green blinded her; 3:33 read her clock.

Aislen was awake.

∞

ALL IN THE SAME MOMENT, Raze felt the hard resistance of the trigger fighting against his index finger, the hard tap of the hammer striking the firing pin, which made contact with the primer, and the sizzle of igniting gunpowder. He felt the click of the casing eject out the side port, and saw the fierce glister from the muzzle as the bullet made its escape. He watched the suspended spin of the slug as it traveled its perfect trajectory.

In that frozen second, he saw her face, covered in ash, streaked with the tracks of her tears, her eyes clenched in anticipation. He watched them open wide when she felt the searing heat of the approaching bullet; the intensity of their green, the sparks of gold alight within them, the calm, the acceptance, the complete tranquility, clear eyes that blazed right back at him.

All in one instant.

Time was irrelevant. Events could be experienced all at once, in an overlapping cacophony, or they could be separated, each aspect of an event removed like the yolk from an egg, then pulled apart like a fresh piece of taffy and slowed down, down, down, to be savored.

As the bullet made contact with the peach-down surface of her forehead, her lips parted to take one last breath and, just as it should have pierced through her skull and absorbed into her brain, she dissolved into a swarm of static.

Raze lowered his weapon.

What the fuck just happened?

He would have believed she was a figment of his imagination if she hadn't left evidence—the curves of her body imprinted in the ash. She had existed, and then she didn't—and that was utterly impossible.

The girl's disappearance created an electrical disruption, touching off a chain reaction in the fabric of Demesne. One after another, the buildings of the city, the cars, the streets, even the two holographic mercenaries that had filled out his squad of four, collapsed into pixelated bits and pieces.

Raze watched the pale of his construction evaporate into the ethers. Within seconds, *Demesne* was gone, and they were standing in the desolate desert of The Stratum.

Raze turned his attention to Blake, who sat slouched behind him, his eyes glazed over in a half-trance. Raze snapped his fingers in front of the little pawn's face. There was no light on.

That was just fucking great. They had completed only half the assignment, the assassination of Scott Parrish, but protocol had required that Blake eliminate himself, as well.

Raze considered his options. He couldn't kill Blake from this space and be assured that it was effective in 3D. With the schema of Demesne deconstructed, he didn't think he could initiate a command sequence that would reestablish enough control to get Blake to complete the assignment. That only left one choice.

Raze reached over, touched Blake in the center of his forehead with his index finger, and initiated the option-lock command.

"Two sticks and a bucket."

Blake's eyes rolled into the back of his head, and he deresonated out of The Stratum.

"That should buy me a little time," Raze said. Now he needed to get back to the Third and confirm that a matching body—the dead body—of Scott Parrish, existed there. He closed his eyes, "Theta 5."

The Womb, as he called his office, responded to his command and slowly began shifting its climate from Delta Phase into Theta.

In Delta, not even the tiniest bit of light illuminated the room. This enhanced his pineal gland's production of melatonin, serotonin, and DMT. The thermostat was set to correspond perfectly to his body's fluctuating thermal readings, confusing his skin's ability to differentiate between itself and its surroundings. A 40 hertz, white noise transmitted a psychoacoustic curve perfect for Raze's auditory perceptions—a sound that could not be named. It wasn't the waves, or the rain, or even the wind, but it caressed his second sense in such a way to be all those things and silence at the same time. Controlling the environmental settings allowed Raze to achieve and maintain the Optimum Octave of Operation: delta brain waves of 2 hertz and gamma brain waves of 70 hertz simultaneously.

As The Womb adjusted to Theta, light began to dawn, similar to the glow of a single candle, and the temperature of the room lowered by less than one degree. Raze slowly became aware of being back in the controlled confines of The Womb, reclining in his zero-gravity chaise. He began to feel the hum of blood flowing through his body.

"Alpha 8."

The Womb replied by increasing the lighting, shifting from white noise to soft jazz, and lowering the thermostat another degree.

Although a part of his brain was anxious to get right to Beta and try to figure out what the hell just happened in Demesne, Raze knew he couldn't just jump out of the chaise without reintegrating first. Plebes do that crap. Their alarm goes off every morning—they jump out of bed, shit, shower, shave and move right into the chaos of the highest Beta frequencies. And as a result, they lived their lives in complete oblivion.

Raze had to fight that aspect of his lower nature. Reintegration was important. It allowed him to pull his experiences in the higher octaves from the Delta and Gamma levels of his brain into his conscious Beta state. Cognizance and coherence were what separated the masters from the noobs.

"Alpha 14."

The chaise tilted forward into an upright position, the lighting dawned into 60-watt full spectrum, a fan circulated the air around him, and Drowning Pool's "Bodies" began blasting through the surround sound.

Raze was beyond vexed. What had just happened was all kinds of wrong—a violation of protocol, a breach of The Stratum, an invasion of Demesne, and the near failure of the Parrish Project.

Demesne was the section of The Stratum that *Raze* created and controlled. Right now, only two people besides Raze had access: Blake and Scott Parrish, courtesy of Raze's unique Surround Vision visors. Even members of the Infiniti 8 did not have access to Raze's section of The Stratum.

No one should have been able to enter Demesne. She didn't belong here. *And yet...*

That girl—whoever or whatever she was—not only got through The Stratum, but also into *his* area, a breach on two levels. Then she vanished before he could eliminate her from both worlds. Raze was not one to be trespassed against. He was the trespasser in this world—he and he alone.

In order to complete the Parrish Project, he was going to

have to report to The 8 and get their buy-in to take other measures. Then, he was going to hunt down that pretty little bitch and eliminate her for good.

Raze stood up from the chaise, straightened his tie, grabbed his suit jacket off the wall hook, and walked out the door.

"Off."

The Womb powered down.

TWO

911 HANG-UP: **508 Magnolia Ave. Male juvenile whispering 'Two sticks and a bucket' repeatedly before disconnecting. No answer on callback.**

Sergeant Mathis stared at the screen. *The fuck?*

Then the MDC's obnoxious ringy-dingy tune blasted through the cruiser, nearly making him spill his coffee. He hammered at the receive button, then pressed his thumb and forefinger into the inner corners of his eyes, breathing deep until his blood pressure settled. It was a pressure point technique he used frequently to keep himself from heaving the computer system into the street and running it over with his patrol car.

The IT department had tried to pick out a pleasant musical tone to alert officers when they were being dispatched to a call. Epic fail. Hearing the same obnoxious, ringy-dingy tune again and again, twelve hours a day, four days a week, was enough to make you want to stick your Glock in your ear and blow out your eardrums. It was fucking annoying.

Once he was sure he wouldn't physically abuse expensive

department equipment, Mathis checked his watch. 4 a.m. This was supposed to be naptime, not deal-with-fucking-bullshit time.

He reached for his Starbucks. Every Friday, he held briefing at the local 'Bucks, making the officer with the fewest arrests for the week pay for the watch's order. That officer only got a reprieve if another officer came in late for his shift. And *that* officer only got off if another officer had been a complete idiot in some way or another during the workweek.

They could all pretty much count on it always being F'in G's turn to buy. The rookie still hadn't figured out his way around the rodeo yet. If he wasn't running late, he was too busy correcting his crap-ass reports to make any arrests, or he was making some other bone-headed mistake.

Tonight's 'Bucks buy had been earned the night before when F'in G decided to key up the radio to inform everyone it had started raining in his part of town. Mathis had to school him on department policy regarding the frivolous use of the radio and remind him that he was a police officer, not the weatherman.

Mathis took a sip from his cup and sucked in a gelatinous film of caffeinated smegma. His Grande, Quad Shot, Non-fat, Caramel Macchiato was now an iced, Grande, Quad Shot, Non-fat, Caramel Macchiato with a head of slime. Spit or swallow were his only choices. With nowhere to spit, he forced it to the back of his throat and swallowed, praying he wouldn't upchuck.

Mathis gouged his fingers into his eye sockets again.

The dispatcher keyed up the radio, breaking what should have been the blessed silence of a seasonably slow winter morning.

"Mary 27, with Sam 21, respond to a 911 hang-up detail at 508 Magnolia. Line disconnected. No answer on callback."

She repeated the basics of what was already written in the call, except now she sounded pissed. Having to pick up her fat left toe and push down on the radio pedal must have been too much for the ol' gal because you could hear the I-already-lifted-my-index-finger-to-send-you-this-fucking-detail-and-now-you-are-making-me-break-from-eating-my-Hot-Pocket-to-talk-to-your-dumb-asses attitude in her tone of voice.

Fuckin' dispatchers.

Obviously, the watch didn't give a gnat's ass about a punk-ass kid prank-calling 911 at zero-dark-thirty in the morning to break from their Angry Birds game and dispatch themselves to the damn call. So, dispatch decided to send F'in G with a Sergeant for cover.

Not. Fucking. Cool.

Briefing topic for next week: dispatch yourself to the fucking call so your sergeant doesn't get sent with the rookie.

Mathis looked up the address on the MDC's mapping system. 508 Magnolia Avenue. Nice neighborhood. Tree-lined streets of old Modesto, classic homes occupied by doctors, lawyers, and business owners with spoiled, punk-ass kids who think they're cute calling the 5-0 at Zero Buttcrack Thirty in the morning.

Well, they were sure getting 'em now. The moment a Sam unit was dispatched as cover, the whole watch hopped to. Mathis watched as all the little po-po cars in the city blipped across the map toward Magnolia. Second briefing topic: every single officer in town does *not* have to respond to a prank call detail... depleting resources... blah, blah, blah.

Mathis shut the laptop screen. Its fluorescent glow was hurting his eyes. At 52, he was getting too fucking old for this. Two years ago, Admin had practically begged him to use up his sick time and go out to pasture so they could promote some ass-lickin' golden boy up the ladder. But Mathis had refused outright. They couldn't make him. It was his career—he got to decide when it was time to walk away.

The brass finally left it alone. Although his no-holds-barred, shoot-from-the-hip style never earned him any bars, Mathis was one of the very few leaders in the department that officers actually listened to and respected—the last of a dying breed.

Which was what really kept him from retiring. The *dying* part. Mathis had a very good gut feeling that if he stopped doing the second-best thing that ever happened in his life, he'd either die of boredom or the overwhelming grief he'd been carrying around inside would finally do him in.

It wasn't that he never dreamed of retirement. He had once. He'd planned his whole career around 3 percent at 50. He was going to sell his house when the real estate market was so ripe, then immediately drive to JZ's and pay cash for the Dream Ride 50-footer with the primary bedroom suite and oversized kitchenette. Then he was going to head out to fulfill his lifelong dream of seeing every state in the union with the best thing that ever happened in his life, Denise.

He was going to be the pilot, Denise, the navigator, just like she had always been, the navigator of his life, the magnetic north of his heart. When the cancer had eaten through to her lymph nodes before they ever knew it had already attacked her breasts, his well-thought-out path toward his Golden Years evaporated from under his feet.

She never had a chance. There was nothing high-maintenance in her death, just as there had been nothing high-maintenance about her life. She was ill for a month, then gone. Nothing long and drawn out. A few kisses, a short goodbye, and just like that, Mathis was left without his compass, without his soul.

Mathis made a left onto Sycamore, then a right onto Magnolia.

Three units were already there. No—wait, four. Officer Simmons decided to break from his nightly Code 7 at his beat-wife's house to show up at the call. Hell must have frozen over.

Mathis parked two houses to the east of the 508 address, noting that F'in G was standing *directly* in front of the house, shucking it up with all the swagger of a douche bag. Piss poor officer safety, that's what that was.

The dispatchers were the ones who christened an officer with his nickname—and they were always spot on. Special Ed, Dingleberry, Speed Bump, Captain Chaos, and F'in G. These were but a few of the monikers that had been bestowed upon fuck-ups over the years. If you were a decent cop, they called you by your name.

"Heeeeeeeeerrrrre's Johnny," hollered F'in G as Mathis pulled himself out of his patrol car.

He must've heard the old-timers at the department call Mathis "Johnny" in the locker room. It was a gentle ribbing about his karaoke inclination. Mathis didn't even sing Johnny Mathis. They shoulda called him Dierks or Merle or Waylon or Willie. Actually, they should just call him Bob. That was his name. That's what dispatch called him.

And F'in G? He shoulda been calling him Sergeant, or better yet, *Sir*. Briefing topic number four: policy review regarding insubordination.

Mathis decided to approach the house with the rookie after all and teach him a lesson about real command presence: making your leather squeak just right, turning up the volume on your portable so the punk-ass could hear the radio chatter, jingling the jail cell keys on your belt and assuming the bladed stance at the door like you were prepared to kick his ass if need be. This would make a very intimidating impression if punk-ass happened to be watching from a window.

Mathis and F'in G made their way up the front path of the white colonial-style home with classic columns on the porch. The front door was painted bright red—some kind of feng shui thing.

Once they reached the door and assumed the position, Mathis rang the doorbell, slow and deliberate.

Diiinng Doooong...

They stood there for a time, allowing the parents inside to have their "what the fuck?" moment. F'in G took this pause in the action as an opportunity to spit some of his chew juice into a potted plant. Mathis thought about adding another briefing topic, but decided briefing was already going to be 30 minutes too long.

"Chew is out of uniform standards," he growled instead. "Get rid of it or gut it." F'in G looked surprised, apparently forgetting he had half a can of Cope in his bottom lip. He scrambled to scoop and spit it out in the planter.

Real. Fucking. Classy.

Mathis rang the doorbell again.

Diiinng Doooong...

Mom should be shooing Dad outta bed about now, urging him to get some chones on and see who was at the door.

After another bit of waiting, it was time to whip out the Maglight and rap on the door, real loud—*Rat-Tet-Tet-Tat-Tat*, five times, with all the authority of the badge.

No one answered the door.

"Shit. It's colder than a witch's tit in a brass bra out here," Mathis said. "You check around the south side, and I'll meet you around back."

"All right, Sarge."

Holy shit! An utterance with some semblance of respect. Maybe the kid was trainable after all, thought Mathis. Then the G smiled at him—his teeth covered with dip fleas. *Yeah, maybe not.*

He watched as F'in G started to work his way around the house, stopping to look into the first window and startling when he saw his own reflection staring back at him. *Yeah, definitely not.* The officers standing out at their vehicles watching this goat-fuck, snickered.

Mathis worked his way around the north side of the house. He stopped at the large picture window facing the street. This was the Christmas tree window for sure. Mathis looked into what these people called the living room, although no actual living ever took place in it. It was pristine—vacuum lines still visible in the carpet. It was decorated like the cover of a magazine and furnished in what Mathis liked to call "Hoity-toity Foo Foo." Nice, but he preferred the "old bastard" chic of his pad.

Mathis made his way around the corner to the side gate. Before going into the backyard, he listened for the rabid panting of the family Fido. He would hate to have to put a bullet in a beloved pooch. That never goes over well.

Once he was sure Cujo wasn't lying in wait, he made his way to the next window. This appeared to be the primary bedroom. It was clean and minimalistic, decorated in crisp white linens and tan walls. That Ralph Lauren dude would have been proud.

Mathis noted that the bed was perfectly made. It was four o'clock in the morning. It shoulda looked slept in. Better yet, Mom shoulda been sitting in it, half naked, while Dad was at the door talking to the police. That would have made the trip worth it. But, no, it was pristine, just like the maid left it that morning. Maybe the parents were out of town and left Mr. Punk-ass alone for the week.

He exhaled. Just another prank call. Waste of time.

F'in G came around from the other side of the house, giving him a shrug. Nothing.

Mathis moved toward the last window. If there was nothing here, they'd clear. There would be no busting down the door to do an interior check. No need for that kind of hoopla. Just 10-8, NR this thing, and everyone could catch a nap or finish their paper for the week.

He paused. Listened.

Silence.

The beam of his flashlight swept across a home office. Mahogany desk. Computer in sleep mode, family photos glowing on the screen. He caught glimpses of a man, a woman, a teenage girl. Then a kid.

Ah, here was their perp. A cute little boy appeared on the screen, fishing pole in hand. In the next shot, he's posing in his soccer uniform, arms around a brand new black-and-white ball, caught mid-laugh, with a dimple in his right cheek.

"Good lookin' kid," Mathis said to F'in G as he sidled up beside him. "No wonder he thinks he can get away with this crap."

The next photo swept across the screen. Same kid, just a bit older, but damn, what a difference. He wore a black sweatshirt with white skull and crossbones splashed all over it. He looked as if someone was forcing him to take the picture, reluctant and petulant. His chin was down, and he looked up through his bangs, shooting a withering glare.

"Yikes," was F'in G's contribution.

Yikes indeed. Mathis's gut itched, and the air suddenly felt heavier. Then something else caught his eye.

The television.

A massive flatscreen. Paused mid-scene on something post-apocalyptic—a destroyed city, a street crusted in dust, spattered with... blood.

A little itch crawled up his spine. He adjusted his flashlight's beam, trying to see if the blood splatter was part of the movie—just a camera effect—or *something else.*

The beam drifted lower. The glow of the screen illuminated the edge of a leather couch.

Something about it made his nerves coil.

He scanned the beam along the base of the couch until he came to the end. He saw a pair of bare feet; the large, hairy feet of an adult male, one foot splayed sideways, the other toes up toward the ceiling. Whoever it was lay on his back.

The hairs on the back of his neck pricked up. Mathis adjusted the beam up a little bit, trying to get a better view. The flashlight beam traced the floor, revealing something dark, something thick, pooled near the couch.

Blood.

Mathis' pulse kicked up. He adjusted the beam, just a little higher.

Something small.

Something rocking.

Mathis froze.

A foot.

No, two.

Bare. Small. Curled at the base of a bookshelf.

And red.

Blood.

The breath locked in his throat. His grip tightened on the flashlight. The world shrank to the beam of light.

The boy sat there, curled into a ball, rocking back and forth, covered in blood.

THREE

AISLEN HAD BEEN STARING at the ceiling for hours. Sleep was impossible after a nightmare like that. The dream looped in her mind—a strange, shifting world where she had lost herself completely. The terror of amnesia, the crushing isolation, the sheer desperation of being utterly alone. The horror of watching a young boy blindly follow his leader's orders. The murder of what appeared to be an innocent man. The haunted shock on the boy's face when he looked at her— and couldn't pull the trigger. Did he have a sudden change of heart? Was he devastated that his resolve had failed—that he couldn't kill her?

And then there was him. The lead soldier. Unyielding. No hesitation before he pulled the trigger.

Even now, Aislen's heart slammed against her ribs at the memory of him—the impossible sharpness of his features. The ruthless discipline coiled in every flexed muscle. Those glacier-blue eyes had sliced straight through her. He was so exquisite it terrified her. She had felt powerless before him, helpless and frozen. She felt ashamed of herself now for feeling so weak. He had only looked at her for a moment, yet it felt like an eternity had passed between them.

And then, he shot her. Just like that.

A chill scampered across her arms and wiggled up the nape of her neck. Heaviness lingered in the air around her. The dream still felt present in her mind and palpable on her flesh.

She'd heard somewhere that if you died in a dream, you'd die in real life. Clearly, that was bullshit. But waking up had been... strange.

For several minutes, she couldn't place herself. The walls of her room had felt foreign, the layout unfamiliar. She had to rebuild her identity, piece by piece, like assembling a puzzle from memory. It was like being born again.

Disturbing. Unsettling.

To have a dream as vivid as this was unusual for her, and it scared the crap out of her. Aislen was not much of a dreamer, asleep or awake. She rarely remembered any of them. Most of the time, she went to sleep and then woke up out of blackness, only knowing that time had passed because the numbers on her clock had changed. When she did remember a dream, it was in vague fragments, a mash-up of the previous day's conflicts mixed with whatever she happened to catch on television before she'd gone to bed. One could wrap a rationale around that.

Aislen wasn't prone to daydreaming, either; silly flights of fancy were a waste of valuable time. She had school, work, and goals to achieve. Girls who were satisfied with whatever life brought to them on a platter could afford to while away the hours wandering in la-la land. One day, though, they would wake up and realize life only brought you mac and cheese and powdered milk if you let it—the stuff of food stamps.

No, Aislen was as realistic and practical as they came. She'd had her fill of that menu and was determined to create a future in which she could choose what was going on her platter. Her preference was to have her cake and eat it, too, thank you very much.

Aislen heard rustling in the kitchen downstairs, and the aromas of coffee and bacon drifted through the cracks of the old ranch house. This was the beginning of the daily grind: Mom making some breakfast, packing Aislen a lunch, and brewing a strong pot of java to get their blood pumping.

At 24, Aislen felt too old to be still living at home, but her mom wasn't exactly pushing her out the door. Quite the contrary, Sabine was insistent that Aislen finish her nursing degree before she had to start worrying about paying rent and feeding herself. She refused to allow Aislen to contribute anything to the household, wanting her to pay for school and save money instead. Aislen's guilt over her mother's generosity mounted daily.

Her mother had worked long, hard hours for years, waitressing at a breakfast joint in town to support the two of them. One wouldn't expect that it would provide them with much, but her mom had managed to buy a house and a couple of decent, although very used, cars, all on her meager waitress salary and the generous tips of her patrons.

Their house wasn't a showplace by any stretch of the imagination—just a modest two-bedroom ranchette in Empire, outside Modesto, tucked beside the Santa Fe Railroad tracks. Passing locomotives rattled the clapboards, swayed the cheap dining room chandelier, and made the lights flicker, but Aislen actually liked the rumble. Having the massive hunks of steel patrol their backyard every couple of hours brought her peace of mind; it was a reminder that someone else was awake in the dark.

While most college students would be chomping at the bit to get out from under parental authority, it wasn't hard living with her mom. Sabine treated her like an adult, no rules, no curfews. And Aislen wasn't the type to go wild anyway. Between school, homework, and nearly full-time hours at the care facility, she had little time for play.

Not that Empire offered much—just a rough corner cantina. And Modesto wasn't much better; its charm was long buried under urban sprawl, and the main attraction was a shopping mall.

Good thing she wasn't much of a social animal, and that she was happy at home. There would be time for traveling and living the high life later on, when she was finished with school and gainfully employed. Then, as a thank you for all her mom had done, she would take her on a real vacation, somewhere exotic and far away.

Aislen had already started planning. Under her bed, she kept a shoebox stuffed with travel brochures and two passports —one for her, one for her mom. She'd secretly applied for them, even taking her mom's picture under the guise of a homework project. Aislen couldn't wait to start filling the small book with colorful stamps from around the world.

She glanced at the clock. Six-thirty. She needed to drag her ass out of bed. Today was going to be a long day. Three classes this morning and a full shift later on. With only four hours of sleep, she was screwed. She shuffled down the stairs to get some coffee and spend a bit of time with her mom before they both had to get their hustle on.

Sabine was sitting at the kitchen dinette by the large picture window overlooking the pruned skeletons of their rose garden, staring off into the horizon. A diaphanous fog clung low to the ground, diffusing the morning light and softening the crooked landscape. She cradled her morning cup of coffee in her hand.

Aislen smiled. Mom always drank her coffee from an

antique teacup. She kept a whole collection of them—twenty-two, each with a matching saucer—carefully arranged in custom-built shelves on the kitchen wall. It defied the laws of physics that none of them had ever toppled off with the passing of a train.

When she was younger, Aislen spent hours gazing at each of the fine porcelain and bone china cups, losing herself in the vivid, intricate patterns. Each year, Sabine had added a new cup to the collection—until she stopped a couple of years ago. Aislen assumed that her mother had again sacrificed something special for herself to help Aislen through college. It was yet another source of guilt and another thing she planned to remedy when she finished her RN program.

Today, her mom was drinking from Aislen's favorite, a royal blue and white lotus cup that sat on a saucer shaped like an open blossom. Sabine was adamant about having her coffee from these cups. A regular coffee mug felt too much like work. There was another house rule: don't talk to Mom until she finished her first cup of coffee, but Aislen knew she was probably on her third cup by now, so it was safe for a conversation.

"Mornin', Mom."

"Good morning, hon." Sabine looked away from the window. "How'd you sleep?"

"Not that good, actually." Aislen didn't really want to go into the details of her nightmare. No one ever really liked hearing people recount their dreams—good or bad. Dreams always seemed interesting to the dreamer, but to the listener? Not so much. "I tossed and turned all night. I must have too much on my mind."

"You? No way. Shocking."

"Yeah, I know." It was the one thing her mother *did* nag her about—her all work and no play philosophy. Sabine never had an opportunity to play at Aislen's age. Being a single mother, she couldn't, and she didn't want Aislen to follow in her footsteps. Aislen sat down at the table, preparing herself for a routine lecture about the importance of enjoying life.

"You know, Aislen, I am really proud of you," she began. "Of how hard you work and how well you are doing in school... I am constantly amazed at how easily you are able to balance everything."

"But..." Aislen continued for her.

"Yes, *but*—I really wish you would take an evening off every once in a while. *Relax*, for crying out loud! You know I wouldn't mind if you wanted to have a little fun in your life. Why don't you call Gen and have a girl's night out?"

Aislen sighed, feeling more than a little guilty. Genesis had been her best friend since kindergarten, when she and her mom first moved out to Empire, but Aislen hadn't been a very good friend lately, too wrapped up in her schedule.

They couldn't have been more different. While Aislen was serious, Genesis was more of a free spirit, a go-with-the-flow kind of girl, wild and mystic. Where Aislen gravitated toward science—facts and proof—Genesis explored weird things, like astrology, tarot cards, and alternative healing. Aislen liked to tease Gen and call her "kooky," but at the same time, she was the easiest person to be around. Aislen always felt immediately at home in the presence of her friend.

"Uh, yeah, I guess we could do that. I can call her later and see if we can hang out," Aislen said, hoping the promise would appease her mother. She changed the subject. "How about you? How'd you sleep?"

"All right, I guess. But I should really stop watching the news first thing when I wake up. It sets the day off wrong."

Mom always worried after watching the news—like the world's chaos might seep into their lives and tear everything apart. But as much as her mom worried, it didn't stop her from watching every 20/20, Dateline, TruStory, Forensic Evidence, Who-Done-It program she could find.

"Well, none of that affects us, Mom."

"Maybe not, but the world's going crazy—earthquakes, freak storms, bombings, the economy in the tank..." She shook her head. "And there was a shooting in town last night. A man was found shot in his house, with his son sitting all bloody next to him. They think the kid might have done it."

Aislen stared at her mother. A creeping sensation wiggled across her back as she recalled the boy in her dream pulling the trigger. "When did that happen?" Aislen asked, thinking maybe she'd heard it on the news before she fell asleep.

"Early this morning. They weren't giving out too many details, and I turned it off before they could. Modesto is still a small town when it comes to this stuff. I am afraid I'll know these people somehow."

Aislen was distracted now. The murder had happened while she was sleeping—while she was *dreaming*. She needed to get out of the room—to get out of the house—and put this disturbing news behind her.

"You know, I need to get ready. I have a long day ahead of me." She got up and kissed her mom on the cheek. "Love you, Mom."

Aislen turned to head back up the stairs.

"I love you, too, Buttercup," her mom replied.

Aislen stopped dead in her tracks. Her mother had never called her 'Buttercup' before. *Not once.* The air in the kitchen turned electric, her skin bristled into gooseflesh. A wave of nostalgia surged through her, the feeling that she had lost something precious, something she loved. It was the same longing she had felt in her dream when the unknown voice spoke to her in the desert.

Aislen looked back at her mother. Sabine was already

gazing out the window, taking another sip of coffee—completely unaware of what she'd just said.

Aislen turned and ran back up the stairs. She jumped in the shower and began scrubbing herself in the hottest water possible, trying to cleanse herself of the heebie-jeebies. She toweled off, dried her hair, and threw on a pair of scrubs.

She stopped to check herself in the mirror. Hair slicked back in a neat ponytail. No makeup. And those damn freckles—permanent as ever. She leaned forward and looked more closely at her reflection.

There it was: the "butt-chin." Strange. She had been looking at herself in the mirror for 24 years and had never noticed the shallow hollow of her chin. She reached up to the mirror and pressed the chin of her reflection.

The humid warmth of the bathroom vanished. In an instant, the air dropped twenty degrees.

Pop.

The sound was sharp as gunfire in the quiet room, but when she looked, the mirror was whole. Steam thickened over the glass. The skin on Aislen's arms prickled, and then—a shift.

She wasn't alone.

"I love your little butt-chin, Buttercup." The voice from the dream desert whispered to her, reaching inside her chest and wrenching her heart. She wanted to run, but something—or *someone*—gripped her and pinned her before the mirror.

"I'll be here when you wake up," a man whispered in her ear, as plain as if he were standing at her shoulder. Another deluge of emotion sluiced through her, filling her with the deepest sadness.

There were no men in her life who would have ever touched her chin in such a way or said such a thing. Aislen never had any boyfriends, and her mom had only a very few dinner dates in all these years. They had no close living relatives. And her father had never been in the picture.

Well, he had been... once, but Aislen could barely remember it. She had only been three or four. But now, a vision pressed itself into her head as if an invisible hand was forcing it inside.

The memory of a small apartment, the doorbell ringing, and her mom opening the door. When her mom saw who it was, she shut the door and spoke to the visitor through a narrow gap in a low voice. The person on the other side of the door answered, again in a low voice that Aislen could not hear. The exchange continued back and forth; the hushed, urgent tones took on a staccato rhythm.

Aislen could tell her mother was not happy. Her voice had the same cadence and insistence that Aislen heard when her mother told her to clean her room, or to stop fussing in the car.

Aislen heard a "no," a "stop," and a "don't." She moved closer to her mother, mostly to reassure her small self that everything was all right. She heard her mother tell the person that she wanted him to leave. A man's voice on the other side of the door asked something with an attitude as firm as her mother's. Mother kept saying no—and got angrier.

"You can't just walk out of our lives... out of *her* life... then just pop back out of the blue. Especially now. Aislen is old enough to know things—to *remember* things. This will confuse her."

"So you named her Aislen after all?" The man did not say her name the way Mom said it. Mom said, "Aaaazlyn." The man on the other side of the door said, "Ashlyn."

Her mother went silent. A wisp of a breeze slipped through the crack, past her mom, and swirled around Aislen. It carried the scent of wood and dirt and leaves, of something unknown and known at the same time. Aislen tiptoed a little closer.

"Sabine," the man's voice said, softer this time. "May I please see Aislen?"

When she heard her name again, said with its foreign lilt, Aislen felt the absolute need to see the stranger on the other side of the door. She came up behind her mother's legs and tried to peek between them. Her mom reached around and placed her hand on Aislen's head, trying to push her back, but that only upset her; being stopped from doing something only made her more obstinate about having to do it. Aislen ducked from under her mother's palm, went around her knees, and pulled open the door.

The man looked down in surprise. He looked back at her mother, a plea in his eyes, then, without waiting for her approval, he squatted down so he was face to face with Aislen.

Aislen didn't take too well to strangers. Attention from anyone except her mother usually instigated an awkward game of peek-a-boo, which ended with Aislen either bursting into tears or running off to hide in another room. But she didn't feel the need to hide herself from this man.

Sandy-haired, he had a soft smile with lines at the corners that made it seem like he smiled all the time. He had lines like that around his eyes, too, and she recognized those eyes. They were exactly like the eyes she saw in her mirror when she looked at herself, grass green with a gold ring dancing within them.

"Hello, Aislen," the man finally said. "My name is Preston."

"How do you do?" Aislen stuck her tiny hand out for him to shake. "I'm Tweedle Dee." It was a gesture she had seen in her favorite Disney movie, "Alice in Wonderland," the one she watched over and over and over again despite her mom's pleas of "not again."

This made the man laugh. He reached out his hand, taking hers in his and shaking it gently. But he didn't let it go, and Aislen didn't pull away. The man named Preston looked down at her small, pudgy hand and smoothed his thumb softly across the top of it.

When he looked into her eyes, his were as shiny as glass. He looked at her for a very long while without saying anything. Then he smiled, reached his pointer finger up, and pressed it in the center of her chin.

"I love your little butt-chin, Buttercup." Then he leaned in, kissed her on the cheek, and whispered into her tiny ear, "I'll be here when you wake up."

Aislen snapped out of the reverie, yanked away from the mirror as if she'd been electrocuted. Profound sorrow ripped through her, clutching at her throat and choking off her breath.

It was him! It was the voice of her father she was hearing—the same voice she had heard when she was lost in her dream. It was his words, transported from a forgotten moment—their only moment—so long ago.

Why in the hell would she have dreamed *his* voice? What was going on that she would pull up such a well-buried memory? And why was it filling her with this sadness, rather than the anger, resentment, or apathy she had nurtured for all these years? He had abandoned her, for Christ's sake—abandoned them!

Yet the memory was back, with fullness and clarity, as if it had happened yesterday. And the look in his eyes, the total love that she saw in them, was imprinted afresh in her psyche.

She looked back at herself in the mirror. The condensation that had veiled her image was clearing away. The sharp *pop* came again—like glass under sudden pressure—but the surface was unbroken. The ghostly grasp released her.

Aislen bolted. Backpack in hand, she tore out of the room, down the stairs, through the front door—fleeing, breathless, before the whisper could follow.

FOUR

RAZE ARRIVED at Headquarters in Palo Alto twenty minutes early for his meeting with the Infiniti 8. The 8 had pre-arranged this appointment back when they first approved the Parrish Project and directed Raze to implement and complete it.

The headquarters of Infinium Incorporated was as sterile as it was anonymous—clean lines, functional surfaces, a façade designed to vanish among shinier Fortune 500 neighbors. Which suited II perfectly: a blank slate, free of identity or belief, ready to absorb whatever mission they projected onto it.

Raze walked down several long corridors, made a few turns, descended a flight of stairs, made a few more turns, and went down several more flights, deep into the inner hub. It had taken him almost a year to learn to maneuver through the labyrinth of the building without getting lost.

Raze caught his reflection in the blank metallic wall—only it wasn't today's face staring back. It was the twenty-year-old version of himself: hungrier, sharper, electric with potential.

The ghost-image pulled him under, and suddenly he was back at the beginning...

The letter—not an email—embossed with the sleek insignia of Quantum Gaming Systems, a subsidiary of Infinium Incorporated, though he hadn't known it at the time.

DEAR RAZIEL TANIS,

We have been tracking your stats in AnnihilNation and watching match replay videos on YouTube for quite a while now. Your skill and strategy are impressive. We would like to extend this personal invitation to attend Quantum Gaming Systems' National Gaming Championships. It will be held in San Francisco next month. If you accept this invitation, we would also like to schedule a meeting to discuss further opportunities. Please contact our offices, and we will make all the arrangements. Please do not let expenses dissuade you from contacting us. Food, lodging, transportation, and entertainment will be paid for by QGS. We hope to hear from you soon.

Sincerely,

Grant Parker

THE DIRECTOR of QGS himself signed it. Raze could feel the indentation where his pen pressed into the paper. It seemed too good to be true, but Raze picked up the phone and dialed the number listed on the letterhead.

"Quantum Gaming Systems, Grant Parker's office, can I help you?" a sexy sounding receptionist greeted him.

"Uh... yeah... I think so," Raze was a little taken aback that the number actually worked. "My name is Raze Tanis," he said, more as a question than a statement.

"Oh, yes, Mr. Tanis. We have been expecting your call. Are you calling to reserve your space at the championships?"

"Uh... yeah... I think so," he answered again. *You gotta be kidding me? This is for real?*

"Very good. Mr. Parker will be pleased to hear that. Let's get some information from you so I can make the arrangements."

The elevator chimed. The doors peeled open, and the past dissolved like pixels breaking apart. Raze exhaled, stepping back into the sterile hum of Headquarters.

That letter had changed everything.

Just like that, he was heading to California. Raze emptied his bank account, packed some clothes and his tournament game controllers, told his family to go fuck themselves, and flew halfway across the country to play video games.

Raze passed by a gold plaque on the wall. Its gleaming letters—AUTHORIZED PERSONNEL ONLY—pulled at him like déjà vu. Not the sign itself, but what it meant. A reminder of the night he stopped being "everyone else" and became the exception.

That night had begun with a suit in a mahogany box.

He'd won his first championship and thought that was the prize. But it wasn't. The real reward came after.

The box arrived via room service, with a handwritten note:

"The driver will arrive at 8." —*Grant Parker*

The suit fit perfectly. Downstairs, a black limousine waited. No one else in the hotel lobby seemed to notice. The driver opened the door without speaking, and Raze was whisked through the glow of San Francisco's hills, all the way to the InterContinental on Nob Hill.

The Top of the Mark. Nineteenth floor. A corner table.

He remembered standing there by the glass, staring out at

the whole world burning gold in the sunset. It was the first time reality felt like a simulation.

A waiter placed a chilled bottle of Dom Perignon on the table just as Grant Parker arrived.

"We know you've been approached," Grant said, sitting without ceremony. "Red Bull, Monster, maybe even Sony. Some impressive offers, I imagine."

He was right. Just the night before, Raze had been at a party that included strippers, shots, and a sponsorship offer worth $250,000. And that had felt like a *dream*.

But Grant? Grant was real. And he didn't pitch.

"You're a gifted player," he said. "But you're also bored. This game's beneath you. Any schmuck can grind XP."

Then he leaned in, eyes gleaming.

"We're building something different. Something that will break the rules—and the world. And we want you in on the ground floor."

The offer:

$250K base salary

A private, furnished apartment wired with top-tier gaming systems

Access to every title in the Platinum NOW network, even restricted content

A concierge service for "any physical or psychological necessity"

There was more, too: sports cars, personal chefs, call girls, a lifestyle engineered to keep an elite gaming developer comfortable and compliant.

But Raze barely heard it. The deal was already done the moment he looked out over the city and saw his name written in its lights.

Raze moved past the metal door and kept walking. The city had welcomed him that night. Infinium had claimed him. And he never left—never looked back. This life gave him everything: power, purpose, pleasure.

And when he did leave, it was on his own terms—slipping through dimensions, walking dreams, bending reality like code.

He moved into company quarters directly from the hotel and, after signing a four-foot stack of contracts and non-disclosure agreements, began work within the week.

Work consisted of testing the company's new gaming system and playing all the new games that were in development. The system employed virtual reality technology, using a full-screen visor, a game controller that was integrated into a pair of gloves, and other accessories.

When playing a fantasy game, there was a shield and a sword that worked in sync with the gloves. If it was a combat simulator, an automatic weapon or handgun controller could be used. The use of real tools and being visually immersed in the game through the visor interface definitely enhanced the experience.

Raze whizzed through every game they had developed. He found their plot holes and operational glitches. He offered suggestions for improvement about everything from scenarios and characters to tools and objectives. After a few months, Grant called him into his office.

"We would like to offer you a promotion."

"So soon?" Raze was a little dumbfounded. He knew he was good, but really?

"It was what we were hoping for all along. We saw something special in you, and these past months have been... well, consider it a test. Not only were you playing our games, but our games were also analyzing you. How your mind works and what other potential you may have. You have demonstrated some unique abilities, and we would like to continue to develop these abilities in a completely new arena. It is an extremely challenging program—few make it through... But it comes with a significant pay and benefit increase. If you agree, you must complete a rigorous training program and sign an exclusive *lifetime* contract with us."

Raze didn't even care about the money. He was already making more than he knew what to do with. And he didn't care about the extra-curricular benefits too much either. No, Raze was intrigued that there was something even more challenging that he could do.

"Absolutely. Absolutely, I'll do it," he agreed, although he had no idea what "it" was, or how radically his life would change.

And boy, how had life changed. Once he became privy to the truth, there was no turning back.

Hard to believe that was almost ten years ago, Raze thought as he made his way into the antechamber and sat down. This was a completely different reality: the *real*, real world. And he hoped that after today's debacle, he could maintain what he'd worked so hard for. To retain his right to stay here, he would need to convince the Infiniti 8 that what had happened in *Demesne* could not have been foreseen; that the project was not a failure, and that he was still the only control operative who could see the project through to completion.

The massive steel doors to the boardroom silently slid open, and Grant Parker appeared.

"Hello, Raziel. The 8 will see you now," he said, gesturing him inside

Raze followed, mildly surprised that Grant was the one escorting him. Grant had recruited him, but his mentorship hadn't lasted long.

They walked toward another set of steel doors.

"I'm surprised to see you here," Raze said.

"I was briefing The 8 on a new recruit," Grant said. "A gifted young man. He may even surpass you."

"Doubtful. But that would be refreshing. Carrying the weight gets tiresome."

"You say that now, but when one comes along that outshines you, you may change your tune."

"Are you speaking from experience?"

Grant stopped. "I did my time, Raziel. I helped pioneer this field."

Raze was unimpressed. Grant had once reached Level V, a major feat then, but time and skill shifts had made him obsolete. He was no longer viable as an operative.

Especially now that they had someone like Raze.

"Maybe I didn't go further because I didn't *want* to," Grant said.

"No. You didn't progress because you couldn't."

"Contrary to your belief, I made a choice. I didn't want to sell my soul. You never had one."

"Don't kid yourself, Grant," Raze scoffed. "You may not actually do any of the real dirty work, but your soul is sold just the same. Only passively—because you're a coward."

"Sorry if killing people isn't my style."

Raze laughed out loud. "I don't kill people, Grant. I just... give them the idea. They jump on their own."

"You're an angel of death."

"And you're still an accessory. The pioneer, remember? We couldn't have done it without you."

They walked in silence to the final doors.

"Good luck in there, Raziel." Grant leaned in closer. "And maybe... watch your back."

With that, Grant turned on his heel and walked out.

Raze watched him, unruffled. Grant was no threat. He was

nothing but a sycophantic pawn who could never accept that Raze had surpassed him.

Once Grant was outside the inner sanctum, Raze turned back to the doors. He placed his feet shoulder-width apart, closed his eyes, centered himself, and concentrated on grounding. He released all other errant frequencies in his space and, when he was ready, he held his hand in front of a glowing plasma screen inlay. He projected his signature energy frequency through the palm of his hand. The Qi panel began to shift colors—swirls of ultraviolet, indigo, gold, and pitch black, blending and turning together. When the combination of colors identified him, the internal door mechanism clicked several times, and the locks within it disengaged. The door slid open, and Raze stepped through into Sanctum Sanctorum.

Located in the third level, subterranean basement of the building, the Sanctum Sanctorum was vast, gleaming, and cold —the kind of cold that lived in the bones, not the air. Flawless stone walls curved upward into a dome so high it vanished into shadow.

Raze's gaze climbed with the curve, past columns of polished metal, to the multi-faceted cut glass skylight that crowned the room, ten stories above. At the dome's apex, gold and platinum intertwined: the infinity sigil, split by two needle-thin capital "I'd." Seams of glass ran down the walls in geometric patterns, carrying the sun from the ceiling to the chamber floor, separating the stone blocks with veins of light. It provided just enough ambient lighting to see by, but not in too much detail. The 8 refused to be scrutinized.

It was a rare exception that anybody even knew The 8 existed. While every employee of Infinium Incorporated and its subsidiaries played a supporting role in its mission, only the elite, integral players understood the true nature of that mission. Raze was one of those players.

The 8 were already seated in eight gold thrones behind an enormous table of illuminated glass that encircled half the room. He walked across the black marble floor and stood before them. He did not know any of The 8 by name, only by their numerical designation. Numbers 2, 4, 6, and 8 were women. They surrounded him to the right. Numbers 3, 5, 7, and 9 were men, seated to the left.

An extra chair sat in the center of the semi-circle, empty. In five years, Number 1's chair had never been filled. It was a mystery—and it would stay that way—because Raze was not in a position to ask questions, only to provide answers.

"Hello, Raziel," Number 7 said.

"Good morning," Raze replied, neutral.

"Parrish Project," said Number 4. "Report."

Raze took a step forward. The lie was ready. Withholding counted as lying, and in here it carried the same punishment. But The 8 relied on him too much to know the truth. He just had to keep them pacified—buy himself more time to figure out what had gone wrong so he could remedy the situation himself.

He decided to start with the good news. "Scott Parrish is dead. He is no longer a threat."

This was the truth, confirmed by the morning's media drip. Found shot in Modesto.

"Unfortunately, Blake Parrish did not follow through with his assignment, as intended. There was a fluctuation in his frequency pattern after he'd shot his father."

Still truth—for now.

"Cause?" asked Number 2.

"This may have been due to interference on the Third, where the actual assassination occurred." The lie slid into place like a loaded round.

Good thing there wasn't a frequency reader here; it would have read the glitch in his energy patterns.

"What could have caused such a flux?" asked Number 5.

Raze noted the guileless tone of the question, so he went on, "Two possibilities. First—recoil and decibel shock. It wasn't a weapon that Blake used in *Demesne*."

This was a stretch. Manchurian assassination techniques weren't new, and they had been perfected in the past two decades to withstand such differences as using simulated weapons during trial runs compared to real guns in actual operations.

"Or it could be attributed to the fact that our candidate was younger than most candidates."

This wasn't plausible, either. Blake, at just under 13 years old, was only slightly younger than the average Manchurian subjects. In the 60s, the government used 24-year-olds who were already in the military, but in the 90s, they started infiltrating younger minds. In recent years, they had success with twelve-year-olds and one as young as 9.

Raze continued, "Blake Parrish wasn't fully immersed in gaming culture, or in an addicted state. Parental intervention may have blunted the effect."

This was not true at all. Little Blake was totally hooked. No matter what intervention his parents had tried, Blake was always able to access the game. Raze had made sure of that. And he had been Raze's perfect little puppet. That is, until that little glitch invaded *Demesne* this morning and interrupted the operation.

Demesne was both a war simulator and a role-playing game, where players used SurroundVision visors and controllers designed as replicas of real weapons to explore and take over worlds.

Raze had developed the game during his tenure at Quantum Gaming Systems, which then produced and distributed it. It was their best-selling game to date.

But *Demesne* was also a portal to a special little sphere within the fourth-dimensional energetic grid called The Stratum.

While The Stratum was policed and controlled by Infinium Incorporated, *Demesne* was created and controlled by Raze—with The 8's blessing, of course.

Through the game, Raze could lure targets into his fourth-dimensional funhouse and, from there, directly seed ideas, manipulate thoughts, and influence the actions of targets as directed by The 8.

Only Raze's unsuspecting targets received his special SurroundVision visors that manipulated the oscillation patterns in their brains and opened the portal that transported them from the 3D game into his 4D, holographic space. There were only two of the visors in existence. Both were sitting at the crime scene in the Parrish house, waiting for Raze to retrieve them once the heat cooled off.

When the stray creature interrupted today's operation, she created a disruption in the oscillation patterns of *Demesne*, so Blake's consciousness, and subsequently the whole construct, fell apart.

But Raze wasn't going to tell The 8 that. He didn't want them to know *Demesne* had been compromised.

He needed to sandwich the bad news with some good.

"Fortunately, when I realized Blake was in flux, I initiated the option-lock command, and I have confirmed that this was effective. Young Mr. Parrish is in police custody under psychiatric observation."

Raze paused and let the state of affairs sink in before he offered his solutions. "The option-lock can remain in effect, or it can be enhanced to place Blake in a vegetative state. I can also attempt to complete the original assignment by getting

Blake to self-destruct via dream seeding or remote influencing. I await your direction."

Raze stepped back, keeping his head lowered as he listened to The 8 deliberate.

"Obviously, none of us are pleased that the goal wasn't accomplished," Number 7 finally spoke again. He always seemed to speak for the group; whether or not he carried more authority than the others was unknown. Raze found that sometimes the more people spoke, the less authority they actually had. "As for what to do, does anyone have a problem with allowing the option-lock to remain in effect?"

"I do," said Number 6 immediately.

"I, as well," said Number 5. "While we have had success with option-lock settings before, it has been with older targets whose brains and memories were already compromised. Due to the age of this target and the resiliency of his brain, I am concerned he could reacquire a stable line to the Third, heal his synapses, and reintegrate. Even if he only partially reintegrates, anything he may reveal is too much information. I vote for remote influencing or dream seeding. Finish this thing."

There was silence again.

"Is there anyone who disagrees with 5?" asked 7.

No one spoke.

Number 7 placed his fingertips together and looked down at the table for a moment as if gathering his thoughts. Slowly and deliberately, he spoke again. "Raziel, you are directed to finish the project. But let us be perfectly clear. No more failures. Or you'll be replaced."

"Yes, sir," Raze replied.

"You may go."

Raze turned and left the room. He had a busy afternoon ahead. The sooner he accessed Blake and got him to kill himself, the sooner he could begin hunting down the girl.

She had invaded his world. Now he was going to burn hers to the ground.

This was going to be fun.

FIVE

MATHIS really just wanted to go home, pop open a beer, and hit the hay for a few hours before enjoying the rest of his week-end, but leave it to a fuck 'em up Friday to ruin those plans.

After spotting the blood-soaked boy cowering in the corner, everything went from big nothin' to clusterfuck, real quick. Mathis immediately called for a perimeter to be set up. Knowing that there was at least one critical victim in the house, Mathis made the tactical decision to have a rapid response team from his own shift attempt to secure the scene. Having the whole watch on scene already wasn't such a waste of resources after all.

They called for anybody inside the residence to come out, but there was no response. So, much to everybody's delight, Mathis let them kick in the back door. As they went room to room, clearing the house, Mathis expected to find it ransacked from a home invasion gone bad. But the house was immaculate, not a single knick-knack out of place. The only people who appeared to have been in the house all evening were the victim, Scott Parrish, and his twelve-year-old son, Blake.

When they entered the den, the boy wouldn't comply with commands, but he didn't put up any resistance either. He sat in the corner next to his father, cradling his knees, rocking himself back and forth, repeating the same nonsensical sentence over and over under his breath.

"Two sticks and a bucket. Two sticks and a bucket. Two sticks and a bucket."

Blake was what Mathis would call a hot mess—slick with blood, snot, and tears—but they got him cuffed and in the back of a patrol car without a fight, where he resumed both his rocking and his mantra. Once the scene was secured, they transferred him to the Adolescent Resource Center on a 5150.

While the rest of the house was pristine, the office looked like a scene from a horror flick. Blood spatter and brain matter made a grotesque abstract work of art on the side wall and across the television screen. There was a deep red Rorschach pattern stained in the Berber carpet.

Mr. Parrish had one bullet hole right between the eyes, with a massive exit wound that was more out of the top of his head than straight out the back. The average fan of CSI could have figured out that the suspect was shorter than the victim, just the height of Blake Parrish. Because of this, and the handgun lying right next to the boy's feet, it was not going to be a surprise when the gunshot residue test came back positive, identifying Blake as the shooter.

By the time Mathis handed the crime scene over to Investigations and got his officers squared away on their reports, it was nearly noon. If he went home and went to sleep, he would be up all night, so Mathis decided to push through the rest of the day and head over to the Old Mill for some breakfast. There really wasn't anything that a four-egg Denver omelet, sausage, bacon, biscuits, gravy, and a strong cup of diner coffee couldn't soothe—not even the cold-blooded murder of a father by his twelve-year-old son.

Mathis had been coming to the cafe since he was a kid. Back then, it was nestled in a scalene wedge of land between two streets and the railroad tracks, the little windmill on the sign spinning lazily over the smell of frying bacon and woodsmoke from the kitchen. His grandfather used to time breakfast so Mathis Jr. could watch the trains crawl past the windows, steel wheels screaming on the rails.

The city had demolished the beloved landmark years ago, but the owners relocated the cafe just down the street. It wasn't the same, but it was his tradition and still served the best breakfast in town. Mathis came here to reminisce about the good old days when Modesto was all rails, rivers, and agriculture. A place where you couldn't come into town without seeing half a dozen people you went to church with and felt at home in the world.

Modesto lost that small-town atmosphere when she spread her legs to the housing developers who cashed in on the real estate bubble, attracted a hundred thousand new residents within ten years, and then dumped her like a two-bit whore. The old girl busted herself at the seams.

But to Mathis, she still had a way about her. Even though the orchards and crops that once graced the landscape had given way to cheap housing developments, their roots were still interlaced, deep in the fertile soil, and sprouted up into her people. Those roots either anchored them to the place for a lifetime or brought them back. Only the lucky few managed to make a complete escape.

Mathis was one of the former, grounded here for a lifetime. He hardly recognized the place anymore, but he didn't mind. It brought him a certain comfort. He felt as rooted here as the trees in the orchards that surrounded the town.

His waitress slid another coffee onto the table without asking if he wanted a refill. "You look like you've been through it today."

Mathis managed a half-smile. "You could say that."

Sabine had been working here for years, and Mathis was a little in awe of her. He always thought there must be a factory in the Midwest that spat out the cookie-cutter diner waitress: the heavy-set, back-combed, netted hairdo, snapping her chewing gum type of broad that was found at Denny's across America.

Well, that waitress factory broke the mold with Sabine. She was definitely not your ordinary diner waitress. Mathis may not have been able to sit at his favorite window and watch the trains go by anymore, but he sure as hell made sure he sat in Sabine's section of the restaurant so he could enjoy a completely different, and ultimately better, view.

Mathis was taken aback when he caught himself admiring Sabine for the first time. He had been buried in grief for so long that he was practically dead himself. But one morning, he noticed the way the light played through the honey-and-caramel strands of her hair, the easy sway of her hips as she sashayed table to table, chatting up the locals, the camber of her back as she leaned over to pour their coffee, and he felt jolted alive.

Sabine seemed to have an intuitive understanding that Mathis wasn't much for small talk. She skirted his table gracefully, respecting his privacy, and although he wanted to, he could never muster up the mojo to say anything to her.

Besides placing his order—please, thank you, yes, and no ma'am—his tongue froze up. He always felt awkward about the "ma'am" part as she was at least a decade younger than he was, but he didn't want to act too familiar and call her by her name. He wanted to pay her a little respect.

Recently, he had been working himself up to attempt a conversation. It had been thirty-five years since he'd hit on a woman—and that was Denise—their junior year in high school. Mathis was pretty sure that shouting, "Hey Sabine, you wanna go steady?" across the cafeteria wasn't how it worked nowadays.

Maybe today he could think of a better icebreaker, like, "Nice weather we're having."

Mathis glanced out the window. It looked like God had sneezed on the city today, leaving a wet, low-lying fog that had enveloped and sealed in one of the malodorous assaults Modesto was known for.

You could never tell what fragrance would greet you on any given day. Some days, the air reeked of maple syrup. The next day, the town would be drenched in a perfume of dairy farm manure.

Today was a dung day, and Mathis was pretty sure that initiating a chat about the nice weather on a day that God's sneeze smelled like cowshit would not elicit a very long conversation—or a dinner date.

Who was he kidding, anyway? He was a standard-issue cop, with a regulation, collar-length haircut, a mustache trimmed to the edge of his mouth, and a body nourished on a widower's diet of beer, barbecue, and half-off Happy Hour appetizers.

What was he doing, considering making small talk with a hot waitress?

Maybe I'll just pay her a nice compliment, he thought as she strolled toward him with his check. He looked up at her as she approached, praying his tongue wouldn't tie on him. Just as she arrived—just as he opened his mouth to say the perfect something that was going to sweep her off her feet—his cell phone rang.

"Are you freakin' kidding me?" he said out loud—not the compliment he was hoping for.

She smirked. "They're annoying little fuckers, aren't they?"

Mathis was stunned. She just said "fuckers." And he may have just fallen completely in love.

The damn thing kept ringing.

"You gonna answer that, sweetheart? Or at least silence the damn thing?"

"Sorry," he stammered, flipping it open. "Mathis."

"Mathis?"

"Yeah, that's what I said." He rolled his eyes at Sabine.

She smiled, lips so perfect they ought to be illegal, and mouthed, *"I'll pick this up in a bit."* She set the check down, winked like it meant something, and moved on—leaving him reeling like a rookie.

Sabine was the kind of dame who inspired the saying, *"I hate to see you go, but love to watch you leave."*

That waitress factory must've spent extra time on her— because damn, that was a world-class ass.

He knew it wasn't politically correct, but hell, no one could police his thoughts.

And did she just wink at him?

The person on the phone had been talking the whole time, but Mathis hadn't heard a word they'd said.

"Uh... I'm sorry. My cell cut out. Who is this?"

"Bob, it's Jackson. I'm calling from the A.R.C."

Jackson was an old department buddy and the lead investigator on the Parrish case. Mathis had trained him when he had started at the department, and Jackson still liked to call Mathis up to get his input from time to time. Jackson was a good cop with good instincts and the right personality. Nothing like the F'in G's they'd been hiring lately.

Mathis leaned back in the booth. "Yeah, buddy. What's up?"

"Not a damn thing, old man. I'm sitting here hosting the world's lamest sleepover. Kid's still in the corner, rocking like he's got his own tide chart. Keeps mumbling that 'two sticks and a bucket' business like he's tuned to a radio station I can't pick up."

Mathis smirked. "Sounds cozy."

Jackson chuckled, "Doc won't release him. Says the kid's not fit for Juvie yet, so here we are. Babysitting."

"Gotta love Fridays."

"Yep. Until the GSR comes back or he quits chanting, I'm just burning daylight."

"Any sign of Mom?"

"Oh, yeah. We reached her. She was out of town; now she's in hysterics. Useless for intel. Big sis is away at college—Mom called her, so now we've got two useless relatives."

"Quite a pickle," Mathis said.

"Seriously. There were no other signs of a disturbance. It looks like Dad was watching a movie, and the kid came in with the gun and just blew him away."

"A movie, huh? Was that what was on the television when we got there?"

"We assume so. The only thing on was the TV."

Mathis stirred his coffee. "What about neighbors? Anyone hear or see anything?"

"Not last night. But the sweet old lady next door said Mrs. Parrish told her that they were having some trouble with Blake —that he was seeing a therapist for behavioral issues, problems at school, defiance, and an addiction to video games."

"Did you get ahold of that therapist?"

Jackson gave a low laugh. "Yeah, we called him. And got a big ol' HIPAA speech. Works at Chrysalis, runs addiction programs. He finally agreed to swing by and see the kid—maybe shake him loose a little. Doubt it'll work. But hell, I once saw a hostage let his grandma talk him out with nothing but a pecan pie, so I'm not ruling anything out.

"But I'm hoping once everything is said and done, this will be a pretty cut-and-dry case."

As if a twelve-year-old killing his dad could ever be cut and dried. Mathis left that unspoken. He wasn't so sure about this case at all. Something about it wasn't sitting right with him. He had an uneasy feeling twisting in his gut that he couldn't shake.

When they took the boy into custody, he lacked both the residual heat of homicidal rage and the bone-chilling stare of a cold-blooded psychopath. Mathis had expected a punk-ass perp, a fighter, all blame and no accountability. Instead, the boy was wounded, completely traumatized; stains of tears dried into a salty rind on his face, lips sticky with blood, and matching bloody kiss prints all over the father's face. That didn't add up to cut and dried to Mathis.

"Whaddaya say I come down there and bring you a cup of coffee?"

"If you're buying, I'll take a grande, quad shot, skinny mocha with whipped cream."

Mathis flipped the cell phone shut. *It was a damn conspiracy.*

He got his wallet out and put enough cash down to cover the tab plus a generous tip for Sabine—for both her service and the pleasure of watching her work. He looked around, trying to find her so he could at least say thank you, or see you later, or let me take you out to dinner, but she was nowhere to be seen.

He told himself it didn't matter—she was just a waitress, just breakfast—but the hollow ache in his gut said otherwise. And somewhere across town, a boy rocked in a corner, chanting to ghosts. Mathis wasn't sure which one of them was lonelier.

SIX

AISLEN CLOCKED in at the hospital with less than a minute to spare. Since running was a no-no at the facility, Aislen did her fastest speed-walk down the hall, threw her bags into her locker, then hustled toward the nurse's station.

She hated feeling rushed, but hated being late even more. She'd been fighting that edgy feeling all day long. Out of sync with the world, she'd dropped things, bumped into people, and hit every single red light on her way to work.

She arrived at the counter out of breath, just in time to help the charge nurse prep medications for the residents.

"Well, there you are," Rachel said when she got up to the med cart. "Running late isn't like you. I was starting to worry."

"I know. I'm so sorry. Today's been insane."

Rachel laughed. "Well, you've come to the right place, then, haven't you?"

Aislen grimaced at her faux pas. When you worked in a mental health facility such as Chrysalis, using words like "crazy" and "insane" was pretty much frowned upon.

"I'm sorry... I am so off today."

"Need a cup?" Rachel asked, gesturing to the little pill cups lined up on the cart.

"Wow. You're incorrigible," Aislen responded, finally laughing a little.

"No different than any other day. After 20 years of working here, I've a well-developed, sick sense of humor. The cart is ready if you want to do the rounds."

"Okay, thanks." Aislen started to push the cart away.

"Oh! Before I forget," said Rachel. "Troy came looking for you before his session started. He wanted to see if you could go with him to an appointment at A.R.C. I told him it was okay and that I'd cover for you as long as you were back by the end of my shift."

A.R.C. wasn't the kind of place you just popped into on a whim. You needed special clearance, and whatever went on behind those locked doors stayed there. The invitation stirred a faint prickle along her arms, though she told herself it was just nerves about working off-site.

"Do you know what that's about?"

"He didn't go into it. But you know how he is, always trying to mentor you with your career," said Rachel, making air quotes around the word *mentor*.

"Yeah, right," said Aislen, slightly embarrassed.

"I think he has a little more interest in you than in career counseling. Lucky girl."

"Okay, stop. It's not like that," Aislen said, flushing a bit at the insinuation.

Troy Kellen was a fairly new therapist at Chrysalis. He was polite and professional, nothing but respectful to all the nurses and aides. More importantly, he seemed completely authentic, without the enormous ego the nurses had come to expect from the other therapists and facility doctors. That alone scored him big points on the floor.

It didn't hurt that he was also cute as hell. Troy wasn't hot in a bulky, bodybuilder way. He was tall, with the lean and sinewy physique of a swimmer. Unlike so many guys, he didn't appear to put too much effort into his appearance—no long hours at the gym, no overly styled hair or mani-pedis for him. He was casual and relaxed, wearing khaki Dockers, long-sleeved shirts rolled up to the elbows, and no tie.

Not Aislen, of course. She couldn't afford to get distracted by "cute." So Rachel's comment was completely ridiculous.

Aislen had worked for Chrysalis Treatment and Residential Facility for four years. After slogging through a semester at the junior college with absolutely no idea of what she wanted to do with her life, she landed a job here as a nursing aide. The busy pace, wide variety of tasks, and satisfaction she got from helping her patients grew on her, and she became an LVN. When she decided to continue with school and work on becoming an RN, she thought the hard part was done. She had expected things to get easier once she made the decision about what to do with her life, but there were so many different avenues—specialties and advanced degrees available—she found herself even more overwhelmed now that she was nearing the end of her program.

Aislen rotated through the various wings of the hospital every few months. Her current assignment was the geriatric ward, caring for elderly patients suffering from dementia, Alzheimer's, schizophrenia, and other disorders. Many of Aislen's patients had lived through a time when their illnesses were treated without their consent, and electroshock treatments or lobotomies left them incapacitated. It wasn't your everyday nursing home. The patients here required more maintenance and structure than other facilities.

Aislen pushed the med cart door-to-door—reverse trick-or-treating for the residents who already knew the drill. Their internal clocks clamored for "med time" as if it were lunch, and most were waiting in their doorways before she even stopped.

She double-checked Rachel's doses, handed out the little white cups of calm, and documented each one.

Out of the corner of her eye, she spotted Troy at the nurse's station, leaning back against the counter and talking to Rachel. Even from here, she could see the easy rapport between them. Rachel, who usually kept the therapists at arm's length, was smiling at him like he was one of the nurses.

"Morning, Sigmund," Aislen said to the elderly male sitting in his wheelchair outside room number 11.

"Good morning, Astrid," Sigmund replied, reaching up with his ancient, spindly fingers. He called every female in the facility Astrid. Whether Astrid was a long-lost love, a departed sister, or a daughter, no one knew. Sigmund Lange had been a resident at Chrysalis for many years, and he never had any visitors named Astrid. Or anything else, for that matter.

"No, Sigmund. It's Aislen," she said. It was important to remind the patients of reality, rather than support their delusions, although it wouldn't do any good with Mr. Lange. Physically, he was actually holding up pretty well for an 86-year-old man, but his dementia was severe.

Besides thinking everyone was some woman from his past, he rambled in a language of numbers. He would sit in his chair, stare out his bedroom window, reciting strings of integers that only an MIT grad could decipher, and tap his fingers together as if counting to infinity.

He looked like a nutty professor—his wispy, pale gray-blond hair sticking out in every direction. His once clear blue eyes clouded over like an overcast sky; he never seemed to focus on anything but the equations and formulas in his mind. Though Aislen was pretty good with math, this language was beyond her ability to translate.

Aislen handed Mr. Lange his med cup. He took it in his shaky hand and stared deeply into it for a few moments. Aislen watched him, wondering what he was looking for. Trying to read the tea leaves of his fate, maybe?

Troy laughed at something Rachel said. That laugh—low, warm—turned heads on the floor without him even trying.

She had to admit there was something about the way he listened—steady brown eyes beneath tousled golden hair, lips with just enough curve to suggest amusement. He made you feel like you were the only person in the room, like your answer to his question was worth hearing.

In quiet moments when residents had settled down for the night, Troy would hang out, asking questions about her life and her goals, what had motivated her to become a nurse, what she liked about working in psychiatric care.

He had been encouraging Aislen to pursue an advanced degree in psychology. While it would've been easier for Aislen to be satisfied with her achievement and settle into a secure career, Troy sparked something within her. As much as she loved her work, she did feel there was something more she was supposed to do with her life.

"Aislen, you are intelligent, capable, and insightful," Troy had said. "I would hate to see you settle because you think this is the best you could do. Not that being a nurse isn't a great profession. I just think you have so much more to offer."

Aislen warmed under the compliment, flattered that he thought so highly of her. Although she'd never admit it, his praise made her a little breathless, especially with that... *that look*. But Aislen quickly reminded herself that Troy seemed to engage like that with everybody, from aide to nurse to janitor, to the most delusional patient. It was just his manner; people shouldn't take it personally. And besides, fraternization between co-workers, while not a violation of policy, was just not professional. Troy was mindful of that. Clear boundaries were important to him. Any kind of flirtation would have been out of character for him. He couldn't help it if he was so freakin' hot.

Aislen marked the dose on Sigmund's chart and was about to move on when his hands stilled, and his gaze locked on her. She met his eyes and noticed that the clouds in them had departed, and they were a clear and bright blue.

"You aren't Astrid," he said.

Aislen was shocked. Never, in the four years she'd worked here, had he had a moment of clarity. A strange pulse rippled through her—a sudden hollow in her stomach—before the words even registered. When they did, she froze.

"Uh, no, Mr. Lange. I'm not. My name is Aislen."

"Ash-lynn," he said, rolling it across his tongue as though he were correcting her.

She hadn't heard it said like that since she was a little girl, and it struck something deep and brittle inside her. The sound of it vibrated through her, like a whisper aimed at the marrow of her bones. It was wrong. Too intimate. Too familiar.

Her blood turned cold, and a knot seized up in her stomach.

"It means 'dream,' you know," he continued.

No, she didn't know. She didn't know it even had a meaning. She could only stare at the old man, speechless.

Mr. Lange leaned over in his chair as if he was going to tell her a secret, and whispered to her, "Are you awake yet?"

Aislen dropped the med chart, sending it clattering down the hall. Her head was in a full spin now. A claw of ice shivered down her scalp and raked down her whole body like fingernails on a chalkboard. The words echoed in her head. Her knees buckled.

A secure, warm arm slid around her waist and kept her from melting to the floor.

"Aislen, are you okay?" It was Troy.

"Sigmund giving you trouble?" he asked, half-teasing but with a faint crease between his brows.

Rachel was standing right behind him.

"What happened, Hon?" she asked. "Do you feel all right? You look like you've seen a ghost."

Aislen caught her breath and shook her head, trying to clear it. She became very aware of the heat radiating off of Troy. He was holding her close against him. She felt the taut ripples of muscle beneath his shirt, and she thought she would faint for real this time, but for a completely different reason. She pushed herself off him, regaining her composure.

"No—I'm fine. Just slipped on something."

Rachel looked down at Sigmund. "Mr. Lange, are you drooling again? Trying to trip up my nurses?"

Aislen looked back down at Sigmund. His eyes were veiled into milky clouds, lost again in his numbers. Maybe that should have reassured her. Instead, she felt as if something had been opened—something that couldn't be shut.

SEVEN

RAZE LEFT Infinium directly after the meeting, hopped into his silver Audi R8, and within minutes was on the 280 northbound toward San Francisco.

The meeting with The 8 had gone better than he expected. In the end, they gave him the permissions he needed to complete the project. He was a little surprised by the threatening stance Number 7 took at the end with his ultimatum.

Really? Although fear was a great control mechanism for the masses, Raze was the last person they should be trying to catch with that net. Attempting to intimidate him during this crucial time in the mission was the equivalent of shooting themselves in the head. Raze was their best. Most operatives never made it past Level Ten, remaining mere bloodhounds in this game of seek and destroy—Raze was a destroyer.

Undaunted—maybe even a little amused—Raze merged onto the 101 and carved through the city's veins toward South Beach. SoMa had gone soft over the years: once a sprawl of warehouses, hobos, and sweatshop grit, now dressed up in galleries, Michelin stars, and high-rent high-rises.

After living in the company compound under lock and key for six years, Raze had finally earned the privilege of his own digs. Living completely on the company's dime had been convenient and extremely profitable. With room, board, and every possible amenity paid for, Raze saved and invested his entire income—off the books, tax-free, and substantial. The compound was far from being a prison, but it wasn't his *own*.

When Infinium acquired an enormous, dilapidated warehouse for a "loss" project, Raze took advantage of his status. He negotiated a bargain price for a 4,000-square-foot section of it and converted it into his own living and workspace. The rest of the building remained rundown and undeveloped. For Raze, it was the best of both worlds. He was able to live in the midst of the dense population yet still enjoy near-total solitude.

The constant rattle and hum of San Francisco suited him. In the bustling metropolis, he could be packed like a sardine in the tin box of a Muni bus or a BART train, breathing into the face of a stranger, and still feel non-existent. People here ignored each other, never making eye contact. It was the perfect place to hide in plain sight. It was the complete opposite of his childhood home in Nebraska, where there was too much space. People not only looked at you, they scrutinized, found your flaws, then picked you apart, deeming you acceptable or, as in Raze's case, *not*.

Raze pulled the Audi into his three-car garage, another luxury in the space-deprived city. At the back door, he placed his hand up to the Qi panel. It was a condition required by Infinium that Qi pads be located throughout the house. Because his residence was both a living and a workspace, access was limited. The Qis controlled admittance to and from each room. Housekeeping and concierge services were limited to the first level. The very rare personal guest could be in the first level and his bedroom, but only if Raze was there with them.

When the Qi panel identified Raze, the locks disengaged and the door slid open. He stepped into the foyer and coded the system for alone status, which allotted him full, unchecked access. All the doors in the house simultaneously slid open, welcoming him home.

He stepped through the hallway and into a soaring living room, vaulted to the third floor. The concrete ceilings and walls were accented with exposed steel beams, original pipes, and ducts. A pair of 24-foot arched windows on the western wall framed the cityscape. Throughout the house, select walls were spray-painted with the vibrant street art of the renowned graffiti gods of The Seventh Letter: Revok, Saber, Push, Reyes, and Retna. Custom stained concrete floors were garnished with bright geometric rugs. An iron spiral staircase connected the staggered, tri-level floor plan, and a catwalk bridged his third-floor bedroom with a private rooftop patio that boasted a 360-degree view of the city and the Bay.

Raze took off his jacket and tie, throwing them on the living room couch. He ripped his shirt off, letting its buttons pop and scatter in six directions, then tossed it on the fireplace mantel. He kicked one shoe off by the recliner and the other toward a far corner of the room. He didn't give a fuck. The maid service could clean it all up tomorrow—*and* mend his shirt. He liked making people clean up after him. He liked reminding them of *their* place in *his* world.

Shirtless and barefoot, he padded into the kitchen and opened up the twin Sub Z's to find himself some righteous nourishment. The concierge service stocked it each morning, leaving it chock-full of pre-made gourmet meals and snacks. Raze grabbed a basket of açaí berries, a handful of almonds, and the pitcher of purified, alkaline water. He adopted a high-vibration diet during his training process, eating only fresh organic foods and completely eliminating alcohol, sugar, and caffeine in order to keep his physical vehicle balanced to better control his gift.

After years of living on a diet of Red Bull, Slim Jims, candy, and fast food, clean living had been a shock to his system and caused severe withdrawals. But the payoff was worth it. He'd had a pretty decent body before, but now it was beyond extraordinary, redefining "ripped" and taking "shredded" into the stratosphere.

Although he was exceptional when it came to keeping inferior energies in check, Raze could feel a persistent nag of stress within his energy field and in his body's cells. A thin thread of current running against its normal flow.

It had been a stressful morning. In his eight years as a control operative, he'd never faced a situation of this magnitude. The question of how a young woman had manifested in *Demesne* and altered events whined in his brain like a candy-deprived child. Raze was itching to pick it up and shake its knobby little head for the answers, but there were other priorities.

He only had a couple of hours before he needed to track Blake down for the kill, and that would take his entire focus. It required a calm and collected mental, emotional, and physical state to do what he was about to do. He needed to release a little tension.

Raze contemplated his options. Anything that would relax him too much—a sauna, a Jacuzzi, a massage—was out. So was sex. That would scatter his focus and drain the energy he needed. A release could wait until after the job was done. What he really needed was a workout and some fresh air. He went into his bedroom, changed into workout clothes, coded the warehouse for away status, and left for a run along the Embarcadero.

It was perfect running weather, clear and crisp.

Surrounded by water on three sides, the seasons in San Francisco tended to be backwards and the weather unpredictable. The summer brought in billows of damp fog and a chill, while fall and winter often brought unexpected warmth. He ran under the steel skeleton of the Bay Bridge, past the Ferry Building, through Maritime Park, up to Van Ness. Instead of allowing his endorphins to run unchecked to produce the euphoric high most runners craved, Raze directed them to burn out the pockets of tension and disquiet in his field. There was nothing better than running to clear his space.

After the alternating currents of agitation and distraction were neutralized, Raze turned around, methodically reacquainting himself with the facts of the Project.

The 8 had called him in on the assignment after they received intel that Scott Parrish had been accessing restricted information regarding Quantum Gaming Systems and Infinium Incorporated.

Level Ten Viewers began tracking Parrish's every move and eavesdropping on every conversation after they found out he'd been sent a top-secret video of a wartime incident that depicted a team of soldiers mowing down a group of civilians.

To Parrish, an award-winning journalist, what was most disturbing about the incident was the glee with which the troops reacted.

They shouted encouragement to each other.

"Light 'em up!"

"100 points for that guy in the stripes!"

"Another 10 if you finish off the one crawling on the ground!"

Also unnerving was that one of them could be heard repeating, "Keep shooting" over and over in a chillingly monotonous drone, until the street was paved with blood.

It was as though they were playing a video game, rather

than participating in a real war, and Parrish had wondered if there was something more. He began working on an article that exposed a military training program that used a video game to create killing machines out of its players.

When Parrish purchased *Demesne* to try to unlock this mystery, Infinium Incorporated was more than concerned. Gaming protocol was a very successful aspect of their government contract, and they did not want to jeopardize it with any unnecessary negative attention.

If Scott Parrish had been a writer for an organization that was part of Infinium's media conglomerate, it would have been easy; an editor would just quash the article. But he wasn't. He was a correspondent for an independent online magazine renowned for its impartial and accurate content. Exposure would be catastrophic; it was imperative that it be prevented.

Raze was called, and the project was initiated.

Lucky for the company, Mr. Parrish just happened to have a member of *Demesne's* target demographic living in his home.

∞

Raze came back from his run, let himself in through the Qi in the front door, stripped off his sweat-soaked clothes, and threw them at the bottom of the stairs.

"Blake Mix," he said out loud.

The voice recognition system of the house began playing music from a playlist specifically created by Raze to remind him of Blake Parrish.

The first grinding metal riff hit—same kind of track Raze had queued during their most chaotic raids in *Demesne*, when he taught Blake to thrive on blood rush and chaos. Music was a basic tool for activating the brain centers, especially the lobes that housed memory and recognition. Even the common maggot used music as a gateway—a song on the radio could throw someone from a good mood into the depths of despair over a lost love, or send them into a joyful butt-dance during their morning commute.

The punk tracks tapped into the kid's half-baked rebellion, just like those side-quests, where Raze "accidentally" let him break protocol and win big. And then, just enough bubblegum boyband to hark back to his more innocent days of only a few months before, when Raze and Blake met for the first time—the noob wandering into the arena, wide-eyed, thinking it was all just a game until Raze took him under his wing.

Raze grabbed some more water, another snack from the fridge, and took the stairs to the third-floor master bedroom suite.

"Tonic," he commanded to the shower.

The shower responded by turning on all 18 heads and heating the water to a lukewarm temperature. Raze stepped inside, allowing the shower to wash off the sweat, then relaxed as it ran through a programmed sequence that stimulated the six zones of his body.

The girl still hadn't left his mind.

No frequency. No signature. No trace.

That wasn't possible.

At least—not by the rules as he understood them.

He filed it away for later. She would need to be handled. Thoroughly.

For now, he drowned himself in the dropped D power chords and raw scream vocals and conjured up Blake in his mind.

Twelve years old, razor-sharp intellect, no armor to speak of. Ripe. Lonely. *Demesne* was the perfect snare—unsupervised hours after school, the hum of his parents' absence, and the kind of game that made gods out of outcasts.

Just having *Demesne* in the house was enough to ensure Blake would get a hold of it. It was the most popular MMORPG on the market. Everyone in Blake's age group was either playing it or talking about it.

After that, *Demesne* handled the majority of the hard work. The game had just the right mix of attributes for creating addiction, especially in one who had a personality type like Blake's. Loneliness and isolation had crept into inviting nooks and crannies to hide within Blake's subconscious.

Raze understood this well.

Studying Blake was like gazing into a mirror—one that reached back through time and threw Raze's own childhood into sharp relief. The same raw intellect. The same aching loneliness. A boy too smart for his own good, too strange to fit, and too unguarded to survive without becoming something else.

Raze had learned to armor up.

Blake hadn't.

Not yet.

Demesne worked her magic, though, engaging Blake in roleplay that allowed him to behave completely different from his normal self. While Blake was completely powerless in his day-to-day life, *Demesne* gave him complete control of everything: weapons, equipment, armies, and people. Intense scenarios stimulated his adrenals, and endorphins flooded his brain, sending him into euphoria.

But what really snagged him—hook, line, and sinker—was Raze himself. Inside the game, Raze befriended Blake immediately. He took the little noob under his wing, showed him the ropes, gave him inside tips, and kept him from getting pwned—leetspeak for being totally dominated by other players. Raze established the camaraderie that quickly brought all the kid's psychological defenses down.

When Blake wasn't in the game, he crashed hard, with a hangover of depression and irritability that could only be alleviated by playing. Blake literally itched and trembled through the insufferably long weekends when his parents were home. His father eventually noticed, changed the passwords, and locked the visors in the gun safe. But Raze made sure the boy got back in.

The night he first shifted Blake's brainwave patterns, opening the portal into 4D space, was the moment the boy truly became his protégé. Within two months, Raze had manipulated, tweaked, and fine-tuned Blake, turning an innocent boy into an on-demand killing machine. A machine programmed to kill his own father.

Well, that was how it was supposed to go down.

The shower completed the relaxation sequence, chilling the water to a brisk, invigorating mode. Raze was both relaxed and completely alert.

"Off," he said, stepping out of the shower and toweling himself dry. He went to his closet to get dressed. While it was theoretically possible to work naked, Raze liked to wear attire that made him feel professional. He selected a pair of black slacks and a form-fitting black turtleneck from his closet. He dressed, ran some gel through his jet-black hair, and slapped on a little of his favorite cologne. He was ready.

Raze stood before the full-length mirror at the far wall of his room. A Qi panel inside the mirror scanned his energy field, then slid open, revealing a set of stairs that led down to the hidden second level of the warehouse. He stepped through the opening, the wall closed behind him, and he descended the staircase into the cold, sterile sanctuary of The Womb.

He called it The Womb—not just for the way it cradled him in perfect stasis while he travelled, but because it was where he gestated new realities—where he birthed new killers into the world.

Today, Raze opted for a remote influencing operation rather than dream-seeding. It was actually easier to manipulate thoughts and influence people while they were still awake. Seeding took several astral visits to fully implant an idea. During sleep, Raze could seed an idea in a subject's mind, but then could only wait and hope; the concept germinated before the subject woke up so that they would follow through.

There were too many variables in seeding. If the subject was under the influence of alcohol or medication, or if they were not evolved enough to pull dream information up through the wavelengths into their subconscious minds, the seed could go latent or perish. Blake would surely be medicated, so Raze wasn't going to waste his time trying to dream seed suicidal thoughts.

Remote influencing could work in one visit. Raze could turn the right screws that would make Blake believe that Raze's thoughts were his own and get him to complete the assigned task.

Raze sat down in the recliner. He checked his energy on the monitor, happy to see that the run and shower had brought his brainwaves down to Alpha 14.

"Alpha 8."

The stereo faded the Blake Mix into a soft, white noise. Raze leaned back into the chair; let his body release its weight, allowed gravity to pull the idea of his body into the Earth. He began taking slow, deep breaths and placed his fingers in a sequence of hand mudras with each breath cycle to coordinate and influence the flow of energy through his physical and astral body.

"Theta 7."

The Womb switched to automatic pilot and began monitoring his brain cycles, adjusting the environment to support him as he traveled.

∞

RAZE PULLED his consciousness into the center of his brain, softly holding his concentration in the space occupied by his pineal gland. An orb of golden light appeared in his mind's eye. Raze evoked Blake's signature frequency, visualizing a scene of colors, similar to an impressionist watercolor painting. He recalled the specific notes on the music scale that were unique to Blake. The process was just like using a phone number to call a friend. Once Raze reached resonance with Blake's signature frequency, the orb would open like an aperture for his consciousness to walk through. Raze would literally step his astral consciousness through the portal and travel into the space Blake occupied.

He waited for the connection to be made, which usually only took a moment, but nothing happened. No alignment occurred. No aperture appeared. It was as if Blake's signature didn't exist—he was disconnected, no longer in service.

This was strange. Even people in a coma still had a faint signature Raze could connect to, but this was akin to the flat line Raze got only when someone was dead. He brought himself back up to Alpha, where he could access his problem-solving processes again.

The newswire said that Blake was in custody, not dead. The option-lock command Raze had used that morning should have only locked Blake's consciousness in place, not erased it completely. The signal line should still be intact. That meant somehow Blake's frequency had changed. Raze closed his eyes, placed himself back in the center of his head, and lowered himself into Theta again.

"GPS coordinates for Chrysalis Adolescent Resource Center, Modesto, California," he commanded.

There was a hushed moment as The Womb's voice replied, "North 37 degrees, 40 minutes, point two, four, six seconds. West minus 120 degrees, 55 minutes, 17 point zero, two, five, six seconds."

Raze attuned himself to the coordinate. The gold orb appeared as he acquired a signal. Descending deeper into Theta, he opened the aperture and pressed his consciousness through the portal.

Raze experienced a slight vertigo, and then, with a snap, crackle, and pop, he was there. He opened his remote viewing eyes and found himself standing at the front door of the A.R.C. Raze shifted his perspective, lifting himself above the building for a bird's-eye view. The A.R.C. was a single-story building, brown and plain, spread out over about an acre of land. Where Blake was inside the building was unknown. Raze tried tuning in to Blake's signature again, but it was still flat. He'd have to do this old school. Raze placed himself at the front door again and pushed himself through it.

Astrally, it was easier moving through actual 3D portals, such as doors and windows, rather than pushing through solid matter. Doors and windows provided the easiest access, but lamps, computer screens, electronic circuitry, even picture frames were also good options. Finding the gaps between the two-by-fours of houses and moving through soft stucco and drywall was possible, but more of a challenge. Brick walls took too much energy to push through.

Once inside the building, Raze moved through the hallway toward an elderly woman who sat at the reception desk. While

Raze could see and feel himself as if he were real, to others in the physical world, he was invisible. His essence could only be discerned by the very sensitive. This old hag was too engrossed in one of the entertainment rags published by Infinium, staring at the latest paparazzi photographs of a celebrity hook-up between some botoxed starlet and the "sexiest man alive." She was oblivious to his presence. Raze moved around her and through the double doors that led into the hospital.

Young patients wandered the halls and chatted with each other while they waited for their next therapy session, meds, or meal. This would not be the area Blake would be in. He'd be in lockdown somewhere. Raze continued down the hallway, looking for signs that would lead him to a higher security area. He spotted one that read Acute Care and pointed himself toward a restricted access doorway.

Locked doors were no barrier for him. He pushed his energetic body through it and wandered down another corridor. He could hear voices echoing from around the corner. He made the turn and saw two men standing in the hallway outside a room. One was dressed in a rumpled blue suit and tie, the other in a dark blue police uniform.

"Bingo," Raze thought.

Raze jumped his essence to a couple of feet outside of the men's energy fields. While people were mostly unconscious of the subtle alterations of the energy around them, sometimes they could catch a drift that shifted their attention. If Raze didn't disrupt or intrude on their fields in any way, he could gather more information.

"Here's your Venti, triple-shot, rama-lama-ding-dong," the man in uniform said, handing a large cup of Starbucks to the suit.

"What the fuck ever, dude. It's caffeinated, and that's all I care about at this point," said the suit. "This is ridiculous."

The old copper looked through a long, narrow windowpane into the room. He grunted. "No change, huh?"

"Not a bit. Still just rocking himself in the corner, repeating his 'two sticks and a bucket' bullshit."

Perfect. Right where I put him, Raze thought with smug satisfaction.

"When's the doc gettin' here?"

"*Therapist.* He made it really clear that he is not a doctor. He doesn't want that kind of responsibility with this kid." The suit checked his watch. "He should be here in twenty minutes. If he's on time. You know how quacks like to keep you waiting. If this dude can't snap this kid out of it, I'm gettin' a rookie over here to babysit and goin' home. Maybe Mommy can knock some sense into him tomorrow."

The cop grunted again and changed the subject. "How's Becky?"

As the suit began a conversation about whoever Becky was, Raze moved himself to the doorway and looked through the window. Just like Suit said, Blake was sitting on the linoleum next to the bed, hunched up in a little ball, cradling himself.

Didn't move an inch. You're making this too easy.

Raze waited for an opportune point in the conversation so he could push himself through the window. When the suit laughed at something the uniform said, he went. The window made a soft tapping sound, and Raze looked back into the hall-way. Too caught up in their idle chitchat, neither of the men had turned toward the sound. Blake didn't respond to the shift in the room either.

Raze surveyed the room. Somewhere between the thera-pist's visit and Mom arriving, Blake needed to be handled —*permanently.* Raze needed to set the stage for Blake to become his own undoing.

His eyes moved over the space, cataloguing its weaknesses

and possibilities. The mirror on the southern wall. The chair in the corner. The steel-framed bed. Every object hummed with potential. If he applied the right pressure, the room designed to keep a boy safe—could be a weapon.

He sat down on the bed, studying Blake and the thin, blue gown he wore.

The gown. The rails. Yes. That would do.

Relief uncoiled in him. The means were there. All he had to do was whisper the right suggestion and let the boy dismantle himself.

Raze looked toward the window, thinking maybe he could get this done now, before the therapist had a chance to interrupt.

He projected an astral hand toward Blake's head. "Hello, little buddy. Remember me?"

There was no response—no shift in Blake's breathing, no reflexive muscle twitch. Raze switched into receiver mode and felt for the presence of an energy signature, much the same way a nurse would take a pulse. Nothing. The body sat there, running its basic programs, but the pilot was gone.

That's... unacceptable. Without a channel to tune into, he wouldn't be able to access Blake's subconscious—he couldn't be the voice inside his head compelling him to self-destruct.

The restricted doors at the end of the hall buzzed open, and footsteps moved toward the room. Raze, like the two gumshoes standing outside the door, was going to have to see if the therapist could pull Blake back into his body. Highly unlikely, but if he did, Raze would be here, ready for the catch—and the kill.

AISLEN WAS MORTIFIED. How embarrassing was it to practically faint in the hallway and have to be propped up by Troy? Yeah. Professional—having a full-blown existential crisis in the hallway. Real nurse material, Aislen. And add to that—flippin' crazy! That's what she really was! With her crazy-ass dreams, weird voodoo vibes following her around all day, and a catatonic psychiatric patient practically waking from the dead to tell her weird shit about her name—it was too much.

She thought she hid her meltdown well with the whole *"oops, I slipped"* excuse. How she came up with such a logical response during a mental health crisis while swooning in the arms of *Prince Charming* was amazing as hell. She didn't realize she had such a knack for lying her ass off.

Rachel and Troy got her back to the nurse's station in one piece and sat her in a chair. Rachel went to the kitchen to get her an orange juice, thinking her blood sugar might be low, and Troy took her hand in his, pressing two fingertips on the crook of her wrist.

"Your pulse is a little fast," he said.

No shit, Sherlock. You're touching me, she said to herself.

He looked up at her, frowning with concern.

"Oh, shit! Did I say that out loud?"

"Say what out loud?" Troy looked even more worried and confused.

"Oh. I guess not. Never mind," she said. She was really losing it.

Troy squinted at her, searching her face, then meeting her eyes. The intensity of his gaze made her heart hammer even harder. She yanked her wrist away so he wouldn't notice.

"I came over here to pick you up for a field trip... but now I'm thinking maybe you should just go home sick for the rest of the day."

"No!" she responded, a little too forcefully. "I've just been having a really, really wild and busy day. And with finals... and work... and almost breaking my neck just now. But it's no big deal—I only slipped." Now she sounded desperate. *God, what is wrong with me?*

She stopped and took a deep breath. "No, I really want to go," she managed to say with a degree of control in her voice. "I've never been to that facility. I want to see what it's like."

"All right," Troy said. "If you think you're up for it."

"I am. I'm sure."

Rachel came back with a big glass of orange juice. Aislen took it from her and chugged the whole thing down in three gulps. Troy laughed.

"Okay then, we should get going. We wouldn't want to keep them waiting."

Aislen handed the glass back to Rachel. "Thanks for covering for me. I'll be back as soon as I can."

"No worries... but try to stay on your feet. I know that may be difficult, given the company." Rachel raised her eyebrows up and down and gave her a knowing smile. Aislen shooed at her with her hand and followed Troy down the hall.

Stepping outside the walls of the hospital was new territory for them, and Aislen immediately felt self-conscious. She always felt more comfortable and self-assured in the structured environs of school and work, hiding behind the masks of erudition and professionalism. In casual settings, such as restaurants, cars, parking lots, *life*, Aislen retreated into a shell. And in the presence of an especially cute guy? Forget about it.

They walked in silence through the lot to Troy's car. Aislen expected to be led to a beige Honda Accord, Toyota Prius, or an older model Volvo, which all the shrink types seemed to be driving these days. Instead, Troy walked her to a vintage but mean-looking moss-green Mustang. He unlocked the passenger door first and opened it for her. No one had ever opened a car door for her. Any dates she had been on had been pretty much fend-for-yourself so far as opening doors and paying for dinners were concerned. She felt flattered by the gesture.

"I'm surprised by your choice of wheels," she said as she slid into the seat.

Troy leaned over the window and smiled at her. "What? Were you expecting a Prius?"

"Yeah, actually I was," she laughed.

"Not my style." He reached up and patted the hood. "This beauty was my inheritance from my Grandpa Joe. It's a 1967 Fastback that he hid in the garage under a quilt for 30 years."

"He must have known you'd appreciate it."

"Yeah... he knew I loved this car. When I'd stay over, I would sneak out to the garage, climb under the quilt and into the driver's seat, and pretend I was Tokyo drifting down the highway. Grandpa would come out, rip the quilt off, and yell, 'This car is off-limits, young man!' He'd be all red and puffy and belligerent, but then he would pop the hood and start telling me all about her. He knew this car would be the first place I'd go, and I knew his anger was all a show." Troy gave a wistful laugh. "He gave it to me when I graduated college, just before he passed away. Crazy."

Aislen was touched not only by the story but also by how sentimental Troy was about it. He was so comfortable in his own skin, just being himself. It was so easy to relax around him.

"We really need to get a move on now. We're late. Good thing this car is fast." He shut her door, rounded the car to his side, and hopped into the driver's seat. "Better fasten your seatbelt, hon." He started the car, revved the engine, and gunned it out of the parking lot.

Aislen needn't have worried about having to carry on a conversation. The deep rumble of the muscle car made small talk impossible. Aislen didn't want to shout over the roar, and she sure as hell wasn't going to lean over and invade Troy's personal space. They sped down the backcountry roads. At an intersection, a driver misjudged their speed and pulled out in front of them. As Troy stepped on the brake, he reached his arm across her and held her in her seat. The feeling of his arm pressed up against her chest sent a flush of heat through her and started her heart ker-thumping.

They whipped into the parking lot of the A.R.C. It was the most exhilarating five-minute experience of Aislen's life. Before she could catch her breath, Troy was out of the car, opening her door again.

"M'Lady," he said, extending his hand to her to help lift her out of the seat.

She reached up and took hold of it. A jolt of electricity coursed through her body, and she thought her heart was going to finally give out on her. "Thanks," she said, suddenly shy again.

"Let's go check in, shall we?"

They walked through the front doors. A silver-haired woman looked up from the magazine she was reading and smiled warmly. "Good afternoon! May I help you?"

"Yes," Troy said, pulling out his Chrysalis ID. "I am here to meet with a Detective Jackson regarding the Parrish case, please. Nurse Walker is with me."

"Oh, yes. I'll buzz you in. Just follow the main corridor to the end. You'll see the signs for the Acute Center on the wall." She handed Aislen a visitor's badge. Troy clipped his ID to his pocket.

"Thank you, ma'am." He gave her one of his signature smiles, and Aislen could have sworn she saw the old lady blush.

They went through the main double doors and started walking down the corridor. The wing was similar to Aislen's facility, only instead of geriatric patients wandering the hall, teenagers loitered there. They stopped talking to give Aislen the once-over and Troy the twice-over as they passed.

"I really didn't have time to go over this case with you," Troy said as they walked. "But just a quick fill-in should do."

"Okay," she replied, distracted by a couple of teenage girls nudging each other and giggling as Troy walked past.

"The client we are here to see used to attend a gaming addiction group I lead at the community health center. It was at the insistence of his parents, so needless to say, because he was forced to attend, he didn't participate much. Apparently, there was an incident at his house early this morning, and he has been displaying some crisis symptoms. I was asked to come over here to see if a familiar face can ease him out of his current state."

"What happened this morning?" A bell started ringing in her head, and a sense of foreboding clenched in her stomach. She knew what he was going to say before he said it.

"The police found him in his house, sitting next to his father... who had been shot in the head."

Aislen stopped walking. "You're kidding, right?" Her head was starting to swim a little more.

Troy stopped and looked at her with concern. "Is this going to be too much for you?"

Aislen shook her head, more as an attempt to shake the vertigo out of it than to answer his question, but he took it as a no.

"I know the situation is disturbing," he continued, "but I have seen how professional you have been with various adult crisis situations and thought you'd like to tag along to observe a juvenile case. I should have explained the situation to you so you could have a choice as to whether or not you wanted to come. You know, it's unclear as to whether or not Blake was the shooter. He could just be a witness."

A needle-bright ringing pierced her ears painfully. "What did you say his name was?"

"Blake. Blake Parrish. Why? Does it sound familiar?"

Yes, it did. Like a really bad case of déjà vu, her dream was haunting her again. She could feel the fierce presence of the soldier and hear the echoes of his command, 'Blake, carry on' reverberating through the crevices of her brain. She shook her head again and managed to choke out a whisper. "No. It just sounds sad."

"It is. Very sad. I wouldn't have seen this coming at all. He seemed like a normal teenager to me. Maybe a little quiet and shy, but he wasn't dark, hateful, or aloof... like most the other kids in the group. He seemed almost confused by the whole concept of why he was there. I'm thinking the shooting had to have been done by someone else, and when Blake found his dad—he went into total shock."

But Aislen knew better.

They walked to the doors of the Acute Center. Troy pressed the buzzer, and a nurse unlocked them.

Aislen felt lost. She felt adrift in the in-between, straddling the dream and the present moment. She could see her body walking down the hall, but could not feel the air caress her flesh or feel the weight of her body pressing into the floor. Words floated in her mouth, evading her tongue, denying her the ability to form them into speech. The woman she knew herself to be, controlled and articulate, didn't exist right now. She didn't know how to think or act.

Aislen tried to rationalize. This was just an ordinary psychiatric situation she was here to witness. She was overreacting, taking an insignificant, unconscious dream and giving it significance and meaning. They have a word for that in psychiatry: *delusional.* The doors opened for them, and they walked down another hallway.

∞

VOICES in the hall grew louder. Raze moved off Blake's bed and to the window. A young man about his own age, wearing a long-sleeved dress shirt with a badge hanging from his pocket, approached the room. He looked a little young to be the therapist, but Raze was a little young to be a mind control operative, so go figure.

There was a lot of handshaking and introductions going on. Raze was able to make out that the therapist's name was Troy, but when the Troy character turned to introduce the person who was with him, Raze felt a slight buzz brush up against his energy field, and a sound of static filled the room. He checked in on Blake to see if it was him, but it wasn't. Blake's energy was still flat.

It had to be originating with Troy or whoever had arrived with him. Raze could not see who it was. He thought about pushing through the window for a better perspective, but decided to move back next to Blake instead. If Blake recognized the doctor when he came into the room and checked back into his body, Raze had to be there to capture the altered frequency, or he wouldn't be able to influence him to self-destruct later.

He hovered around Blake and watched the door.

∞

TROY HAD BEEN SPEAKING to her all the way down the hallway, telling her about the different areas of the facility and what each section was responsible for, but Aislen couldn't keep track. She felt like she was swimming underwater. She could see his lips moving, but she could only hear her own breath. Her vision narrowed as they walked the hallway, and the loose knot she had been holding in her stomach tightened.

They turned the corner and approached a police officer and a man in a suit who were waiting outside a door. Aislen watched in a fog as Troy extended his hand to the detective, "Good afternoon, I'm Troy Kellen." There was a round of handshaking and name exchanges. Aislen could barely hear any of them. The shrill tinnitus fluttering in her ears had intensified. "This is Aislen, a nursing student and one of my assistants."

The police officers offered to shake her hand. But a blurring of her vision made it hard for her to focus. She looked up at the ceiling to see if one of the fluorescent lights was burning out and making the hallway strobe, but all the lights were glowing steadily.

Troy walked over to the door and peered through the window. He turned to Aislen. "This shouldn't take too long, if you want to watch from the observation window with the officers."

She nodded at him, although she hadn't heard a word he said. The officers went into the adjacent room as Troy opened the door and stepped inside the room with Blake.

∞

RAZE SAW the doctor's face appear in the door window just before he opened the door and stepped in. He wasn't a bad-looking dude, this Troy, a little loose around the edges, but he seemed confident. Being in the same room with a psychopathic child didn't seem to faze him in the slightest.

Raze tuned his receptors into Troy and evaluated his signature as he pulled up a chair and sat down in front of Blake.

"Hello, Blake. Do you remember me? I'm Troy Kellen. You've been in a few of my classes."

He was so sincere, Raze wanted to puke. He could easily feel and see Troy's signature, a smooth and lolling frequency—waves of blue and green—as calm as a sea.

Raze paused. Troy's frequency looked normal—almost too normal. Like it had been flattened and repainted. Manufactured calm.

But he seized it and banked it away. Every pattern could be

weaponized, given the right breach. Then he returned his antennae toward Blake, who was still non-responsive.

A fierce vacillation was volleying around the room like an errant ping-pong ball. It was so strong, Raze had to start compensating to remain anchored in the view. Not Blake. Not Troy. Something else entirely. And something about it was starting to feel very familiar.

∞

AISLEN REMAINED IN THE HALL. She didn't know what she was supposed to do. Disorientation affected her vision and hearing to the point that she was nearly incapacitated. She watched the officers moving toward the observation room and thought she should follow them, but her feet refused.

At the same time, she felt an irresistible, almost magnetic, pull toward the door that Troy had just walked through. The intensity caused a revolting twist in her stomach, yet at the same time, it had a seductive appeal.

Aislen moved toward the doorway and peeked through the slat of glass. Troy had pulled up a chair and was sitting with his back to the door. Just beyond his shoulder, she could just see the dark, tousled crown of a small head resting face down on his knees. The force luring her toward the little boy became too intense for her to resist. Aislen opened the door.

∞

THE GRATING sibilation turned into an obnoxious jackhammering, forcing Raze into overdrive. He checked Blake's energy for any signs of life. Still nothing. He rechecked the doctor's space again to see if he was the source. He wasn't.

What. The. Fuck?

Raze saw a flutter of movement behind the little shaft of window. A shadow of a face peeked in, and the room flooded with another tsunami of energy. Raze was thrown back and pinned against the wall. He had to compensate by pulling his field in close to retain his grip on Theta. He was determined to hold on so he could find out who was causing all this chaos.

Raze watched the door slowly crack open. A fury of unseen force sliced through the room, nearly pushing him out, but he held his ground. Troy, hearing the door open behind him, turned in his chair.

"Aislen?" he said, surprised and a little confused.

"Sorry," a female voice said. But rather than leaving, the door opened further. A young woman slowly walked into the room.

It was her! The stray strumpet he booted from *Demesne* this morning. Raze was stunned, which caused his control to falter, and he started to slip out of the view.

The room became frantic with static, like bees swarming in a hive. His hold on the space felt like it was being plucked at, one ethereal finger at a time. He gripped the space with all of his might as she walked further into the room and over to Blake.

Raze glanced down and saw that Blake had stopped rocking and was slowly raising his head off his knees.

Shit! Blake was back! But the vortex in the room was overpowering. Raze couldn't split his signal—Raze couldn't maintain the space *and* capture Blake's frequency. Not with her distorting the field like a tuning fork on fire. He watched helplessly as Blake looked up, straight into the woman's shocked face.

Blake cocked his head to the side. "You're the lady from *Demesne*." He smiled at her, not with the sweet eyes of an innocent boy, but with a glower of someone sinister. "I knew you would come."

The room exploded with the force of a nuclear bomb, and Raze was slammed back into his body in The Womb.

"FUUUCK!"

∞

AISLEN HEARD a loud crack inside her skull. Her brain felt like it was ripping apart, her heart stuttered, and time stopped.

She was standing face-to-face with the boy from her dream. He really existed—and he knew her! Only this was not the same small creature she felt pity for in the dream. His smile was twisted and evil. She felt something reaching at her throat, trying to crawl inside of her.

Her stomach curdled, and she turned and ran out of the room. Sinister fingers clawed at her back, trying to grip her and pull her back. She ran even faster, back down the halls, and out the front doors of the hospital, where she vomited in the shrubs.

NINE

AISLEN DIDN'T KNOW how long she'd been on the curb. Cold bit through denim. One tilt and she'd be Humpty Dumpty and shatter into a million pieces.

The late afternoon air was laced with crystalline particles of winter, and she wrapped her arms around her knees, resting her frost-nipped face against them—not so unlike Blake's had been, sitting in his cell.

She had a little mantra going on in her head, too. It went something like, "What the fuck just happened? What the fuck just happened? What the fuck just happened?" And although the idea of it soothed her, she left out the rocking. No need to ice the crazy cake.

Footsteps approached behind her, and she braced herself. She had no idea how to explain things to Troy. What could she possibly say? "I had a bad dream last night, and that little boy was in it?" Yeah, right. She had already ruined any good impression he had of her by intruding into his session, and she didn't want to make it worse by confirming she was a nutcase.

He crouched down behind her, and the heat of him wafted

around her. He placed his hand on her shoulder, searing its print through her coat, sweater, and into her skin, making her shiver with something not at all weather-related.

"I called Rachel," he said softly, his breath tracing the contours of her ear. "I told her that you're really sick and can't come back to work. I'm going to take you home."

Her stomach twisted. The humiliation was unbearable. He hadn't asked, just decided. Finally realized she was "really sick." Her emotions started to get the best of her. Tears stung the back of her eyes; she was determined to keep them in check. She was not a weeper, damn it! She refused to appear weak and broken.

"I'm so sorry. I've ruined everything," she lamented.

"It's okay," he said, "and you didn't ruin anything. I don't know what on earth possessed you to come into that room, but it triggered a reaction in Blake that nobody else has been able to get. So that's a positive. At least we know there's a light on in there somewhere."

"I don't know what I was thinking. I *wasn't* thinking, that's the problem."

"Yeah, I was more than a little surprised when you walked in, that's for sure. But when he *spoke* to you—I almost fell out of my chair. Do you know him from somewhere?"

She *did* know him! He wasn't just a figment of her imagination, and yet he was. But she couldn't explain that to Troy. If she couldn't understand it, he surely wouldn't. She lifted her head, wiping her face on her sleeve.

"I've never seen him before in my life," she said, aiming for steady. She was getting really good at this lying thing. At least she still knew the difference between knowing someone in the real world and dreaming them.

"Blake said you were the girl from *Demesne*. Maybe he recognizes you from there."

"What?" Aislen was confused. She had no idea what Troy was talking about. "I've never heard of *Demesne*. Where is it?"

"*Demesne* isn't a place—it's a game... a video game. So you don't play video games?"

Aislen shot him a look that said, "Does it look like I play video games?"

"No? But you so seem like the type." His face relaxed with the joke. "Demesne is a role-playing game. Dystopian. Lots of destruction and debauchery. You know exactly what all the kids want these days. It's the game that Blake's parents felt he was addicted to, and why he was sent to my group." He explained the game smoothly—like he'd given this speech before.

Aislen's skin prickled. *Demesne* sounded too similar to what she'd dreamed, and if he told her any more, she would really lose it. "Never even heard of it," she said.

Troy let it go with a little shrug. "Maybe you remind him of an avatar he knows in the game. You do have that fantasy anime look, you know." He gave her ponytail a playful tug. "Do you think you can get up so I can get you home?"

She nodded. He took hold of her hand and helped her up off the sidewalk, sending her emotions spinning again.

Why did he have to be so considerate? Why did he have to be so cute and so smart? And why did she have to be such a mental case? She could actually start to like him. Then, she had to admit, she already did—*a lot*. And in a very *un*professional way. But after this afternoon, he was probably all too ready to get her crazy-ass home and as far away from her as possible.

They walked back to his car, where he opened her door for her again. Now she was suspicious. Maybe he wasn't just being sweet. Maybe he really thought she was a pathetic invalid. That would make more sense.

He got into the car and looked over at her, "So where's home?"

She started to give him directions to her house, but thought better of it. "You know, could you just take me back to my car? I can drive myself. I'm feeling better now." He could think what he wanted about her, but she wasn't about to continue playing the damsel in distress.

"No problem," he readily agreed.

Aha! It was just as she suspected—he *was* eager to be rid of her. Although he drove in a more civilized manner back to the facility, the engine was too loud for conversation. Aislen glanced over at him a couple of times, but he appeared to be lost in thought. He pulled into the Chrysalis parking lot, turned off the engine, and looked over at her.

"Are you sure you're okay?" he asked, with the same sincere look on his face that she was beginning to believe was nothing but a great performance.

"I'm all right." She watched her hands instead of him.

"You know, Aislen. After doing what I've been doing for the last couple of years, I've gotten really good at reading people. And I can kinda tell—you *aren't* all right."

Just freakin' great. He can already see I'm cracked at the seams, and now he's going to point it out. She bit back a withering retort and looked down at her hands.

"I think we have gotten to know each other pretty well over the past few months, and I hope you know by now that if you need to talk about anything, I'm a damn good listener."

"You know, it's been a really strange and stressful day for me, and I really just want to be alone for a while and decompress." *And scream. She really wanted to scream. And cry. She really, really wanted to cry.*

"Okay. I understand."

She reached for the door handle to let herself out. "I'm sorry about everything today."

"And like I said earlier, you don't have anything to be sorry about."

She sighed. She disagreed but wasn't in the mood to argue about it. She got out of the car.

"Hey, Aislen," he stopped her. "You know, I am the one who should apologize. You were under my supervision today, and I was obligated to make sure you were all right. I shouldn't have put you through that."

"Obligated?" She spat the word back at him. She didn't know why, but it made her angry. Of course, he felt *obligated* and responsible for her. She was his subordinate. They weren't equals. They weren't really even friends.

"I get it. No worries," she said, sounding angry. She slammed his car door and stormed across the lot to her car. She fumbled with her keys, eyes blurry with frustration and unshed tears. She managed to unlock the door and get inside. The windows fogged. She glanced into the rearview mirror. She could see the shadowy figure of Troy through the haze of the back windshield. He had gotten out of his car and was watching her. She needed to get away—the faster the better.

She started the car, floored the gas pedal, and sped off, leaving Troy standing in a sputter of exhaust. It was not as impressive an exit as the Mustang, but it felt good making the tires squeal, slamming on the brakes, whipping around the corner, and making something else her bitch for a change.

She drove down the road in the completely opposite direction of home. The last place she wanted to be was home. She didn't want to have to face her mom or answer her questions about her day and have to lie, yet again. She knew exactly where she wanted to be.

She drove fast and furious, cutting in and out of traffic,

making her way to Route 108 and following it out of town. As businesses grew sparse, the landscape was taken over by dormant orchards and unplowed fields. Just before she reached the river, she pulled onto a private, dirt road and under a tall, vermilion torii gate, almost completely shrouded by overgrown oleanders. The sign on the gate had once read 'Lotus Garden' in gold flake paint, but time and weather had stripped it of both its "u" and its gilding. Aislen parked the car, put on her coat, and walked down a steep hill into the garden grounds.

Gen had brought her here during one of their adventures when they first got their driver's licenses. It had been a stifling June afternoon at the peak of the bloom. The main field had been green and lush, and the long, shallow ponds that surrounded it were overflowing with majestic blush and hot pink lotus blossoms. They spent hours admiring the flowers, peeking into the tranquil pools for frogs and turtles, and lounging under the shadows of the weeping willows, intoxicated by the exotic fragrance that permeated the air.

Being in the garden had filled Aislen with a deep sense of peace that she had never experienced before. She felt free of every expectation, content to just be—rather than have to do or think. After that first visit, she came back often, when she found herself feeling overwrought with the pressures of school or needing to tune out the chatter of her own head.

Today, large, rotting lily pads blanketed the scummy water. Dry, brown stalks jutted upward from the bogs toward the stark, gray expanse of the sky, seed pods dangled at their tops, as if mourning the loss of the sun. Aislen walked across the burnished fawn of grass toward the river's edge, past ornate stone statuary and a golden, laughing Buddha that hid in the midst of a bamboo thicket. She walked up a grassy staircase toward a large, wooden water tank that had been converted into a shrine, opened one of the red doors, removed her shoes, and stepped into its stillness.

Crepuscular rays beamed down through windows that encircled the top of the tank, alighting upon sacred objects that graced the room: a brass gong, prayer scrolls written in Chinese characters, and banners with woodcut drawings depicting mythological creatures. One in particular caught Aislen's eye, a dancing chimera with an elephant's trunk, a tiger's body and paws, and the tail of a cow. It seemed to gaze directly at her with wide and benevolent eyes.

Although the gardens were abandoned this afternoon, someone had been in the shrine earlier and had lit the candles on the altar. Aislen took a stick of incense from a vase and went to the altar. Lighting her incense from a candle, she placed it in a brass holder, watching as ethereal wisps of smoke spiraled up and fingered out into the waning ladders of sunlight, filling the room with the soothing scents of spice and wood.

She sat down in the center of the temple on a straw mat, took a deep breath, and finally let herself weep. Wracking sobs and streams of hot tears poured from her, releasing the fear, uncertainty, confusion, and frustration that had been gripping her all day. All that she knew herself to be—composed, independent, and confident—felt like an illusion. She didn't know who she was. Yesterday, she knew herself. Today, she did not.

She wept for a long time, purging herself until she was completely spent and felt heavy with exhaustion. She lay down on the mat and rested her head on her arms. The only sound was the faint drip of water in the bamboo thicket outside, each hollow *tok* echoing like a metronome through the quiet. It steadied her breath, lulled her deeper into stillness. She allowed her mind to wander, staying clear of the mundane aspects of her life and the profane land mines of the day.

She slipped into her imagination: saw herself driving

through a city in a car that wasn't hers. She was speeding, feeling a desperate need to get to her destination, but she couldn't figure out exactly where that was. It wasn't home, it wasn't school, it wasn't work, but it was someplace very important. She whipped through the asphalt grid, but every time she came to an intersection that felt familiar, there was a roadblock, signs, and barricades denying her access. She kept having to turn around and drive another direction, only to be met again with more obstacles: an enormous sinkhole in the middle of one street, a decrepit old lady crossing another. She made U-turns and detours until she finally came to one open junction. There were three roads she could take; she could turn left, right, or go straight, but she didn't know which one led to where she needed to go.

She sat in the car, contemplating. Each way looked exactly the same. She was about ready to play eeny-meeny-miny-mo when she noticed a homeless man standing on the corner. He was watching her intently, holding a cardboard sign with "The Father Knows The Way" scrawled across it in black Sharpie.

Religious freak. She shook her head and looked down each street again, then looked back toward the homeless man. She jumped. No longer standing across the street, he was now standing right at her passenger window, peeking over a hand-lettered sign that read, "Can I wash your windshield for you?"

She mouthed to him, "No, thank you." But the man paid no attention and set about washing windows that were spotless and didn't need cleaning.

She rolled down her window, stuck her head out, and shouted at him, "Sir, no! No, thank you... really... the windows are fine. Sir, please... it's already clean." But he kept squirting fluid on her windshield and rubbing it with a filthy cloth. Soon, the window was completely smeared with a grimy film, and she could no longer see through it at all. The man came to her open window and reached his palm in to her, waiting for his pay.

"No," she yelled at him. "I didn't need my window cleaned! And look, you've made it worse!" She looked at the mess of her windshield with dismay.

"You don't know where you are going anyway, Buttercup."

She gasped and looked at the homeless man's face. Underneath a veil of greasy hair, a pair of green and golden eyes gazed back at her intently. It was her father.

She reached down toward the button to roll the window back up, but the man reached inside and grabbed hold of her hand in an intense but painless grip.

"Aislen," he said tenderly. "Just give me one second. I know what you are going through. Believe me, *I know*. And you are going to need my help."

"Leave me alone!" She screamed at him, her eyes clamped shut, refusing to look at him. "I never needed you before; I sure as hell don't need you now!"

"Ah, but you do." The soothing calm of his voice made her breath catch in her throat. "You have always needed me, but you need me now more than ever." She tried tugging her hand away from his viselike grip, but he held her fast. "I understand why you feel the way you do, but I can't explain anything to you in a way that you would understand right now. You wouldn't believe it—especially coming from me. But listen to me, Aislen. You are waking up. You need help and protection, and I need you to let me in to help you."

Aislen tried again to pull her arm away from him, but his strength was supernatural. Tears slipped out from her sealed lids and rolled down her face. She felt his other hand reach up and gently wipe them away.

"Aislen," he whispered, "just do one thing for me... for

yourself." His voice was right next to her ear. "Ask your mother about the tea cups." He released her hand.

Her eyes snapped open. She was lying on her back, staring up at the roof of the shrine. Her face was soaking wet from crying. The sky beyond the windows had turned from heather to steel; the fading light barely illuminated a ceiling thick with cobwebs.

She grabbed her shoes. Barefoot, she sprinted through the dark garden to her car.

"Tea cups." The words beat in her skull all the way to the ignition.

TEN

RAZE JUMPED up out of the chair without waiting for himself to reintegrate. He was full Beta now, and he needed to break shit—*bad*. He wanted to tear the fucking place apart. He looked around for something to destroy, but everything in The Womb was too valuable. If he broke anything in here, it would compromise the work.

He stormed out of The Womb and back upstairs, scouring the house for any object he could smash to smithereens: a mirror, a window, a painting, a vase, his own fucking hand into a cement wall. He couldn't find anything insignificant enough that he didn't mind shattering. That only enraged him. Since when had he given a shit about *anything*? He kicked a chair over. Very fucking unsatisfying. He needed to get out.

"Away," he told the house, setting the security system as he stalked out into the street. He walked for blocks trying to cool the fury. His blood was boiling, his brain on fire with a rage beyond anything he had experienced in years.

A murderous desire to crush something returned, and he looked around for something to take it out on. Raze started kicking the shit out of a dented trash can, metal shrieking in protest. The sound jarred something loose—memories of bedroom walls back in Nebraska, peppered with holes from the same fury.

He didn't start out as a rage case. As a boy, he'd been bright, quick to laugh, the delight of his Air Force father and stay-at-home mother. But even then, there was something uncanny about him. While most kids stumbled through first words, he was already reading. Duplos bored him—he preferred taking radios apart, laying their guts out in color-coded rows. Even "Sesame Street" couldn't hold him; he'd climb his bunk to stack books into precarious towers, testing how far he could push balance before it all came crashing down.

A couple passed on the sidewalk, laughing too loudly. Raze shoved his hands in his pockets, jaw tight, and kept walking.

His downward spiral had started in kindergarten, when the adoration at home was replaced by disdain at school. Raze made people uncomfortable. Teachers avoided his gaze. Classmates whispered "Creeper," "Damien," "Zombie." His alabaster skin, jet black hair, and unearthly blue eyes scared people rather than attracted them. By middle school, even the bottom-feeders of the social order took swipes at him. He learned to shrink back, but his silence only made him more of a target.

With nowhere to turn, Raze sought asylum in his room where he could play with his erector set, read his favorite books again and again, or just lie on his bed and stare out into space.

A car horn blared behind him. Raze snapped his head around, pulse spiking, until the noise passed.

Then one Christmas, his grandparents delivered the Quantum3—the holy grail of consoles. People had fought each other in the aisles, hoping to get their hands on one. A stampede of shoppers trampled a poor, elderly woman who just wanted a George Foreman Grill.

The Quantum3 consumed him. He tore through every arcade and racing game, then pushed his parents for harder titles. Relieved to see him engaged, they obliged—and he devoured each new challenge with obsessive ease. Schoolwork fell away. Instead of homework, he sketched characters and maps for games of his own, his notebooks filling with worlds more vivid than anything in class.

He began failing. But because his teachers didn't want to see him again the next year if they flunked him—no child could ever be left behind, after all—they passed their F student along with generous C's and D's.

His home life began to deteriorate. His parents, who had so much pride and hope for him when he was younger, couldn't hide their disappointment. But even though they always threatened to take the Quantum3 away, as punishment for bad grades or fighting, they never followed through. Gaming kept Raze in his room, and when he was in his room, he wasn't around to remind them of their own failings. So, instead, they continued to buy every upgrade and game that he requested.

For his sixteenth birthday, he convinced them to buy him the new and improved Q3 console. The Q3 was a solid, onyx cube, a perfectly square monolith, seamless and shiny as an oil slick. There weren't any openings for game disks, because disks were no longer necessary. The wireless console came with access to Quantum's NOW Network, an online service that allowed players to connect and play any game on the network, 24/7.

Once a four-walled prison that locked him away from the world, his room became a sanctuary—his gaming console, the portal through which he made his escape—and the game, AnnihilNation, his new world.

Online, he shed his name and became *CrazE*. The handle stuck fast, whispered with awe and contempt across the NOW Network. He didn't just outplay opponents—but was gifted with an almost psychic ability to predict another player's strategy. He took his opponents totally by surprise, used their own tricks against them, and destroyed them before they ever had time to react.

Tournaments followed, and with them cash prizes and notoriety. For the first time, checks arrived in his name, and strangers showed up to watch him play. His parents, who once threatened to take the console away, now bragged about their son, the prodigy gamer. The more he won, the more he fed on it—money, reputation, control.

He acquired fans, a live following of people who idolized him. They showed up when he played, emailed him love letters, and asked him to mentor them. Girls actually wanted to meet him, hang out, and have some real-time game time. In gaming circles, his dark, brooding looks made him mysterious and alluring, bringing him the kind of attention that had evaded him all his life. He quickly grew accustomed to it.

In the digital world, he was untouchable, and some of that ruthlessness began to bleed into the real one. He started working out—running and lifting weights in his garage every day. Although it took a couple of hours away from his gaming practice, there were side benefits that made it worthwhile.

It helped him burn off the overpowering itch he got to beat, break, or destroy shit. Raze had countless holes in his bedroom walls to show for that rage.

It also gave him the to-die-for six-pack and massive guns that suddenly made him popular. The same girls who used to sneer at him now couldn't keep their hands off him. He wasn't going to pass up the opportunity to take advantage—sex took the edge off, and he played better when he was loose.

He also liked knowing that most of the ass he was getting belonged to the fucksticks who had been tormenting him for years. When the gloating wore thin, he turned on them directly, whooping *their* asses for a change. This led to suspensions, of course, but if he timed the fights a few weeks out from a big tournament, it gave him more hours to practice.

Everything started to turn in his favor. He looked awesome. He had money and a ride. He got laid whenever he wanted. And nobody fucked with him anymore. Raze felt invincible. The complete opposite of how he felt at this moment.

He stopped walking.

The full realization of his situation dawned on him. He had lost control. He lost control of the viewing; his energy had been swatted out of the space like it was nothing but a pesky gnat. He lost control of Blake; the option-lock Raze had initiated in *Demesne* wasn't effective, as evidenced by Blake's signature practically evaporating, only to completely resurface in the presence of that girl. He'd lost control of *Demesne*—his very own construct—when it disintegrated around him this morning. And he was on the verge of losing control of the Project, which could mean the loss of everything he had worked for. And the chaos of the day revolved solely around one thing... *that girl.*

A flicker of light caught the corner of his eye. A neon green martini glass of the local dive sizzled into full illumination. He let up on the trash can and considered a stiff one. Drinking was completely against his personal standard of operations; it dimmed the wits and made views less controllable.

Fuck it. It couldn't make anything worse. Raze walked through the swinging doors into the sticky, sweet stench of the tavern. It was packed with bodies, the new working class of the financial and dot-com era getting their Friday night happy hour on before taking a ferry home.

Raze bellied up to the bar and scoped out a bartender. He

spotted a dishwater blond with a weak energy field, cranked up the magnetism in his own field, and directed it at her. It worked just like a tap-tap on her shoulder. She immediately looked up and over at him. She handed a customer the beer she had just pulled from the keg, then bypassed twenty waiting customers to wait on Raze first. That was more like it—the world *should* bend at his will.

"Mark Manhattan, lose the cherry," he demanded. "I'll be at the corner table." He walked away and sat down with his back turned to the crowd. She was pretty prompt on the service, too, setting his drink on the table within a couple of minutes.

She set the glass down with a nervous little laugh. "Fastest drink I've served all night."

Raze didn't even look up. "That's because you knew who to serve."

The laugh died in her throat.

"Start me the next," was how he thanked her.

He didn't savor his drink—he slammed it—feeding fire with fire. The heat of it burned down through the center of him, settling into the pit of his empty stomach. He closed his eyes as the warmth spread from his belly into his bloodstream, down his shoulders into his arms, into his brain, slowing down the synapse explosion that was creating havoc in his head.

The second drink was placed on the table. The waitress, seeing the empty glass already waiting for pick up, knew well enough not to linger. He took another drink, an appreciative sip this time, and looked out the window at the Bay. His heartbeat slowed in time to the scintillation of the city lights reflecting on the undulating waves.

Aislen.

That's what the therapist had called her. Raze was starting

to reintegrate now and pulled up the memory. He might have been too dismissive about the benefits of bourbon.

She was a real person after all, not a wayward dreamer or accidental, astral tourist. *And* she was just an average, everyday girl. Raze was amazed, but confused. How had she accessed *Demesne*? And why?

Aislen. Raze allowed himself to envision her now that he was a safe distance away from the energy vortex that had walloped him in the view. She appeared so timid and tremulous when she walked in that door, and yet she packed the ferocious, energetic punch of a lioness on crack.

Irritation stirred up inside him again, but he extinguished it with another swallow of his drink. All of his failures today revolved around her, and failure was not an option. The 8 didn't tolerate weakness, let alone failure. If word of today's collapse reached them, he'd be swatted out of existence faster than *Demesne* this morning.

Aislen was the thread that the skein of his reality was unraveling around. He needed to find her and put her in her place of non-existence. But how?

Then he remembered. He'd had the sagacity to capture the frequency of the therapist, Troy. He could evoke that frequency and track him to get to her. His fury started to settle now that a plan was starting to come together. He ran a quick assessment.

Blake was still a problem, but maybe not as big a one as Raze thought. Even if he came totally out of the option-lock and started talking, after the state he'd been in all day, and the event of that afternoon, the authorities would give very little credence to anything he said. He would either stay in the hospital or be remanded to custody for killing his father. Eventually, Raze would get to him and finish the deal.

But he also needed to cover the company's tracks. If Blake

reintegrated and started talking about the game, the police might want to take it and the visors for evidence. Raze could not let those visors get into the hands of the wrong people. He was going to have to get them from the Parrish house. Immediately, before anyone else laid eyes on them.

Now that he had an agenda, he started feeling more like himself. First, he'd take a nap to burn off the alcohol, and then he'd take another astral trip back to Modesto to sniff around for Miss Aislen, then scan the Parrish house for the visors. If he got a lock on them both, he would take a trip to the valley and deal with them in person.

It would be much more of a pleasure to deal with Aislen in the flesh.

He got up, leaving the rest of his drink on the table. *Consider it a tip*, he said telepathically to the waitress.

ELEVEN

THE AFTERNOON WAS TOTALLY FUBAR. Mathis and Jackson had barely gotten situated in the observation room when the young nurse walked into the padded cell with the therapist and Blake. Mathis didn't think that was in the game plan, but, lo and behold, the boy came out of his stupor. He said some cockamamie bullshit to the nurse and scared the living crap out of her because she spun tail out of the room and took off running down the hall.

"What the fuck just happened?" Jackson said, staring through the window.

"I have no fucking idea," Mathis said.

The boy stared at the doorway after the girl for a long moment. The therapist, Troy, tried to engage Blake in a conversation again, peppering him with questions, but the boy didn't react to him at all. When it was clear that the girl wasn't coming back, he slowly retreated back into his brain stew.

The therapist was smart enough to know when to give up. When he came out of the room, Jackson stormed into the hallway.

"What the hell was that all about?"

Troy shrugged his shoulders. "I don't know, but it was pretty intense."

"Gee, is that your professional opinion?" Jackson never could hide his sarcasm when he was upset.

"I don't know what you're expecting. It could be that he thinks he knows her. It could have been a fluke response to us being in the room. It could be that he is malingering, but that would be a really good act for a twelve-year-old to pull off. It could be a lot of things, but the cause may not matter right now, does it?"

"Well, does she know him? Does he know her?"

"I don't know that either. I don't think she does. She would have said something to me. Of course, I'll ask her, and if she does, I'll get her in touch with you."

Mathis came into the hallway. "What is *Demesne*?"

"*That* is actually a good question," Troy replied, throwing Jackson a sharp glance. "*Demesne* is a game. The game that Blake's parents felt he was addicted to, and why they brought him to my group in the first place. At least half the kids in my group are obsessed with it. It is what they call an MMORPG, a massive multiplayer online role-playing game, and it is one of a few games out right now that are thought to be extremely addictive."

"Could somebody be so addicted to a game that they kill someone, say, *their dad*, because of it?" Jackson was asking both Mathis and Troy.

"No way," said Mathis.

"That's a controversial subject," Troy said. "There have been studies, but gaming has only been shown to slightly increase aggressive behavior. I'm sorry if this didn't accomplish what you were hoping for, but at least you know all isn't lost. It may just take some time."

Jackson let out an exasperated puff of air. "Looks like it will be a babysitting job until tomorrow."

Mathis looked back through the window, watching the boy rocking and gibbering. Instinct was scratching around inside him, and it didn't feel like a byproduct of too much Starbucks. "Something's rotten in Denmark," he mumbled.

"You say somethin'?" Jackson asked.

"Just talking to myself."

"Well, we got enough of that goin' on around here, so knock it off."

With that, Troy took his leave, and Mathis wasn't far behind, leaving Jackson on his own to find a babysitter.

It was Thursday night. Mathis thought about changing and heading over to Sammy's for a beer and karaoke. Some people had golf. Some people had the gym. Some people had Fantasy Football. Mathis had karaoke. After Denise died, only two things grounded him: his job and karaoke.

It began as an idea to drink himself to death in a red leatherette booth at Sammy's Sushi Boat, surrounded by barflies and badge bunnies. The ratty dive turned out to be a live version of an American Idol reject show. Who knew so many people really thought they could sing? They came in droves, bedazzled tees and cowboy hats, handing slips to the KJ, then knocking back a couple before it was their turn to make the dogs howl.

Months passed, Mathis wallowing in grief and beer to the keening of *Modesto Don't Got Talent,* without kicking the bucket. One night, after realizing beer wasn't the elixir of death he'd hoped for, he threw back a couple of shots of Jack and asked for the mike—opting for suicide by mortification instead.

He moseyed up onto the makeshift stage, boots tugging at the liquor-candied carpet. Without a word, everyone knew his story. They'd been reading it for months in his hunched posture, the stack of peeled beer labels, the weight of grief on his face. They went silent as the solo strum of an acoustic guitar began. Under red paper lanterns and a spinning disco ball, Mathis sang.

"The road is long, so long. The years stretch out ahead of me."

The sad slide of steel guitar followed.

"Now that you're gone, it's all wrong. I cry tears for what will never be."

He closed his eyes and sang for Denise—to Denise, if there was a heaven.

When the last chord faded, a hush fell over the bar. Then a crescendo of applause erupted as the regulars honored Mathis with a standing ovation. And gave him a hobby.

Every Tuesday and Thursday night, like religion, Mathis was at Sammy's. Never weekends—he left those to the drunken bachelorettes. But Tuesdays and Thursdays, he owned the stage, getting in three or four songs from his little CD folder. He was hooked. Sometimes he even wished there was a geriatric version of *American Idol*. He'd *so* win.

He hadn't missed a Thursday night in three years, but today Mathis was done and doner. He was two decades past being young enough to pull a 24, so at hour 28, he finally decided to head for home.

When he finally made it inside the warm dark of his humble bachelor's abode, he dropped trou in the laundry room and prowled into the kitchen in his skivvies. He dug out a Hungry Man Salisbury steak dinner from the freezer and nuked it in the microwave. Then he shopped the beer crisper for a brew, pulling out two Newkie Browns, the first for its slam factor, the second to savor with his snack.

With a hot plate in one hand and a cold brew in the other, he flopped down in the man-chair and turned on the tube. He scrolled through the guide for some mindless programming, skipping ESPN (too stimulating), CNN (too boring), and FOX (too aggravating). MTV was playing a *Jersey Shore* marathon, but there was just no fucking way. It was mindless all right, but he hated anything that needed closed captioning because he couldn't understand what the fuck they were saying. And who calls themselves "The Situation" or "Snookie"? And where did the "M" in MTV go?

Mathis settled on the Food Network. Giada was at home— the next best thing to porn. He devoured his meat and potatoes while she stirred, sampled, and moaned over her creation.

"Jesus Christ," he muttered, shaking his head. "Old cop, drunk on cleavage."

Still, he couldn't help thinking Giada looked a little like Sabine—or at least what Mathis imagined Sabine would look like if she were done up for a night out with her hair down and a nice dress on. Maybe it was time to grow a sack and ask her out at the diner. Worst she could say was no. But what if she said yes? The possibility was worth the risk of disappointment.

Mathis thought about pulling himself out of the La-Z-Boy and hitting the rack, but couldn't overcome inertia. Instead, he reclined the chair back and in less than a minute his snoring filled the room, but under it, something else gnawed at him—an echo of the boy's voice, soft as a dream.

Two sticks and a bucket.

TWELVE

AISLEN SAT in her car in the driveway of her house, trying to corral the thousand thoughts running through her mind. The day had found truth in what she had dismissed as pure fantasy. But what of this new vision? She didn't feel like she had been asleep in the shrine. She had felt deeply restful but still awake and present. She could hear the muffled babbling of the river below, smell the sandalwood incense burning on the altar, and see the light dwindling beyond her closed eyelids. Yet she was also entirely immersed in the vision—it was bright and present, as vivid as her dream from the night before.

This is how it starts, she thought. The slow drift from reality. She'd seen it often with her patients—how someone could appear steady, even lucid, only to suddenly slip into places no one else could follow.

Take Mrs. Crowley, for example. She could talk clearly about her childhood: her father running liquor during Prohibition, her mother's tragic death, and the years in foster care. Then, mid-sentence, something unseen would catch her attention. A voice, maybe two, maybe more. She'd respond as if in a conversation, her focus shifting to people no one else could perceive. Sometimes her hands would reach out, batting at the air, as though she were fending off an invisible presence.

And yet... what if they were real to her? What if the rest of the world simply lacked the ability—or the willingness—to see?

The thought made Aislen's stomach turn. Entertaining it meant stepping onto the same uncertain ground. She tried to steady herself, but fear pressed in. All her plans, her future, everything she'd worked toward—it could all unravel before she ever had the chance. She wanted to help people in those facilities, not become one of the patients.

And then there was Troy. She was sure he'd have a professional opinion about what she was experiencing. It had been a mistake to have ever had personal conversations with him. She should have kept it strictly professional. Now, if he suspected she was losing it, not only would their relationship deteriorate further, it could affect her work.

She thought about talking to her mom. But her father had played such a significant role in her hallucinations. She didn't want to risk reopening her old wounds. There was only one answer: She needed to do her best to bury it all, down inside of herself. She needed to move forward as if this day had never happened.

"Go inside, beg exhaustion, go upstairs, and wake up tomorrow morning, on the right side of the bed—the *sane* side of it," she told herself.

A light was on in the kitchen. Her mom would be in there, making dinner. Aislen checked her reflection in the rearview mirror. The puffiness in her eyes had diminished, and her nose was no longer swollen and red. *Objects in the mirror are closer than they appear.*

"Shut up," she told herself, taking one last, deep breath for fortification.

She got out of the car. The air had sharper teeth in it now; it gnawed at her in the wind that had kicked up. Down the track, a train let out a wail as it headed toward town. Batten down the hatches, it warned.

Aislen fumbled through her backpack for the house key, but it kept slipping from her gloved fingers. The train's rumble swelled, a foreshock shaking the ground, as if the world itself was forcing her to wait. She thought of the dream desert shifting into a city with just such a tremor, and dread whispered her real life might do the same.

Finally, her fingers closed on the key, but when she tried the lock, it jumped, clattered off the porch, and skittered into the dirt. She scrambled after it, heart pounding as the roar bore down. The rafters rattled, the porch light swung like a pendulum. She jammed the key back into the lock just as the iron horse screamed past. The door gave way, and she tumbled inside, the cold chasing her heels, the whole house shivering as the endless line of boxcars thundered by.

She took off her coat and gloves and wandered toward the warm glow of the kitchen. Under the veil of the train's cacophony, Aislen could hear her mother sobbing. She stopped; dread coiling up inside of her. Never in her life had she seen or heard her mother cry. She stepped hesitantly into the kitchen and found her mother sitting on the floor, bent over the shattered fragments of a teacup and saucer. Aislen could make out the sapphire blue and white of her beloved lotus teacup in the jagged shapes that littered the floor. She knelt beside her mother on the linoleum and put an arm around her.

"Oh, Aislen! I'm sorry, I didn't hear you come in," she said, trying to wipe away her tears, hoping Aislen wouldn't notice.

"Mom, what happened?"

"Stupid train," she said. "It finally knocked one of them

down after all these years. Don't worry about it. It's a stupid teacup." More tears spilled over, belying her true feelings.

Aislen looked at the shards of porcelain.

"*Ask her.*" She could hear her father in her head—feel his pleading.

She pushed him away, but an icy hand pushed back with unrelenting pressure. "*Ask her.*"

She reached down and touched the particles of dust. Tears welled up in her own eyes, and her throat choked with grief. "This was my favorite cup."

"I know." Her mom could barely whisper. "It was mine, as well."

"*Ask her.*" A swell of emotion filled Aislen's chest. She knew she couldn't deny him... she couldn't deny her own desire to know.

"Mom," she said softly. "Tell me about the tea cups."

Her mother dropped her head in her hands and began to cry in earnest. "Oh, Aislen! I don't even know where to begin."

Aislen put her arms around her mother and held her. "Begin at the beginning."

Her mom shook her head.

"Please, Mom, I need to know," she tried again.

Sabine lifted her head, dried her eyes, and finally said, "They came from your father."

Aislen looked down at the shattered cup, then back up at the neat row of survivors. Her chest tightened. "I don't understand."

"I know," her mother sighed. "I've thought about telling you for so long, but I thought it was best to leave well enough alone. You never asked about him—not once—so I tried to act as if he'd never existed either." She pushed the broom into the pile of porcelain, hands trembling.

"I always knew," Aislen whispered. "I just knew better than to speak of it. For your sake...and mine."

Sabine set the broom aside, poured the fragments into the old gift box, then pressed a folded piece of paper into Aislen's hands. "Sit. Read."

The handwriting was neat, deliberate.

Love travels a straight line, from my heart to yours.
Distance, time, death cannot disrupt the connection.
Every drop of my love belongs to you and Aislen.
From across eternity,
Preston

The words blurred as Aislen reread them. Her mother busied herself with the kettle, pulled two cups from the shelf as though they were holy vessels, and poured coffee heavy with honey and cream.

"I was seventeen when I ran away from my family's ranch in Utah," she began. "We belonged to a strict sect that believed marriage should stay inside the family. My father expected me to wed an uncle—something they all called normal, but I couldn't stomach it. When I tried to escape, he caught me and beat me until I passed out. Weeks later, my mother crept into my room with two hundred dollars from his wallet. Her last words were, *'Get far away and never look back.'*"

She took a sip, gaze far away. Aislen gripped her cup, afraid it might slip.

"I thought I'd make it to Hollywood, be discovered." A humorless laugh. "I barely made it to Modesto. Fifteen dollars in my pocket, a fleabag motel, and a job at the diner because of a *Help Wanted* sign in the window. God, I was a terrible waitress—spilled more coffee than I served. And then one morning, Preston walked in."

Sabine's eyes softened. "He sat in the corner booth, the sunrise behind him like a halo. He wasn't much older than me, but he looked so tired, so worn out, he seemed twice his age. But underneath all that exhaustion, my God, he was so handsome. I thought my heart was going to explode.

"I pulled out all the stops for him. I gave him *both* the wrong order, *and* I spilled his orange juice all over the table and into his lap. I began to panic. I tried to wipe up the mess with a cloth, but it just spread the juice around the table. I was about ready to burst into tears when I looked up at him and found him smiling at me. He reached his hand out, placed it over the top of mine, and said, '*Shhh. Settle.*' And for the first time in my life, I did."

"Aislen, I cannot describe it. The world stopped turning. All the wrong that had been spinning through me for as long as I could remember stilled, and in that one moment, I fell into his eyes and rightness began spinning in the opposite direction." She looked up at Aislen, then added quickly, "I know, sounds like a soap opera, huh?"

Aislen should have laughed—yesterday she would have. But after everything she'd seen and felt, she couldn't. Instead, she whispered, "No... I believe you."

"I only knew him for a few months. I'd work the breakfast shift, then slip into his rented basement room. We drank percolator coffee from a single cup, talked for hours—well, *I* talked. He dodged questions about himself. At night, we picnicked under the stars, but he was always looking over his shoulder, like something, or someone, was following him. I wondered if he was an escaped convict, or a runaway like me, but when I'd ask, he would tell me not to worry and change the subject, make me laugh, or tell me how much he utterly adored me."

Sabine stopped talking and looked out the window toward the tracks that led into the night.

"One afternoon, he woke me from a nap. He said he had to leave. I was stunned. Devastated. I cried. I begged him not to go. He took both my hands in his and brought them to his lips and looked me in the eyes, in that same way he looked at me in the diner, the way that stilled everything to a hush."

Aislen's stomach knotted. She pressed her palm flat to the table to keep from shouting.

"Then he said, 'I love you. Beyond time. And if I don't leave—all that stops. For your sake, and for our baby's, I have to leave. Now. Please forgive me.' Then he got up and walked out the door."

"I didn't even know I was pregnant," Sabine whispered.

Aislen couldn't speak. Bile rose inside her. She wanted to shout, *"How did he know? Why would he do that? Know that you are pregnant and just leave? Disappear forever?"* but she bit her tongue. She could see that her mother was barely keeping it together.

"He left money with the landlady so I wouldn't be thrown out. Weeks later, men in black suits came asking questions. She kicked me out on the spot. That night, a letter arrived from Mexico with a thousand dollars and instructions to rent a place of my own. Six months later, another package arrived from England."

She pushed the square box across the table. Inside was a creamy yellow teacup with gold trim, and another note. Aislen carefully unfolded it.

Please name her Aislen.
My love to you from across eternity,
Preston

"That was our cup," Sabine said, brushing the rim with her fingertip. "You were born the next morning."

Aislen resisted the urge to smash the cup. "Why did you do it, Mom? Why would you do anything that he asked after what he did?"

"I don't know how to answer that. It was something inside of me. The love that contained him was as real and tangible as you were in my arms. Of course, I was angry. I was hurt, even bitter. But though I wished for it, the love I felt just wouldn't roll over and turn into hatred.

"And every year... near your birthday... another box would arrive, with another teacup inside." Her mom looked up at the shelves, the sacristy for the teacups.

"When you were four, he showed up on our doorstep— desperate to see you... insistent. He said he needed to rest his eyes on you, to touch you just once, to assure himself that you existed in the world. I tried not to allow it, but you were as persistent as he was."

"I remember that," Aislen said.

"You do? I'm surprised, and at the same time I'm not."

Aislen wanted to tell her everything right then and there. About how she hadn't remembered it at all until just the night before—about everything that had transpired throughout the day. It would be such a relief to get it off her chest. But the cold hand that had been gripping her all along pushed against her chest, and she couldn't find her voice.

"That was the last time I... we... ever saw him. An extra-large box arrived on your birthday that year. Inside was the lotus teacup, with the note you read earlier... and $30,000 in cash. There was a second note stuck inside the money that read, 'Buy us a home.'"

Sabine looked around the house. "So I did." She looked back out the window and didn't speak for a long time. "I always thought he'd come back, you know? I thought that was what he meant by the 'us' in the note. But eventually, I realized the 'us' he was talking about was the part of him that was in you."

She looked back at Aislen and smiled. "You look so much like him... your eyes are exactly the same. And the looks that pass across your face... sometimes it takes my breath away."

Aislen didn't know what to say. "I'm sorry."

"Why are you sorry? Don't be silly. You are the very best thing that ever happened to me."

"No. I'm sorry for what he did to you. That he left you like that. That he was so weak and irresponsible. All he could do was send money and teacups? I never hated him as much as I do right now."

THEY SAT IN SILENCE, staring at the fragile cup on the table. Aislen tried to absorb her mother's revelation—that though he'd abandoned them, his presence lingered with every birthday, every ritual, every sip. Then it struck her.

"But Mom, there are only twenty-two cups. Shouldn't there be twenty-four? You used to get one every year...then you stopped. What happened?"

Her mother shrugged. "I wish I knew. Each year, another cup arrived, postmarked from somewhere new. The note was always the same: 'My love to you from across eternity.' I kept believing he'd be here if he could—that maybe he'd come back. But two years ago, the packages stopped."

Aislen sat with that, thinking of her mother's life held hostage to waiting. Work and raising her was all she had, nothing in return but porcelain and cash. Where was the love? The support?

Sadness twisted into anger. She thought of the hallucination, of him begging her to ask about the cups. *Fuck you,* she seethed. She wanted to dive back into that vision and punch him in the face.

The phone rang, breaking the silence. Aislen got up from the table and answered it. "Hello?"

"Aislen! Girl! What are you doing? I haven't seen or heard from you in forever!"

"Hey there, Gen." Aislen looked at her mom and mouthed, "It's Genesis" to her. Her mom threw her a "no shit" look and got up to clean off the table. "What have you been up to?"

"I finished my certification hours today!"

"That's awesome, Gen! Congratulations!" Aislen did her best to sound enthusiastic, though it had completely slipped her mind. What kind of friend was she? She had been so caught up in her own drama that she forgot her best friend was graduating and about to get her Holistic Health Practitioner's license.

"Ready to hit the town and celebrate? Because I am so ready!"

Aislen felt like complete crap. She had promised Gen a night of celebration, and now she was going to disappoint her. "Gee, Gen, I'm really sorry... but tonight isn't a good night for me. I've got some... stuff... going on."

"What? What stuff? What's wrong? And why haven't you called me about it?"

"Just stuff. And I don't want to bug you with it."

Aislen felt a hand rest on her shoulder. Her mom whispered in her ear, "Go, Aislen. It will be good for you."

Aislen shook her head vehemently. The last thing she needed right now was time with anybody, let alone a crowd. She wanted to bury herself in her comforters and hide.

"Come on, Aiz," Gen pleaded. "I have been looking forward to this for months. And you are the only one I want to celebrate with. Just come over. If you don't want to go out, we can chill. I can make us a snack, you can tell me about 'stuff', and I can practice my new voodoo skills on you."

Aislen felt torn.

"I am fine, Aislen," her mother said. "You need a little time with a friend. Let all this go for a while and embrace something happy for a change. Please? Do it for me."

Aislen hesitated. It went against everything she was feeling inside, but she would do it if it would make both of them happy. "All right," she said to them both. "Let me get some clothes together and I'll be over in a few."

Gen's ebullient squeals twinkled through the phone line, making Aislen smile. Maybe this was what she needed after all.

THIRTEEN

AISLEN RANG THE DOORBELL. "COMING!" She heard a shout from inside. Genesis appeared, fairy-princess bright—pixie hair, blue eyes, and dimples in her cheeks when she smiled—which was always. Adorable, effervescent. But pity the fool who mistook her for a dumb blond, because with the flick of her sharp wit, she could cut him to the quick.

Genesis threw her arms around Aislen and embraced her. Relief loosened her shoulders. Coming here had been the right choice.

"Goddess, I have missed you," Gen squealed. "Get in here out of that cold!"

Aislen stepped into Gen's apartment, small but unmistakably hers. Unlike Aislen, Gen had left her parents' house years ago, carving out independence with her massage-therapist hours at the day spa. The space glowed in calming sages and tans, alive with potted plants and rescued furniture arranged with meticulous feng shui. A curl of sage smoke drifted from a dish on the counter, twining with the citrus tang of massage oil.

The whole place shimmered somewhere between spa retreat and fairy den—pure Genesis.

"I made us a happy hour happy," Genesis said as she skipped into the kitchen. She returned bearing two martini glasses containing a day-glo aqua concoction with a fiery red cherry floating in it.

"This does not look organic at all."

Gen giggled. "It isn't. I am breaking from my organic-holistic-puritan traditions for the evening. A girl needs a little fun once in a while." Genesis put the drink in Aislen's hand and held hers up. "A toast! Here's to health, happiness, and maybe a future that includes a little dancing! Cheers!"

Genesis clinked her glass to Aislen's, and they both took a sip of the electric blue juice. The sugar and chemicals clung to her tongue, nothing like the earthy teas she preferred.

"Interesting. What is it?"

"I call it The Avatar!" Genesis swirled her glass with a flourish. "Hpnotiq, vodka, and a splash of energy drink. A few of these, and everything will be backwards, the dream will be the real world, and we will be the dream," Genesis laughed.

Aislen blanched and set the cocktail back on the table, not sure she had an appetite for it anymore. It was just like Genesis to unwittingly hit the nail on the head.

"Gee, was it something I said?"

"No. It's nothing."

"Don't try to fool me! Girl, you need to remember who you're best friends with. Does it have to do with your so-called 'stuff'?"

"Kind of, but not really." Aislen really didn't want to talk about it. She came here to get away. But who better than Gen to talk to about the strange and absurd? "It's just that I've had a couple of strange dreams lately—disturbing, really. And I seriously would not want to flip-flop the real world with them."

"First of all," she pointed to her glass, "this is a cocktail, not a magic potion." She picked Aislen's drink up off the table and handed it back her. "Second. It was only a line from one of the best movies ever... not an invocation. And third? You need to tell me about these dreams, pronto."

Aislen felt warm and relaxed for the first time all day. Only Genesis had that effect on her. She could tell Gen anything, never fearing that she would be criticized or judged. And without fail, Gen would have a perspective completely off-kilter from the rest of the world: fresh, out of the box, and perfectly right.

Aislen twisted the stem of her cherry between her fingers. "Okay, so last night's dream was...different. Disturbing."

Genesis leaned forward, eyes shining. "Spill."

"There was this mutant world—dark, twisted. And I heard my dad's voice. It pulled up memories I didn't even know I had. Then this soldier showed up. Ruthless. Magnetic. He..." She swallowed. "He killed me."

"Whoa. Zero stars, would not recommend that dream."

Aislen gave a weak laugh and pushed on. "...and then there was this boy named Blake... who shot a man in the dream. And today I actually saw him. Like, in real life. Same face, same energy."

Genesis blinked. "Wait—dream boy Blake really exists?"

"Yeah. And get this... he might have killed his dad."

"Holy crap."

Aislen rubbed her forehead. "Then this afternoon, I had this vision in the shrine. My dad again, but dressed like a homeless man. He told me to ask Mom about the teacups."

"Teacups?"

"Mm-hm. And when I got home, Mom was crying over one of hers. Shattered all over the floor. And then she told me the whole story of where they'd come from. It's like the dream reached into real life and cracked it open."

Genesis sank deep into the cushions, eyes and mouth wide. "Holy shit, Aiz! That's freaking intense! No wonder you are so off tonight."

"...Do you think I'm losing it? Like I'm heading for a full-on meltdown?"

Genesis burst into a fit of laughter and took Aislen's hands in hers. "No way. I think you had a premonitory dream *and* a message from your father."

"Well, I think that sounds pretty, freakin' bonkers."

"You would. I hate to be the bearer of bad news... but what you hold as real isn't the only real that there is. Maybe that's really what your problem is. Your 'what you see is what you get' philosophy makes you feel comfortable and safe, but something happens that strays outside of the provable, and you are thrown into 'I must be crazy' panic." Genesis wagged a finger at her, half-serious, half-playful. "So the question is... do you want to stay in your comfort zone? Because if you keep rationalizing it away, you'll drive yourself mad. Or..." She grinned. "You can get the world according to Genesis."

"After today, I'm game for anything. Do tell, oh wise one!"

"Okay. Your dream last night was obviously precognitive. I mean, it was symbolic, but it was definitely a vision of an actual event. Precognitive dreams are not uncommon, but for you, not being used to this kind of stuff, it would be shocking."

"Really? Not uncommon?"

"Absolutely not. People have precognitive dreams all the time... like dreaming of a plane crash, skipping the flight, and then the plane actually goes down. Even Abraham Lincoln—he dreamed of his own death three days before he was assassinated! Weird? Maybe. But common? Yes."

"Scary."

"That, too, sometimes."

Aislen mulled this over. She should have called Gen earlier. Even though it seemed nuts, the idea that it was common to have dreams that actually occurred in real life reassured her. Just a little, but enough.

"So, what about my father? Why him? I haven't thought about him for years. Yesterday, I couldn't have told you a single thing about him. And today, I can hear him and picture him as if I had always known him."

"Well, there are different theories. Some people think that people in our dreams are not really those people, but just aspects of ourselves. Maybe all these dreams and visions are surfacing because of the stress you're under with finals and work. Maybe your subconscious is diving down deep for resources, pulling up a lot of repressed stuff, like the memory of your father's voice and his visit when you were young. In some way, you might be reaching for that lost aspect of your life for strength. Or it may be surfacing now because it's something that needs to be healed so you can move forward into the next chapter. *Or...*" Gen paused, contemplated something, then seemed to think better of it, "Never mind..."

"No way!" Aislen playfully hit Gen on the arm. "You started it. Now finish it."

"Well..." Genesis took a deep breath, then spoke the next sentence super fast. "Maybe your father is really trying to speak to you, so he's coming to you in your dreams." She closed her eyes in a wince, ready for Aislen to punch her again, but harder this time. When it didn't happen, she opened one eye. Aislen was staring at her.

She thought about her father, how he had known her mom was pregnant. How he timed his first package with the night of her birth. How he always seemed to be one step ahead of every event in their lives. She thought about how his voice actually helped her in her dream and how that afternoon he'd told her she was going to need help.

A shudder rippled through her. She grabbed the Avatar, swallowed it in one gulp.

"I think we need to go dancing after all," she said, jumping off the couch. "How about you make me another Avatar, call us an Uber, and I'll get ready?"

"Atta girl!" Genesis exclaimed, jumping to her feet as well.

Dancing felt ridiculous after everything she'd just told her. And yet, the idea of losing herself in rhythm—in something beyond thought—tugged at her.

Maybe if she kept moving, nothing could catch her.

FOURTEEN

THE FIRST STRIKE of the bowl began the clock's golden ratio progression. Raze heard the harmonic chime resonating from a long distance away, deep under a sea of black silence, adrift in a mind unadorned with form or thought, resting in oblivion.

Precisely three minutes and forty-eight seconds later, the bowl sang again. Raze began a slow ascent toward the surface, riding the mellow overtones of B on a steady 232 Hz wave. A third gong, two minutes and twenty-one seconds later, brought him to the crest of consciousness. He recalled his name, his life, and his purpose with his first waking breath. While chilling in low Alpha, he stretched out in the bed and began the process of tracking Mr. T, Raze's code name for Blake's preppy therapist from the hospital. Raze pictured Troy in all his casual confidence, messy brown locks barely brushed out of his eyes, cute enough to make Zac Efron jealous. Once Raze got a lock on his image, he selected his sound.

"Fusion Jazz," he said aloud. The house responded, and the loquacious groove of Joshua Redman's tenor sax began to dance off the walls. That seemed to work, and Raze put his feet on the floor and walked to the shower.

"Brisk," he said as he stepped inside. The shower went through a three-minute sequence of pummeling his body with freezing water at full throttle. He stepped out, dried off, got dressed, and headed down the stairs, fully alert and ready for a productive evening.

"Alpha 8, and keep the tunes." The jazz was definitely putting him in the zone. He could feel the signal line syncing up. Tracking Mr. T wasn't going to be difficult at all.

Raze reclined in the lounge, closed his eyes, and re-accessed Mr. T's signature from the cognitive storage area of his brain. An algorithmic kaleidoscope of cerulean and sea foam broke across the velvet black of his inner vision. To anyone else, it might have looked like chaos, but to Raze, this matrix of color and sound was the control panel of his world. Every hue, every spiral, every frequency meant something he could tune, twist, or break.

An aperture appeared in the center of the radiating sine waves and cyclones of color. Raze regulated his breathing, slowed his brain cycles down, and tuned in for the match. An opening burst into brighter whirlpools of radioactive lime and azure, giving Raze a strong and accurate portal.

"Theta 7." Raze pulled his consciousness into an orb and moved himself into the line. He fell through the supernova, traveling at warp speed, and was pushed out of the tunnel in a flash of blinding white.

It took a moment for his vision to adjust from the soft grays of the Womb to that of the viewing. As it did, Raze found himself in a more Cimmerian atmosphere. Neon veins lit the ceiling, lasers skittering over the walls. The playful jazz sounds of the Womb cross-faded into grimy, wobble bass and syncopated drums.

Raze knew better than to project expectations, but he was surprised to find Mr. T in a nightclub spinning EDM and not at home cooking dinner for a lady friend and sipping Pinot.

As he integrated more into the view, Raze saw that he was on the second-story perimeter balcony overlooking a very crowded dance floor. The upstairs area was filled with tables, each lit with blue flame candles. A fire burned in the fireplace in the corner, surrounded by couches and puffy chairs. The place was saturated with bodies dressed for the prowl, holding drinks, chatting, and checking each other out.

Raze scanned the room for his target and spotted him at the bar next to a couple of his bros who were talking up a couple of trim. Mr. T wasn't paying much attention to his pals as they worked the getting-laid angle. Half sitting on a barstool, he was taking stock of the room while nursing a drink.

Raze moved into closer proximity. Rather than casual business attire, T was in a pair of dark blue, almost black, hand-sanded jeans, lace-up loafers, and a dark chocolate sweater that lay smooth against his chest—stylish, but not too metro. He was fit but not buff. His drink of choice appeared to be Scotch on the rocks. Hmmm... there were more provocative facets to Mr. T than what he presented to the world. Raze was almost impressed. *How refreshing to have a target more complex than a piece of cardboard,* Raze thought.

Something caught T's eye, and Raze watched him zero in on a couple of females walking up the stairs across the room. One was a spritely little nymph with short blond hair wearing a fuchsia mini dress. Her friend was taller and was rocking a shimmering cream dress that clung and slipped against each perfect curve as she moved, her body coruscating like a disco ball. Her long, copper hair cascaded in waves around her shoulders.

She was smoking hot, and T's eyes were on her as she

crossed the room to a table overlooking the dance floor. There was something familiar in the way she carried herself. And there was also something familiar in how the room suddenly reverberated with a riff that wasn't being spun by the DJ, a buzz of electricity that sent ripples through the little space Raze had staked out in the view.

Her Royal Hotness turned around to survey the room, eyes wide with vulnerability.

It couldn't be! There was no fucking way that piece of eye candy was the same chick from Demesne and the hospital! Raze watched her as she turned back and said something to her friend. The way she moved, the way she spoke, the way the energy radiating off her pressed against him. It *was* her.

Mr. T must have been thinking the very same thing; his mouth dropped open.

Score! Raze couldn't believe his luck in finding her so soon.

But he wasn't going to wait around for homie to make a move. She was the one he was really after. All he needed was to snatch her signature, and he'd be on his way. He had other business to attend to before he could deal with her, but as soon as his other shit was handled, she would be his highest priority. And he didn't want to be rushed when he dealt with her either.

Rather than moving in quickly, pouncing on her, and risking getting zapped out of the view by her voltage, Raze measured the oscillations of her field from a distance. She was relaxed. Her guard was down. There was still a lot of spark in her, but it wasn't the same nuclear power she brought with her earlier. She might be attainable tonight.

"Aislen," he said her name to himself as he stalked the outer edge of the room. He took cover within the heated skin and musk of the bodies crowding the room, all the time keeping his eye on the prize. She was engaged and laughing with her firecracker friend.

"Good girl," he said silently to the sprite. "You keep her on ice like that for me." He had a better chance of apprehending Aislen's essence if his presence remained undetected. He wouldn't want to frighten the little thing and throw her into any power surges.

The DJ was spinning a sludgy mix; the bass was low and thick and made the very air of the room palpable. Aislen would be distracted by that flux and might not feel his energy differential if he moved in closer. He slid himself behind a large column right beside her table.

He didn't see her skin or her dress anymore, not really. Only the whorls and spheres, the language beneath flesh that told him what she carried. He could feel her signature spiraling around his own. Rather than being greeted by her usual resistance, her signature was alluring and inviting. Colors weren't decoration; they were data. Violet told him who she was, gold told him how strong she burned.

He was pleasantly surprised and opened his field up to her disposition, letting it roll across him, savoring her and enjoying the scent before he reached in and plucked the flower.

Just as he flipped his switch to receive her, a sharp dissonance shot through him, kicking him out of the flow.

"*Now what?*" Raze peeked around the pillar, thinking she must have become aware of him, but saw that Mr. T had found his swagger and had presented himself at her table. Aislen responded to his appearance by battening down the hatches and throwing up some highly charged barbed wire. Maybe it wasn't just Raze. Maybe she wasn't into guys. Raze moved out from behind the pillar, using Troy's lolling field for cover, so he could get a better view of the scenery.

"Well, hello to you," the sexy sprite said, giving Troy the once-over and flashing him a dimpled smile.

Aislen looked way less pleased. She looked at Troy through

narrowed eyes, then reluctantly introduced them. "Gen, this is Troy. We work together. He's kind of a boss of mine. Troy, this is my friend, Genesis."

"Your best friend since forever," Genesis corrected her playfully.

Troy extended his hand. Raze mirrored him with his own phantom fingers, tuning into Genesis and snagging her vibration key. *Like taking candy from a baby.* It should have been just as easy with Aislen, but against his better judgment, he'd lingered a little too long.

Normally, he would've moved in, swift and merciless. That was the way he worked. But tonight, with her here—of all places—he found himself hesitating. Watching. Drawn instead of driving. The hesitation shocked him almost as much as her presence did. He should have taken her signature the moment she laughed, quick and clean. Instead, he lingered like some gawking fool.

What the hell was wrong with him? Raze didn't watch. He took. Yet here he was, spellbound, and hating himself for it.

"Nice to meet you," Troy said as he shook Genesis's hand. "And I am *not* her boss. We're co-workers." He gave Aislen a pointed look, "and friends."

A mixture of wistfulness and doubt passed over Aislen's face. Raze felt a whoomp-whomp in her energy as her defenses weakened and then, on a second thought, went back up again.

"A total pleasure to meet you." Gen flashed him another smile. Aislen looked from her friend to Troy and back again. Raze felt her energy take on another, sharper layer.

Is that jealousy? he wondered.

He checked out Genesis again. She was adorable—sassy and sparkly, wrapped up with a little bow of naughty. Raze could see why Aislen would feel threatened, but only because Genesis had an easy energy, flowing and golden, like honey.

Aislen, on the other hand, was stunning and dynamic, but she was tightly coiled and didn't give anything away. Troy could totally go for Genesis. It was the path of least resistance, but to Raze, there was something much more tempting in Aislen's challenge.

"So, I guess you're feeling better?" Troy said to Aislen.

She bristled a little. "Yeah," she said before turning a cold shoulder and looking down at the dance floor. The silent treatment created an awkward moment at the table, and Genesis picked up the slack.

"She's had a rough go of it lately, but nothing that a little time with a friend, a couple of cocktails, and some dancing can't shake off. Right, Hon?" She reached across the table and rubbed Aislen's hand to try and soften her up.

"Yep, that's right," Aislen responded, trying to put up a good front, if only for her friend.

But Raze wasn't having it. This girl was a mess. How could someone who seemed so weak and insecure have such a powerful field? All that trepidation Aislen transmitted should leave her ripe for the plucking. Raze should have been able to ravish her with ease. Fear was the most disruptive of frequencies. Fear, anger, depression—any intense, dark energy weakened a target's grid, leaving them exposed. It was the perfect weapon for control: amplify a person's fears, and you can capture, imprint, and track them anywhere. Jack up their fear frequency to terror and you own them.

Instead, Raze had to hold on for dear life in her presence or get knocked on his ass.

Raze looked at her intently. She was literally breathtaking; her vivid green eyes, lit up with a golden ring of fire, were clear and bright with intelligence. Yet she reeked of fear. Her vulnerability triggered something in Raze, and an unfamiliar feeling wriggled around inside, making him uncomfortable.

She has no idea what she carries, Raze realized. *If she did, she'd be invincible.*

"Can I buy you two a drink?" Troy asked.

"Oh, absolutely," Genesis said. "I would love a Lemon Drop."

"I'll have whatever you're having," Aislen said half-heartedly.

Troy lifted a brow. "Scotch? On the rocks?"

"Yeah. Problem with that?" she shot back, though she'd never touched the stuff in her life. Admitting that would feel worse than choking it down.

He grinned. "Didn't peg you for the Scotch type." He winked at Genesis, who giggled. "I'll be right back."

Raze stayed with the girls as Mr. T left to get their drinks. Genesis couldn't help checking out his ass as he walked away.

When he was out of earshot, Genesis turned to Aislen, breathless. "Holy shit, girl! He is freakin' delicious! Why haven't you told me about him? No wonder you've been so stressed! He's enough to tie any girl in knots."

"Well, it's not like that. We *work* together." Aislen must have realized she was completely unconvincing and sighed with exasperation. "And it doesn't matter now, anyway. I totally ruined any chance of anything else because I made a complete fool of myself today."

"Oh, Aiz, it couldn't have been that bad. He came over here specifically to say hello to you, and now he's over there buying you a drink! Geez, get a clue! But really, Scotch? You should have asked for a Lemon Drop."

"I don't like lemons."

"Well, you won't like Scotch! I guarantee it. Your liquor palate hasn't graduated to that kind of lightning yet, love."

Aislen dropped her gaze to the table. "See? I blew it. He probably thinks I'm a total idiot." She winced as soon as she said it, knowing how pathetic it sounded, but that was the truth she trusted Genesis with.

Aislen looked over to the bar. Troy was leaning against it, waiting for their order to arrive, looking back at her. He smiled.

A storm of energy began whipping around her again, and Raze had to grip the space so he wouldn't get thrown from the viewing. "I'm going to the restroom," Aislen said as she jumped up out of her chair and walked off.

The energy battered Raze until she moved a good distance away from him. *Jesus Christ, woman!* He thought. He would have followed her, but with the turmoil she was in, he wouldn't be able to get close enough. He needed to wait and see if she would settle down, because if she did, he wasn't going to hesitate. When the moment was right, strike while her field was open.

Troy returned with the drinks and set them down on the table. He glanced at Aislen's empty seat, disappointment apparent on his face.

So... he likes her, too, thought Raze.

"Mine," he growled, startling himself with the word. He didn't claim things. He erased them. So why did the word taste like hunger?

Genesis saw Troy's reaction and smiled. "Don't worry. She'll be right back. She just ran to the bathroom real quick. Have a seat." Troy sat down in Aislen's vacant chair.

"You know, Aislen is the sweetest, smartest person I know," Genesis continued. "Don't let whatever happened with her today fool you."

"I know," Troy said. "All I see is sweet and smart—except for tonight that is."

Genesis laughed. "I know, right? I am taking complete credit for that dress. She has no idea how beautiful she is and no idea how to show it off."

"And contrary to what she may think, I have nothing but the utmost respect for her," Troy responded. "Today was an exceptional situation. I realize that. She responded accordingly. It doesn't change how I feel about her at all."

Raze felt the familiar buzz of Aislen agitating the space and looked up to see her making her way back toward the table. She stopped short when she saw that Troy was sitting with Genesis.

"I probably shouldn't speak to you about this," Troy said, gazing down at his glass. "You being her friend and all... it's probably not appropriate. But I have been trying to get close to her—trying to figure her out. But I can never get around all the walls she puts up. I think she's amazing and I'd like to ask her out to dinner or something—"

"Yes!" Genesis interrupted, clenching her fist victoriously. "I mean, that's cool... great you want to ask her out and everything."

She tipped forward, the low-cut dress doing half the talking. "I know what you mean... Aislen has had a one-track mind most of her life. It's all seriousness and school, not much play. Play makes her nervous, and when she gets nervous, she shuts down and pushes people away."

She flashed him another mischievous smile, reached across the table, and grabbed his hand enthusiastically. "Maybe I could help you out? Drop a couple of hints? Well, they may need to be more than hints to get the point through her thick skull."

Troy laughed, making no moves to remove his hand from hers. An enormous punch of energy shuddered Raze's space. Raze looked back at Aislen. Her energy was full fury now, watching the interchange between Troy and her friend. Obviously, she assumed the wrong thing about the visual chemistry.

"That's really nice of you," Troy continued. "But I'm a big

boy, I can get my own dates. I guess I just wanted to make sure it wasn't me."

"It isn't, but suit yourself. This should be fun to watch."

The force grew more intense as Hurricane Aislen made landfall at the table. Raze distanced himself, not wanting the gale to blow him out.

"Hey, guys!" Aislen said, a little breathless. She looked down at the table just as Gen pulled her hand from Troy's. "You know, you two seem to be enjoying yourselves here. I'm going to leave you alone for a while."

She reached down, picked up the Scotch, threw it back like a sailor, and slammed the glass down on the table. The fire hit her throat, but she forced herself not to cough.

"Thanks for the drink," she said to Troy. She spun on her high heels and stormed away, before either of them could make a move to stop her.

Troy gave Gen a "See what I mean?" look.

Raze chuckled. This was all very entertaining. He watched Aislen move toward the stairs, admiring the way her body radiated in the form-fitting dress and the bolts of lightning in her field.

He decided to follow her. She was still way too hot to get close to, but that Scotch would work its way through her pretty fast. That, plus the hypnotic groove of the music mixed with a little bump and grind on the floor, was an equation that was sure to work in his favor.

He slithered behind her down the stairs to the dance floor to wait for the perfect moment. He just needed a little taste. Then he could call on her whenever he wanted.

∞

AISLEN WAS ANNOYED—NO, she was *pissed*. Mostly with herself. She couldn't blame Gen. It wasn't Gen's fault that Troy was irresistible. He may have been cute at work, but tonight he was— she didn't even have words. It was criminal to be that good-looking and act like you have no idea.

And then seeing him talking to her with such intensity. It made Aislen want to throw up. He was always charming, but she had never seen him speak to anyone with a look like the one he'd had on his face just now—raw, longing.

What frustrated her even more was her own behavior. She had no idea what to do with herself, what to say, or how to act. She just didn't have the effortless interpersonal skills that Gen did. If she did, she would be the one up there, hopelessly, and probably very successfully, flirting with him.

The whole place, with all its beautiful people, smiling and laughing, batting their eyes and grinding against each other on the dance floor, made Aislen feel like a fish out of water.

How had Gen talked her into pouring herself into this dress and coming here? She had no idea. It was the drinks. Aislen had been feeling reckless and giddy when she shimmied into the dress and strappy heels. All Gen's oooing and ahhing had drowned out Aislen's voice of reason.

She pressed herself deeper into the mass of writhing bodies, letting their heat embrace her. She'd found the music cloying when they'd first walked in, but now the deep bass throbbed in her chest, down her arms, into her thighs, vibrating across her skin. It practically moved her body for her.

The Scotch—awful going down—had already made a straight shot to her brain, softening thought to jelly. Lights bled into orbs of color. Flesh brushed slick against her. She felt warm, fluid, entranced. The colors weren't just in her head anymore; they pressed against her skin, seeping in.

She closed her eyes, tilted her head back, and gave herself

to the rhythm. She never sensed the predator already curled around her field.

Crisp air slipped through the crush of heat, threading over the curves of her body, cooling her skin even as her insides flushed hotter. The presence licked across her in invisible arcs, a frisson of voltage scattering through her nerves. She surrendered to it, intoxicated, spinning faster and faster, until delirium pulled her down into a siphon of white.

Arms wrapped her waist. A hard body pressed against her back. Warm breath grazed her neck.

"Aislen, I think it's time to go," was all she heard before the dark took her.

∞

HE ONLY INTENDED to dip his fingertips into her—to dabble in her field just enough to take what he needed. But as soon as he touched the outer edge of her space, the sharp static of her downshifted to a more pleasant vibe, a *much* more delectable essence. And just a touch hadn't been enough after all.

Surprised by the sudden accommodation of his presence, Raze caressed through her outer layers, watching as her face softened, as she seemed to revel in his energetic touch. He moved in closer. Their energy played off each other, pulling and pushing in an effortless dance.

Before he realized it, he had stepped right into the middle of her etheric center, his spinning liquid silver within her ultraviolet and gold vortex. He lingered in the rapture, tuning in to the sweetest spot of her, absorbing and knowing every facet of her in a dazzling array of light.

An explosive blast suddenly threw him out of her field and completely across the room. The percussion disoriented him and diminished his integrity, but it didn't throw him out of the view. He grounded himself and turned back toward Aislen. She was in Troy's arms, and he was carrying her off the dance floor toward the front door.

Raze could see Genesis through the haze, waiting for them on the sidelines, a worried look souring her otherwise angelic face.

Raze took a deep breath. He could still feel Aislen's essence in his midst. He wanted to bask longer in the glow of it, or better yet, follow her out and taste more of her, but he needed to come up for air. Plus, he had one more project to consummate for his night to be complete. He glanced at Aislen one more time as Troy carried her out.

He had her now. Wherever she was. Whenever he wanted.

"Alpha 9," he said reluctantly.

FIFTEEN

MATHIS WOKE WITH A JOLT, slamming into the chair with such force he felt as though he were dropped from the ceiling. His head was swimming. His heart pounded in his chest. One thought was on repeat in his head.

I have to get the game.

He sat upright in the chair and tried to rub the grog out of his skull.

Images of women removing facial hair off of each other were playing out in comic exaggeration on the television, telling him it was *infomercial:30 in the morning*. He grabbed the remote and pressed the info button. 1:11 appeared on the screen. He had been asleep for at least six hours. So why did it feel like he hadn't slept a wink?

Get the game.

"What the hell for?" he argued out loud.

Because we say so, his brain and gut gnawed back.

He thought about calling Jackson and suggesting that he send a crime scene tech over there to confiscate the console, so he could go back to sleep, but his stomach twisted up like a pretzel at the idea.

That's not good enough.

It was right. The game needed to be examined, not just booked into evidence. Well then, maybe he could meet Jackson over there; they could get the console and investigate it a little further.

You need a search warrant, idiot.

"Fuck it then," he said, sitting back in the chair and closing his eyes. This was not his problem. He wasn't a dick anymore. He was just a ground pounder. Let people above his pay grade figure out their own shit.

But the itch in his belly wouldn't let it go. There was something more to this, and it had to do with that game. The certainty of it sang in his bones.

"So what you're suggesting is... I actually break into the house... and *violate the law* to get that game?" There. That was a dose of reality that would shut 'em up.

He wobbled out of the chair, still feeling a little dizzy, wandered into the bathroom to take a whizz, then stumbled down the hall and fell into his bed for another six-hour snooze.

But the cogs of obsession were already turning: wondering, whying, and worrying, all clamoring for the same thing.

THE GAME.

He could not shake the intuition that had latched onto him. The answer to the Parrish murder was in that game. He just couldn't provide evidence to bring it to reason. And it wasn't going to let him go. The compulsion was too great. It had to be done—and he was going to do it. He was going to get into that house and get that game, even if it was breaking the law.

"Fuck me in the ass," he grumbled as he rolled out of bed. And if he got caught, the State Pen would be more than happy to oblige.

You are too close to retirement to be risking this, his rational mind tried to argue.

"Yep," he muttered as he changed into a clean uniform.

And in uniform! When you're off-duty! You are out of your goddamn mind!

"Yep."

Mathis put his badge on. He strapped his duty belt around his thick waist. Dug out his 1980s nightstick and slid it into its holster, just in case he had to put the wood to someone.

Don't let that happen. Felony 459 and 187?

"Yep."

He checked himself in the mirror. Brushed his teeth. Stared at the man dumb enough to risk prison for a goddamn video game. His gut still sang the same refrain.

Get the game. Get the game. Get the game.

He grabbed his keys, got in his pickup truck, and headed across town.

SIXTEEN

A VOICE BROKE through the buzz still rattling her eardrums. "Felt the need to tie one on, eh?"

She tried to move her body, but she was twisted and tight, hot and sticky with sweat.

"You should listen when your friends tell you that you aren't big enough for Scotch, yet."

"Genesis?" Her own thought throbbed against her skull. "Troy?" Each guess only sharpened the headache. Her mouth tasted sour with the residual flavors of alcohol and bile, but she didn't remember throwing up. Oh, wait. Yeah, she did. A flashback of a gutter and a nice pair of loafers replayed in her mind, and acidic juices lurched into her throat.

A cool hand from out of nowhere rested on her forehead, instantly quelling the spinning and silencing the hissing that harassed the cochlea of her inner ear.

"Egh, Aislen, what were you thinking?" The voice was right next to her ear, speaking her name with its foreign inflection.

Her first reaction was to jump up and run away, but she

found herself frozen—pinned in place by a force stronger than the gentle hand pressing on her forehead. A scream rose in her throat, but she could not find her vocal cords. She could only lie frozen and mute, staring up at her father sitting beside her.

"Shhhhhhhhh. Settle," Preston said gently. "It's only a dream." Then he laughed softly.

He removed his hand. "I don't like imposing my will upon you, Aislen, but this is for your own good. So here is the deal... I am going to hold you here, with me, until you hear me out. Then, you are going to make a decision, and we will go from there, okay?"

She struggled against her own numb flesh. "Noooo!" She screamed at him in her brain.

"Like I said, you don't have a choice right now, but you will, I promise." He got up off the bed and sat down in a nearby chair. A metal chair with a cracked green cushion, the kind you'd find at the DMV—or in a psych ward.

She wasn't even in a room. Just a void—fog thick as milk, bed and chair floating in emptiness.

"First, a recap," her father said. "You've been drinking tonight."

No shit, Sherlock, she thought, glaring at him.

"Sarcasm intact. That's a good sign." Preston chuckled.

Her stomach dropped. *Did I...say that out loud?*

He carried on as if nothing was strange. "Problem number one is, you aren't a drinker, so your body's processing it like poison. You're still quite intoxicated."

The 'no duh' of the century, she fired back, testing him.

Preston laughed again, which was really starting to irritate her. "I'm not here to lecture you about what you already know —just about what you don't. Like the fact that drinking dulls your control. Which is why I can keep you pinned here so easily. If you were sober, I'd have to work a lot harder to hold you still."

What?

"It is very tempting to drink or use other pharmaceuticals. You might think it will suppress all this," he waved his hand around the space, "that you can bury it all back down and pretend it doesn't exist. But drinking won't cover it up. It won't put it back in the box. It only makes you lose control. Are we clear on that?" He looked down at her in the bed, waiting for an answer.

Her anger flared hotter than her nausea. She hated being told what to do—especially by him.

Who do you think you are? You can't tell me what to do! She yelled at him, but with a tongue still hijacked and hog-tied. She glared at him, hoping she still had control of her eyeballs and could get her point across.

"I'm not telling you what to do, Buttercup. Just trying to impart some extremely important advice, especially for you."

Oh, great. A pep talk from Dad-of-the-Year.

Preston chuckled softly. "Hey, I'll take the promotion. Better than 'Deadbeat of the Year,' don't you think?"

She was shocked. *Had he heard her?*

Yes. It's called telepathy. His lips didn't move, but she heard it in her head as clear as day. Just like when she was in the dream. And when she was in the kitchen with her mom—

And I told you to ask her about the teacups, he finished her thought, again without speaking.

If you can hear me, prove it.

"I just did," Preston answered, maddeningly calm.

That is very fucking annoying, she thought back to him.

"Yeah," he admitted with a sheepish smile. "I hated it when I first realized I could hear others, too. Be grateful, you tune most of it out. Otherwise, you'd be hearing everybody's obnoxious chatter. Usually, only really capable people who have a strong emotional connection to you can get through."

I don't have a strong, emotional connection to you, she thought.

He didn't say anything. After a moment, he got up and started wandering about the space.

Aislen realized that he no longer looked like the deranged, homeless man from her earlier vision. He didn't look like the man who came to the door when she was four, either. He looked middle-aged, the age that he would be in real life. He was slim and fit. The sandy blond of his hair was flecked with a little gray. He was handsome, just as her mother had said, and there was a magnetism about him. A very calming force drew her in and held her in a feeling of safety and belonging that she didn't want to leave, even though she hated his guts.

Aislen could understand how her mom fell so hard for him and remained hopeful for so long. Thinking of her mother pining away for this man, who just up and left them to fend for themselves, rekindled her anger.

Preston stopped pacing, came to the side of the bed, and sat down beside her.

"I don't know how to tell you all the things that I need to, Aislen. I hope that after what you experienced yesterday, you understand that I *know* what is going on with you and that I can help."

This is crazy, she thought. *I'm going fucking crazy.* She started trying to fight again, her mind kicking and pushing against her body, yet it remained hopelessly motionless on the bed.

"Easy now. You're not broken, Aislen. Just rattled. Happens to the best of us. But that brings us to problem number two: what *is* happening to you. It would be easy just to label yourself as crazy and medicate it away. But that is not what is happening. The skills that have been lying dormant inside of you, your whole life, are starting to activate.”

What does that mean? Skills? That doesn't make any sense!

“I know it doesn't. That's why I am here, to explain it and try to help you with it. You are in the process of, well, it's like waking up. Only you aren't waking up from this world back into the world you call 'real'. You are waking up from that world, into something... different. And I know it feels unfair, but this isn't madness. It's ability. It's an inheritance.”

This is too much for me... I don't want it! I want to be the way I was. I just want to be normal!

“I know. God, I know. But you've never been normal, Aislen. Not in the way the world means it. Your genetics are coded for this. And that's not a curse. It's survival.”

So I am a freak? That's what you're saying? Great! Just. Fucking. Great!

“Well, you're in good company.”

With who? You? That's good company?

Preston didn't respond. Aislen couldn't read his mind the way he could read hers, but she could read the pain on his face well enough.

“No. Not just me,” he finally said. “There are others like you, like us, in the world. A few of them actually realize it and use it in a way that is beneficial. Some have experienced it but suppress it. Like you would like to do. But you aren't going to be able to. Your abilities are too strong. You need to understand it, learn how to control it, and you need to do that really fast. Because there are also those who understand it and will utilize it to their advantage. And those people are very, very dangerous.”

Preston frowned slightly and shook his head. “I never wanted this for you. I wanted you to have a normal life. And safe—I wanted you safe. When you made it through childhood and adolescence and into adulthood, still dormant, I thought that it might be possible. But you are waking up, Aislen. There is no way around it. I missed too many of your firsts, Buttercup. But this one—this waking up—I can't miss. I won't."

How do you know anything about my childhood or adolescence? You weren't here for that!

Another shadow passed across his face, and he looked away from her. She could tell he was trying to maintain his composure. When he looked at her again, the gold was alight in his eyes.

"I have *always* been near you, Aislen. As near as your next breath. It hasn't been in the way I have wanted, or in the way you have needed. It has been the most painful aspect of my life. You can never fathom how sorry I am for that. I am very, deeply sorry."

The apology sat heavily between them. Finally, Preston spoke again. "Aislen, I need to help you. I am the only one who can. And if I don't... if you don't let me... your life... your mother's life... and any other people who get in their way will be in grave danger."

He held her in his intense gaze and slid closer to her on the edge of the bed. "It's going to be hard for you, but I need you to trust me." He placed his hands together and closed his eyes, as if he were about to pray. A lambent flame began to radiate in the space between his palms. As he pulled his hands apart, the glow clung and flickered around his fingertips. He placed his hand on her head and gently ran both thumbs across her forehead.

Aislen immediately became alert. The agonizing pounding in her head and her queasiness vanished. The paralysis released its grip, and she could tell she was free to move and speak again. She also knew she was in a dream—and that, if she wanted to, she could wake up and be away from her father and this madness.

She sat up in the bed and looked at her father's face, directly, for the second time in her life. Only this time, she was the one who had the choice of whether to walk away or not.

His eyes didn't waver from hers: verdant, alive, and pensive. A large part of her wanted to hurt him, to turn away from him, to wake from this vision and never think of him again. But the fear that her mother could be harmed somehow was too disturbing.

"What do you mean by danger?" she finally asked him.

He let out a breath. "It's a very long story and probably beyond what you can understand right now... but the short version is—the people who have been looking for me for most of my life, if they figure out that you are my daughter... they will look for you and they will not stop until you are dead."

"What?!" A million questions riddled her mind at once. "But what did *I* do? What did *you* do? Why do they hate you so much they would kill me? Are you a criminal?"

"I am not."

"But you've been running all this time, just like Mom said!"

"Yes, I have. I have spent most of my life running and hiding—because of who I am and what I can do. If they find out who you are... they will know *what* you are and what you are capable of. And if they can't control you and use you for their own purposes, then they will eliminate you."

"But what am I?"

He met her eyes. "You're a Walker."

Aislen bristled. "That's Mom's name. She gave it to me because you weren't there."

His expression softened, almost pained. "She gave it to you because I asked her to. Walker was mine. An alias, a mask. The only way I could stay tied to you without painting a target on your back."

"I never told her my last name at all," He continued. "She only knew me as Preston. See, I knew I wouldn't be able to stay for very long—no matter how much I wanted to. No matter how in love I was, I couldn't stay with her or you without bringing harm to you both. But I gave her the name that I used so we could be connected that way. So I would always be able to find you."

"So your name is Walker, too?" The idea of it was repugnant. She had always been proud that she had her mom's name, that they were independent of the man who walked away from them. "I guess you lived up to your alias, didn't you?" She meant it to be hurtful and was satisfied when she saw it had found its mark. But Preston pressed on with his explanation.

"Names carry a signature that can be tracked. My real name carries a signature that has been tracked since I escaped from my original life. I never speak the original name. It would be enough to send the hounds sniffing our way. But I needed a name to use as I traveled. I came up with Walker because it was the best way to describe what I had found myself to be."

"A *Walker*? What the hell is that?"

"It's really hard to explain in a way that won't make you flip out. But here it goes, Aislen. You have the ability to transmigrate dimensions." He stopped and watched her.

She stared at him blankly.

"Everybody is capable of it. It's a natural aspect of being human. But when they do it, for the most part, they do it unconsciously and don't remember. You, on the other hand, are able to walk your consciousness from the third dimension into other dimensions, at will."

"Are you freaking kidding me? Do you even hear yourself? And you tell me *I* can't use drugs? What are *you* on?"

"I know it is a foreign concept for you, but that's the gist of it." He shrugged his shoulders as if it was really no big deal, even though he was blowing her mind.

"There are other dimensions that exist just beyond your normal, sensory perceptions, Aislen. Your corporeal consciousness normally tunes them out—it has to in order to function within the 'rules' of 3D. Your body is only capable of experiencing one, very thin slice of the spectrum of existence. But your consciousness, the essence of who you really are, isn't limited to the confines of your brain. It transcends the physical altogether. Always has and always will. You are being forced to operate on a new level now, whether you like it or not."

"Alright, enough! This is all sounding a little too 'woo woo' for me.

"Well, welcome to the woo woo, kiddo. The thing is—you don't get to opt out."

She could only stare at him. It sounded completely outrageous, but was it? When she applied it to what she had experienced the past twenty-four hours, what she was experiencing now, it kind of made sense.

"So these dreams I've had?"

"Were travels to another plane—the Fourth, actually. People call it different things: Mundus Imaginalis, Alam-i-Malakut, Olam-Hadamut, the Astral. The people who will be interested in you call it The Stratum.

"Your little journey last night, your *dream* as you say, took you to a place in The Stratum where you weren't supposed to be. You saw something you shouldn't have seen. They'll be looking for you because of that."

Aislen thought of the dark soldier boring holes through her with eyes of ice and a bullet of lead, and a shudder went through her.

"But it all comes down to you," Preston said. "I told you

that you have a choice. You cannot change what is happening to you. Your abilities will continue to develop, whether you like it or not. And people are already looking for you. Trust me, if they find you, find out who you are, and what you can really do, they will hurt, maim, or kill anything that gets in their way. Your mother. Your friends. They don't care.

"You can choose to go this alone, like I did. Or you can choose to let me help you."

Aislen didn't know what to say. It seemed ludicrous to her that anyone would think she was that important or dangerous that they would go to such lengths as to kill anyone to get to her.

You are dreaming, she reminded herself as she looked up at her father. His eyes blazed with conviction. As much as she wanted to hurt him by cutting him off and denying him, she couldn't. The words that rang in her head, the emotions that played upon his face, were full of truth.

"What do I have to do to keep Mom safe?"

RAZE SPRAWLED IN THE CHAIR, loose and lazy, lingering on the cusp of Theta, enjoying the afterglow of his Aislen assignment. He had been spot on about the confluence of music, booze, and movement breaking down her walls and giving him the gap he needed to move in close enough to find her baseline.

It had left him feeling a little intoxicated himself. He was tempted to reopen the aperture and take another spin.

Her baseline had left a trace in him, still humming like a second pulse. That wasn't standard. Hardware didn't linger. Signatures didn't stain. But Aislen had seeped under his skin, and that was the hook. One obsession at a time, he reminded himself. Routine was survival. She was anything but routine.

Still, he forced the aperture closed.

"Alpha 14."

The Womb turned up its luminosity and cranked up the volume on the jazz.

"Metal," he instructed. The Womb switched tracks: Pantera roared through the speakers.

"Perfect," Raze said, grinning at his own reflection in the console glass.

He got out of the chair, went to the control console, and pulled up the programming app. With a few taps on the keyboard, he initiated the homing device on the visors. He knew the GPS coordinates of the Parrish residence, but he did not know where the visors were inside the house. He wasn't about to waste his valuable time playing hide and seek with a pair of inanimate objects when he had a much more tantalizing game to play with Miss Aislen.

The visors were just hardware. Replaceable. Trackable. But Aislen? She was a volatile equation walking into the restricted zone. A living breach. And breaches like that could undo everything.

"North 37 degrees, 39 minutes, three point nine, eight, five, two seconds. West minus 120 degrees, 59 minutes, 46 point eight, one, two, six seconds," he said to the Womb. Once the sequence was initiated, he lay back down in the chair.

"Theta 8."

The Womb descended through the cycles. Brainwaves aligned, heart rate slowed, synaptic chatter dimmed. Standard sequence. Raze could've done it in his sleep—hell, sometimes he had.

The Womb recited the coordinates back in her flat cadence, like a flight computer running pre-launch. To Raze, it was background noise, protocol. To anyone else, it might have sounded like a summons whispered through the void.

"North 37 degrees, 39 minutes, three point nine, eight, five, two seconds. West minus 120 degrees, 59 minutes, 46 point eight, one, two, six seconds."

As simple as e=mc^2, the coordinates slotted into his mind with the precision of a key clicking into a lock. To Raze, it was muscle memory—drop the coordinates, catch the signal line, step through. Just another commute through a wrinkle in reality.

EIGHTEEN

MATHIS PULLED his truck onto a side street and walked around the corner to Magnolia, trying to appear officially casual, like he was supposed to be there. If anyone happened to be looking out a window at this hour, seeing a uniformed officer wouldn't cause them to call the cops. But the sleepy little neighborhood was just that, sleeping. All houses were dark, and the streets were deserted.

He checked to make sure no new vehicles were parked in the driveway or garage, that Mom or Sister hadn't made it home yet; then he sidled along the easement between the Parrish house and its neighbors, tracing the same path he'd taken last night.

He went to the back patio door. They had broken one of the multiple panes of glass to unlock the door. In a convenient case of incompetence, the broken pane had been covered in nothing but cling wrap and masking tape, rather than nailed over with plywood.

"Thank God I work with a barrel of monkeys," Mathis said to himself. The last thing he wanted to attempt was hefting his fat ass through an unlocked window. He stuck his hand through the edge of the window, ripped the tape with his fingers, and placed his hand on the inside latch.

He took a moment to say a quick Hail Mary, of which he only knew the words "Hail Mary," flipped the lever, and popped open the door.

This was breaking and entering. Flat-out burglary. With a badge on his hip. *Jesus, what the hell was he doing?*

He paused at the threshold, listening for the timed beeping of an alarm system. The house was silent except for the soft purr of the refrigerator.

Mathis stepped inside and quietly shut the door behind him. He wasn't about to lollygag now. He needed to grab it and ghost. He went directly to the den and the entertainment center, careful to walk around the still-damp bloodstains on the carpet where Mr. Parrish had lain less than twenty-four hours earlier. He located the black cube on the bottom shelf and set about unplugging and untangling cords as quickly and methodically as possible.

Every tug on a cord sounded like a gunshot in the quiet house. Evidence tampering. Career suicide. Prison time. All for a damn video game. His gut screamed it was worth it—but his pension sure as hell didn't agree.

What little he understood of video games, he at least knew he needed some kind of hand-held controller, so he started searching the shelves for one. He located a shelf littered with an array of tools: A plastic pistol, a toy sword, and some kind of sci-fi power glove. Jesus. What kind of Nintendo-from-hell was this kid playing? He scooped up the lot of them and placed them next to the console.

It was then that he noticed a red light somewhere in the room. The red strobe washed the walls like a pulse. For a second, it felt less like a toy and more like the room itself was breathing. He scanned the room to find its origin. After a few flashes, he traced it to the far corner of the living room.

Lying on the floor, under the splatter pattern of Scott Parrish's brain on the wall, were what looked like a pair of shades only elderly men who'd just had cataract surgery would wear. The lenses were massive, large enough to cover half a grown man's face, and even in the low light, Mathis could tell they were mirrored with the particolored gleam of an oil slick, similar to the game console.

The mirrored lenses threw back the red strobe in sickly rainbow flashes. They had to be part of the setup, though Christ only knew how. Mathis scooped them up, dumped them with the rest of the loot, and stared at the growing pile. He only had two hands and, because he was unskilled in thievery, he hadn't brought a bag along. He needed to be selective about what to take with him.

God Almighty, listen to him—weighing loot like some two-bit burglar. If Internal Affairs could see him now, they'd have him cuffed before sunrise.

The thought cut short with a sharp pop, like a small rock had been thrown at the glass. Mathis froze. Then, with reflexes closer to an arthritic housecat than jaguar, he threw himself on the couch and held his breath.

NINETEEN

RAZE STEPPED through the portal and into the den of the Parrish residence. A sluggish movement from the corner of the room caught his eye, a large, lumbering presence hurtled itself onto the couch.

Jesus Christ! Could anything be routine? Even in the middle of the night, in a dead house, disturbance found him. He held very still, watching the space where the burly creature fell and hid itself.

He only had to wait a couple of minutes before a massive man-head peeked up from the back of the couch. He looked directly at Raze, but Raze knew he could only see the window that was behind him. After making sure the coast was clear, the man, dressed in full police regalia, stood up.

Well, I'll be damned! It's the fuzz from the hospital! What the hell is he doing here? Raze bided his time, watching to see what the officer would do. *This oughtta be good.*

The officer walked over to the television and started grabbing items off the floor. He rolled up a glove and shoved it into a pocket, picked up a plastic gun and stuck it in his waistband, then picked up the visor, blinking red from the homing activation, and slid it on top of his head.

Holy shit—he's taking the visor!

Of all the people to stumble into the Project, it had to be this bull-headed cop. Worse, he wasn't just grabbing evidence; he was trusting his gut, acting without a plan. That kind of unpredictability was the one variable Raze couldn't account for. The cohesive thread of the Project was fraying into an irreparable mess, more convoluted and out of control by the hour.

Raze watched as the officer fumbled frantically with the game pieces. *What could he possibly be thinking?*

Raze slipped in behind him, etheric palm pressing the back of his neck, and switched into receiver mode. Fear spiked through the man's signal—muddy maroon and amber pulses, thick with panic.

Get the gear. Move. Don't screw this up. There's something in this game—I can feel it!

The thoughts blared raw and jagged, conveying that the cop knew the game was more than it looked.

Raze siphoned the officer's base frequency and encrypted it into his internal registry—a spectral signature he could trace anywhere, like a wolf memorizing the scent of prey. Then he slipped around to the front of him, noting the stripes on his arm and the name tag on his chest.

He moved out of the way as the man stumbled past, in an obvious hurry to leave.

The sergeant had only taken one set of visors. Raze needed to get a lock on the second so he would know where to find it when he came in the flesh to repossess it.

He scanned the room searching for a signal from the second visor. No beacon. No blinking pulse. Which meant someone had already claimed it. That fact gnawed at him harder than Mathis's theft.

He turned his attention to the desk and checked the computer. The screen was asleep, but a green glow from the monitor told Raze that it was still powered on. That was good. The Intercept program he'd set up in The Womb would be able to access the hard drive and fry it with no problem, wiping out all the incriminating information about Infinium that Scott Parrish had accumulated.

The cop's meathead bobbed past the window, wearing the visor like a prize.

Raze leaned back into the signal line, retreating to The Womb.

"Enjoy your head start, Sergeant Mathis," he murmured. His jaw was tight.

Because when I catch up, the game won't save you.

TWENTY

MATHIS COULDN'T GET BACK to his pickup fast enough. His pulse hammered, breath tight in his throat. That crack at the window had nearly made him shit himself—and even after convincing himself it was just the old house settling, the feeling of being watched clung like static.

Ghosts weren't real, he told himself. But this was the house of a fresh murder victim, and his conscience wasn't letting him forget it. It breathed down his neck like a warning: *you're making a mistake.*

And he had. Christ, he'd just stolen evidence. Felony theft. A direct violation of everything he'd sworn to uphold. His gut churned.

He slid into the driver's seat and glanced at the pile of electronics beside him. The visor's red light pulsed faintly, like a heartbeat. What the hell had he done?

What had seemed like a good idea five minutes ago now looked like career suicide. God forbid if he ever had to explain this to someone, like his future defense attorney. He gripped the wheel until his knuckles whitened, telling himself it was just exhaustion, madness brought on by too many shifts without sleep.

The truck engine turned over, loud in the quiet neighborhood. A porch light flicked on down the street.

Mathis cursed under his breath and peeled away from the curb. The sooner he got away from that house—and from what he'd just done—the better.

TWENTY-ONE

"WHERE TO BEGIN?" Preston said, mostly to himself, as he jumped off the bed and started pacing around the space again. "I don't want to put you into too much shock. Not that you haven't had enough of that today." He stopped and turned to her. "You know you are in a dream state now, right?"

"Yes."

"Okay, so the first thing I want you to do is wake up. Then—I want you to fall right back asleep and come back here, got it?"

She didn't get it.

"It's really easy. I promise," he tried again. "The important thing is that when you wake up... don't let yourself get too awake... don't get out of bed, don't go to the bathroom, don't start trying to make sense or analyze anything... Allow yourself to wake up, take a moment to see where you are, then go back to sleep and come back here. Baby steps, okay?"

"Okaaay... I guess," she said. Although it seemed quite impossible to her, she might as well try. Worst-case scenario, it didn't work. Or maybe that would be the best case.

Aislen lay back down on the bed and closed her eyes. Her mind was spinning with doubt and uncertainty, but after a while, she felt herself relax, and she started drifting off to sleep.

"Wake up, Aislen," she heard her father say from across the room. She opened her eyes, expecting him to be standing next to her in the empty space. But she wasn't there anymore. She was in the dark. She could make out the shapes of a dresser, a mirror, a window, and some posters on a wall.

She put the pieces of the room together and realized she was in Gen's bedroom, not her own. She could feel her friend's warm body sprawled out next to her and hear her breathy, little squeaks. Only Gen could snore and sound adorable.

Okay, she thought to herself. *Let's see if this is real or not.* She closed her eyes again, breathed deeply, and relaxed into the comfort of the bed. She thought about Preston, the soothing sound of his voice, and the chiffon oasis she had shared with him just moments before.

"See? You're a natural."

She opened her eyes. She was sitting back on the bed, and her father was sitting in the chair across from her, a beaming smile on his face.

"Wow. I can slip in and out of delusions with ease. I'm sooooo relieved," she said.

"Very funny," he laughed. "Come on, admit it. You're impressed."

"Well, okay, maybe a little. But it doesn't prove I'm *not* crazy."

"No. But by the time we're done, you may need a new definition for crazy. You want to do something really crazy? Something so crazy that it may not be so crazy after all?" He stood up and held his hand out to her.

She hesitated.

"It's only a dream, Buttercup. Remember?" There was a

tease in his smile and a challenge in his eye. She never could resist a challenge. She took his hand and he pulled her out of the bed. "Okay, this time I'm going with you. Close your eyes."

She obeyed. He kept hold of her hand and moved to stand beside her.

"Let's go visit Mom, shall we?"

Aislen opened her eyes to look at him.

"Ah, ah, ah! No peeking." He brushed his hands over her eyes, closing them again.

"All right," he said, his voice becoming soft and melodic. "Take some deep, slow breaths. Get back down in that warm, liquid, sleepy space. Now, I want you to think about home. Imagine you are looking at it on a map, then imagine that you are a bird hovering above your rooftop. Can you see it?"

"Yeah."

"Now pull that image into a little ball about as big as your fist."

Aislen watched the image roll itself into a small sphere of energy.

"See what you did there?" Preston asked.

Aislen squinted at the glowing sphere. "Yeah... made a glowing stress ball."

He laughed. "That's evoking. You just called forth an itinerary—a path. We call it a signal line. This one is made from a geo-coordinate, tied to a place on a map. But let's do something more advanced, shall we?"

"Now I want you to picture your mom. Feel what it is like being around her, what makes her unique and special, and pull that feeling into an image, like you did with home."

Aislen thought about her mother, how she moved around the kitchen and the house with graceful purpose, her gentle strength when times were hard, and how comforting it felt being wrapped in her arms.

"Next, take that image and those feelings and imagine them as color and shape."

Aislen watched as her pictures melted into mellow amber and warm gold and spun themselves in a slow whirlpool in her mind.

"Got it?"

"Yes," Aislen said.

"Now, put that into a ball of energy in front of you."

Preston gestured to the second orb of color coalescing in front of her. "That one's different. That's a signature frequency—a sig-freq line."

Aislen frowned. "So... a GPS for people?"

"Exactly," he said. "A geo-cord gets you to a place. A sig-freq gets you to someone, even if you don't know where they are."

She gave the sphere a wary glance. "That's not creepy at all."

"It can be," he admitted. "Which is why I'm teaching you the right way to use it. We are going to use the signature frequency to visit Mom."

"Visit Mom? What???" Aislen opened her eyes and looked at him incredulously.

"Fasten your seatbelt, Buttercup," Preston said with a grin. "Time to get inside."

Aislen blinked at the golden ball hovering before her. "Uh, yeah. I'm not Thumbelina. I don't fit."

"Your body doesn't," he corrected. "Your body's still in bed. This—" he tapped the orb with a fingertip, making it ripple "—is where your awareness goes. Just close your eyes and imagine stepping in."

Aislen folded her arms. "You make it sound like I'm logging into a video game."

"Pretty much," he said, unbothered.

She sighed, shut her eyes, and focused. For a heartbeat, nothing happened, then she felt her skin stretch, loosen, unravel—like threads pulling free of a sweater. In the next instant, she was inside. Whorls of color wrapped around her like ribbons in a storm.

A flash of light burst open in front of her, expanding into a hole of brilliant white that sucked her inside. Suddenly, she was flying, or falling, she couldn't tell which. Before she could scream, her ears popped loudly. Startled, she opened her eyes. Her father stood beside her, and together they were in her mother's room, right beside her bed.

"Holy dog shit," Aislen let out in a long breath. She looked down at her mother, sleeping peacefully. The auburn of her hair was loose and fanned out like a flame across her pillow. "Are we really here?"

"Yes," Preston answered.

Though she had the whole bed to herself, Sabine was sleeping on the far right side, leaving the left side of the bed empty. Aislen knew she always slept that way. There was a noticeable indent on that side of the bed. It was as if her mother held that space open, thinking that one day she would open her eyes and someone would be there, looking back at her.

"This feels wrong," Aislen whispered. "Like we're... spying. On Mom."

"We are," Preston admitted without hesitation. "And the fact that you feel it? That's good. It means you have ethics."

She tore her gaze from her mother and glared at him. "So not everyone does?"

His jaw tightened. "No. Some people treat the unconscious as fair game. They say if someone isn't aware, then boundaries don't matter. To them, a sleeping person is no more than an animal, or worse, a maggot."

"Maggots," Aislen muttered, the word sour in her mouth.

Preston nodded grimly. "Exactly. They cross any line they want, convince themselves it doesn't count because their victim never knew."

"But it *does* count," Aislen shot back. Her fists clenched at her sides. "It matters."

"Yes," Preston said, softer now. "That's why I'm teaching you. So you'll know the power, and the cost, and where not to cross."

Her mother stirred in the bed and opened her eyes. She looked directly at them, squinting her eyes to try to see better.

Aislen gasped.

"Still, Aislen," Preston said.

They stood motionless while her mother looked in their direction for a while, then drifted back off to sleep. Aislen glanced at Preston, but he was still looking at her mom. Longing was evident in his expression, along with the deepest sadness that she had ever seen.

He pulled his gaze away and looked back at Aislen. "Close your eyes, Aislen, and go back the way we came."

Aislen closed her eyes, thought again about how they got to her mother's room, about the seamless blend of color and shape. Her ears popped, and they were both standing back where they started.

Aislen plopped down on the bed, dumbstruck. Preston pulled the chair up and faced her, waiting for her to speak.

"You do that all the time, don't you?" she finally said.

"Yes."

"I've felt it."

"Yes. So does she."

"Why? Why do you do that? Why do you torment her that way?"

"Because... " His voice faltered. He looked down at his feet for a long time, then looked back up at her. "Because I can't get near you any other way. Not without putting both of you in danger."

The bitter ball she'd carried in her heart for a lifetime ruptured. Realization crashed over her—he hadn't abandoned them out of selfishness, as she had believed. He had wanted to be with them. He had loved them. The truth overwhelmed her, and she broke, sobs shaking through her as Preston wrapped his arms around her.

She thought of birthdays marked by an empty chair, of nights she'd wished he was there to chase away the dark. The ache split wide open—and then it burned, hardening into anger. Anger at whoever had stolen him from them, denying her and her mother the life they should have had together.

She drew a shuddering breath, wiped her eyes, and looked up at her father.

"Who are they, Dad?"

Preston looked surprised, his face softening with emotion. Aislen realized it was the first time she had used the endearment with him. She thought of all the suffering he must have gone through, all that he had been denied during his lifetime. She got even angrier.

"Who are they? I need to know! Why are they after you? What are they doing?"

Preston shook his head. "Not yet, Aislen. I know you want answers. And over time, you will get them. I promise. But there is so much more that you need to learn first, so you can be prepared.

"Right now, you need to get back. It's nearly morning. You need to take it easy today. Rest. Drink lots of water. Think about what has happened tonight, but try not to judge it, invalidate it, or explain it. Your brain will try to, but just let it be. Don't talk about it with anyone just yet. And whatever you do, don't mention my name. Later, if you are ready for more, come back here."

"How will I know how to get back?"

"Do what I said, and when you are ready, follow this."

Preston held his palm face up in front of him. An orb materialized and hovered in the center of it, and he extended it toward her. It was breathtaking; a multifaceted diamond that flashed with sparks of every color and hue in the spectrum.

"Take it, Buttercup. And come back to visit me."

Mesmerized, she reached a finger up to touch it, but it instantly absorbed into the palm of her hand. She gasped and opened her eyes into the blaze of morning sunshine.

TWENTY-TWO

MATHIS HAD TO PEE. He'd been tossing and turning for hours, trying to ignore the ballooning pressure of his bladder. Reluctantly, he flopped himself out of bed and shuffled down the hall, one hand clamped at his fly like an old man warding off disaster.

He sat down on the toilet. This was for the best—no need to risk painting the walls like a busted hydrant—and rested his head in his hands, nearly nodding off while he pissed.

He was parched. He shuffled toward the kitchen with his eyes closed, hoping to wet his whistle and get back in bed before he fully woke up. It was a straight shot down the hall from the john to the fridge. He knew it by heart. He opened the refrigerator door, reached into the beer bank, pulled out the first thing that caught his finger's attention, twisted the top off, and guzzled half of it down.

Then he made his first mistake of the day. He opened an eye. He had no good reason for doing it. He had been managing blind just fine. But his right eyelid cracked open involuntarily mid-swallow and spotted the shiny, black monolith sitting on the counter.

Good morning, it seemed to say. Then it watched him silently as he sprayed beer across the counter.

"Jesus H. Christ!" He had completely forgotten about his felonious foray to the Parrish house.

"Jesus!" He shouted again, half hoping that the good Lord would show up for his second coming right about now, because it would make his current situation way more insignificant.

Mathis stared at the cube.

The cube stared back.

Mathis slammed the rest of the beer down, grabbed another from the fridge, opened it, and slammed that one down, too.

He looked back at the box.

It was still there.

"Okay," he said to himself. "I must've done this for a reason." He thought about the murder and about Blake Parrish. He thought about the young nurse and the only words Blake uttered being about the game. Something about the game had bothered him.

He went to the box and reluctantly picked it up. It was smooth and seamless with two little holes at the base. It wasn't going to give up its secrets by just looking at it. He was going to have to interrogate it from the inside out.

Mathis squinted at the glossy surface. "All right, box. You gonna talk, or do I have to sweat you under a lamp?"

The thing sat silent, black and perfect.

"Why does it feel like you're already watching me?"

Warmth pulsed through his palms where they rested on the glossy surface—like the thing had breathed.

The hairs on his arms prickled.

He quickly walked it over to the television, set the box down on the carpet, then gathered all the other accessories he had acquired and arranged them on the floor. He contemplated the pile. As a self-proclaimed technophobe, he wished he'd thought to grab the manual.

"What a dumbass," he said out loud, looking at the box.

Totally, the box seemed to agree in silence.

He picked up a cord, tried jamming it into the wrong port twice, swore, then flipped it over only to find it still didn't fit. "Figures," he muttered. "I spent thirty years running perps down alleys, and now I'm outsmarted by a plug." He shuffled through the rest of the pile, not sure what went where, until finally the cube gave a faint click and lit up on its own.

"Well, shit," Mathis said. "It runs itself. That's not creepy at all."

The edges of the box began to glow purple, then faded back to black again. He grabbed the remote and turned on the television. A violet 'Q' illuminated and filled the screen. Animated blue and purple lightning bolted from it in sporadic intervals. Mathis moved away from the television and noticed that the animated bolts seemed to intensify and follow him when he moved.

"What the hell?" Mathis sashayed side-to-side and front to back, as the bolts of white lightning tracked him, pinpointing exactly where he was in the room at all times. For a second, his throat went dry—then he forced a laugh and went back to the pile of accessories.

He was savvy enough to know what a game controller looked like, but nothing in the pile looked familiar. He picked up the glove with its flexible plastic digits and slipped it on his hand. The edges of the cube surged with purple, and the television screen went blank.

"UNIDENTIFIED PLAYER" typed across the screen in orchid cyber-lettering.

Mathis stared at it for a while, not knowing what to do next.

The screen went black again, the cube surged with light, and more letters typed across the screen.

"STATE YOUR NAME FOR THE Q."

A keyboard appeared at the bottom of the screen.

Mathis was lost. He scratched his bed head with his gloved fingertips, and an arrow on the screen shadowed the movement of his hand. He pointed his finger at the keyboard and poked the air in position over the keys.

"M-A-T-H-I-S"

He poked his finger at the enter button. The cube surged with purple, and the screen dissolved into electric confetti.

"Welcome to The Q, MATHIS. Wanna play?"

A YES and a NO button appeared below the question. Mathis hesitated, his gut screaming this was a bad idea. But he had come this far. He needed to put his hunch to rest. Even if he ended up being wrong. Even if he ended up in prison.

He placed a gloved finger in the air and pushed the button, "YES."

∞

"GAME ACCESSED," The Womb decreed over the house sound system.

Raze was still in bed. He'd been dozing on and off throughout the morning, catching up on some much-needed rest while waiting for the sergeant to figure out how to access the game. As soon as he'd reintegrated from the Parrish house viewing, he set up a security watch on the console.

He snickered to himself. He had only put one name in the system to track. MATHIS. It was a calculated guess that it would be the moniker the sergeant would sign in under. He was a noob. And he was old. There was no way he would know what he was doing or be imaginative enough to create a clever game name.

Raze sat up in bed, propping several pillows behind him. There was no need to even get dressed for this. He was going to sit back and watch Mathis bumble around Base Camp. It should prove as entertaining as Saturday morning cartoons. Then Mathis would decide that the game was just a game and dump the evidence of his—and Infinium's—crimes into the dumpster for the next garbage day pick up, and three-quarters of Raze's problem would be handled.

"Q on," Raze commanded.

The original RETNA mural that covered the entire wall in front of his bed began to move. The lounging nude goddess, with her incandescent, mandala halo, projected toward him several inches and then slid apart, revealing a recessed wall. Hanging on the wall was his 73-inch laser television. The Q sat alone on a shelf beneath the TV. It powered up, violet light throbbing through its ebony skin. Raze grabbed his game gloves off the nightstand and slipped them on.

The television came to life in a blazing exhibition of lightning that cycled around the screen until it honed in on Raze, reclining naked on the bed.

"Welcome, CrazE," the Q said, in a voice programmed to sound like his own. "Wanna play?"

"Yes," he responded with a flick of his index finger.

"Name your game." A list of games appeared on the screen. *Demesne* was number one on the list, not only because it was his baby but also because it was the number one game on the planet. He had created this world, and the world was obsessed.

With another flick of a finger, Raze brought up the search engine and typed 'Mathis.' The network instantly located the sergeant meandering in Octave 1, the base layer of *Demesne*. He was probably trying to learn how to walk.

Raze modified his avatar, CrazE, into an average-looking grunt and walked him into the teleportation booth on the screen. While most players had to earn their way through the different strata of *Demesne*, Raze, as master of this universe, could jump to any Octave he chose. He was instantly transported to base camp, where he could observe the little nooblet.

Base Camp, *Demesne*, 3020. The starting pit. Mathis would rot here until he scraped together enough skill to join a clan and claw his way upward, navigating other octaves, jumping strata, universes, worlds, and time in an attempt to reach Earth 2020 and stop humanity from destroying itself.

Of course, no one ever would. The game was engineered that way. Players burned out on the main quest, then slipped into the diversions—building virtual lives, businesses, relationships—until they forgot why they logged in in the first place.

Just like real life. Nobody was ever going to save the world.

Raze spotted Mathis right away. While most players crafted dream avatars, the sergeant had made one that looked exactly like himself—paunch, wrinkles, and all. He shuffled around in a jerky, half-broken walk, drawing stares from the other avatars. A few even pointed and laughed.

Raze couldn't stomach it. He picked up his simulated SIG P220, walked straight up to Mathis, and shot him in the head. The cop's avatar disintegrated in a burst of pixels.

"Pathetic," Raze muttered, stepping back into the teleportation booth.

He logged off, peeled off his gloves, and pushed out of bed. Mathis was going nowhere in his world.

Time for a run.

TWENTY-THREE

AISLEN SLIPPED OUT of Gen's bedroom, shutting the door softly behind her. Gen was still squeaking little snores and oblivious to the world. Aislen padded into the kitchen to scrounge for some breakfast. She was famished.

Rather than suffering from the symptoms of a justifiably massive hangover, she felt great, energetic, and refreshed—better than she had ever felt first thing in the morning. She wasn't sure if it was beginner's luck or if her father's dream ministrations had actually healed her. She couldn't help but wonder. During the first part of her dream, she'd felt ghastly, but after he did his version of the Vulcan mind-meld, she felt fantastic.

She also felt unusually upbeat. The demons of judgment and hounds of self-doubt were silent. The bitter emotions about her father churned up the previous day had transformed during her night's journey, healed by understanding. She found herself wishing she could have lingered in the reverie a little longer to get to know him better.

It was only a dream, her head chimed in. *None of it was real, you know.*

"Shut up," she cut the voice off. It all seemed as real as walking into this kitchen and looking into this piss-poor excuse for a refrigerator.

But it wasn't. Your brain is just trying to fix a fucked-up situation by creating a fantasy around it.

Aislen slammed the refrigerator door, annoyed that she had allowed logic to get a word in edgewise.

It was nice thinking there was another side to the story, that maybe he had good reasons, that maybe he was protecting them by not being around. Of course, that reminded her of the parts of the dream that were off-the-wall and disturbing—that her life, and her mother's, could actually be in danger.

Maybe it was all just a fantasy. Who would give a shit about two typical women who lived on barely the right side of the tracks? They weren't a threat to anybody. As logic began obliterating her burgeoning paradigm back to the ranks of 'it was only a dream,' there was a soft knock at the front door.

Aislen went to the door and looked through the peephole. Troy was standing on the landing, holding a large paper bag overflowing with groceries. The last remnants of her warm, fuzzy blanket of tranquility were violently ripped from her. Disjointed clips from the night before stuttered back to life: a replay of him practically eating Genesis with his eyes, her subsequent fit of jealousy and slamming of Scotch, the rapture of the music, the lights and movement, and then—nothing except a very vague recollection of her puke splattering Troy's really nice shoes.

She froze, hoping that he would think they were still asleep and leave. But a distorted, fish-eye hand materialized in front of her eyes and rapped on the door again, a little harder, echoing loudly through the small apartment. He was going to wake up

Gen with this racket, which would be totally rude. She swung open the door to give him a piece of her mind.

"Aislen!" His eyes opened wide when he saw her. "Wow! I'm, like, really surprised to see you up and about." He gave her a once-over. "You're actually looking pretty damn good for someone who drank a little more than they could swallow."

She hoped the narrow-eyed look she shot him looked like anger rather than the wince of embarrassment. "I'm sorry to disappoint you."

"Nothing is disappointing about that at all."

"Well, Gen's still sleeping, so you may want to try back a little later."

"I'm not here to see Gen, silly. Well, I *expected* to, because I expected *you* to still be three sheets to the wind. I was planning to play the hero and make my mom's famous Hair of the Dog soup and miraculously cure you. But it appears that you don't need it."

"No. I don't." She stood at the door, hoping he'd take the hint that she didn't need his remedy and leave, but he didn't.

"You must have good genes—most people would be wrecked," he said. "May I come in?"

She wanted to say no, but remembered she was in Gen's house, after all, and maybe Gen would actually welcome his company.

"I was just getting ready to leave, anyway," she said as she stood aside and he slipped past her.

"After I went through all this effort? Like hell you are!" He took his bags into the kitchen. "Pull up a chair and keep me company. Even if you are a perfect specimen of health, a girl still needs to eat."

"I'm not hungry," she responded, still standing by the door. Her stomach growled in defiance, loud enough that the whole building could have heard.

Troy peeked his head around the corner, giving her a quizzical eye. "Your stomach just called you out. And anyway, you are obviously not leaving, yet." His eyes swept over her, a smile tugging like he knew a secret. She followed his gaze. She completely forgot she was only wearing a pair of Gen's pajamas, a soft pink ensemble that left little to the imagination. She looked back up and found him smiling at her.

"Busted," he said with a laugh.

She shut the door and stamped across the floor, harrumphing into the stool across from him. She wanted to make sure he got a clue that she was disinterested and inconvenienced. Unfazed by her antics, he unpacked the bag: Campbell's Chicken and Rice Soup, eggs, lemons, ginger ale, Alka Seltzer, bottled water, and a bottle of Johnny Walker.

"What the hell kind of recipe is that?"

"These three are for the soup," he said, pointing to the eggs, lemon, and soup cans. "If that fails, these are secondary, tertiary, and final-final options," he said, pointing to the ginger ale, Alka Seltzer, and Scotch in that order. "When all else fails, the real hair of the dog never does. But look at you..."

His gaze lingered, just long enough to make her pulse quicken.

Aislen crossed her arms across her chest and tried to keep herself from blushing.

"I see Genesis was able to get you situated all right. I offered to help, but she had it handled." Troy gave her one of his classic, heartthrob looks.

It didn't even cross her mind how she had gotten out of the piece of fabric unfit to be called a dress and into fabric unfit to be called pajamas. How tiny Genesis had managed to undress and redress Aislen's dead-drunk weight was unfathomable. It crossed her mind that maybe she had help after all.

Aislen reddened further. "I don't remember that part."

Troy laughed. "Yeah, well, you were pretty gone by that point. What *do* you remember?"

She thought for a moment, replaying the fragments again.

She skipped over the love scene she witnessed between him and Gen. "The scotch," she said.

"Check."

She thought about the dancing again: how entranced she was by the music, how good the heat felt on her skin, how it felt like someone was dancing with her, moving in sync with her, around, with, and through her.

"The dancing," she said.

"Double check. Very impressive by the way."

She looked up at Troy. Maybe he had been dancing with her, after all. But she had looked around and nobody was there. And she would have remembered Troy being that close. Absolutely, no question.

"Is that it?" Troy said.

Aislen thought about it. There was a blank gap of amnesia from the dancing until the next image.

"Your shoes," she said sheepishly.

He laughed.

"Sorry about that."

"No worries. Nothing a wet paper towel couldn't handle. That didn't happen until we got you here. So you don't remember me rescuing you from the dance floor and carrying you out of the club?"

"No." Her voice sounded small.

"How about being sprawled out across my lap in the back seat of the cab?"

"No." She really needed a rock to crawl under about now.

"Anything that you said in the cab?" He was looking at her intently. Amusement glittered in his eyes.

The embarrassment was too much for her. She didn't want

to know what she said to him in the cab. She changed the subject. "Do you want me to wake up Gen for you? She could probably use a good bowl of soup." *And be thrilled to see you again,* she added silently.

"Uh, no, actually. I'm enjoying spending time with you."

Aislen was suddenly suspicious. "What are you? A player?"

"A player?" He chuckled, a shrug in his tone. "Not my game, Aislen."

She might as well confront him. It wasn't as though this was going anywhere. "I saw you talking to Gen last night when I was coming back from the restroom."

"Yeah, so?"

"You were holding her hand... and you were talking... and you were looking at her like... like... I don't know, like..." Aislen stammered.

Troy crossed his arms, rested them on the counter, and leaned in close until his face was only inches away. "Like what, Aislen?" A hint of a smile played on his lips.

"Like you are looking at me now! Like you were really, *really* into her!"

Troy didn't say anything for a moment and just looked at her. "I was talking to her about you, Aislen," he finally said. "I was talking to her about how I am really into *you.*"

She faltered, shocked by the revelation. "Oh." It came out as a breath rather than a word.

"Yeah. Oh," he mimicked her quietly. He moved his face even closer, eyes unwavering. An exquisite ache melted through her body. She couldn't hold his gaze any longer and dropped her eyes, but he lifted her chin so she was looking at him again, his thumb brushing against her cheek.

She felt intoxicated again. Her head spun, and her body felt ablaze with fire. She closed her eyes. She felt the fever of his breath, then the glance of his lips as they brushed against hers.

The bedroom door burst open, and Genesis staggered into the living room. Aislen jolted upright, almost falling backwards off the stool.

"Oh, geez! I'm sorry! I forgot you were here," Genesis said to Aislen. Then she noticed Troy leaning forward on the kitchen counter. "Holy crap! Hey there, Troy..." She stopped, noticing the body language, the mood, and put two and two together. "Uhhhh. I can go back to my room if you want."

"No! Not at all. It was nothing." Aislen jumped up, vertigo almost knocking her off her feet.

Troy shook his head and rolled his eyes. "Yeah, she just had something in her eye, and I was helping her get it out."

"Oh, I see," Genesis said, smiling back at him, totally in on the joke.

"We were going to make some kind of soup to help you feel better," Aislen added, trying to ease the awkwardness.

"Au contraire," Troy protested. "I was going to make soup for Aislen, but it appears she made it through the evening unscathed. You, on the other hand, look a little emo right now. I'd be glad to whip it up for you. You strike me as someone who likes things bright."

"I'm willing to try anything if it will take this headache away." Genesis sat down in the stool Aislen vacated, holding her head in her hands.

"Great! An appreciative and willing patient!" Troy found a pot and began his kitchen wizardry, opening cans, adding water, mixing in lemon juice, and cracking and separating eggs. He whipped up the yolks in a bowl and then poured them slowly into the soup. In less than ten minutes, a steaming bowl sat before each of them.

Aislen looked down at it. It was the most unappealing meal

she had ever seen: a bowl of thick, bright yellow liquid with floating chunks of mystery meat. She grudgingly picked up her spoon and took a tentative taste.

Genesis had no qualms about it. She plunged in heartily. "Wow! This is delicious," Gen said between spoonfuls.

She was right. It was pretty damn tasty for looking so... *yellow*. And with each spoonful, Gen seemed to get more of her sparkle back. She drained the rest straight from the bowl and shoved it toward Troy. 'More, please.' By the second serving, she looked almost brand-new.

"You've got to be kidding me," Aislen said to both of them.

"Told you so," Troy responded.

"So Ais," Restored to her normal bright-eyed and bushy-tailed self, Gen turned to Aislen. "How'd you sleep? Any more wild dreams?"

Aislen blanched. She glared at Genesis, mortified that she mentioned her dreams in front of Troy.

"What dreams?" Troy asked, looking over at Aislen.

Her stomach flipped. "Nothing. Never mind." Her tone had an edge to it, sharp as a razor. She threw Gen the evil eye.

"It's not a big deal, Ais," Gen protested. "I had some humdingers last night myself."

"Could we talk about this later?" Aislen hissed, but Gen continued.

Gen leaned forward, oblivious, eager to share. She didn't even realize she was about to cross a line until it was already too late.

"No, because I had this one with you in it, and I want to tell you before I forget." Genesis rattled on without taking a breath. "There was this older man with you—blond, green eyes. He showed you how to make balls of light, and then you both jumped into them and disappeared."

Aislen nearly choked. It couldn't be! That was exactly

what Aislen had done with her father, but how was it possible that Genesis would see what Aislen had been doing in her dream?

"Whoa! That is really wild." Troy chuckled, but something in his eyes flickered—like maybe he was laughing to cover the unease.

"Yep. Sounds pretty crazy to me, too," Aislen said through gritted teeth.

"Really, Aislen? That's the last thing I expected to hear outta you. With all you told me about yesterday," Genesis rolled her eyes. "Not everybody thinks dreaming is crazy, Aislen—only *you*. You think that everything is always physiology, chemistry, and neurology. You ignore all other possibilities, because you can't prove them. And you have *proof*, Aislen, try to say that you don't."

In all their years of friendship, Aislen had never been so mad. Maybe she did have proof—especially now. And maybe she wanted to share this with Genesis—*alone*. But that Gen had brought it up in front of Troy was unforgivable. "I don't want to talk about this right now, Gen."

"So... let me get this straight." It was Genesis who was angry now. "You dream about a boy shooting a man in the head... and then you see that *same* boy yesterday, and he may have *shot his father* and—"

"Shut! Up!" Aislen yelled, slapping the palm of her hand down hard on the counter. The spoons rattled, broth sloshed over the rim. Gen flinched, color draining from her face.

Then a slow shame dawned on her face as she realized she'd betrayed Aislen's confidence.

Aislen turned to Troy. He was looking at her with a flat, steely intensity, a mixture of disdain and confusion. She couldn't see which one was winning, but the "really into her" was not playing there anymore.

"Is that true, Aislen?" he asked her, his voice tight, devoid of its usual warmth.

Aislen was speechless. She wanted to call Gen an outright liar. But the words wouldn't pass her lips. Her heart seized up in her chest.

"Yes," she confessed.

"You had a *dream* about *Blake*? And he shot a man in the head in it?" Disdain took the lead, but disgust was fast on its heels.

Agony rippled through her, but she couldn't lie. She nodded.

"Why didn't you tell me this yesterday?"

"I couldn't. I've never had anything like this happen before —I don't have dreams that I usually remember—or that seem real—or that are actually true! I thought I was going crazy."

"And you're telling me this felt real to you?" His tone was careful, like he didn't want to spook her, but didn't buy it either.

They stared at each other in silence. He gripped the counter, waiting for her to answer. Tears welled up in her eyes, and she looked at Genesis, who was awash in remorse.

Aislen couldn't be mad at her. She had told the truth. She realized, with sudden clarity, that Genesis would always believe her—even if Troy never did. And maybe that mattered more. She looked back at Troy, directly. If he couldn't accept the truth—so be it.

"It did feel real," she said, a calm descending over her. "And I know it sounds unhinged. I can't explain it, but it happened. And," She looked at Genesis and covered her hand with her own. "I had a dream like yours, Gen. Exactly what you saw—was exactly what I did. It scares the hell out of me, and I know I may sound delusional, but I can't lie about it anymore. I'm sorry I yelled at you."

"No. I'm sorry, Aislen. I don't know what I was thinking."

They both looked at Troy again.

He leaned on the counter, jaw tight, his eyes unreadable.

"Why don't you go shower. I'll clean up." He turned away, all trace of warmth erased.

Aislen watched his back for a while, thinking about how, just a few moments ago, he had confessed to having feelings for her. He definitely still had feelings for her, but they appeared to be quite different.

She got up and walked out of the room. She knew he would be gone when she came back.

TWENTY-FOUR

MATHIS HAD BEEN at it for hours. Empties lined the coffee table, and a crushed bag of Ruffles lay on the floor at his feet. Every time he respawned, he expected something—anything—that explained Blake Parrish. Instead, it was the same recycled scenery and pointless scraps of combat. No sinister secrets. No hidden agenda. Just a grown man grinding level one like a chump.

It was obvious, even at the beginning level, that the game was addictive. Before Mathis realized it, it was after two in the afternoon.

After the first player walked up to him from out of nowhere and shot him in the head, other players in the base camp started doing the same, apparently just for fun. Mathis felt a competitive urge just to learn how to walk like a human, so he could blend into the crowd and avoid getting knocked off every five minutes. Once he mastered walking, his next challenge was figuring out how to use the sword and the handgun controllers with a certain degree of accuracy. That didn't take as long.

The next step was joining a clan, or rather, being accepted

and initiated into a clan, so they could move together as a group to a different level of the game. The game didn't allow you to go at it alone; you had to develop alliances, or you went nowhere.

Mathis would have preferred the Lone Ranger route, but if he was going to stay out of prison, he needed to get out of the first level, to find out if his hunch was right.

He wandered around the base camp trolling for "friends." A group of young lads was standing at a column of light, getting ready to change levels. Mathis sauntered up to them.

Me go with you, he pantomimed, pointing to his own chest, then pointing at the group, then pointing to what looked like an elevator contraption. They laughed at him, got into the glowing tube, and vanished.

He tried another group, using the same sign language, only this time pounding on his chest forcefully, more of a demand than a request. Well, that went over like a fart in church. The alpha male of the clan walked over and kicked him in the chest, knocking him down into the dirt, a blessing, because if he had shot him in the head, Mathis would have had to start the game over from scratch. *Again.*

Maybe this was like high school, and trying to join an established clique wasn't the best idea. Mathis decided to build his own team and approached a solo player wandering in the street.

He raised his palm to the fellow. Hi.

The player turned and walked in the opposite direction.

Mathis did this several times, with the same effect. Finally, one of them stopped. His head bobbed at Mathis, like he was trying to tell him something, but Mathis didn't understand. He tried his "me go with you" gesture again. The player jiggled his head again. Mathis tried the chest-pounding act. The player threw up his hands and walked away.

"What the fuck," he said out loud. He stood in the middle

of the street, turning himself in circles, looking as lost on the screen as he felt in his own living room.

Then Mathis spotted another player standing in the doorway of a futuristic tavern, smoking a cigarette and watching him. He was an incredible game specimen with massive arms and chiseled abs that could be seen rippling beneath his uniform. His stance was self-assured and intimidating. Mathis wasn't about to risk his current status in the game by trying to ally with this menace, so he continued to stand in the street, waiting for a more approachable character.

The merc took a slow drag, smoke curling unnaturally thick in Mathis's visor. It smelled real, too—burnt and acrid, nothing like a kid's game.

Mathis watched as the streets slowly emptied and players moved inside buildings and out of sight. It was like they all knew this guy was bad news and didn't want to get caught in the crossfire. Mathis stood alone in the street, feeling very exposed. He looked back at the doorway. The creep flicked his cigarette to the ground and stepped on it, then marched directly up to Mathis. He braced himself for a shot to the head.

A black bubble popped up on the screen between them, and neon green letters typed quickly across it.

"Put the visor on, Noob."

The visor? Shit! He had forgotten about the visor! He turned his back on the monster and plucked it up from the floor. It had stopped flashing its red light at some point; maybe that was why he'd forgotten about it. He put the visor on.

Through the visor, his living room dimmed into shadows, while the TV still glowed ahead of him. It was like squinting at the game through a pair of blackout sunglasses.

"How in the hell am I supposed to play when I can't see?"

Something blipped on the television. He lifted the shades. Another dialog box was on the screen.

"Turn them on, dumbass."

Mathis pulled them off, located the only button, and pushed it. They came alive with a purple pulse, and an earpiece released from the frame. Genius!

This time when he slid them back on, the living room receded like an afterthought. The world snapped into focus—too sharp, too vivid. Colors on the screen popped with intensity and depth snapped into place, objects hovering just shy of his face. The TV wasn't a screen anymore—it was gone. His living room dissolved until the visor's world was all there was.

The dirt under his boots wasn't flat texture anymore; it looked wet, clotted, like the aftermath of a gunshot. He blinked hard, but the red smear stayed. This wasn't how games were supposed to feel. Not like memory. Not like life.

A translucent bubble ballooned inside his visor, text hovering in midair as if someone had projected graffiti across his living room. He half-reached to swat it, forgetting it wasn't really there.

"Uh, the earpiece?"

Mathis slid the earpiece into his ear.

"Jesus Christ, it's about time! I was about to shoot you in the head." A derisive and raspy voice sounded in his ear, a cross between Simon Cowell and Clint Eastwood.

"How do I talk?" Mathis asked.

"Like that, dipshit."

"Oh! Neat."

"Yeah, real neat. Neato skeeto. Fuck, why do I even bother?"

"Sorry. I've never done this before."

"Gee. No one could tell."

Mathis decided to keep his mouth shut. Now that he could talk and see clearly, maybe he could make a friend. "Well, thanks for the help. I really appreciate it," he said to his minacious savior.

The mercenary continued to stand in front of him, sizing him up and down and lighting another cancer stick. Mathis wondered if there were cigarette controllers available to buy for kids to use in the game. He wouldn't put it past Big Tobacco to capitalize on such a thing.

The street was still desolate, not another player in sight.

"So? Do you want to get out of this joint?" the beast asked. "You could tag along with me to a couple of other octaves if you want."

Mathis almost gushed. A friend! Yay! He could get into the elevator thingy now! But he played it cool, shuffling his feet in the dirt and shrugging his shoulders. "Yeah, sure. That would be, uh... cool, I guess."

The mercenary stared at him. Mathis thought he was going to change his mind.

"Follow me." He turned on his heel and walked toward the column of light.

This was how dumb kids ended up in the back of vans. But hell, he didn't have another option. He stepped into the light and let it take him.

TWENTY-FIVE

AISLEN STOOD IN THE SHOWER, letting the scalding water pummel her back until it ran cold. The past two days had been a downhill plunge to hell, nightmare after nightmare with barely a breath of peace.

She got out of the shower, toweled off, and took her time getting ready, giving Troy plenty of time to clean up and beat feet out of the apartment. Aislen couldn't bear to remember the rush of passion that had coursed through her body when Troy had confessed he was interested in her or the fire that had ignited her lips when he kissed her. But her revelation had dampened that flame, as was evident in the scornful haze that had clouded his face and extinguished the light of affection.

She sat down naked on the bed, combing her hair. Rather than torturing it straight with a blow dryer or forcing it into her usual severe ponytail, she scrunched it dry into loose ringlets. It was time to try something different, time to be *someone* different. She pulled on her favorite pair of Sunday jeans and a soft, chenille sweater, then went through Gen's makeup. She'd never spent any time pampering herself before. It felt good. She massaged moisturizer into her skin, brushed her lips with creamy lipstick, and studied her reflection.

Underneath the crushing sadness she felt about Troy—and what could have been—there was a steady calm. She was relieved the cat was out of the bag. It had been unbearable, pretending to be something that she wasn't. She gazed at herself in the mirror. Serene, almost ethereal—as if she finally fit together. Strange, that a few small choices—looser hair, softer lines—made her feel more real than she ever had.

If Troy or the rest of the world thought she was certifiable, so be it. Gen didn't see the world the way that everyone else did, and she seemed to be doing fine. Maybe there was a life for Aislen that wasn't precisely mapped out.

She gathered her things into her bag and went back out into the living room. Genesis was sitting on the couch, looking utterly miserable, and Troy was nowhere to be found, just as Aislen had expected.

"I don't even know how to tell you how sorry I am," Gen said. "You have every reason to hate me for the rest of your life."

Aislen sat down beside her. "I don't hate you, Gen. I could never hate you. It all had to come out sometime. What happened isn't going away. It could get worse. So I have to come to grips with it now, try to understand it, and learn to live with it."

"I think you'll see that your dreams aren't a curse, they're a gift." Genesis leaned over and hugged her.

Aislen returned the embrace. "And I think you're one of the best parts of my life."

After they said their goodbyes and made promises to get together again soon, Aislen walked down to the parking lot and put her bags in the trunk of the car. When she turned around, Troy was standing behind her.

"What do you want now?" Immediately, she was angry and defensive. "You know, there is nothing you can say or do that could make me feel any worse."

"You lied to me."

"Of course I did."

"I told you... you could trust me, and you didn't."

"No, I didn't. Good judgment on my part, don't you think?"

His eyes narrowed. "I want you to take me to the garden."

"Really? Gen told you about that, too?"

"She was under duress."

"How so?"

"I told her I would never speak to you again unless I knew everything that was going on." He stepped closer and leveled his eyes with hers. "We need to talk. I want to know about the dreams."

"I have nothing to say."

"Oh, yes. You most definitely do."

"Well, how about I save that for my therapist—or psychiatrist—or whatever it is that I need? But not you."

"You haven't given me a chance, Aislen."

She opened her mouth to say something, but had nothing to say to that. Had she really given him a chance? She realized she hadn't. She hadn't been open or honest. She had never given him anything of herself that he could use to earn her trust. Until she gave him something, she wouldn't know if she could trust him.

He held up his hand. His car keys dangled from his fingertips. "Take me to the garden."

She contemplated his face again. The anger that was so evident earlier wasn't there, just an earnest plea. For once, his bravado had slipped, and what stared back at her was raw need. That—more than his demand—made her snatch the keys. She snatched the keys from his hand and walked over to his car.

"Do you know how to drive a stick, young lady?"

"Guess you'll have to wait and see," she said as she slid into the driver's seat.

They drove in silence, Aislen whipping down the side streets, toward the perimeter of town, taking the long way so she could open the Mustang up and let her fly. She'd never driven a car with more than four cylinders or 140 horsepower. It was invigorating. She glanced at Troy a couple of times to see if she could catch him white-knuckling it, but he stayed perfectly calm, unreadable as ever.

When they arrived at the gate, Aislen shifted the Mustang into neutral and let it coast into the dirt lot as quietly as possible, not wanting to disturb the serenity of the gardens with the roar of the monster.

She got out of the car and tossed Troy the keys with a defiant grin. He caught them and slipped them into his pocket.

She paused for a moment. Why she had decided to bring him here, she didn't really know. This was her special sanctuary, where she came alone to think things through. The hush of water and faint incense clung to the air, the kind of silence that soaked into her bones. Here, she never had to perform. She didn't have to hide.

Troy stood patiently, watching her, his gaze steady, almost measuring.

This is his chance to prove himself, she thought. And she walked down into the garden, leaving him to follow.

She didn't want to talk. She didn't want to diminish the space by playing tour guide. Although it was much more spectacular in the full flush of summer, the sedate quality of it now, in its dormancy, was equally special and deserving of reverence.

She followed the pathway, taking her time strolling past the ponds, stopping every so often to glance back at Troy. He was taking his time as well, keeping his distance, kneeling beside the pond to engage a small turtle, and stopping to watch a great heron trying to play statue in the tall grass.

He had only asked that she take him to the gardens, but if he talked to Gen, Aislen knew what he really wanted to see was the shrine. After confirming that he was adequately respectful, she kept moving toward the sound of the river and disappeared through the shrine's red doors.

She removed her shoes, lit two sticks of incense, and went around the room lighting all the candles she could find. A warm glow illuminated the shrine, and its artifacts came to life. She took a seat on the grass mat in front of the altar, closed her eyes, and waited for Troy to arrive.

She suddenly felt extremely vulnerable. Just as she began to think that it was a mistake to let him this far in, the door behind her creaked open. She held her breath.

Troy removed his shoes and began walking softly around the perimeter of the room. He took in the artifacts one by one, contemplating the prayer flags and the glistening, brass gong. He picked up the padded mallet and leveled it at the gong. Aislen winced, preparing for a harsh clamor, but a deep, mellow tone shimmered from it. The ring lingered long and clear, resonating around the room in ripples, embracing them within it.

Troy moved next to the banner of the mythic, dancing creature and studied it for a long time.

"Do you know what this is?" He said, looking over his shoulder at her.

She shook her head.

"It's called a baku. They are usually carved into the wood columns outside the shrines to ward off evil spirits." He walked over and sat down beside her on the mat, facing the altar and the banner. "They are considered supernatural beings who protect the sleeping and devour nightmares."

The words should have comforted her, but a chill licked her skin. She couldn't tell if it came from Troy's voice or the creature's stitched eyes.

"I'd venture to say that this little place you discovered is a Chinese version of a sleep temple."

"A sleep temple?" She looked at Troy again.

"Uh-huh. They were common in ancient Egypt and Greece. People went to them when something was disturbing their peace of mind. A priest or priestess would induce them into a trance with chanting or drumming; the patient would dream or have a vision, and then the priest would analyze it for them." He smiled at her. "Did you know that about this place?"

She shook her head again, looking back around the shrine. Her whole body began to tingle with the revelation.

"Do you believe in synchronicity, Aislen?"

"What's that? Fate?"

"No. Fate is the idea that there is a predetermined course of events, a destiny you cannot escape. Do you believe in fate?"

A chill tickled up her arms. "I didn't use to. I used to believe that what happened to you was only what you did for yourself. If you wanted something, you had to make it happen. But that was yesterday. Today is way different. I don't know what I believe anymore."

"Well, what you believed yesterday is called causality. You create a cause, and an effect happens. Hindus call the effect karma."

"Then what is synchronicity?"

Troy turned his body so that he was facing her. "Synchronicity is— synchronicity is like a little miracle—meetings and happenings aligning up without intention. Say you create an event—like coming here, to this shrine, when you are stressed—and then another event happens that you didn't intend, but it has significant meaning and powerfully relates to what you created—like not even realizing that this is the perfect place for your kind of troubles."

"How do you know all this?"

"Jung."

"Hung?"

He chuckled, "No, silly, Carl Jung. He's the psychologist who first described synchronicity—among many other things you would probably be interested in, given your current situation."

"What situation?" she said, her voice taking on a defensive tone. *Here it comes*, she thought, as she prepared herself for the name of the disorder he was going to diagnose her with.

"Your dreams, Aislen. Jung was a pioneer in the area of dreams."

"Oh." She was caught off guard and a little ashamed that she had assumed he would label her.

"Jung was big on lots of ideas that you would probably call crazy." He was teasing her now. "Dreams, synchronicity, alchemy, astrology, mythology, the collective unconscious."

"They taught you this in school?"

"Yes... he was actually a pretty big part of my education. And one of my favorites. Jung had his own personal experiences with visions and hearing voices, and he worried he was becoming schizophrenic. But rather than fighting it, he embraced it. He began inducing what others would call hallucinations, but what he called his 'active imagination'. He journaled the whole thing in a red leather-bound book he called, go figure, 'Red Book'. He filled it with amazing illustrations and descriptions of the spirits he said visited him."

Aislen sucked in a sharp breath.

Troy stopped talking, watching her carefully. She sensed he was giving her space to talk, but she didn't want to.

"You know, my profession may seem to be all about analyzing, diagnosing, medicating, and controlling the brain, but did you know that psychology literally means 'study of the *soul*'? Yeah, we're trained to assess and treat mental disorders, but that doesn't mean all of us have abandoned our roots. Psychology is really closer to philosophy than biology."

He paused and looked down into her eyes. "When I told you yesterday that you could trust me with what is bothering you, I meant that. I am not here to invalidate, judge, label, medicate, or institutionalize you, Aislen. I am here as someone who cares about you and would like to help. If you'll let me."

Aislen looked up at him, then at the Baku hanging on the wall. Its brown eyes twinkled at her. She looked back at Troy. They both were telling her she was safe.

"So you would be a synchronicity then?"

He smiled, then reached up and took her face in his hand. "Yes. I would be *your* synchronicity."

He bent down and kissed her, his lips pressing fully into hers. The fingers of one hand moved up into her hair, as his other hand moved down her back and pulled her closer to his chest.

Her body surged with warmth and electricity. She could feel the tension and energy coursing through his arms. He moved away from her lips and pulled her head back, placing hot kisses down the length of her exposed neck, then pushed her lips back up to meet his. Just as she thought they were going to slide right on into second base, Troy pulled away from her, gently setting her back in her place on the mat.

He looked at her, his eyes dancing with intensity, taking her in while she caught her breath.

A shiver trickled down her spine, out of place against the

heat still lingering on her lips. For a heartbeat, it all felt too perfect—but she smothered the thought before it could spoil the moment, drowning it in the heady rush of his closeness.

He reached up and brushed a stray curl out of her eyes, traced the side of her face with his fingertips, then held her by the chin.

"Will you tell me about the dreams, Aislen?"

TWENTY-SIX

AFTER THIRTY-SIX HOURS of working in the viewing arena nearly nonstop, Raze felt like a caged animal, experiencing the DTs that only came from the lack of moving his body. In desperate need of release, he ran from the Bay Bridge to the Golden Gate, blasting his music and tuning out everything in existence.

He barely noted the other humans. He passed them by as if they were mere boulders in the flow of his river, inanimate objects not worthy of a thought.

He relegated the stray agitations of *Demesne*, the Womb, Infinium, and all the loose ends of the Project into a quarantined compartment of his brain, focusing only on his body: the timing of his breath, the burn in his lungs, the impact as his feet met the pavement. The expansion and contraction of his quads, hamstrings, buttocks, and calves.

When he reached Fort Point, he turned around and ran toward the warehouse. A brisk, January breeze was blowing in from the Pacific, pressing hard at his back, a thin thread of heat laced within it.

As Queens of the Stone Age riffed in his ears, the warm rays of the sun fingered down his spine in time with the rhythm, sending a shudder of electricity through him.

Without warning, the opaque fabric that Raze purposefully wove to keep himself disconnected from the world dissolved. He stopped mid-stride as he was suddenly overwhelmed with sensory input.

A border collie leapt in the air to snatch his Frisbee from flight, simple delight alight in its face.

A father lifted his tow-headed boy onto his shoulders to better see a pod of dolphins playing in the swells.

A young couple strolling on the path stopped to gaze at each other. He spontaneously kissed her on the forehead. She lifted onto her toes to kiss his lips. His lips moved, 'I love you.' Hers responded, 'I love you, too.'

The world was flush with life, each moment stilled in freeze-frame. For the briefest moment, he couldn't remember if he was running or standing still, if the world was moving past him or into him.

Raze inhaled deeply as his breath caught up with him. He could smell the brine in the air and taste its salt on his tongue.

He noticed clouds hovering over the city skyline, creating a violet and silver halo, and he was reminded of her—of Aislen— and of the liquid violet and silver field they created when their energy merged on the dance floor the night before.

The vision of her trespassed his mind as easily as she had into *Demesne*: the copper flow of her hair, the shimmer of her body in the lights, and the fire in her eyes. She had invaded him like a virus. He felt drawn to her like a moth to a flame. But she was supposed to be the moth and he, the flame. She was the one who was supposed to burn, yet he felt her fire incinerating his core.

No. He would not let this stand. He would not be the one consumed.

Bile rose inside him. He wanted to rip her out of his flesh— purge her from his system. Yet, at the same time, he did not. The contradiction tore at him, and the only answer was movement. He broke into a sprint, as if speed alone could burn her out of his blood.

Years ago, Destiny had knocked on his door, and Raze had answered. She came bearing gifts: wealth, power, prestige, everything a man could want, and Raze had embraced them. He wasn't about to let that go. He wasn't about to let Aislen untether him from the life he'd created.

He'd been a natural from the start, mastering the first five levels of the operative program in record time. Level I: learning how to acquire signal lines of locations around the world, simply by tuning into coordinates. Level II: obtaining five-sense data: what the location looked, smelled, sounded, and felt like. At Level III: adding emotional details. And Level IV, Raze started gaining control of his viewing, able to move his awareness through the target location as he gathered detailed intelligence. An etheric recon scout.

As a Level V operative, Raze was able to access and re-access any place on the planet, at will. The company used him exclusively for its most important missions—when sending a physical body to a location was impossible. Raze could sit in the lab in Palo Alto while his astral body and consciousness freely roamed the globe, gathering priceless intelligence. Because of Raze, Infinium Incorporated was awarded an incredibly lucrative contract as an intelligence contractor for the government. Infinium, in turn, rewarded him for his skills.

Raze scanned himself back into the house. Still unsated, he stormed into his gym and drove his fists into the 150-pound

Hydrocore bag. The bag swung back, and he hammered it again, each strike dragging up memory.

Left jab—Level VI. No more maps, no coordinates. Now it was people he tracked, each one carrying a frequency signature as distinct as a fingerprint.

Right cross—Level VII. Not just finding them, but holding them in his sights. Watching their movements in real time, like puppets on invisible strings.

Hook—Level VIII. He could slip into their rhythm, see through their moments, catch them in the act: the politician rutting with an escort, the banker conspiring to crash a market, the drug lord charting shipments, the terrorist praying before the blast.

Uppercut—Level IX. He was the ghost in the room, silent and unseen, a shadow breathing down their necks.

Another hook—Level X. The apex. The bag jolted on its chain as he struck harder, remembering the raw power of it: not just to witness, but to intervene. His reports fed The 8, and they bent the world around them. If it broke the right way, it was because Raze had been there.

He struck again, harder. It was always his job to make sure everything went as planned.

He punished the bag until his body screamed, until the rhythm of fists and breath finally dragged him back into himself —flesh, blood, sinew. When the last blow landed, he let the bag swing free and turned away, sweat slicking his skin.

Spent but steadied, he climbed the stairs to the third floor, crossed the catwalk, and stepped onto the patio. The Bay stretched east, the bridge cutting a line across the water like a marker of distance traveled. He had come far—too far to stop now.

Only two others had climbed as high as he had—Thomas

Reed and his son, Preston. Both had stopped at the edge of the next tier, the one that demanded more than spying, more than control. Assassination. They'd refused to cross that line. And then—they vanished.

Raze clenched the railing, jaw tight. He wasn't built for refusal. Lines weren't there to stop him. They were there to be broken. Killing had been the cleanest line of all. At least a target stayed dead when you eliminated it. Easier than what Aislen was doing to him.

It was one thing to control the masses—an easy thing. So elementary it was ridiculous. Human beings were maggots—easy to herd, blind to anything beyond the net. Once penned in, the smallest nudge could send them stampeding—or drop them docile again.

Infinium had a full arsenal for that. The simple levers: media feeds stoking fear, bots churning propaganda, mindless television and glossy trash feeding insecurities, video games severing them from real life. The subtler tools cut deeper: low-frequency vibrations, electromagnetic pulses, pharmaceuticals, and—most effective of all—the schoolroom. Layered conditioning, cradle to grave, until the hive moved exactly as directed.

Every so often, though, one wriggled loose. Someone who dared crawl past the curtain. Most froze there, clutching their revelation in silence, terrified of the swarm turning on them. But the few that didn't—the ones that wanted to drag others into the light—those had to be dealt with. They made a control operative like Raze necessary.

Scott Parrish had been one of those. He crossed the line, and when the remote techniques failed to reel him back, Raze was sent in.

Blake had been meant to be nothing more than collateral. That was the assignment. Then Aislen—skillful and dangerous

—and Mathis—persistent and suspicious—complicated things. Now the mission had grown. Three targets. All of them had to go.

Raze went back inside the house and into his bedroom. He needed to see if the Sergeant had figured out his ass from a hole in the ground or if he'd given up and disposed of the console altogether, solving one third of his problem.

"*Demesne*," he told the Q. The television turned on and the game initialized.

"Locate: Mathis."

The screen lit up with a layered, topographic map; each octave stacked like a sandwich one upon the other. A gun sight icon appeared on the screen and began scanning through Octave One: Base Camp. Mathis wasn't there.

Good! Just as Raze had expected, the first circuit had proven too much for the old dog, and he'd given up. But the 'Player Unavailable' window did not pop up on the screen; the sight icon kept moving through the layers of the map.

That meant Mathis was still somewhere in the game. No big deal. It took players months to get anywhere significant. He probably just got sidetracked by a role-playing circuit like a strip club or a poker game.

The sight jumped through several octaves, finally landing in Octave 6.

"Mathis Located," the pop-up screen read, as it zeroed in on not one, but two, moving players. They were standing dangerously close to Raze's hidden portal—the doorway out of the game and into The Stratum itself. Raze's jaw clenched. Old dog had sharper teeth than he'd given him credit for, and now he was sniffing at a place he shouldn't be.

The Stratum had already been breached once—the Aislen invasion. If Mathis stumbled through next, it wouldn't just be a crack in the system. It would be collapse.

"Damn it!" Raze yelled as he grabbed his gloves and put on his visor.

"Octave 6. 50 meters with cover."

The game teleported CrazE into Octave 6.

Precision. Elimination. That was what he did best.

TWENTY-SEVEN

ANOTHER FOUR HOURS of the day had slipped past with Mathis following his new buddy around *Demesne* like a puppy. His ally, a reticent fellow who went by the name Ichiban, allowed Mathis to tag along behind him but didn't utter a single word. Mathis understood right away to keep his mouth shut and pay attention.

They maneuvered through the first few levels quickly, stepping in and out of teleportation tubes and into different scenes and settings. It was mind-boggling. One world was a bustling metropolis of gleaming metal and glass, another an ancient stone ruin, the next an elaborate series of underground caves.

Although there were people engaged in many other activities, as far as Mathis could tell, the game revolved around combat. Beating other clans, taking their assets, and gathering higher statistics in order to move to higher levels of the game.

Combat situations arose several times. As a two-person team, Mathis and Ichiban were always outnumbered. Gangs of at least four and sometimes up to eight players saw them as easy pickings and confronted them with glee.

Being good with a gun, Mathis was able to hold his own, keeping himself from being killed and getting in a few kills himself. But Ichiban was a beast, seemingly invincible. He plowed through every battle, taking no prisoners and leaving only mangled bodies in his wake.

Mathis must have proven himself worthy, because when they teleported into the sixth level, Ichiban finally began to speak.

"First of all," he began in a bored rasp, "they are not called levels. They are called Octaves."

Mathis felt like Ichiban had been rummaging through his head and knew that he had been thinking of them as levels.

"Eight Octaves. Eight thresholds," Ichiban continued. " Each one is designed to separate the strong from the weak, the disciplined from the indulgent. Most fall long before the end."

Mathis grunted like he understood, but he was stupefied by the game's complexity. He had a million questions, but was afraid that if he asked, Ichiban would get exasperated by his stupidity and ditch him. Mathis knew he would never make it back this far without him.

They sauntered through another glowing vortex. This one moved them sideways.

"Some portals will take you up and down through Octaves," Ichiban said. "Others, like this one, move you sideways from one circuit into another within the same Octave."

The movement stopped, and the portal opened.

"This is the 9th circuit of the 6th Octave. It is one of the most popular circuits in all of *Demesne*."

They both stepped into a gigantic room of pure, blazing white. Spotlights rotated through a series of filters that doused the whole room in jeweled colors. An open space in the middle was dotted with round, stage-like platforms. On some of them, avatars were grinding and gyrating in erotic dance. On others, avatars engaged in a variety of sexual activities as an audience of avatars in various states of undress feasted on the depravity, clapping politely at each performance.

Most of the avatars were not even human. Players had cloaked themselves as humanoids, animals, robots, and even nondescript shapes. A three-dimensional, twelve-pointed star with a large set of human knockers floated past Mathis into a recessed alcove where an all-out orgy of polygons was taking place.

Mathis moved a couple of feet backwards, trying to stay clear of the debauchery. *Maybe the Food Network isn't that kinky, after all.*

Ichiban's voice rasped, heavy with disdain. "Decay. They dress rot in jewels and call it freedom. A waste. There are only a few bodies that matter. The rest? Expendable."

Then he turned back to Mathis. "You interested in getting in on any of this action?"

Mathis didn't know how to respond to that. What did Ichiban expect him to say? Maybe this was his thing, and he was testing Mathis to see if it was his thing, too. But it was making Mathis uncomfortable, so he had to tell the truth. "Uh, no."

"Good answer," Ichiban said. He turned around and stepped through the portal, back into the jungle-like circuit they had just come from.

Mathis was relieved, but felt like he needed a shower.

"Like I said," Ichiban started again, "there are countless circuits within each Octave. That was only one of them. Many people come into *Demesne* for the combat aspect of the game but get over that as soon as they discover its more wanton diversions."

"There's more than just that?" Mathis was agape.

Ichiban snorted. "Oh, yeah. That was nothing. There are

circuits for every freaky fetish imaginable. *Demesne* has even created a few fetishes that were unheard of before. Take "The Shapers," for instance, like that star with the tits... they were created here for people who get off by being a rhombus or an isosceles triangle. I'm pretty sure all those people are rocket scientists."

"Weird." What more could Mathis say? He was old-fashioned that way. A real body in a soft bed was as perverted as he got.

"Yeah, but there are normal circuits as well. Circuits where players can enjoy concerts or perform in them. They can participate in theatre, bands, or sporting events. There are comedy clubs, nightclubs, art galleries, even shopping malls. People have sexual encounters, but they also date, get married, and have virtual families. There are college circuits that hold virtual classes and churches that have services. Real people put their game faces on, come into *Demesne*, and live an alternate life. And, for most of them, this life is way better."

Mathis could see how easy it would be for a person bored with his life or in need of escape could become entranced by this place and over time have difficulty separating from it. He himself had been in the game for over ten hours already.

Ichiban didn't say anything for a long time, but he didn't make any move to travel any further in the game either. Mathis wondered if this was the end of the line, and he was failing to get the hint. He started to turn away to try to find a way out when Ichiban suddenly spoke again.

"There are those of us who understand the inner workings of *Demesne* and know its real purpose."

Mathis stopped and slowly turned back toward Ichiban. The revelation got his attention. He'd already discovered that there was a lot more to *Demesne* than what the box advertised, but was there something that could explain the Parrish murder?

He'd learned so much about the game by keeping his mouth shut, but Ichiban had stopped talking again. Mathis could not read his expression through the polarized visor that covered most of his face. His lips were sealed in a tight line.

Mathis didn't want to risk displeasing Ichiban or give too much away about his suspicions, but he really had to know.

"So, what is the real purpose of *Demesne?*"

∞

THROUGH HIS VISOR, a panoramic vista of an otherworld rainforest opened up before Raze. He knew right away Mathis and his teammate were near the portal to the 9th circuit. He was God in this world. He knew his garden.

Raze had placed the 9th circuit here for specific, strategic purposes. The maggots either flocked to it and got trapped by its temptations, or they were completely appalled by it and stayed far away. Either way, it was perfect. Just on the other side of the circuit was Raze's secret portal into the 8th Octave, known by the very few as The Stratum. The 9th circuit kept players' brainwaves stimulated too high and too base for access. But with a few frequency tweaks, Raze could invite them right in to his personal, fourth-dimensional, mind-fuck.

A small map in the bottom left corner of his visor pinpointed Mathis and his new friend. They were close. Raze put himself into stealth mode, making his avatar invisible inside the game, and moved toward them.

He aimed his viewfinder on the friend. "Player vitals," he spoke to the Q.

He wanted to know all the particulars of Mathis' new

friend, especially how advanced he might be. He couldn't be that advanced. Raze tracked all the top players, looking for real talent and possible threats. If he were that good, the Q would have sent him an alert.

"Access denied," the Q responded.

Raze stopped cold. Access was never denied to Raze. All access was granted and controlled *by* Raze. This was absolutely impossible.

He moved in closer, close enough to hear the new player explaining to Mathis about the variety of activities available within the circuits. Raze lifted his gloved sensor and pointed it directly at the player.

"Player vitals," Raze commanded again.

"Access denied," the Q responded immediately.

"Player tag," he tried instead.

"Denied."

"What the fuck!" Had the game been hacked? Raze had to fight the urge to pounce on the fucker and send him back to Base Camp permanently, but he needed to know more about him first and analyze the threat level.

"...Real people put their game faces on, come into *Demesne*, and live an alternate life. And, for most of them, this life is way better." The player stopped speaking. A long, uncomfortable silence ensued, the player staring at the Sergeant, the Sergeant growing more uncomfortable with each moment. Mathis finally gave up and turned to walk away when the player spoke again.

"There are those of us who understand the inner workings of *Demesne* and know its real purpose."

What the fuck did he just say? Raze's blood was ice now.

Mathis appeared as shocked as Raze was. He didn't respond right away, looking like he was considering his options and measuring his next move.

"So what is the real purpose of *Demesne*?" Mathis finally

asked. He was playing dumb. Raze could tell. The light was totally on, and he was trying to get the ally to disclose more, to validate his hunches.

The ally remained silent, stoically regarding Mathis. Then he smiled crookedly. "I can tell you what you want to know," he said in a measured tone.

Raze held his breath. Mathis looked like he was, too.

"But in order for me to tell you what you want, you need to give me something that I want."

What the hell could the sergeant possibly have that this monkey-fuck would want? Raze thought.

Mathis was thinking the same thing. "Uh, well, okay, but I have no idea what that could be."

The crooked smile slipped from the player's face. "I want the girl. She doesn't belong here, and yet she does. She is necessary. You tell me how to find her, and I'll tell you why *Demesne* exists."

Raze ripped his visor off and threw it across his bedroom.

"Game off," he commanded.

The game was no longer secure. The Womb, the project, nothing was secure anymore.

And Raze knew exactly who that fucker was.

∞

MATHIS'S GUT tensed up at the mention of the girl. He didn't know what to say. He knew not to deny knowing what Ichiban was talking about. Mathis knew exactly who he was talking about.

"Well, I don't exactly *know* her," he said. And he didn't.

She was just a nurse's aide whom he thought created a fluke response in Blake Parrish.

"You may not know her," Ichiban said. "But you know how to find her."

Mathis didn't attempt to deny that, either.

"I need her last name or her address. Give me one or the other, and I'll give you the information you want to know. If you give me both, I'll take you there."

"Take me there?" Mathis lost his poker face. "But we're already here."

Ichiban shook his head. "No. *This* is only a game." He gestured to the jungle around him. "You tell me how to find the girl and I'll take you where the real action happens."

Mathis's spidey sense was tingling. There was something more to this game after all.

"But why the girl?" Mathis asked. "What does she have to do with this?"

"She's my business. You tell me how to find her, and your answers will be revealed."

With that, Ichiban blipped out of sight.

Mathis stood frozen, the jungle pressing in around him. He'd come looking for answers about Parrish. Instead, he'd found something far bigger—*and it wanted the girl.*

TWENTY-EIGHT

RAZE WAS in The Womb faster than a predator scenting blood in shallow water. He checked the Qi reader. His brainwaves were spinning at the highest Beta cycle, neural pathways screaming on overload. If there was ever a time he needed his skills, it was right now.

There was no point in trying to go straight into Theta—his agitation wouldn't allow for that—and fighting it would only increase the resistance. He'd have to take it step by step, acknowledge the interference that blocked him, so it would let him go.

"Beta 15."

He inhaled long and deep, allowing himself to fully feel the most intense current coursing through his meridians.

Rage.

Wrath was coiled tight and ready to strike. He'd been played like a newbie in his own game. But rage wouldn't take him where he needed to go. He sucked the emotion deep into his belly, absorbing its venom and taking from it the motivation he needed. Then he exhaled forcefully, releasing the chaff in an explosion—pushing it far away from him.

He inhaled again.

Confusion.

A massive wad of "how the fuck?" churned in his mind. How the fuck had all this happened? How the fuck had he missed the signs? No—worse—how the fuck had he let it happen? He lassoed each question one at a time, with a breath, and exhaled them in a propulsive blast. He'd get all his answers soon enough, but he needed clarity now.

With every inhale, he acknowledged another useless emotion, and with each exhale, he expelled it, let it go, and locked it out. After five minutes, the throbbing in his jugulars subsided, and the static in his field dissipated.

Raze checked the Qi again. Beta 12. Not good enough. An underlying discord still hummed off-key within him, denying him access into the zone. It was a faint, yet familiar, buzz of emotion. Raze recognized it, like a distant acquaintance from long ago, its name just on the tip of his tongue. But he refused to speak it. He had defeated that demon years ago. There was no way it could have taken up residence within him again.

He continued breathing, trying to find an alternate route around the block, working his fingers through the mudras like an idiot savant, and pulling his scattered energy in close around him. But it was no use. Raze wasn't going anywhere until he acknowledged the dissonant chord and called it out for what it was. Reluctantly, he sucked another deep breath into his constricted chest.

Fear.

The word struck like a gut punch, folding him from the inside. He'd thought he'd cut it out years ago, buried it. But here it was, waiting like it had never left.

The worst had happened. Not only had he completely lost

control—he never even had it in the first place. All this time, he had believed he was the one working the strings, and yet, in reality, he was the one dangling on the other end of the line.

If Mathis stumbled through—or if that phantom forced his way deeper—reality itself could crack. The world as people knew it would collapse. And with it, the empire Raze had built for himself.

He stood at the end of a dark tunnel. No light could be seen shining from the other side, and what lay within was unknown and could very well destroy him. But Raze wasn't about to just stand there and let fear have its way with him. He would not be immobilized. He would not be castrated. He knew who he was. He knew he hadn't even scratched the surface of what he was capable of. He would confront whatever, *whomever*, he found in the hinterlands and hold his own against them. He would be the one to choose how his day would end.

And with that, Raze felt the alignment click into place.

"Alpha 8."

White noise came on, and the chaise went into zero gravity. Raze worked the sequence and continued spiraling down the cycles until he felt the final shift into low gear.

"Theta 7."

The Womb went into automatic.

"North 37 degrees, 40 minutes, point two, four, six seconds. West minus 120 degrees, 55 minutes, 19 point three, four, two seconds," she said in her serene monotone.

The luminescent globe appeared immediately, hovering in front of his mind's eye. Raze watched as the aperture blossomed, and then he stepped through the opening to confront the only person who knew about Aislen.

TWENTY-NINE

FINGERTIPS RAN THROUGH HER HAIR, gently pulling and twirling the long tendrils and fanning them around her head. Soft caresses brushed across her forehead, her cheeks, her lips, before playing around her ear and down her neck.

She took a deep breath and sighed.

"Hey there, Sleepyhead."

Aislen opened her eyes and looked up at Troy's smiling face. The smoke from the incense and the dusky, afternoon sunlight created a dreamy haze around him. Her head was resting on his lap, and she felt her heart starting to race as his fingers went back to working their way through her curls. It couldn't be real.

"Am I dreaming?" she asked.

"I don't know. Maybe," Troy said, smiling bigger. "If you are, then I am, too." His fingers traced the side of her face, to her shoulder, then down her arm, leaving chills in their wake. Then he pinched the back of her hand—*hard*.

"Ow!"

Troy laughed. "Nope. Not a dream." He kissed his own

fingertips, then brushed them lightly over the spot that he pinched. "All better?"

Goosebumps blossomed up her arm, answering his question for her. It felt better than better. A powerful thrill tingled inside of her, reminding her of their kiss earlier. The heat and passion of it had consumed her. Troy was so tender with her, so considerate, that she felt completely safe, sheltered in his arms like she belonged there.

So when he asked her to tell him about her dreams, she did —finally trusting him enough to share the truth. He hadn't lied; he *was* a great listener, completely engaged, without a hint of judgment or criticism, as she told him the gory details about the dream with Blake and how she had watched him shoot someone in cold blood. The honesty alleviated a burden she'd carried, but it also left her feeling completely exhausted. She must have drifted off while lying in his lap.

"I can't believe I fell asleep. How rude!"

"It's totally fine," Troy murmured. "I was enjoying the view."

She blushed again, sat up, and stretched. Then she realized that for the first time in two days, she had slept without dreaming. Could it be possible that just talking to Troy had cured her? Sure, talking with Genesis had been helpful, but the fact that Troy accepted her affliction put her even more at ease.

But then Aislen thought about her father. If she were cured of the dreams, would she see him again? She had actually started to like him, and the idea of not seeing him—of him being a figment of her imagination—renewed the ache of loss.

"What's wrong?" Troy asked.

"What makes you think something is wrong?"

"Aislen, please. You wear your heart on your sleeve. Every emotion you feel runs across your face before you even know it's there. You couldn't hide from me if you tried. So tell me—what is it?"

"I just realized—I didn't dream just now. For two days, I haven't slept without having some kind of strange or disturbing vision. I'm kind of relieved, but kind of sad, too, I guess."

Troy's eyes softened, though his gaze lingered a moment too long. "Gen mentioned something... a dream about a father? She wouldn't tell me more. She said it should come from you. And she was right. I'd rather hear it from you."

Aislen thought about her father, a man she had only seen once in her whole life and rarely thought about until the dreams came. In all of her talks with Troy, she had never gone into any detail about her life. He knew that she lived alone with her mother, but she'd never told him about her father or that he'd abandoned them. It was way too personal to share with a co-worker. But now that they were becoming something different, something more, maybe she could go there.

"Are you sure you want to hear about it?" she asked. "I don't want to bore you to death."

"Absolutely, I do," Troy said, sliding himself behind her and pulling her back against his chest. His arms closed around her with gentle strength, holding her as if she'd never slip away. "There is nothing I would rather hear about."

THIRTY

RAZE STEPPED through the blazing white aperture and into the room on the other side.

Blake was curled in the fetal position on the sheetless, stained mattress of his bed, moaning and rocking himself back and forth. He looked scrawny and pathetic in his thin, paper gown, but Raze was no longer fooled.

He glanced through the windowpane into the hallway. An oily-faced police officer, who must have drawn the short stick for babysitting duty, was planted in a chair just outside the door. The guy was lost to his phone—doomscrolling, sexting, or numbing out on porn. A little tête-à-tête between Raze and Blake wouldn't even register.

Raze turned back to Blake and waited. He knew there was no need to disengage the option-lock command because he knew now—it had never worked in the first place. Right on cue, the tantrum stopped, and Blake slowly rolled over. He sat up at the edge of the bed and looked directly at where Raze's invisible presence was standing.

That took longer than expected, Blake said—not aloud, but with the clean snap of telepathic certainty.

Sure enough. A puppet had hold of the strings.

Raze wished he had brought his body along with him so he could beat the crap out of this little shit—but he put that energy back in check. Discipline first. Violence later.

Blake raised an eyebrow at Raze. *I see you're finally getting a grip on your anger issues. The challenge has been good for you.*

Raze blinked, surprised both by Blake being able to read his signature fluctuations as well as by the massive balls he had apparently grown overnight. The petulant, lonely schoolboy act was gone. The cadence of his voice didn't belong to a twelve-year-old. It was older. Ancient, even.

I am full of surprises, aren't I?

There was no way Raze was going to allow this brat access to his thoughts. He locked his field into a flat line. Now that Blake was back inside his body, he could grab hold of his frequency so he could keep his mind's eye on him from now on. Raze turned on his receptors and tuned in to Blake's space.

That isn't gonna work, Blake said, smugly.

Raze ignored him and scanned. At first, Blake's field was a dull, tar-black smear. Then, without warning, it flickered—static across his receptors—before flipping blood red. Another shift: blinding yellow. Then back to static. Then another hue. Blake was changing his frequency transmissions as easily as flipping through channels on a television set, volleying back and forth between static and various colors of the spectrum. All of them inaccurate and therefore useless to Raze.

Told you so. Blake snorted.

That was enough. Raze balled a knot of hot electricity in the palm of his hand and launched it. It cracked against Blake's temple with a satisfying sizzle.

"Ow!" Blake hollered out loud, as the voltage threw him backwards.

Raze glanced at the window to see if Blake's yelp elicited any interest from the gunny sitting watch outside the door. When he failed to appear, Raze looked back at Blake. He was sulking now, rubbing the spot where the energy absorbed into his brain and acting like the twelve-year-old he was.

"What'd you do that for?" the boy whined.

Raze said nothing.

I don't understand. Ichiban told me you'd be pleased.

Who? Was there someone else involved in all this? *Who's Ichiban?* Raze demanded, finally breaking his telepathic silence.

He's the Master of Worlds, of course, Blake said, rolling his eyes as if it was a total no-brainer.

Master of Worlds? Only an egomaniacal prick would come up with such lame bullshit. *How did you meet him—this Ichiban?*

He'd come play with me in Demesne—after you left—but he would show me all kinds of things that you never did.

Like what kinds of things?

Like how to change my force field so nobody could ever catch me... and how to get in the game without the visor after Dad took them away from me... and how to access the hidden level of the game.

So Blake *was* working for someone else. And he was able to access Demesne—and even bleed into Raze's part of The Stratum—without the visor. The only thing was, there wasn't a single person even close to being adept enough to show Blake how to do those things. Raze's fury was piqued again.

I don't understand why you're so angry. Ichiban said you'd be pleased.

The little shit had found his way around his firewall and read his field again. Raze readjusted his frequency.

Why would he think I'd be pleased? Raze asked.

Ichiban said that you have too much work to do—that you have to do everything—all by yourself—and that you needed a helper.

Raze recognized the sentiment as his own. *Someone is using my own words against me,* he thought to himself. And there was only one person it could be.

Grant Parker!

Of course it was Grant. It fit too perfectly. The words. The timing. The betrayal. Who else could it be? Who else would be arrogant enough to turn his own words against him?

And Raze just had that conversation with him yesterday—where he'd told Raze that he had his eye on a new talent... someone who could surpass him. He must have been talking about Blake, which meant the asshole had been trying to undermine Raze and the Project all along.

Raze moved in closer and got his phantom face down into Blake's. *Then why didn't he tell me about you? Why didn't he tell me that the plan had changed and that we weren't killing you after all?*

Feeling the menacing proximity of his presence, Blake pulled his head back. His brain began to stutter. *Uhhhh... well, uh, he said that... that no one was supposed to know about me yet. That I'm a secret.*

Raze's jaw clenched. Grant had sworn he told The 8 about his 'new prodigy.' More lies. More betrayal. Was that fawning sycophant so bold as to do what he wanted, with blatant disregard for The 8's objectives?

Ichiban says The 8 are buffoons. That they can go fuck themselves. Blake answered, finding a way around Raze's firewall yet again.

Raze's vision flared white. It took everything in Raze's power not to knock the smart aleck unconscious. He updated his firewall again, locking Blake out, and moved toward the far wall of the room.

The Grant Parker he knew would never say that. The 8 *made* him. Propped him up, saved him from irrelevance. And now he thought he could bite the hand that fed him? The ungrateful bastard. He was a fucking traitor, and that was a death penalty offense within the Protocol of the company. Raze would be all too willing to handle that assignment himself.

...He says your talents are wasted with them, Blake continued. *That you should look out for yourself. That's the only thing that matters now: the pretty lady.*

At the mention of Aislen, something cracked inside Raze. She was supposed to be *his* secret.

Did you tell him about her? he asked, trying not to let the charge of apprehension leak through the transmission.

Blake shook his head. *I didn't have to.*

What do you mean, 'You didn't have to'? Someone had to! You and I were the only ones in Demesne when she showed up.

No, we weren't. Ichiban was there.

Raze thought back. Blake was wrong. The only conscious entities in *Demesne* that night were Scott Parrish, Blake, Aislen, and Raze himself. Parrish was dead before the girl reared her pretty head, and the drones were nothing but holographic shells.

Where? Raze demanded. *If he was there, where was he?*

Blake tapped his forehead. *Because he was there. With me.*

Raze reeled. Not watching—inhabiting. Riding the boy's consciousness like a tick buried deep in the skull.

Is he in there now? Raze demanded.

Blake frowned. *No. I think you knocked him out with that*

lightning. But he'll wait for me in Demesne. He says that when we meet Mathis, he will tell us where the lady is.

The unfamiliar sensation of possessiveness fisted up again. Raze could feel it twist underneath the steely reserves of apathy that normally fortified his interior.

Ichiban wants you to meet us there, too," Blake continued. *And when we find out where she lives, he wants you to go and get her for him."*

Me? Go get her for him?! Raze was increasingly unsettled.

Yep. Ichiban wants her captured. Not killed. He has plans for her.

What plans?

He says she's the key. Better than what he was fishing for that night. He wanted someone else, but she showed up instead.

Who else was he trying to lure? The thought needled him, but the boy's smile froze it in place.

Blake hesitated, then parroted flatly: *None of your business.*

Raze lashed him with another bolt.

Sorry! Blake yelped. *That's just what he told me. None of your business. All we need to do is find her, bring her to him, and he will handle the rest.* Blake's eyes lit up again, and he smiled. *Then he says my work will be done and that he'll take me to my Dad.*

The words rattled Raze. Didn't the boy understand that his father was dead? Or maybe—with another consciousness channeling through him that night—it wasn't Blake who pulled the trigger. It would have been Ichiban. It would have been Grant.

Raze's fury spiked.

Some emotions were prohibited in his line of work: pity, guilt, jealousy—any weakness that suggested he still had a heart. If even one caught hold of him, it could destroy him from the inside out. Raze realized it might be too late.

The thought of Grant's hands on Aislen made something primal and murderous claw its way up his throat.

If Grant wanted her, Raze would get to her first.

And sometimes, the only way to beat a rival was to play along.

What does Ichiban want me to do?

THIRTY-ONE

AISLEN RELAXED IN Troy's arms for another hour. She felt so comfortable in his presence, so secure that he wouldn't find her crazy. It was easy for her to open up and tell him about her other dreams.

She shared the vision of her father as a homeless man and how he'd begged her to ask her mom about the teacups. She explained to Troy about her father abandoning them before she was ever born, how she had only met him one time in her whole life, but that he had sent her mother a teacup from a different place around the world every year.

Then she told him about her dream that morning, how her father had held her with an invisible force to make sure she would listen to him and that he had made her illness go away with practically a wave of his hands.

"He told me I was waking up," she said. "That I had special abilities that were activating and that he needed to show me how to use them because I could be in danger."

Aislen felt Troy stiffen behind her, and he sat up straighter. "What kind of danger?" he asked, sounding pensive.

Aislen didn't want to worry him, so she backed off. "Nothing bad," she said, hating how false the words tasted. "Just that people would be looking for me, wanting to use these abilities for themselves."

"What kind of abilities was he talking about?"

"I don't know all of them. He only showed me how to do one thing."

"And what was that?"

Aislen opened her mouth to answer, but the distant whistle of a train interrupted her—a long, hollow cry that seemed to stretch itself into a single word: *Don't.*

She remembered that her dad had told her not to talk about her dreams. But he wouldn't have meant Troy. Troy was being understanding and helpful.

"Well, he taught me how to travel to different places using balls of energy," she decided to tell him. "It was just like Gen said this morning. We created these orbs of energy—he called them signal lines—just by thinking about a place. Then we stepped into them—and went to that place. It was amazing! And don't you think it's strange that Gen would dream something that actually happened in my dream, too?"

Aislen felt Troy's body tense up again and thought that maybe she had gone too far. Maybe it was beyond what Troy could handle.

"Go on," he said, but his voice was tight, almost stern.

"Are you sure?"

"I'm positive," he said.

The sound came again, nearer this time, sharper, more insistent—like the tracks themselves were screaming, *Stooop!*

Aislen sat up and turned to face Troy. The intensity that had clouded his face at breakfast that morning was written there again.

"Are you changing your mind now? Are you starting to

think I am crazy?" You know, maybe the dream is crazy, but I still find it weird that Gen had a similar dream—and I want..."

"Wait, wait, wait," Troy said, cutting her off. "It is unusual, yes, but I don't think you're crazy. I am very interested in what you have to say."

Out of the blue, he reached up, pulled her face to his, and kissed her. She closed her eyes. The warmth from his lips coursed through her, and she felt her defenses melt.

A hush descended upon the shrine as if it had been thrown under a blanket. The sounds of the birds singing outside and the river babbling at the bottom of the hill were muted. The silence was complete. She could only hear her own breath in her ears.

When he pulled away, his face had softened into his usual good-natured expression. "So you were saying that he showed you how to make orbs of energy, and you travelled through them? Where did you go?"

Feeling secure again, Aislen continued. "We went to my house. Almost instantly, we were in my mom's room. I stood right by her window and watched her sleep. Then she woke up, and I thought she could see us, but she went right back to sleep, and we left."

"What happened next? Did you wake up?"

"No. We went back to the original space, and he told me how I could find him if I wanted to see him again."

"And how are you supposed to do that?"

When the locomotive thundered across the trestle just outside, its voice fractured into a guttural wail, no words left in it—just a raw, aching moan that rattled the walls as if the world itself was begging her to listen.

"Well?" Troy said. She could see his lips move, but he sounded like he was much further away. Aislen knew she was awake—and she knew that a train could not speak to her—but the atmosphere felt fictive, like the whole shrine had slipped from time.

She shook off the ominous feeling and continued. "Well, he gave me another orb to use. I'd never seen anything like it before. It was beautiful! Almost like a..."

The gong in the corner began to sing of its own accord, cutting her off with a circular humming that harmonized with the train's deep bass.

"It was like a what?" Troy asked.

Aislen could only stare at him. Her thoughts were cloudy and incoherent.

"The orb your father gave you..." he prompted. "You were saying it looked like something. What did it look like?" He encouraged her with a reassuring squeeze of her hand.

She looked into his gentle eyes, at the smile on his lips, and her mind wandered to how nice it had been kissing those lips. "Well... it was kind of like a diamond, clear like a crystal, but it flashed with colors like I had never seen before."

The gong grew louder, overpowering the lamentation of the locomotive. The walls of the shrine felt like they were closing in around her, squeezing her in a tight embrace.

Aislen looked at Troy, wondering if he had noticed the change in the shrine. But he seemed to be oblivious to its convulsions. He was watching her—looking at her in a way she had never seen before, like he was seeing her for the very first time and yet knew everything about her.

Troy broke his gaze and looked down at her hand instead, holding it as if it were a fragile and delicate treasure. He brushed his thumb across the back of it with a feathery touch, sending fresh shivers from the bottom of her throat down through the center of her. Her limbs went weak.

"Funny you've never mentioned him before," Troy said. "What was his name?"

"His name—" Her ears popped with a loud crack, and she heard her father's voice in her head.

Do not speak my name!

Aislen gasped and snapped out of her trance. She suddenly remembered what her father had told her—names carry a signature that could be tracked—that just speaking his name could send people looking for her and put the people she loved in danger.

"I don't know," she blurted out. She shuddered at the thought that she had almost put Troy in danger by speaking her father's name.

"You don't know?"

"No! I don't know his name. I never knew his name." The lie felt uneasy on her lips, but her ears popped again, and the constrictive grip around her released itself instantly. The silence lifted. Aislen could hear the evening birds, the river and the train rumbling further down the track. The shrine gong trembled out a final resonant whisper.

"That's too bad," Troy said. "I mean, if you knew it, we might be able to find him. You obviously have unfinished business with him; your dreams are telling you that. If you could find him, you could confront him and deal with it once and for all."

She looked at Troy's face. The severity she had seen on it a moment ago was gone—a phantasm that faded away, leaving the genuine, gorgeous face she knew.

From far off down the track, the train let out a feeble moan. While it didn't actually say anything to her, it reminded her of the danger her father warned her about. She felt an overwhelming need to check on her mother.

"You know, it's getting late, and my mom will be worried if I don't check in. We should go."

Troy sighed, looking disappointed. "Sure, I can take you back to your car if you like."

"Would you mind just taking me home?" she asked, anxious to make sure her mother was all right.

Troy perked up at the request. "I don't mind that at all," he said, standing up and pulling her to her feet. "In fact, I'd love to see the place you call home."

THIRTY-TWO

MATHIS STOOD on the front porch of the clapboard ranch house. Though charming and well-maintained, he was surprised that the old girl was still standing. The five o'clock Amtrak had just roared past, almost heaving him off the porch.

After his strange encounter in Demesne with the even stranger Ichiban, there was no hesitation on Mathis' part about finding out the whos and wheres of the little nurse from the hospital.

He'd immediately called Jackson and asked if he had jotted down her name. He had. Then he rang up dispatch and had them run out all the particulars on a Miss Aislen Walker. She was clean as a whistle, not so much as a traffic citation in all of her 24 years. The only thing they could find on her was the address listed on her driver's license.

Mathis hopped in his pickup and headed out to the depressed little spit of a town. While he had no intentions of just handing the girl's info to some weird, video game freak, he did have a few questions he wanted to ask her. In less than forty-eight hours since the murder of Scott Parrish, she had generated the rabid interest of two people: the catatonic son and probable killer of the victim, and this bizarre Ichiban character.

It couldn't be a coincidence. She had to be connected—no doubt about it. And Mathis was going to put on his best 'bad cop' persona to get the truth out of her.

Standing on the warped floorboards of the porch, he waited for the train to pass before he rang the doorbell. He was sure no one could hear themselves think over that kind of racket, and wondered why anyone would ever purchase a home in such an undesirable location.

He pulled his shoulders back, widened his stance, and slipped his thumbs into his belt, doing his best Captain America impression. Truth was, he looked more like Mighty Mouse—and not even the kids' Saturday morning kind. Years on the job had worn the shine off him, left him with too much gut and too little sleep. He hoped the badge and uniform might still carry the weight he no longer did.

The porch light came on, the door opened, and standing before him was a dream come true; a vision in a clingy red sweater and faded blue jeans with her hair hanging long down her back, rather than up in the bun of a diner waitress. Mathis was immediately at a loss for words.

A worried furrow crinkled her brow when she saw him standing on her porch. "Hello, Sergeant. Can I help you?"

"Good evening, ma'am," Mathis said, feeling ashamed of his sham now that he was standing in front of Sabine. "Uh, I'm sorry to bother you, but I'm looking for an Aislen Walker. You don't happen to know her, do you?"

Please don't, please don't, please don't, he thought to himself, but it was obvious they were related. He could see the resemblance in her face to that of the girl he met at the hospital.

She raised an eyebrow. "Yes. She's my daughter. Is something wrong? Is she okay?"

Her answer took all the hot air right out of him. "Nothing's wrong, ma'am. I just want to ask her a few questions about an incident that happened yesterday. Does she live here?"

"Yes, but she isn't home right now. What kind of incident? She's not in any kind of trouble, is she?"

Mathis wished he had something else to hem and haw about. This was not the kind of situation he had hoped would facilitate a conversation with Sabine. "No, ma'am. She's not in any trouble. We had an incident in town night before last—a murder—and we have a boy in protective custody while we try to sort it all out."

"I heard about that! But what does that have to do with Aislen?"

"More than likely, nothing," he said, now hoping that it was actually the truth. He didn't want to date the mother of a murder accessory. "It's just that she came to the facility with the boy's therapist, and the kid acted like he recognized her from somewhere. No one else has been able to get through to him, but she walked in and he snapped out of it and spoke to her."

Sabine's brow knit, but her voice stayed even. "Strange. She didn't mention anything. But honestly, Aislen keeps to herself. School, work, home. If she knew that boy, I'd have heard about it."

"Well, it could have been nothing, but I didn't have a chance to talk to her and I want to cross my i's and dot the t's, you know."

Sabine laughed. "Okay. But the other way around would work better for you, doncha think?"

Mathis thought about it, realized what he'd said, and

mentally kicked himself in the ass. What was it about this woman that reduced him to a bumbling idiot?

"Would you like to come in?" Sabine asked, opening the door wider for him. "Aislen stayed at a friend's house last night, but I expect she'll be home soon."

Mathis shuffled a boot on a crooked board. He really should just come back another time, or give Sabine a number for Aislen to call later, but the opportunity to stay in her presence a little while longer was irresistible. "If you don't think it will be long, I suppose that would be fine."

He stepped through the open door and followed Sabine into the dining room.

"Can I get you something to drink? I've got coffee, tea—a beer?" She laughed at her own joke, knowing that he couldn't drink while he was on duty. Mathis kicked himself again for coming in uniform under the guise of official business. He'd much rather sit on the porch, a cold beer in one hand, hers in the other.

"That's okay, ma'am. I'm fine." The last thing Mathis wanted was Sabine waiting on him, especially in her own home. He'd like to break that routine completely—get to know her for herself. Get her a cup of coffee for a change... make *her* breakfast... in bed... then build her a better porch.

"All right. But, could you do me a favor? Can you call me Sabine? The ma'am thing isn't doing it for me."

Mathis smiled. "Deal."

"Have a seat and make yourself comfortable," she said as she turned and walked into the kitchen. Mathis' eyes followed her. Jeans on that woman were even hotter than the waitress uniform, if that was possible. When she came back in, he averted his eyes, pretending to admire the collection of teacups on a shelf.

It struck him how long it had been since anyone poured

him a cup of coffee without expecting something in return. Most nights, he ate alone, half-watching the TV just to fill the silence. Sitting here, even for a few minutes, felt like a glimpse into the kind of life he thought had passed him by.

"So what kind of questions do you have for Aislen, Sergeant?" Sabine asked, coming back from the kitchen, balancing a delicate teacup on a saucer. "Maybe I can answer some of them for you while we wait."

Mathis didn't want to mix business with something he really wanted for pleasure, so he changed the subject. "Well, first, if I'm going to call you Sabine, you can call me Bob."

"Bob, huh?" Sabine said. "Is that short for Robert?"

"Yeah, as a matter of fact, it is."

"Could I call you Robert? It seems to fit you better."

No one had ever called him by his given name before. Denise had always called him Bobby. His family always called him Little Bobby, and the guys either called him Bob—or Johnny when they wanted to fuck with him. Mathis liked the way Robert rolled off Sabine's tongue. It made him think of all the ways she could say his name. She could call him whatever the hell she wanted.

"Sure. You can call me Robert if you'd like," he said.

"All right, Robert, so what do you want to ask Aislen about?"

Mathis so didn't want to go there. Not now. In fact, he just wanted to forget the whole thing altogether. What was he doing this for, anyway? It was none of his damn business. He should just let Jackson handle it. Keep to his business on the streets. Better yet, he should drive down to the department right now, fill out his retirement paperwork effective yesterday, and get on with enjoying what was left of his life. Like taking this beautiful woman out to dinner.

He looked at Sabine. What were the odds that he would be

sitting here at her dining room table? Mathis didn't believe in luck or coincidence or any good lord watching over him. But looking at her, he felt like he'd been handed a gift—an opportunity—and he would be a fool to pass it by.

Cases had rules. Evidence, suspects, motive. But this one bent sideways, like gravity didn't apply. First the kid, then the video-game freak, and now this girl. Mathis wasn't built for whatever this was. Out of his depth, he clung to the one thing that still felt solid: the way Sabine looked at him.

It was now or never.

"Could I get your number so I could call you and maybe take you out to dinner sometime?"

Sabine's eyes opened wide. "That's what you wanted to ask Aislen?"

"No. It's what I want to ask you—what I've wanted to ask you for a long time, actually, but have never been able to muster up the gumption."

Sabine arched a brow. "That's your big line? Pretend you came here for Aislen just to ask me out?" Her tone had bite, but the corners of her mouth betrayed a smile.

"No, ma'am... I mean, Sabine. *No!* I would never—I mean, I really did come over here to talk to Aislen. I just didn't expect to see you... and I, I..."

She leaned across the table, snagged his pen without asking. "About damn time." She scribbled fast, tore the page out, and slid it across the table. "I was beginning to wonder if you'd ever grow a pair, Robert."

Mathis picked up the paper, staring at her number in shock. And just as his heart felt like it was going to explode in his chest, the front door burst open.

THIRTY-THREE

RAZE PULLED his consciousness backward through the signal line and came out of Theta. He sat in the chaise in The Womb, chewing on what he'd learned from Blake.

All that "Ichiban" wanted was for Raze to monitor the game until Mathis entered base camp and track him until he met up with him. As soon as Mathis revealed Aislen's address, Raze was to drive to Modesto, locate and apprehend her, then take her to a safe place to await further instructions as to where an exchange would take place.

According to Blake, Ichiban was going to make it very worthwhile for Raze for assisting and completing this assignment. But because Ichiban also promised to take Blake to his *dead* father, Raze was not so enthusiastic.

Grant wasn't in any position to make Raze any offers worth his while. Everything in *both* of their lives was given to them by Infinium and The 8. Besides, Raze already knew how to find Aislen. He didn't need Mathis. He had access to her any time he wanted. He held her like a key in his pocket.

As far as Raze was concerned, the mission was pointless.

There was nothing in it for him. Mathis may be an old fart and a techno-troglodyte, but he didn't seem like the type who would throw a young woman under a bus for selfish, personal reasons.

Raze thought about convening an emergency meeting with The 8, to expose Grant for what he was—*a traitor*—and get permission to eliminate his sorry ass. But there wasn't time for that. If Raze was wrong about Mathis and the Sergeant did feed Aislen to the wolves, Grant could just as easily have someone else run the intercept mission to bring her to him. And that was unacceptable.

But why? She should mean nothing to him. And yet the mere idea of her—of Grant wanting her for himself—made his pulse spike and chest tighten until he could hardly breathe.

From the moment he laid eyes on her, his world began falling apart. The instant he channeled her frequency into his memory banks, it had surged through his veins and short-circuited all of his wiring. Her name was a constant, unavoidable hum in his head.

And Raze wasn't the only one with an Aislen obsession. She was important to Grant, too. What did Grant need her for? Who had he been hoping would show up that night? Maybe the answer to Raze's Aislen problem could be found in figuring out why she was also Grant's problem. He needed to know the truth, needed to figure out what made her so valuable before Grant could find a way to get his hands on her. All Raze had to do was pull up her signature, find her, and snoop around for the answers.

He surveyed The Womb. The large Qi reader on the wall was still on, monitoring his field. He couldn't search for Aislen here. He couldn't have her telling his secrets to Infinium.

"Womb off."

He went upstairs to the bedroom and looked at the bed. It was situated in front of the Q, another machine equipped with a field reader that tracked people and fed their information into Infinium's data banks.

He continued roaming through the house, looking for a safe place from which he could hunt Aislen. There wasn't a space anywhere inside the warehouse that wasn't furnished with a Qi pad.

He had all the trappings of a successful life: the house, the car, the clothes. But they were exactly that—a trap. The Womb, his portal to freedom, only took him to places he was told to go, not places he chose. His home was virtually a prison, the Qi pads the guards. Sure, they constantly monitored for intruders, but he wasn't so naive as to think that they weren't monitoring and absorbing everything else about him as well.

But Aislen's frequency was different. It hadn't been assigned, logged, or scripted. It had hit him raw, unsanctioned—like oxygen after years of recycled air. Maybe that's why he couldn't let it go: she represented a freedom Infinium would never permit him to taste.

He thought about dismantling the Qis. But that would trip an alarm at headquarters, and a half-dozen Men in Black would be through his door within the hour.

There was only one space that didn't have a reader. Raze bounded up the staircase, across the catwalk, and onto the roof. He raked a hand through his hair and let the words slip out before he could stop them: "What the hell are you doing to me, girl?"

Raze evaluated the patio, looking for the perfect place to set up a makeshift Womb. A large, slate fountain sat at the corner, creating a continuous waterfall. Mist cooled his face, the scent of wet stone filling his lungs — more alive than anything Infinium ever fed him. Running water was a natural jammer. Rivers, waterfalls, even ocean surf created negative ions that shrouded frequency. The constant cascade here would throw enough static into the signal to cloak him, at least for a while.

He grabbed a cushion off one of the patio chairs and set it in front of the waterfall. This was going to be antiquated, but it had worked for yogis for thousands of years. If both Blake and Aislen could travel without the sterile environs of The Womb, Raze surely could.

He sat on the cushion, crossed his legs, and closed his eyes. Using the same sequences that he had in the Infinium lab and in The Womb, he drifted down into the recesses of his subconscious and then out to find Aislen.

THIRTY-FOUR

AISLEN ITCHED the whole drive home, on fire from head to toe. Something was wrong. She knew it.

At the dead end of a desolate country road, Troy stopped, leaning close. "Which way now?" he asked, resting his hand on her thigh.

It should have been calming, even exciting, but instead his touch made her nerves flare hotter, her dread spike. She couldn't get words out, so she pointed him toward her house.

"It's all going to be just fine. Don't worry," Troy said with a smile.

Aislen smiled back weakly. She should be grateful to have him there, instead of feeling and acting so uptight. Yet as they got closer to her house, the more intense her anxiety became.

When they finally turned onto her street, she understood why. A strange, white truck was parked in her driveway. Her mother never had company. The sight of it pushed her to near-hysteria. She felt as if she had no barrier between herself and the world—just a ragged bundle of raw nerves exposed.

Troy barely got the Mustang parked before Aislen leapt out

of it and bounded toward the front porch. Through the picture window, she could see her mother sitting at the dining room table, writing something down on a piece of paper. When she was finished, she handed it over to the police officer sitting next to her. Aislen recognized him immediately. *The same one that had been at the hospital.*

Her heart jackhammered. What was he doing here—and why was her mother writing something down for him? Was she helping the police without realizing the danger? Fearing the worst, Aislen burst through the front door.

Startled, her mother turned to her. "Geez, Aislen, you scared the crap out of me."

"Mom, are you okay?" She couldn't help but shout, but before Sabine could answer, she turned on the officer. "What are you doing here?"

"Aislen! Don't be rude!" Sabine chastised. "I'm fine. And Sergeant Mathis just came here to ask you a few questions, that's all."

"A few questions about what?" The officer still looked down at the piece of paper in his hand, a half-smile tugging at his mouth, distracted. Then he folded it carefully and slipped it into his pocket. It took everything in Aislen's power not to snatch it away and rip it to pieces.

"Whoa, girl! Where's the fire?" Troy entered the house. He glanced toward the table. "Oh! Good evening, sir. Sergeant Mathis, right?" Ever polite, he walked over and shook the officer's hand, then turned to her mother. "Good evening, ma'am. I'm Troy, a friend of Aislen's."

"We work together," Aislen blurted out abruptly.

"We're friends," Troy reiterated, narrowing his eyes.

"Well, that's wonderful! It's nice to meet you, Troy. I'm Sabine, Aislen's mom. Though right now I hardly recognize the girl." Sabine frowned in Aislen's direction.

Aislen had no patience for pleasantries. "What kind of questions?" she growled at the officer again.

"Honey, what's wrong?" Sabine asked. "This isn't like you."

"Nothing's wrong! I just saw that strange truck parked out there, and I knew you were here alone, and I was worried. That's all."

"Well, everything's fine, sweetheart. You can calm down."

"Yeah, I'm sorry about that," Mathis put in, finally coming out of his daze. "I'm not officially on the clock. That's why I'm in my own car. But things have come up in the Parrish case, and I had a couple of questions that couldn't wait. I was hoping you could help answer them."

"Me? What does your case have to do with me?" Aislen tried but failed to keep the shrill tone out of her voice.

"I already asked Mr. Kellen here yesterday, but I wanted to ask you personally. Do you ever play video games?"

Sabine laughed out loud. "I could have answered that for you."

"No," Aislen answered, hoping that would be the end of it.

But apparently, no wasn't good enough. Mathis tried again. "Well, do you have any friends who play? Could you have been around a friend while they were playing?"

Aislen did not attempt to hide how stupid she thought the question was. "None of my friends play video games. This is crazy."

Yet Troy had asked her the same questions yesterday, and although it was ludicrous, Aislen couldn't help but wonder. Her father had told her she had wandered into a place she shouldn't have been. Had she wandered into a video game? Was that even *possible*? A tremor coursed through her.

"What do video games have to do with your case?" she decided to ask.

"That kid, Blake, was allegedly addicted to a particular

video game—*Demesne*—and when he saw you yesterday, he acted like he recognized you from the game."

Aislen thought about her dream. Was that *Demesne*? Her father had called it something else—The Stratum. Was this game *Demesne* the same place as The Stratum? Aislen shook the nonsense out of her head. Trying to connect the real to a fantasy was just the next step to full-fledged delusion.

"That's not where he knows me from." The words slipped out before she could stop them. Heat surged up her throat as Mathis' gaze sharpened. Should she lie again—or confess the bizarre truth? Her pulse hammered, vision narrowing.

"So you *do* know Blake?" Mathis asked

"I don't play video games," she said firmly, trying to cover up her mistake.

"Okay... but you know Blake?"

Aislen's mind raced, trying to figure out how she should answer him. Should she lie in front of her mom and in front of Troy, who knew the truth and hadn't taken well to any of her deceptions? Or should she just confess the truth, as bizarre as it was, and get it over with?

They were all watching her intently, waiting for her answer. The white-hot energy racing through her veins built itself up to a flashpoint. Her vision narrowed, and her head began to spin.

Just as Aislen felt like she would suffer a complete meltdown, there was a soft tap at the window, and a cool draft wafted through the room. Aislen heard it loud and clear. The crisp breeze moved around her, dousing out the fire on her skin. She could practically hear it sizzle. Though she felt faint, there was a substance within the nothingness of the air, propping her up and keeping her on her feet.

She knew what this meant now. Somehow her distress had called out to him, and he had come to help her.

Her father was here, and she knew what she had to do.

∞

OUTSIDE THE CONTROLLED environs of The Womb, under a twilight sky and with the white noise of rush hour in the background, Raze was surprised at how easy it was to conjure up a clear signal line for Aislen. The aperture manifested with very little effort. Raze stepped through it and directly into a raging fire.

Aislen was standing in front of him, but he could barely see her for the white-hot vapors around her. Mr. T was there, standing next to a woman who could only be Aislen's mother, sitting at a table next to Sergeant Mathis.

From the looks of it, Raze had walked into an interrogation. All eyes were on Aislen, and her field was responding accordingly. Her energy blazed through the room, crackling and erratic. The most powerful energy Raze had felt thus far in her presence.

He carefully moved closer, mindful that she had knocked him out of the viewing space at half this power. In spite of the fact that her ohms were on a rampage, he was actually able to move right up against her. As soon as his field came into contact with hers, rather than amping her up, her flaming incandescence extinguished, switching off like a light.

Raze was surprised by the reaction. Almost instantly, her field mellowed into a gentle lull, completely unlike anything he had seen before. She took a deep breath and looked directly at Sergeant Mathis.

"I have never seen that boy before yesterday afternoon," she said to him. She could only be talking about Blake, and Raze knew she was lying. She had seen him all right, but no one would know it from the calm, straightforward way she said it.

Aislen glanced sideways toward Troy, who looked down at his feet, expressionless. Raze wondered what she was thinking. He moved around her, synced up his receptors, and tuned in to her mental and emotional transmissions.

Her field shifted again, but rather than powering up her defenses, she let them down even more, practically inviting him into her space.

It's all going to be okay, she was telling herself. *Whether Troy is disappointed or angry with me for lying, it doesn't matter. I am doing this for everybody's own good. If he doesn't understand, so be it.*

So she had confided in Troy, Raze thought, making note of yet another problem that would need to be remedied.

"Hmm," Mathis grunted from across the table. "That's really strange."

"What's so strange about it?" Aislen said. Raze was impressed by how collected her energy was. She'd developed some fortitude, right quick.

"You see, something about that game's been bothering me," Mathis said, rubbing the back of his neck. "Ever since the boy mentioned it. I couldn't help but wonder if the game could mess with a kid's head—enough that he would off his own dad." Mathis sighed. "It sounded ridiculous, but I couldn't shake it. So when I came across a copy—and, hell, even bought a console —I figured I'd... poke around. Just to see." He winced, like the admission embarrassed him. "Not exactly my usual beat."

Troy looked at him. Mathis had his full attention now. "So did you find anything?"

"Well, I'm definitely not an expert," Mathis said. "But it seemed like a regular video game to me. A little twisted in some parts. I could see how some people could get addicted to it. But there was nothing that struck me as out of the ordinary. Until later on..."

Mathis turned his attention back to Aislen. "You wouldn't happen to know anyone who goes by the name of Ichiban, would you?"

∞

THE COOL BALM on Aislen's skin suddenly prickled. "No. What kind of name is that?"

"It's a gaming name, a moniker for a player I met. While I was trying to figure out how to play, this character, Ichiban, befriended me. He was beyond weird, but he let me tag along with him and kinda showed me around the place. I wouldn't have been able to get very far without him.

"But after a couple of hours—completely out of the blue— he asked about you." Three pairs of eyes turned to Aislen again.

The icy hand dug its nails deep into her flesh, reinvigorating her with fear. People *were* already looking for her, like her father had warned.

Mathis continued. "He started talking about some kind of secret level where all the real action happens, and he demanded to know about you before he would take me there.

"I found it more than a coincidence. Two people associated with the game have mentioned you. Both of them are very insistent about it, too."

Mathis and her mom were watching Aislen expectantly. Troy stared incredulously at Mathis. Aislen didn't know what to say. Part of her—the very scared part—wanted to confess everything right then and there.

The presence at her back moved even closer to her. It felt insistent. She could feel it trying to press itself into her head. Was her dad trying to tell her something? She closed her eyes and tried to relax so she could hear what he had to say.

∞

THE MENTION of Ichiban and The Stratum made Raze's blood boil. He didn't know what Mathis was up to. Maybe Raze had him all wrong. Maybe he *was* all about himself. Maybe he *was* planning on giving her up to Grant.

He needed to figure out why Aislen was so important. He extended his mind toward Aislen's and pressed himself forcefully into her head.

Who are you? he asked her silently, reaching through her skull and scouring her consciousness for the answers. Rather than resisting him, he felt her give in.

What? What are you trying to say? I can't hear you? she asked.

Raze yanked himself back out of her head. She was talking to him! How did she know to do that? The girl he met two nights ago was lost and confused, and now she not only knew he was there, but she was trying to communicate with him. He pressed himself back into her head, and she addressed him again.

You were right. I believe you now. And I know you are the only one who can help me.

What was she talking about? Raze was definitely not here

to help her. He was here for himself—and for some answers, damn it.

I'm totally lost, she continued. *I don't know what to do or what to say. I need help with this. Please, Dad, tell me what to do.*

Raze shot back out of her head again. Dad? Is that who she thought he was—her dad? Who the hell is her dad? Raze's chest, throat, and gut all gripped up tight, telling him he was close to the truth. He needed more information, and he wanted it now.

Raze stepped up close behind her and placed his etheric lips up against her ear.

Get. Rid. Of. Them.

∞

AISLEN HEARD him as clearly as if he were really standing right beside her, whispering in her ear. But he didn't sound like the kind, patient man from her visions. Her dad sounded angry —outright demanding. The situation must be far worse than she thought.

She finally looked at Mathis. "I have no idea why anyone in that game would ask about me," she said, trying to sound as impatient and bored with the questioning as she could. All she cared about now was getting everyone out, like her father had said. "I don't play video games, I don't know that kid, and I defi-nitely don't know anyone who calls himself Ichiban."

Mathis sighed, obviously not happy with her answer, but defeated nonetheless.

"Well, none of it adds up, but if you say you don't know any of these people, then all right. I have to tell you, though—this whole thing makes me feel very uncomfortable. I think, given the circumstances, until I can figure out what this Ichiban is up to, you two should be extra careful."

He reached into his pocket and pulled out a business card. "If anything unusual happens, here is my cell phone number. Please don't hesitate to call me."

He handed the card to her mother. "Promise me?"

"Absolutely," her mom promised.

"Okay then, I should get going," Mathis said as he stood up from the table.

"You know, I should probably go, too," Troy said abruptly. Aislen could tell he was upset. "It was nice to meet you, ma'am," he said to Sabine before shooting a glance at Aislen. His glare sliced through her like a razor. "I'll catch you later." It sounded like a threat. Before Aislen could think of a response, Troy followed Mathis out the door and into the night.

Aislen's heart sank under Troy's glare, sharp as a blade. But when the door shut behind him, the pressure she hadn't been able to name — the same crawling heat she'd felt the whole drive home — lifted with him. She let out a shaky breath, strangely relieved.

It really was for the best that he stay away. He'd be safer that way, and it was one less person she had to carry like fire under her skin.

The breezy presence of her father circled her again, pacing around her in an agitated whirlwind.

Her mother came over and put her arms around her. "Is there something you need to talk to me about, honey?"

Aislen clung to her mom, aching to spill everything. But Sabine had spent her whole life protecting her—it was Aislen's turn now.

"No, Mom. I'm just tired. And I really don't know what's

going on, or what these people are talking about." It was no lie. She really didn't understand any of it. But she could. She just needed to talk to her dad to find out. His presence whipped in close behind her, practically pushing her to move.

"I'm really beat, Mom. I'm just going to head upstairs and go to bed."

"Okay, Hon. But know that I'm here if you need to talk about anything," her mom said, kissing her on the forehead. "Sweet dreams."

Fat chance, Aislen thought to herself as she turned to head up the stairs—the cold breeze following hot on her heels.

THIRTY-FIVE

RAZE FOLLOWED Aislen up the stairs, drifting on the tantalizing tendrils of her wavelength. When she reached the top, she turned and walked into a bedroom, pausing a moment at the threshold to allow him inside. As if *that* made a difference. She shut the door behind them and whipped around to face him.

"Holy shit, Dad! This is crazy!" She began pacing quickly back and forth across the floor. "I didn't really believe what you told me last night, but it's all true!

"People *are* looking for me. That Blake kid remembers me from the dream, and now this person in some video game is asking about me and getting the police involved. None of it makes sense, and I don't know what to do."

She stopped pacing and looked around the room. "Dad, are you still here?"

Raze did a quick scan of the room for any other signatures, but there was no one else there. Just him and Aislen, alone for the first time.

"I need you," she pleaded. "I need you to help me understand—tell me what I should do."

Raze realized that if he was going to do anything, now was his moment. Aislen was at her most vulnerable; her guard was down. She was allowing him practically unlimited access to her mind and space because she thought he was her dad. She thought she was safe. She was open, his for the taking.

The Raze of two days ago would not have hesitated. He would have slipped in for the kill, sucked the energy out of her flesh, and left an empty bag of bones on her bedroom floor. *That* Raze would have relished the triumph.

But standing there watching Aislen flounder, drowning in her own helplessness like a bird in an oil slick, he was immobilized. Foreign amplitudes and frequencies moved through him. Emotions he didn't have names for. In her presence, he was just as helpless as she was.

"Please talk to me," Aislen said softly.

The static hum of her voice sent ripples across the room that penetrated his space with a buzz even more intoxicating than it had been on the dance floor. Her allure dislocated all his remaining resolve and wrenched him from his place across the room. Under no volition of his own, he found himself moving closer to her. The utter lack of dominion over his own will perplexed and frustrated him. He was better than this, damn it —stronger than this. He struggled against the riptide of her energy, but to no avail. Soon, they were face-to-face.

Aislen sucked in a shallow breath when she felt his presence brush up against her flesh.

"I'm scared," she said in the barest of whispers.

Raze could taste her words in his mouth. Her chest rose and fell rapidly. He could feel each sigh as if they were his own. The rhythm of her heartbeat pulsed through the atmosphere around them, the composition of her shifted from double to triple meter, creating an irresistible baseline.

Disconnected from his own will, his essence reacted in opposition to all his intentions, and he watched helplessly as his etheric hand reached up and traced the contour of her cheekbone. The fine, downy hairs on her skin rose up to meet his phantom touch, sending an exquisite torrent tripping through his spectrum. Aislen gasped as though she felt it too, and looked directly at him with unseeing eyes.

Like gravity, her field tried to pull him even closer, demanding that his energy coalesce into her own. It took all of his endurance to keep himself from melting completely into her.

Who are you? he said, a rhetorical question not meant for mortal ears, but Aislen jumped back.

"Dad? Is that you?" she asked, reaching up, trying to feel for him like a child lost in the dark. When her fingers connected to his incorporeal body and brushed lightly down the front of his chest, another kick of bliss shuddered through him. She must have felt it, too, because she jerked her hand away.

A sudden rift of energy scorched through her space, reversing the pull of the tide and pushing him back several feet as she attempted to put a boundary between them. She definitely knew he was there now—and she definitely knew he was not "Daddy."

"You have to tell me," she tried again. "Give me a sign. Are you my dad?"

She paused, waiting for an answer. Raze dared not move, dared not think, in case she amped up the anionic vibes and tossed him out of the viewing arena, or worse, demolished his transmundane integrity altogether, sending him into the ethers permanently.

When she didn't get any response, Aislen became more demanding. "Dad, is that you?" she asked with a harsh whisper. "Tell me now! Is this Preston?"

A concussion of cold voltage inundated him, snapping him fully conscious and throwing him further outside her boundaries. Had he heard her right? Did she just say *Preston?* The name set off alarm bells in his brain.

Raze slinked back even further, giving himself more space to regain his composure. She couldn't be talking about Preston Reed, could she? *The* Preston Reed?

Reed. The ghost of Infinium. A talent beyond compare, able to slip past the Fourth and bring back revelations no one else could match.

Like his father before him, he'd refused to bow—and vanished without a trace. Infinium never stopped hunting. They made every operative study his signature, memorize his frequency, chase him across the grid like a catechism. But no one ever caught him.

And now... his *daughter* stood right in front of Raze.

Raze looked at Aislen. A stunning clarity swept away the muddy interference and confusion that had been stupefying him. It couldn't be! *She* couldn't be! But it was the only thing that made sense. Preston Reed had a daughter, and she was standing right in front of him.

If it was like Blake said—that Ichiban had broadcast a signal to lure Preston Reed—it was completely possible the signal had snagged a genetically similar signature and pulled its owner helplessly into The Stratum.

It explained everything. But it was still only speculation until he could prove it. And there was only one way to do that.

Raze accessed his database of signatures, pulling up Preston's last known frequency equation, and quickly created a signal line based on its values. Instantly, an orb began to manifest in front of him, a sphere of gleaming, molten gold, so pure and dense it seemed almost physically tangible.

He gently took the orb into his phantom hand and slowly approached Aislen with it. If he was right, the orb would act as a skeleton key. Not only would it open the doors through her harshest defenses, it would protect him in the process. If Aislen's field responded to the sphere by going into resonance with it, Raze would know the truth.

He easily slipped through the jagged grid of protection she'd thrown around herself without so much as a flicker of resistance, and Raze smiled with the first taste of validation.

I know who you are now, Raze taunted Aislen in a tele-pathic sing-song, making no attempt to conceal himself.

Aislen's eyes opened wide. "Who are you?" she whispered.

There was no mistaking it; she could actually hear him. She began a slow retreat backwards.

Clairaudient, are we? Raze continued toward her. *You know, people who hear voices are considered crazy in this world. You'd better keep that to yourself.*

"You aren't my father."

Well, you're right about that. I am definitely not your father. Raze laughed softly.

"What do you want from me?"

I just want to know you, Aislen—to know the truth about you. Once I know, I can figure out what I am going to actually do with you. There's nothing to be scared of... yet.

Aislen shuddered visibly, continuing to retreat until her back was pressed against the wall. The ultraviolet foundation of her signature bruised into a dark purple as fear turned to horror.

"Stop!" she shouted, then looked to the door, hoping her mother couldn't hear. She looked back toward Raze and switched to telepathy.

I'll tell you anything you want! Her thought-voice trembled through the link. Terror pulsed in the current between them, but tangled inside it was something else—raw, rising, like she was learning to ride the signal instead of drown in it.

Raze stilled. This wasn't the wild, accidental contact from before. She was doing it deliberately now, her field threading into his with unnerving precision. Fear, yes—but also intent. *My, my,* he sent back, letting the words coil slowly and deliberately. *You're not just hearing me. You're answering.*

I'll tell you everything I know, she continued, *on one condition."*

Raze snorted derisively. *That's very sweet of you, but I can find out all on my own, thank you. Besides, I don't negotiate.*

The deep purple haze of her space warped and distorted as her fight-or-flight response ignited. Before she could make a run for it, Raze used his free hand and threw a cord of control at her, effectively roping her down and freezing her in her place.

Not so fast. You're far too interesting to let slip away.

Panic clawed at her throat, but she forced it down. If she begged, he'd devour her. If she resisted, he'd snap her in half. All she could do was stall, stretch seconds into lifelines until she figured a way to protect Mom.

Aislen looked wildly toward his invisible presence, her eyes like an insect trapped in a web. *"Please,"* her voice begged in his head. *I'll do anything you want.*

Anything? Careful, Aislen. You don't know the half of what that could mean. But unfortunately, we have to do this my way.

Tears welled up in her eyes, and her body began to tremble, frozen to the bone by terror. *Please—whatever you do to me, I don't care. Just leave my mom out of this.*

It's okay, Aislen," Raze said with a voice as smooth as honey. *I have no interest in your mother.*

Raze took a final step toward her. *Nope. Just you. Only you. Oh! And your father, of course.*

Aislen's face blanched. She opened her mouth as if to say something, thought better of it, and shut it again. But she didn't have to say a word. Raze could read the truth all over her; her face, her body, her aura, all sang the truth. He was right. He knew it. But just for shits and giggles, he decided to continue with his little experiment. There was no use wasting a perfectly good signal line.

Don't be scared, he said, as he released the orb from his palm and slowly projected it deeper into her field. *This part shouldn't hurt a bit.*

He stepped back again to enjoy the show. The sphere glowed brighter as it moved into her field, bursting each membrane of her aura like soap bubbles. The amethyst overtones disintegrated, and her aura spun to gold, pulsing in perfect synch with the sphere. Exactly as Raze suspected it would.

Raze began to laugh, the full rush of victory upon him. This was his proof: Aislen *was* Preston Reed's daughter. A priceless treasure, indeed.

But his glory was short-lived. A deep bass roared in the room, so loud that all four walls of the room creaked and snapped audibly. A brilliant beam of golden light serpentined from above Aislen's head and down through her spine, grounding out the remaining high-band fear frequencies. Simultaneously, each energy center in her body burst open and showered the room in a deluge of liquid gold raindrops.

Aislen closed her eyes and took a long, deep breath. Raze watched as her signature cycled down, down, down into the lowest levels. When it hit Theta, another loud percussion shook the room, sucking out all sound and flatlining all modulation. Aislen and Raziel stood in a complete vacuum.

Aislen took another breath and opened her eyes. They met his directly.

"It's you," she said.

Raze was speechless. She could *see* him! It was a rare medium that could physically see the unseen, but what happened next shocked him even more.

A mirror image of Aislen stepped forward from her body, a ghostlike duplicate peeling away from her like a sheet of sunburned skin. The eidolon took two steps forward before Aislen realized what was happening. Both faces registered an identical look of surprise just before her flesh and bones collapsed in a faint at her gossamer feet.

She glanced down at her crumpled shell, then looked back up at Raze. The gravitational forces around her amplified once again. Raze, again, tethered to her by an invisible rope, began moving uncontrollably toward her. Surprisingly, Aislen moved toward him as well. When their etheric bodies met in the middle of the room, both of their essences sizzled with the proximity, like fire meeting ice.

Aislen raised a hand as if to push him away, but Raze reached up and grabbed it. Their fingers met with an auriferous explosion, and a shrill screech pierced the silence as their palms merged together as one.

Before Raze could figure out what was happening, the golden orb exploded, opening into a huge aperture that filled the room. Aislen was ripped away from him into a tunnel of light.

The opening immediately collapsed into itself, vanishing from the room and leaving Raze standing alone with Aislen's lifeless body on the floor.

Oh my god, I killed her. The thought slammed through him just as the vortex snapped him backwards into pitch black.

THIRTY-SIX

MATHIS FLOPPED down in the La-Z-Boy. His fact-finding mission at Miss Walker's house did not go down like he'd hoped —*at all*. He'd gone there to get some answers, damn it, and all he had was a shit-load more questions. And a phone number. Sabine's number.

Mathis reached into his pocket, pulled out the thin slip of paper, and contemplated the neat and deliberate numbers. Maybe it wasn't a complete loss. Hell, maybe it was the only kind of win he still had left. The job had eaten most of his life already—Sabine's number felt like a reminder there might be something more waiting for him, if he could ever climb out of this mess.

In fact, it could have been the only reason to have gone there in the first place. What were the odds? Stray bits and random pieces of life all lined up in just right in order and handed him something he had been wishing for all along. Maybe that was the only thing that mattered.

He pulled out his cell phone and carefully punched the numbers into his address book. The Great Whatever had gifted him with the digits. Now it was up to him. He needed to make sure he dialed the damn thing and asked the lady out.

Of course, *now* was definitely not a good time. He'd basically just accused her daughter of being associated with a murder. She was probably wishing she'd never written down her digits after all that. It was certainly not going to get him very far. No, he'd need to give it a few days before he called her. Even better, he really needed to get this murder shit solved. Sabine would be hell of a lot more open to having dinner with him if he could exonerate her daughter.

But that might be easier said than done. Aislen Walker appeared to be a smart, upstanding young lady, but she didn't seem at all forthcoming. She may have been adamant in her claims of ignorance, even incredulous, but Mathis knew better. He could see the knowingness behind her eyes.

The saving grace was that, along with that glimmer of cognizance, there was also a very healthy dose of fear. Not the type of fear that goes with guilt when one's about to get arrested. She was just plain ol' scared. There was a difference.

Fear of guilt made people sweat, fumble, slip up. Fear of something bigger made them shut down, go rigid, look for exits that didn't exist. Aislen wasn't dodging like a liar—she was bracing like someone out of her depth. That scared him more than anything she'd said out loud.

Mathis didn't know what Aislen's story was, but she definitely had a story to tell.

He looked down at the obsidian game cube sitting on his living room carpet. If she won't talk, maybe this bastard will. Sure as shit, somewhere within that box and the world it created was an answer. And Mathis was going to go in and find it.

He was a cop for Christ's sake! A professional investigator, an expert interrogator. He was capable of squeezing some little video game geek for the truth—and he didn't need to give anybody any God-damn information to get it, either.

Come hell or high water, Ichiban was going to give him the nitty-gritty and take him to that "place where the action happens."

Mathis snatched up the gun, slipped on the glove, and turned on The Q. He grabbed the visors and slid the shades over his eyes.

Christ. His *first* bust in cyberspace

THIRTY-SEVEN

RAZE FELL WILDLY through the darkness, thrashing and churning in every direction. He no longer felt the harness of the signal line that connected him to his body. The silvery thread that was ever attached to the viewer as they travelled was nowhere to be found.

He was severed from 3D. That was a bad sign.

A viewer without a tether was nothing but cosmic debris—lost forever if they didn't find an anchor fast.

He was not traveling the signal line he'd created for Preston Reed, either. A good signal line was a direct and instant pathway through space/time. There was no chaotic tossing around in a clear line. When Aislen entered that signal line, Raze had been sucked into a wormhole of unknown origin—a really bad sign.

As Raze tumbled further through the melanoid tunnel, images flashed across his mind. Snapshots, stills, and animated clips replayed with a speed faster than light: the sterile palate of The Womb, all white and sterling silver; the rust red of the Golden Gate Bridge against the clear, azure sky; and the dry, ochre landscape of The Stratum. Faces appeared before him: Grant's pasty mug as they walked through the halls of Infinium; the grim faces of The 8 hovering above him. Blake, the innocent; Blake, the corrupted; and Scott Parrish, dead in the gray ash.

Raze realized he was falling backwards through time, his life literally flashing before his eyes. This was the worst sign of all.

The playback slowed. Fragments from a different life surfaced: riding a bicycle with the warm spring wind at his back; his father lifting him high to see the dolphins at the zoo; his mother bending close, kissing his forehead as she tucked him in.

"I love you," she said.

"I love you, too," he heard himself answer, in a child's voice.

The words struck like a blow. His gut seized, his chest locked. He doubled over as the memories kept coming, strange and alien, like intruders he had no defense against.

Emotions regurgitated from the depths of him, an incapacitating sickness that tore through his chest and split his heart wide. He didn't have names for them—didn't want names for them—but they flooded him all the same, raw and ungoverned, as if some buried infection had been loosed.

The tunnel broke open, and Raze was violently ejected out into a dense and infinite blanket of stars. His somersault in the void offered a momentary respite from the emotional deluge, but then a vision of Aislen appeared before him. She was dressed in only a blue flame nimbus that licked and caressed her body, hinting at the bare skin beneath it, dancing across the cosmos. Her face was tranquil, otherworldly—too still, too perfect—as if painted on the inside of his skull.

Another wave hit him, hotter, sharper—an ache in his

marrow, a hunger that clawed his insides raw. It pulled him toward her, need without name, craving without end.

As he watched her travel across the galactic expanse, a gnawing déjà vu tormented him. She felt familiar, as if glimpsed in some place he couldn't name, some time that didn't exist anymore. The ache of recognition without memory drove him half-mad.

Nostalgia overwhelmed him. How desperately he had missed her! Yet here she was, in front of him the whole time. How had he not realized that?

He tried to call out to her, but his tongue was thick and useless, and she continued drifting further into the infinite.

Game accessed. It sounded like a woman's voice, and a force began dragging him in the opposite direction.

"But I just found her again," he protested, though no one was there to hear.

Raze willed himself to swim after her, but the empty space around him felt like granite, and every muscle in his body cramped with the effort. No amount of strength could break him free.

"Game accessed," the voice said again, and he began to recognize what that meant. But Aislen seemed more important. He had to get her back. He reached toward her fading presence.

"Game accessed," he heard again, and he was snapped backwards violently.

"Noooooo!" Raze heard himself cry, but the unrelenting force reeled him in at warp speed until he slammed back against a surface so hard it knocked the wind out of him.

"Game accessed," the woman repeated, just beyond the ringing in his ears.

Raze could feel his flesh encasing him again, and an excruciating pain at the back of his head. He opened his eyes. The black expanse of the universe was still there, but Aislen was not. Few stars remained, and those that did were distant, slowly fading into a mist of fog.

"Game accessed." The voice was insistent.

The twinkling lights of the night reemerged from their backdrop, and Raze could now see the lights of the skyline that towered above him. He began to hear squealing tires and sirens blaring, and he recognized the sounds of the waterfall melodically tickling his ears. He was still alive.

"Game accessed."

His mind cleared. He was back on the rooftop of his warehouse.

"Game accessed." The Womb called out, and Raze was instantly and fully alert. He leapt to his feet with a desperate urgency.

Mathis was in the game. And if Aislen was still alive—and God help him, she had to be—then Mathis was about to send her straight into the fire. And Raze was the only one who could stop it.

THIRTY-EIGHT

AS SOON AS he entered Base Camp, Mathis went on the prowl. His first hardcore stint in *Demesne* had taught him more than a few lessons. He knew that in order to begin his journey through the Octaves, he needed a partner. A clan would be even better.

He wasn't here for XP or loot; he was here to keep a mother and daughter out of a grave he half-suspected he'd already started digging with his own damn shovel.

Ichiban wasn't going to come hold his hand this time. That egomaniacal superfreak was sure to make him work for it. He would expect Mathis to seek him out, prostrate himself at his feet, hand over the info on Aislen, then grovel to be taken to where "the action happens."

Well, it wasn't going to go down like that. Mathis didn't actually have a plan for how it *was* going to go down, but he knew he was going to get what he wanted without leading the virgin to the sacrifice. Aislen and Sabine would be kept out of all this and Mathis would get his answers.

Rather than audition for the pros, Mathis decided to scope

out the newbies. They'd be grateful for a mentor and wouldn't have an agenda of their own yet. He'd even learned a bit of geekspeak to help him blend in with the goobers. Not a fact he was proud of, but there was no way in hell he'd be getting ganked this go around.

He marched into Base Camp with all the swagger he could muster and did a quick once over of the fresh meat. A half dozen noobs postured about, each a clone of the next, looking like what every new player looked like—a buffed and badass mercenary. There was no way to tell which one of them actually had any skill. But beggars couldn't be choosers.

"You!" Mathis yelled, punching his finger at an exceptionally beefy one, "and you!" he barked at another, who was fucking the air with a sword. "Come with me!"

The two newbians fell in line with him, no questions asked. Mathis considered that a win, although it also proved how stupid they were. He took one last glance around the room at the remaining pool of players. It would have been nice to have more expendable bodies on the team, but Mathis didn't want to be hindered by all the inexperience he saw loitering about. His not-so-fearsome twosome would have to do.

Just as he turned to march them toward the door, a player spawned out of thin air into Base Camp: a squat troll with a sickly green tint to his skin, dressed in what looked like nothing more than a burlap sack. He waddled directly up to Mathis and looked up at him with eyes that protruded three inches from his head and spun like whirligigs in their sockets.

Mathis's cop brain flagged him immediately: wrong proportions, wrong gaze, like a perp who could see straight through him—and wasn't even trying to hide it. The only thing remotely attractive about the hideous creature was the massive, semi-automatic weapon strapped on his back.

"Hey, dude. I need a lift," the troll said, fixing one telescopic eye on Mathis, while the other one rotated around, scoping out the other players in the arena. "Can I join your little clan, here?"

"You've got to be kidding me." Mathis thought, but before he could actually say it, the troll continued.

"I know what you're thinking, man. But I get a lot of action lookin' like this, if you know what I mean." He gave Mathis a grotesque wink.

Mathis opened his mouth to protest, but the troll interrupted him again.

"Look. I'm an original playa from back at Beta. I know my way backwards and forwards in this joint... *and,*" he thumbed a crooked stub toward the weapon on his back. "I got Big Bertha here.

"I need to get back to the 9th circuit so I can use her on the whore that just fragged my ass. And since this game doesn't let you go Lone Ranger 'til the 5th, I need a team to piggyback on."

Mathis ears lit up at the mention of the 9th circuit. It was right where he needed to be. He sized up the whole three thick feet of the varmint, discouraged. He really didn't need this shrimp slowing him down, but if he was really that good, it would save Mathis from having to waste time grinding his way through the Octaves.

"What's your name?" Mathis asked.

"I go by Dookie."

That didn't help.

"You don't like it?" Dookie said lightly, parroting Mathis's expression. "That's not really about the name, is it? It's about control."

Mathis sighed with resignation. Without the troll along it would be the blind leading the blind. "Alright... *Dookie.* If you can help us get to the 9th circuit as quickly as possible, you can join us. I have some business to take care of there myself."

"Hehe, I'm sure you do, big guy," the troll smiled slyly, revealing one rotten tooth. "I'm sure you do."

Mathis made a mental note not to look at the beast lest he gag. "Let's get goin' then," he said.

The troll weeble-wobbled out the door, leading the way. Which was fine with Mathis.

∞

RAZE FUMBLED his way into the house and stumbled like a drunkard across the catwalk toward his room. Not yet completely assimilated back in his body, he misjudged the position of the doorway and slammed hard into its metal frame. A sharp spasm ripped through his shoulder and he had to prop himself against the wall to catch his breath. The pain actually helped him remember the boundaries of his flesh. Here was his arm. There was his neck. He found his fingers and wiggled them.

"Game accessed. Game accessed. Game accessed." Though it was her usual serene voice, on repeat, The Womb sounded maniacal.

Raze rested his face against the cool concrete, letting it soothe the throbbing in his head. He couldn't let his sense of urgency turn into panic or he would be even more useless. He pressed himself off the wall and shuffled into the bedroom, making it safely to the soft cushion of his bed.

"Game on," he said to The Q as he grabbed his gear off the nightstand.

"Find Mathis," he commanded, after the console powered up.

The target icon zipped across the screen and through the Octaves, pinpointing the sergeant in the 5th along with three other players, none of which appeared to be Ichiban. Raze had to wonder how Mathis could have made it this far without him.

The game did not allow players to level up without earning it. It was designed to maximize the players grind time, making them engage in repetitive, boring tasks. Once they were used to the game, players became like little rats, not wanting to figure out a new maze to get their hit. They didn't want to try new things or take on challenges. Instead they would rather repeat a familiar scenario again and again to get to their desired goal.

It took even the best players several hours to make it this far when they started a new session and Infinium raked in big bucks off them in subscription fees. Mathis had made it too far, too fast. No maggot climbed this high without help. Either Mathis had outside backing—or someone was moving him like a pawn across the board.

Using a gloved finger, Raze selected the soldier bringing up the rear and accessed his stats. He went by Neo4253, which meant he was the four thousandth, two hundredth and fifty third Neo in *Demesne*, which was four thousand, two hundred and fifty-three too many. Not only did the tag prove he was an ubernoob, so did his stats. This was his first time in the game; he had no assets, no kill count, and no skill points. The poor kid hadn't even popped his cherry yet. He brought nothing to the team.

He selected the soldier hoofin' it in front of Neo The Zero next. GrimGriever had a better name and smidgen more game, with three kills and a pouch of gold in his belt. But that wasn't near enough to have gotten this clan this far.

Finally, Raze selected the green dwarf that was leading the league of losers and he found his answer. Dookie was an Alpha player, a tank with so many experience points racked up, he never needed to waste his time grinding through the octaves. He had almost as unlimited access to the game as Raze did as the Puppetmaster. There was a rare cast of characters that made it to the Master list, and Dookie was not a name Raze recognized.

Still, something about the troll's rhythm—the way he spoke, the pauses he left—itched like a frequency Raziel had tuned to before, faint but undeniable.

"Player profile," he told the Q. He wanted to know the real-life details on this cat; like what his real name was and where he was from.

"Access denied," the Q display read.

Really? Again? Raze stared at the screen, almost disbelieving, and yet, all too accustomed to these high speed curveballs.

Raze wondered if Grant, fearing Mathis would not trust his Ichiban character anymore, reinvented himself as this harmless looking ogre.

"Locate Ichiban," he told the Q.

The scope icon flew across the screen, skipping to Octave 6 and the jungles outside the 9th circuit. Standing in nearly the same spot as the last time Raze saw him, was Ichiban. So much for that idea. Raze contemplated the scene. If Grant and Blake were still as one in Ichiban, then who was the little gnome?

Raze fought the urge to enter the game. He so wanted to phase in and fucking blast them all back to Base Camp, but what good would it do? That was not a permanent solution. It would only delay the inevitable. Grant would eventually find his way to Aislen—and through her, to Preston Reed. If he interfered at this point, Raze wouldn't be protecting Aislen or Infinium's interests. He needed to play it wise, remain behind the curtain and bide his time until the a real opportunity to change this game presented itself.

He continued to sit impotently, watching as Mathis and his clan entered the teleport tube and slid into Octave 6.

∞

THE DOORS OPENED and Mathis followed Dookie into the jungle he remembered from his last visit. If he was right, Ichiban would be waiting in the clearing just beyond the first grove of trees.

Now that he was nearly there, Mathis needed to figure out how he was going to ditch the clan. He didn't need them anymore and it would be best if he confronted Ichiban on his own. He wouldn't be able to play bad cop to full effectiveness with an audience and there was no way Ichiban would take Mathis where he wanted to go with the tagalongs.

He wasn't worried about the troll. Dookie just wanted to exact some revenge on one ho in the 9th then maybe knock naughties with another, but the other two geeksters needed to go.

As if on cue, Dookie turned around. "Here, let me take care of that for you."

He whipped Big Bertha around his body, grabbed hold of it with both nubby hands, and lit up the two players standing behind them with bullets of electric blue light. Mathis watched in shock, as they both exploded in a rain of blood, guts and pixels. He stared speechlessly at the chunky, gut puddle.

Pixel gore or not, his stomach turned. He'd seen real shootings, but never anyone enjoy them this much. The line between game and crime scene blurred—and the fact it rattled him pissed him off more than the mess itself.

"Works for me. Does that work for you?" Dookie asked.

Mathis turned back to face Dookie and stared down the barrel of Big Bertha, now pointed at him. Dookie pulled a pair of shades out of his pocket. They matched the pair Mathis wore exactly.

"So this is how it goes," Dookie said, sliding the visors over his bulging bug eyes. "You are going to take me to this Ichiban character. You are going to get that motherfucker to take us to this secret level of his. Then I am going to handle the rest. Comprendez?"

No. Mathis did not comprendez. How did this squat fuck know about Ichiban? How did he know about the secret level? And what exactly was he going to handle? With the deadly end of Big Bertha in his face, Mathis was not on the asking end of those questions.

"You're spiraling, Sergeant," Dookie said with eerie calm. "And anyway, you don't really have a choice. He rotated one eyeball in the direction of the gut puddle in the dirt. "Not unless you wanna end up like them. And trust me, you don't."

"*Who are you?*" Mathis asked against his better judgment.

The troll snorted. "Who is *anybody?*" He flicked the muzzle of the gun toward the jungle. "Get moving. I got some shit to take care of."

Mathis had told himself he was in control. But deep down, he knew better—he wasn't playing the game. The game was playing him.

THIRTY-NINE

RAZE SAT at the edge of the bed, immobilized by shock. What had just happened blew his mind.

Besides slaughtering the two noobs without warning, the troll had just taken Mathis hostage and was now demanding that he get Ichiban to take them both into The Stratum. Most disturbing, he had a pair of visors that, even in two-dimensional CGI, looked like the missing pair to Raze's set.

That explained why Raze didn't find them in the Parrish house. Someone else had them! The question was who? Who was this green little shit?

Still, the troll wasn't moving like a maggot. Too sure of himself. Too practiced. Whoever he was, he wasn't one of Infinium's pieces—but Raze had no read on him at all. That made him more dangerous than Grant. If Ichiban was Grant, then this troll was a wild card Infinium hadn't accounted for— and Raze hated wild cards.

"Take the visors off, Mathis," Raze said to the sergeant through the television. "Get out of this while you can."

But Mathis was too caught up in the game to think of such a simple solution, and began walking into the jungle with the troll trailing behind him.

∞

RELUCTANTLY, Mathis slogged through the thick vegetation toward his rendezvous point with Ichiban. The troll tailed him like a shadow. He stepped out into the clearing and immediately spotted Ichiban standing in the distance, arms crossed, tapping his foot impatiently.

"I was beginning to wonder whether or not you would show," he said as Mathis approached.

"Uhhhh... yeah... uh, sorry. It took me a while to find what you are looking for."

"So you found her? You know where the girl is?" Ichiban lost his normally cool disposition, excitement causing his voice to tremble.

"Uh... yeah. I guess I did."

"Well, let's have it. Where is she?"

Mathis stalled. He didn't understand what kind of game these fools were really playing, but he knew that if he told Ichiban where Aislen lived, there would be no incentive to take him to the hidden level, which was the only reason he was here. Ichiban would just take the info and run with it. Then Aislen and Sabine would be in a world of hurt.

It crossed his mind then that he could just take the damn visors off his face, turn off the cube, then burn it like a Ouija board in his backyard and forget he ever ventured here. But that wouldn't solve a murder, and it wouldn't protect Aislen or Sabine from these freaks. No, Mathis needed answers first. He had to go to that hidden level.

"Well, I do know where Aislen lives," Mathis started cautiously. "As a matter of fact, I saw her there not an hour ago. I'd be happy to give you that address, but first, I want to be taken to that special Octave you were talking about."

"What? You don't trust me?" Ichiban said, feigning hurt.

"No," Mathis replied with a slow shake of his head. "I don't." His gut said he was broadcasting every ounce of fear, but sometimes bluffing was all a cop had left.

Ichiban chuckled. "Good guess. Maybe you aren't as dumb as you look."

"What? You mean to tell me you weren't planning to take me there?"

"Yeah, no. It really isn't a very good idea."

"You can't back out now!" Mathis was livid. "That was the deal. I bring you Aislen's whereabouts—you take me to this secret level and show me how the 'real action happens.' You take me there, or I don't give you Aislen."

Ichiban deliberated for a moment, his mouth working, between a pout and a frown. Mathis hoped Ichiban couldn't tell he was bluffing. There was no way in hell he was giving him Aislen, but he had never been a good poker player. Copious sweating always gave him away.

Mathis reached up and swept a cold palm across his forehead. He could feel the clamminess on his fingertips. He said a quick prayer and shifted his weight from one foot to the other.

"You really do not understand the consequences that going to that Octave may bring," Ichiban said.

"I don't give a shit about consequences," Mathis responded. What consequences could there be from a video game?

"Life as you know it—reality, as you perceive it—may never be the same."

Christ, they really believed their own bullshit. Or worse, maybe it wasn't bullshit at all. "Whatever. We had a deal."

"Fine," Ichiban finally gave in. "But you may end up regretting this."

Mathis already regretted *everything*. He should have just left the whole mess to Jackson and Investigations from the start. But he was in too deep now. He had to see it through.

"Take me there," he demanded.

"Fine. But don't say I didn't warn you." Ichiban said with irritation. "Blake! Activate his visor."

The name cracked across him like a whip. *Blake?* Was it just a coincidence that he yelled for another player who happened to have the same name as a kid that was sitting in a padded cell right now? No. Nothing in this nightmare was coincidence. His cop brain screamed connection, even if he didn't know what it was yet.

Mathis scanned the jungle, expecting another player to appear, but there was no one else around. Mathis turned back and watched in horror as Ichiban's neck broke in half, twisting perpendicular to his body. Muscles bunched and spasmed under his skin, crawling like worms, before his head snapped upright with an audible pop.

"Don't say he didn't warn you," Ichiban giggled in a squeaky falsetto. Mathis could have sworn that it was someone else's voice speaking out of his mouth.

"Better hold onto your underpants," Ichiban said. He leaned toward Mathis, speaking slow and deliberate.

"This. Is. Not. A. Game."

FORTY

"HOLY FUCK!" Raze shouted as Ichiban recited the activation phrase.

"Visors activated," The Womb announced calmly.

Raze leapt up off the bed and made a mad dash for The Womb. Within thirty seconds, all three players would disappear off the television screen, out of the game, and into Raze's section of The Stratum.

Raze knew now that Mathis had no intention of telling Ichiban where Aislen was. He was a terrible liar. He just wanted to solve his little murder and rightly suspected the "secret game level" was a tool in that.

But how dare that motherfucker Ichiban activate the visors. Those were Raze's property, meant to access *Raze's* realm of control. Grant had no right to take Mathis there without permission. It was bad enough that he had already trespassed there himself.

He shouldn't be transporting Mathis to *any* part of The

Stratum at all. It was a violation of Protocol of the highest order. Maggots were to be contained by The Stratum, not taken there. They weren't supposed to know it existed.

Grant could explain Aislen to The 8. They would understand if he was trying to catch Preston Reed and ensnared her instead. They'd give the asshole a fucking bonus for finding her!

But Mathis? He was a different story. There was no good reason to take him there. The punishment for such a violation was worse than death. If The 8 found out about it, they would have Grant's brain wiped and scrambled. He would be sitting in an institution somewhere, slobbering on himself for the rest of his life. Grant would never risk such a thing, which only meant Grant was *not* Ichiban.

Raze dove into the chaise. "Theta 4. Stratum access," he demanded. The Womb activated, throwing the room into darkness and bringing up the brown noise. Raze didn't have time to cycle down properly. This was an emergency. If Mathis disappeared into The Stratum, this wasn't just about Aislen anymore. Infinium's whole leash system was fraying—and Raze had no control of who was yanking the chain. He had to stop this madness and figure out who Ichiban really was.

As The Womb swallowed him, Raze could only pray he wasn't too late. On the other side of the visor, Mathis was already falling.

∞

MATHIS FELT a vibration tickle his temples where the visor frames touched his skin. The tingling sensation wiggled across his scalp until his whole head felt charged with electricity. He tried to speak, tried to ask Ichiban what was happening, but was suffering from a severe case of lockjaw.

As the current worked itself through his brain, his frontal lobe went numb, and his vision was overcome by black and white static. The world felt like it was toppling end over end, and the vertigo made him violently nauseous.

A sudden burst of orange light pierced his eyeballs, radiating pins and needles through the rest of his body. As the orange faded out, Mathis slowly recovered feeling in his limbs. He shook the last of the fog out and looked around.

No longer in the verdant and overgrown jungle, instead he stood alone in a desert landscape that seemed to be somewhere between Barstow and Mars, surrounded by miles and miles of absolutely nothing.

This was it? This was the *special* place?

A vortex of particles and light appeared in front of him, and Ichiban materialized.

"Well, here we are. You happy now?" His voice had changed back to its more mature timbre.

"What the hell is going on here?" Mathis demanded.

Ichiban laughed, a deep chortle, completely unlike the boyish giggle from just a moment ago. "What do you mean, Sergeant? Not what you expected?"

"No! There's nothing here!"

"Well, that isn't true. This desert is here." Ichiban strutted around in a circle in the dirt, surveying the arid wilderness. "It's just enough for you to feel like you are somewhere, and not realize you're really nowhere."

"What are you talking about? That doesn't make any sense."

"Of course it doesn't. Because you are a fool."

That was it. Mathis was done. The game held no answers

for him, and Ichiban was right—he *was* a fool. But he wasn't fool enough to stick around. He was out. He reached up, yanked the visors of his face, and tossed them.

Instead of watching them fall onto the moss green shag carpet of his living room, he watched as they smashed into the red, desert dirt and shattered into a million pixels.

That wasn't right.

He looked back up. Ichiban was still standing there with a stupid smirk on the lower half of his face. And he wasn't just an image on his television set. They were both still standing in the desert.

"What the fuck?" Mathis yelled at him.

"What the fuck, indeed," Ichiban said. He reached up and removed his visors, revealing a pair of milky gray eyes; eyes too wizened for the youth of his body. He looked at Mathis and smiled.

"It's a trip, isn't it?" he said. "But that's nothing. Watch this." He lifted his arm above his head and brushed an open palm across the sky. "Demesne," he commanded.

The atmosphere responded, rippling as if he had brushed his hand across a pond of still water. The ground began to quake, groaning and creaking. Roads and then layers of ash appeared beneath Mathis's feet. Skyscrapers began to sprout up around him like daisies in grass. Instantly, a city in ruins was constructed around them. Mathis recognized it immediately. It was the scene that was frozen on the Parrish television set, minus all the blood.

Mathis's gut plummeted. "How does a game do this?"

"A game *doesn't*." Ichiban's cloudy eyes glimmered. "Your mind does—with help."

"You're saying this is real?"

"Just as real as the place you think you live." He leaned in. "Now. Where is the girl?"

"No. I want answers."

"Don't make me angry, Sergeant. You don't want to see me angry. I gave you what you wanted; now you give me what I want. Where is she?"

Mathis stalled. *Never give up your witness, never give up your suspect.* "What does Aislen have to do with the murder of Scott Parrish?"

The name detonated like a mine. Ichiban's body jerked back as if Mathis had just shot him. His neck snapped sideways, and the gray clouds in his eyes evaporated. He now looked at Mathis with a clear set of blue ones. "What did you just say?" he asked, in a thin squeal.

"I said," Mathis started again, watching Ichiban carefully. "What does Aislen have to do with the murder of Scott Parrish?"

Ichiban's head snapped to the side at an exaggerated angle again. A whine issued from him. "What? What do you mean? Ichiban! What is he talking about?" Then he let out a plaintive cry, "Ichiban, what happened to my dad!?"

That voice—that squeal—wasn't just childish. It was familiar. *Blake's* voice, bleeding through a monster's mouth.

Ichiban's head snapped upright again. "Enough! Get back and stay!" Ichiban roared in a deep, gravelly voice.

Mathis jumped back. He had no idea how any of it was possible, but he was pretty sure that there were two people inside of Ichiban. And one of them was Blake.

Ichiban cracked his neck and straightened his uniform, smoothing his hands down the front of it. Once composed, he looked back up at Mathis, his eyes a pale, cloudy gray.

"You shouldn't have upset him like that," Ichiban said.

"Who?" Mathis was afraid to ask, but even more afraid of the answer. "Blake?"

Ichiban sighed. "Yes, Blake. Poor lad didn't realize his father was well, you know..."

Mathis was shocked. "Are you saying that Blake doesn't know his dad is dead? That he doesn't know he killed him? He did kill him, didn't he? They were the only ones in the house that night."

"Well, Blake's finger did pull the trigger, but his mind wasn't in it. That was me."

Mathis was appalled at the idea of this monster possessing a little boy and getting him to kill his own father. "Who are you?"

Ichiban laughed. "Well, if I told you that, then I'd have to kill you! Seriously.

"So, what was it we were talking about?" Ichiban continued. "Oh yes. The girl. You asked if she had anything to do with Scott Parrish's, how should I put this, departure? The answer is no. She didn't. She has to do with me. I need her and I need her now. So where is she?"

Mathis didn't know what to do. He didn't know how to leave—how to wake up from this nightmare, because that was the only thing it could be. He was out of options.

"Peekaboo," Dookiel popped out from behind Mathis. The wink-and-grin troll was gone. This voice had teeth. Predatory.

Mathis had completely forgotten about him, and Ichiban startled, jumped back. Dookie stepped around from behind Mathis and aimed Big Bertha at Ichiban. Ichiban took another step back, and Dookie shot a warning blast that missed him by mere inches.

"Do not even *think* about skipping out on me," he yelled at him.

"Who are you?" Ichiban hissed at the troll.

"I would like to ask you the same thing, *Ichiban.* Who might *you* be?"

Ichiban took another step away from the troll without

saying a word. Dookie fired off another round even closer to his head.

"Do not test me, or I swear, Big Bertha here will zap you back 100 millennia. You'll come back as a salamander in your next life."

Ichiban stopped and put his hands up in a gesture of surrender. "I need to find the girl," he finally said.

"So I've heard," Dookie said, approaching Ichiban. "And I'm so curious about that. Why? What is she to you? You know her from somewhere, perhaps? While I'd sure like to know, I have a few friends who would be even more interested."

On the other side of Ichiban, Mathis spotted a laser beam of white light cutting into the city landscape. It tore through the wall of a building like it was nothing but a thin veil of fabric, and a man, dressed in black from head to toe, emerged from the gash of light. He carried no weapons. He wore no protection, but he marched up to the group without fear, like he owned the place.

Mathis had never seen anyone like him before. He looked human only in silhouette. The air around him was too still, too heavy, as if the world bent itself around him. The man shot an icy look his way, and for the first time, Mathis felt deathly afraid.

"It's about time you showed up," both Dookie and Ichiban said in unison to the man.

The dark stranger turned his glare toward both of them, one then the other, before he growled in a low voice. "I don't know who either of you are. But both of you are trespassing here. *Demesne* is mine. Leave or die."

Ichiban was the first to step back. "My apologies," he said. "You're right. I trust you can handle things from here." He gave the man a slight nod before vaporizing in a swarm of static.

Dookie looked toward the now-empty space that Ichiban had occupied.

"Damn it! I wasn't done with him yet," he said. Then he looked at the man in black. "Raziel, I can explain everything. But let me take care of this guy first."

Dookie turned toward Mathis. "Sayonara, Sergeant," he said, aiming the weapon at the center of his chest.

"Don't!" the man named Raziel shouted, but it was too late. Dookie had already fired, and Big Bertha's electric blue bullets were headed directly for him.

Raziel raised his palm toward Mathis, and a white ball of electricity shot out of it. Both blasts of energy hurtled toward Mathis. The white sphere was faster, and it caught up with Dookie's ammunition. They collided and exploded upon contact, but a small amount of their mingled energy was still propelled forward and hit Mathis in the dead center of his chest.

The charge reached inside him, grabbed hold of his heart, and sent burning spasms throughout the muscle. Mathis fell to the dirt in agony.

The man in black was suddenly standing above him, a dark angel staring at him with the icy eyes of death. He knelt beside him and placed a hand on his chest. Another shock of pain ripped through Mathis. This time, a sucking pressure pulled at his heart, and the pain began to subside.

The man in black took his free hand and placed it across his eyes. Mathis felt another current enter his brain as he heard the man whisper, "Go now."

For one fractured second, Mathis saw them all—girl—mother—boy—cop—killer—braided in light.

Then the cord snapped, and everything faded to black.

FORTY-ONE

HE OPENED HIS EYES. The dark-haired devil who had been hovering over him, one hand on his heart, one on his head, had vanished. Mathis was flat on his back, staring up at the popcorn of his ceiling. Ugly, ordinary, and real. Only hell would keep that feature alive.

His television screen swarmed with an array of black and white chaos. The static on the TV bled into his ears until it became the roar of blood rushing in his head.

He managed to roll over to his right side and came face-to-face with the dreaded gaming console. Only it was no longer inky black and throbbing with purple light. It was now just a cube of gray ash, a spent piece of charcoal barely holding itself together on the plush green of his carpet. One last gasp from Mathis would blow it into dust. The visors were nowhere to be found.

The only thing that he brought back with him from the game was the unbearable pressure sitting in his chest, the knowledge that the game really wasn't just a game, and that

Blake really didn't kill his father. He also knew that Aislen and Sabine were in terrible danger.

Mathis tried to push himself up off the floor. His chest seized, ribs locking like a vise had clamped down on him. Cold sweat slicked his skin, soaking the carpet beneath his cheek.

He let his body roll backwards again. He was going to die here if he didn't figure something out.

He lolled his head over to the left and spotted a flashing green beacon on his coffee table. His cell phone! If he could just make it the two feet to that table, he could call 911.

Another spasm tore through his chest. This wasn't just exhaustion. It was his heart—grinding itself to a stop. Mathis knew he didn't have much time. With a mighty shove, he threw himself over onto his stomach, schlepped his body in a slow, army crawl to the table, then flung his good, right arm toward the phone.

Thankfully, it hit its mark. The phone slid off the table, landing just inches from his face. As his vision tunneled, the edges darkening like curtains pulling shut, all he could manage to do was reach a finger up and push the green call button on the phone.

Mathis could hear the sweet sound of a woman's voice—far away, like someone calling from the bottom of a well.

"Hello?" Sabine answered.

"Help," he managed to whisper before everything went black again.

FORTY-TWO

SOARING through a kaleidoscope of brilliant white and gilded amber, Aislen felt whole and complete. All the fear, doubt, and insecurity she had been burdened with her whole lifetime was effortlessly shrugged off with the body that had fallen to her feet.

It had been a curious feeling to look down upon her own flesh as it lay empty on the floor. She hardly recognized it. It was familiar, but it was so flat—so two-dimensional—so limited. Now, flying through the unknown completely free, rapture ignited her heart, filling her with total joy and complete peace. Her whole body hummed like a struck bell until the tunnel ripped away beneath her, and she thumped down hard onto a solid surface.

When she regained her equilibrium, she got up and looked around. She was standing in an enormous room, on a polished chrome floor that gleamed like a mirror, domed one hundred and eighty degrees around and above her by clear glass. On the other side of the glass lay a dense blackness stippled with a billion iridescent stars. Towering clouds of vibrant gases and several spiraled galaxies hovered both near and far. The whole spacescape reflected on the mirrored surface she stood upon. It was like standing in a bubble in the center of the universe, looking out at all of creation—immense, elegant, and breathtaking.

"You did not use the signal line I gave you," Aislen heard him say from behind her, and she turned to face her father.

No longer the middle-aged man from her visions, Preston looked as he did when she first met him as a child. Young and handsome, like all age had fallen away from him. Overcome with relief, she ran to him and threw herself into his arms, holding on to him as if her life depended on it. He wrapped his arms around her and returned her embrace. They remained like that for a long time, neither of them wanting to release the moment. It was Preston who finally pulled away.

Though he looked at her with gentle, loving eyes, his voice was stern. "This was not the space we were to meet. How did you get here?" His words cut through her joy like glass splintering underfoot.

"I don't know," she said. "Everything happened so fast. One of the men from my dream came to my house. At first, I thought he was you. But then he said he knew who I was and that he wanted to find you."

Aislen stopped, feeling overwhelmed. "I'm sorry. It's all too much."

Preston put his hand on her shoulder, and she immediately felt calmer. "It's ok, Aislen. Take your time."

"He created an orb," she continued. "Not like the one you gave me. It was golden. And he threw it at me, and my body collapsed. I was still standing, watching myself on the floor. When I looked back, he was there... I could *see* him."

Aislen shuddered. She had recognized him at once—the black hair, the chiseled face, the blue eyes—the soldier from her dream who had shot her. "It all happened so fast," she whispered. "One moment, he grabbed my hand—" She paused, remembering the ecstatic connection. "— and then I was sucked out of the room, flew through golden light, and landed here." She looked around at the universe surrounding them. "Am I dreaming again? Where are we?"

A shadow of sadness slipped into her father's eyes. "Where this is does not matter for you yet, Aislen. You have strayed too far, and if you stay too long, you may not be able to return."

"But I need your help," Aislen said, grabbing his hand. "Too many people are trying to find me—*and you!* And I can't protect Mom on my own. I need you to come back with me!"

"I can't go back with you. You don't understand."

"You're right! I don't understand! At least tell me where you live, and I will bring Mom with me. You can teach me what I need to know, and we can be together."

"I am very sorry, Aislen, but that is impossible. And, unfortunately," his voice caught in his throat, and his expression grew even more pained. "Unfortunately, this may be the last time we will be able to meet each other."

The truth snapped into place: he had just reappeared in her life! And now had to leave again? Aislen's hands clutched his sleeve as if it would hold him in place. "What! What do you mean? Why?"

"They are onto you, and if I get near you, that will only seal your fate. If they find me, they will think that you are no longer necessary and kill you on sight. They do not know the treasure you are, yet. And they cannot find that out."

A cold, hollow ache opened under Aislen's ribs.

Preston lifted her chin, forcing her to look into his eyes. "You still have so much to learn. It is imperative that you learn about your abilities and how to use them. And you need to learn about your history—*our* history—so you will understand *why* you are so important. You have no idea how much is at stake here.

"Once you understand... once you realize your potential, you'll be beyond their reach—as I am now—only better, because you will be able to use your gifts in the world in a way that I cannot."

"But I can't do this without you," she said.

"You can and you will, Aislen. This is your destiny. And there will be people to help you. I'll make sure of that. Now, we don't have much time, and this will be the only chance I can teach you these basics—so listen well."

Preston stepped back and, with a curl of his fingers, sketched liquid silver lines in the air. "You view reality as length, width, and depth." A single vertical line, a crossbar, a third stroke: the lines spun and knit into a cube. He turned it in his palm until it softened into a sphere and then contracted into a miniature Earth.

"You live inside that box," he said. "It's useful, but limited—like thinking the world is flat until someone proves otherwise." He slipped a hand through the hologram and pulled her into it. A moment later, she stood on her own front porch.nHer pulse quickened; she wanted to ask more, but Preston kept going.

"See that garden hose?" Preston asked, pointing.

"It's just a green line from here," she breathed.

"Now be the ant."

Like Alice in Wonderland, she began to shrink until she was extremely small and was standing on top of the shiny green rubber tube.

"Perspective changes what's real. It's a completely different world from this perspective, isn't it?"

"It is," she said, even more amazed. The vision disintegrated into a billion particles of colored sand, and Aislen was once again in front of her father inside the glass dome.

"Reality only *appears* three-dimensional, but you are *more* than three-dimensional."

Preston began to draw again as he spoke. "When you step out of the box, a different world opens.

One after another, he drew sweeping spirals of sterling light. He layered each one on top of the other and then intertwined them.

"The ultimate reality is made of many interpenetrating zones," he said, weaving spirals of light. "Lower planes are denser and more material; higher planes are finer, more energetic. Higher frequency doesn't mean 'far away'—it simply expresses differently, subtler to ordinary perception."

The spirals rotated together, folding in and out like a carousel turning inside itself. Her father moved around the holographic creation and stood beside her, admiring its perfection with her.

"See how they interpenetrate each other and how they all occupy the same space," Preston pointed out.

The separate layers of light moved in consort with each other, the outer cyclone rotating down and around like a carousel and then back up into itself in the opposite direction. It created an illusion of twisting inside out, then outside in.

In that constant motion, Aislen caught flashes of pattern: a rose unfurling, the chambers of a heart, an eye, a brain, then the double helix of DNA—one master pattern reshaping itself as she watched.

"The only thing that makes these planes appear separate," Preston continued, "is your perception. Only a shift in your perception is needed to step from one dimension into another."

"It sounds so easy," Aislen said.

Preston laughed. "Ah, if only that were true. To enter into a higher frequency plane, you have to resonate harmonically with that plane. And too many things work against you in the

Third for that to be easy. First being fear. Fear bolts the doors of the 3D world; it takes courage to open them."

"The fact that you have been able to travel at all is a testament to the power of your abilities. I can only imagine the places you'll go when you conquer your fear."

"Other places like this?" she asked.

"Yes, and grander and stranger and higher than this," he replied. "Another obstacle to dimension walking is the cellular makeup of the body. Your physical body has to be trained to handle higher levels of frequency, or, like a light bulb, if it gets too hot, too fast, it can blow out its filaments.

"That is why you have to leave, Aislen. This plane vibrates too high for you, and the longer you stay, the more you run the risk of your body not being able to process this frequency when you go back."

"There has to be a way to make my body handle it—can't you teach me now?"

"Not now, but I can guide you and send others to assist. But the journey is yours, and the soil and struggle of Earth teach a body how to hold those frequencies. If you really want to, and if you really work at it, you can find your way back to me. It will not be easy, but you, of all people, can do it."

She nodded, as if her world depended on what he'd say next.

Her father turned back to the circling complex manifold hovering in the air. He rolled his fingertips together, creating a tiny orb of crystalline white light between them, a miniature version of the one he had given her before.

"To get here," he said, placing the sparkling orb onto one of the spinning spirals, "you must carry and integrate these frequencies."

Preston continued to create tiny balls of colored light: red, green, blue, and purple, until there were nine of them, spinning in different orbits. He placed each one within the silvery hologram.

"You must be able to travel dimensions at will, and then find your way back. You must not fall back into the amnesia of 3D, or the journey will be worthless. You must *remember*."

He reached into his luminous creation, grabbed it with both hands, and collapsed the whole thing between his palms. He turned back to Aislen and opened his hands like a book. A platinum amulet lay within them, an elaborate, spiraling path. The nine colored orbs were now brilliant jewels, embedded in orbit around a diamond center.

"A labyrinth," Aislen said, breathlessly, in awe of its dazzling beauty.

"Yes," her father said. "The ancients knew more than modern civilization gives them credit for."

He picked it up from his hand, pulled a silver chain from it, and carefully placed it around her neck. "Listen to it carefully, it will guide you and help you learn to carry each frequency into your body. Someday, it will guide you back to me."

He looked her in the eyes again. This time, his own were moist with tears.

"It's time for you to go, Buttercup. You must get back before it's too late."

Aislen knew not to protest, but could not stop her tears from spilling down her face.

He pulled her into his arms and gave her one last, long embrace. "I love you, Aislen. I always have." He kissed her on the forehead and pressed his finger on her chin. "Remember, I am always with you. Always just a breath away."

The glass dissolved around them, and Aislen began floating off the chrome surface, away from her father, drifting into space.

"I don't want to leave. Please let me stay here," she cried

out to him, though he was getting infinitely smaller and further away.

"You can come back at any time," she heard him say in her head. "You just have to remember."

She closed her eyes and continued to weep in the darkness. She stayed like that for a long time, floating in an abyss of grief and loss, until she felt numb.

"Wake up, Aislen," she heard. Thinking it might be her father, hoping that he had changed his mind, she opened her eyes. Instead, she was sprawled on her bedroom floor, her face soaked with tears, and he was nowhere to be found. Her heart ached afresh.

She lay there in a daze. Aislen shook her head, trying to figure out how she had ended up on the floor. And why was her face drenched with tears?

She realized she had been dreaming, but the details of it were fading fast. All she could remember were stars—billions of stars. And color, the most dazzling colors and shapes. And her father's face. She could see him still, too, just barely. He had told her something really important, but what was it? The vision was quickly beyond her recollection's reach.

There was a sharp knock at the door. "Wake up, Aislen!" her mother called. "Honey, open up—now!"

Aislen pushed herself to her feet, lightheaded and off balance, and stumbled to the door. Her mother's face was all worry. "Something's happened to Sergeant Mathis. He called me asking for help, then stopped talking. I called 911—they found him unconscious at his house and are taking him to the hospital. We have to go."

"Sergeant Mathis?" Aislen repeated, foggy. "What—how bad is it?"

"I don't know," her mother said. "I just need to get over there."

Protection. She remembered the word out of the blue—her father's promise from the dream. There would be people around to protect them. Suddenly, Aislen felt a pressing urge to get to Sergeant Mathis as quickly as possible, too.

She reached for her jacket and the room tilted.

"Mom, can you help me with this?" she asked, handing the coat over before she could topple.

"Of course." Her mother shrugged the jacket on, buttoning it the way she'd done since she was a little girl. At the last button, she paused, eyes widening. "Dear God, Aislen—what is this?"

Aislen followed her mother's hand to her throat, to a polished platinum labyrinth studded with nine bright jewels.

The cool of the metal and humming pulse against her skin finally registered. And with it came a single, undeniable truth—it wasn't a dream after all.

Aislen looked back up at her mom, remembering.

"It's a map."

FORTY-THREE

RAZE WAS SQUATTING in the dirt, looking at the empty plot where Mathis had just been, wondering if he had done enough, while Dookie was yelling like someone who'd been denied dessert his whole life.

"What the fuck did you just do?" Dookie yelled, flipping his visor up. The bug-eyes were all bluster; Raze felt the accusation like a punch to the ribs. "If you had just stayed out of it, Mathis would be having a massive coronary right now and dead by morning!"

Like the troll, Raziel also wondered what the fuck he had just done. Saving people wasn't in his wiring—least of all the ones who threatened his existence. If Mathis lived, he was going to be a problem, and Raze would only have himself to blame..

But who was this shit bag to point that out? Raze stood up and slowly turned to face the troll.

The tirade continued. "I don't get it. What were you thinking—saving his fat ass? You didn't do us any favors, that's for sure. Now he knows that Blake isn't really a killer, and worse, he's confirmed that your game isn't just a game." Dookie shook his head and expelled an angry gasp of air. "You royally fucked this up."

Raze was on the troll faster than a wolf snapping at an exposed throat. He yanked the collar with a rough jerk and lifted him until they were face to face.

"Look, runt," he snarled. "I don't know who the fuck you are, but you're in my territory. You don't tell me shit about what I do or how I do it.

"There are a lot of unknown players in this racket doing their fair share of fucking things up. Take you, for instance." He jabbed a finger into Dookie's chest. "Who gave you any authority to come in here? Who gave you permission to eliminate the sergeant? Not me—and I'm the only one who counts.

"You're going to tell me how you got my visors, how you know that police officer, and why the fuck you're even here. Or I'll kick your gnarly ass from here to eternity."

Dookie never flinched. "Here, here, Raziel. Let me clarify things for you." His dangling legs began elongating, stretching obscenely until two normal-sized feet, wearing a nice pair of leather loafers, planted themselves into the ash. The burlap sack Raze gripped in his fists crumbled between his fingertips, the molecules of the coarse brown fibers refashioning themselves into a pressed blue dress shirt.

Raze watched as the protruding eyes contracted back into Dookie's skull, his green tint paled into natural, human skin tones, and a perfectly tousled mop of golden brown hair sprouted from his head. In a matter of seconds, the ogre folded into a man: neat loafers, a thesis smile—Troy Kellen.

Raze released the shirt and stepped back. Stunned. Speechless. Of all things, he didn't see this one coming.

"Apparently, you know me already," Troy said, raising an eyebrow at him. "Stalking me, are you? Well, glad to finally meet you." The handsome therapist extended his hand toward Raze. Raze looked at it, then back up at Troy. He had no intention of shaking his hand. Troy dropped it, unperturbed.

"Mr. Parker was hoping we would be introduced properly, under different circumstances. Unfortunately, the situation took a turn for the worse, and an intervention was necessary."

Raze did his best to keep his confusion and his burgeoning rage hidden behind a stony expression.

"Mr. Parker has told me a lot about you, Raziel... none of it good, I might add."

"How do you know Grant?" Raze asked, his voice laden with derision.

"We've been working together for quite some time, actually. When I was writing my thesis on gaming addiction, I started playing *Demesne* as part of my research. Got pretty good at it, actually. You may remember me—as MUTEnt. Word is, *you're* the one who brought me to Mr. Parker's attention."

Raze did remember. Over a year ago, a player called MUTEnt rocketed through the octaves, breaking record after record. Per protocol, anyone who is that good got flagged for vetting. Promising subjects were groomed; duds were booted with a convenient terms-of-service violation.

MUTEnt had vanished, so Raze had assumed he was one of the rejects. Clearly, he'd been wrong. MUTEnt wasn't discarded—he'd been recruited. And now he was Grant's protégé.

"Mr. Parker may hate your fucking guts, Raziel," Troy said with a sly smile, "but he listened to you. We met under the guise of me becoming a consultant for the company, but he ended up having bigger plans for me."

Raze narrowed his eyes at Troy. "Bigger plans, huh? Such as?"

"Aw, I'm sorry," Troy said, his smile fading into a mocking pout. "That's classified."

Raze's blood rolled to a boil. Troy hadn't been around QGS or Infinium long enough to pass any training levels in the operative program. He hadn't shown any quantum awareness or used any techniques during Raze's viewings. Troy was 3-D all the way.

"What do you mean? Classified?" Raze asked. "How do you have clearance for something *I* don't? You couldn't even get into The Stratum without my visors."

Troy smirked. "I dunno. I'm thinking it may be because I have skills you lack, Raziel. Self-control, maybe? Consistency? Uhh... people skills? *Hello?*

"Not everything needs to be handled from your little ghost world." Troy flicked a dismissive hand at the surrounding city. "In the *real* world, I deliver results."

"I deliver *untraceable* results," Raze argued, hating himself for sounding defensive.

"Too bad for you, I happen to be delivering a lot more than you lately. And I've got *everyone* eating from the palm of my hand. Grant. The 8. And especially that sweet Aislen Walker."

Raze restrained the reflex to punch Troy in his pretty-boy mouth. He needed to keep it together long enough to figure out what kind of game Troy was playing and how much he really knew about Aislen.

"Who cares about her?" Raze said, throwing down a bluff. "She's nothing—a nobody."

Troy wasn't buying it. "You care. I have no doubts about that." Troy began to walk a slow circle around Raze, watching him with amusement.

"You've been a very bad boy, Raziel. You didn't tell anyone about her, did you? Grant? The 8? About how she slipped through all your so-called impenetrable defenses and showed up here the other night? Or about how Blake remembers her—and Sergeant Mathis is asking about her? Or about how Ichiban wants to find her? All of that would make you look bad. Real, *real* bad.

"So because they can't track you here and find you out, you withheld that juicy tidbit," Troy licked at his bottom lip and pulled it between his teeth. "And she is a juicy little tidbit, isn't she?"

Raze squeezed his hands into tight fists. A searing pain burned through his body as his muscles went rigid with restraint. He so wanted to rip the vile smirk off of Troy's face.

Troy stopped walking and leaned in toward Raze. "Well, thanks to that tasty morsel, I know all about it. I know she was here. I know she saw Parrish die. I know she saw *you*." Troy snickered.

"She keeps trying to convince herself it was all just a bad dream. But did you know she keeps having these so-called dreams? Dreams about her dear, ol', deadbeat daddy? His telling her she has a gift? Did you know about that, Raziel?"

Raze clenched his teeth together until he thought they would crack and swallowed the violent desire to kill this asswipe. He said nothing.

Troy continued circling him, talking to himself as much as to Raze. "Ichiban really has a jones for her, too, which is amazing. He's a corpse in every sense that matters. Yet she woke something in him. Care to guess why?" Troy stopped and looked at him.

Raze looked toward the space where Ichiban had last stood. "Do you know him?"

Troy feigned surprise. "Why, yes. I do. You don't?"

It killed Raze to have to admit that he did not. "I thought he was Grant, possessing Blake's consciousness so he could get in here because he can't do it himself."

"Grant!" Troy hollered and let out a loud hoot. "Hell, no! Mr. Parker is far too squeamish about killing people. He wouldn't want the blood of Scott Parrish on his hands!"

Raze wanted to kick his own ass for thinking that Grant was behind all this, but who else could it be?

"That guy, on the other hand," Troy pointed to where Ichiban had been, "is not squeamish about anything. Twisted fuck, that one is. In fact, if he wasn't Infinium's enemy numero uno, he'd be my hero."

Raze was astonished at Troy's sociopathic tendencies. He disguised it so well under his great looks and all that charisma—something Raze had never been able to do. "Who is he, then?" Raze asked. He knew of no enemies other than Preston Reed, and he knew Reed was not Ichiban.

"Sorry," Troy said with another condescending snarl. "That's classified."

Troy changed the subject. "So, Raziel, what's really going on here? What's going on with you? From what Grant has said, you are a ruthless, stone-cold killer. And don't tell him I said this, but I could get behind someone like you, over him, any day of the week. But from what I saw just now, I'm disappointed. Why did you stop me from killing the sergeant? And how come Blake isn't tits-up by now? And what's the deal with Aislen?"

Raze swallowed a hot retort and thought for a moment before answering him. Troy knew who Ichiban was, but not why he wanted Aislen. Raze knew who Aislen was and why everyone would want her. She was his ace.

As far as he could tell, Grant and The 8 didn't know about her yet. Raze needed to make sure *he* was the one to inform them before Troy figured it out and did it himself.

"It's really none of your business," Raze started. "But before you go and screw things up any further, I'll tell you. During the course of this project, I discovered something...

valuable information that The 8 will be extremely interested in. But I didn't want to take it to them until I was completely sure."

Raze faked a sigh of exasperation. "You have no idea how hard it has been—not eliminating these maggots as I would normally do. But I have to get a lock on this. It could be the biggest find of all time for The 8."

"Really?" Troy said, his interest piqued. "What is it?"

Raze mirrored Troy's pompous smirk right back at him. "That's classified."

Troy's demeanor blackened. He glared at Raze and stalked up to him until they were chest to chest.

"I suggest you get on that then," he seethed. "Figure it out—before I do. Because if Aislen has the answers, it won't take me but a shot of Scotch and a couple of come-hither twitches of my fingers, and she'll be moaning it to me as she's calling my name." Troy put two fingers in Raze's face and wiggled them.

"You won't get to her before I do," Raze hissed back, eyes narrowed. "I'm already there."

"Oh, that's right," Troy laughed and stepped away from Raze again. "You go ahead and do your thing. Stay in that little cage Grant and Infinium has you in and do what it is you do best: be the last resort. In the meantime, I'll be handling reality." Troy turned to walk away, but turned back to say one more thing.

"You know, Raziel, I pity you. You never get the pleasure of seducing your young, virginal targets—suckling their juices dry and then slitting their supple throats. It's so much more satisfying than your invisible mind-fuck.

"Hurry along now," he said, shooing Raze off with a flick of his fingers as he backed away. "Because if I give Grant and The 8 what they want before you do, you're going to need to find a place to hide."

Troy reached up, lifted the visors off the top of his head, and severed the frequency modulators from his brain.

∞

RAZE WATCHED HELPLESSLY as Troy began to evanesce from *Demesne*. His last threat was the final straw. The rage Raze had swallowed throughout their encounter reached its tipping point. He charged toward the disintegrating body, wanting to rip Troy apart, but grabbed hold of nothing but a billion splintered particles.

He bellowed, a roar so loud it rattled the glass in the towering skyscrapers that surrounded him—*like a cage,* he thought.

Troy was right. Raze was just a pawn on the board, pushed around by the unseen fingers of Grant and The 8. Their go-to boy when they couldn't handle something themselves, yet constantly under their thumbs.

It never bothered him before. He enjoyed what he did. He got off on using his ability to push people around, punishing them for all their stupidity—and cruelty—and sins. And he had everything he really wanted, didn't he? He'd been given every worldly possession. He had been living the dream.

Now he was waking up to the nightmare it actually was.

Fury rose up from deep in his belly like bile. Raze let out another long, primal scream that sent a powerful shockwave through the atmosphere of *Demesne*. Her buildings responded by spontaneously exploding, propelling razor-sharp shards of glass, brick, and mortar across the horizon faster than his eyes could entertain. The remaining foundations collapsed and melted into the earth.

As his creation atomized into nothingness, Raze was left alone, standing in the desert of The Stratum.

He had managed to destroy one prison only to find himself in another, incarcerated in a nesting box of hells, forever doomed to solitary confinement. He was more of a hostage than any of the maggots on Earth. At least they were blind to their bars. At least they had the illusion of freedom.

On the verge of madness, Raze roared again, spewing the wrath from his body. Fiery rays and molten orbs exploded from the palms of his hands with rabid ferocity. Raze hurled them in every direction, hell-bent on destroying The Stratum once and for all.

Soon, it was completely ablaze. Raze stood on a bubbling bed of lava, surrounded by a new cage of flames. He wished for the walls of the inferno to close in on him, to devour him. He longed to feel the blistering of his flesh and the incineration of his bones. But he could not. His form lay cool and safe within The Womb, while his phantom soul stood in Purgatory, unable to destroy itself.

Raze leaned his head back, raised his fists to the sky, and tried to scream again. Through the roar of his own destruction, he caught a ghost-note of her frequency—high, piercing, impossible to shut out. It cut deeper than fire, a reminder that she had already rewritten him.

Something cracked inside of him, and his wail came out a whimper. He had nothing left. Broken, he fell to his knees and dropped his head into his hands.

As a single drop of water fell and hit the liquid fire of the ground. The tiny puddle boiled in the lava, coagulating it to ash. He watched as another, and then another, fell to the flaming earth, dousing it back to its original state of dry, ochre dust.

Were those tears? The thought of it cracked something in him; shame rushed in faster than fury. Raze pounded his fists into the ground. He would not be broken, damn it! Damn Grant, and Troy, and The 8 to hell! Damn all of Infinium! And damn Aislen! She had ruined him; rearranged his circuitry, altered his frequencies, and brought him to his knees.

The sizzling grew louder as more and more droplets of water fell to the ground. Steam and smoke billowed up around him. Raze looked through the haze at the cool rain falling from The Stratum sky, baptizing his face and calming his rage. He reached up and wiped his cheeks, so relieved to realize they weren't tears, that he almost wept for real. Across the landscape, the massive flames surrendered to the gentle shower.

Through the veil of smoke, Raze noticed movement on the horizon. A shadowy outline of a man walking toward him through the dying firestorm.

What now? *Who could that possibly be?* Raze rose from the ground and gathered himself, ready to confront another possible threat.

You can't destroy this place, Raziel, he heard the man say telepathically. *At least not on your own. You're strong, but not strong enough.*

"Who are you?" Raze yelled at the figure across the desert.

There was no answer. The patter of the falling raindrops silenced, the heavy globules crystallizing into flakes as the stranger walked closer. Prisms caught the soft light and danced with color as they floated to the ground, icing on the charred earth a frosty white.

"You are on the wrong side of this," the blond stranger said when he finally stood before him. "You have been using your gifts for evil purposes for too long." The man's familiar green and gold eyes bored into him.

"Preston Reed," Raze said with a growl that was both awestruck and territorial.

"You allowed the circumstances of your life to turn you, and like a whipped dog, you became vicious, attempting to exact revenge on humanity for the wrongs of a few. You think you were made stronger by all this? You weren't. You were diminished by it."

"We've been looking for you."

"Is it really *we*, Raziel? I don't think so. *They* may be trying to find me, but trust me, they won't."

"You're here, aren't you? What's to say I don't seize your signature and start making you my mission in life?"

"Don't pull your bullshit with me. You don't think I've moved beyond that? I wouldn't be here talking to you if I thought you were capable of tracking me. You aren't. Give it up."

"Then why are you here?"

"Because I need you," Preston said. "To help Aislen."

"To help *Aislen*?" Raze was taken aback. "Why would I help her? She is responsible for the—"

"She's not responsible for anything," Preston interrupted. "There was no intent behind her actions. She has no understanding of how her abilities work or how strong they are. But she *needs* to understand. She needs to learn. And now that I am being actively hunted again, I can't get near her to teach her. Or protect her. I need you."

"You're out of your mind." Raze scoffed. "You think I am the one to teach and protect her?"

"I know you are."

Raze stopped laughing and stared at Preston. The man was serious.

"It isn't too late for you, Raziel. You can get on the right side of things. Aislen needs you. *I* need you to help her. At least get her out of harm's way, so she has a chance to discover and develop her gift."

"And why would I help her? Everything I know and am is barely hanging on by a thread. Why would I risk my life for her? That's what it would be, you know, if I got between Infinium and Aislen. *My life.*"

"I do know." Preston nodded his head solemnly. "But I also know that you are her only hope."

Raze had no words.

"It's not just Infinium that I am worried about. It is someone far worse."

"Someone worse than Infinium and The 8? That isn't possible."

"Oh, but it is. And if he gets his talons into Aislen, you will see just how much worse it can be. You don't want to see that, trust me."

"Who is he?"

"My grandfather—Sigmund Lange. The architect of Infinium."

Raziel went quiet—cold dread pooling behind his ribs—Sigmund's name a splinter at the base of his skull.

"Raze, you can continue selling your soul to the highest bidder and cling to your perceived power, or you can do the right thing for a change. It's up to you. But I need to know. What's it going to be? Stay a puppet, or be the man who stops his own maker?"

FORTY-FOUR

THEY SPED through the empty streets, Aislen and her mother, beneath the leafless trees that sat black and crooked against the midnight sky. The world outside passed by like she wasn't even a part of it. Her dream, although she could remember so little of it now, had felt more tangible, more real than actual reality did.

Aislen couldn't help but notice how tense her mother was. Her concern for Sergeant Mathis was apparent, but it was more than that. She obviously had feelings for him, and Aislen didn't know what to feel about that.

She'd always wished that her mother would try to find some happiness for herself—even a little romance—and although Mathis seemed like a nice enough guy, he'd been asking too many questions, trying to associate Aislen with Blake and the murder of his father. For all she knew, he wanted to have her arrested.

Now that Aislen knew that her father had been around, watching over them and loving them all these years, she realized she didn't want her mother moving on after all. She found herself carrying a small hope that one day her father would come back and they could try being a family.

Her fingers found the amulet at her throat. The smooth spiral hummed faintly beneath her touch, and she told herself it meant she was safe. Then—so soft she thought she imagined it—a melody threaded through the hush of the tires on asphalt.

"Do you hear that?" she asked her mom.

"Hear what?" her mom said, intensely focused on the road.

Aislen let go of the necklace and reached toward the radio to see if the volume was turned down too low. The music stopped, but the radio was already off.

She sat back in her seat, baffled. Strange. She could have sworn she had heard something.

They were nearing the hospital now. Aislen could tell by the sickly fluorescent aura it projected into the sky. She would normally feel completely at home in a hospital, but now she felt a flutter of anxiety in her chest. She unconsciously toyed with the pendant again. A barely perceptible vibration tickled her fingertip, and the lilting refrain serenaded her again. Calm immediately settled upon her.

She lifted her finger off the pendant, and the song stopped. She *was* hearing something. The music was coming from the amulet.

Aislen ran her finger around the spiral one more time and listened closely. As it circled the metal, the hauntingly sweet note played. When it brushed across one of the nine jewels, Aislen heard the faint chime of a bell. She placed a second finger in rotation, and another tone played in harmony with the first. It reminded her of the crystal wine goblets her mother would play at holiday dinners. Just by wetting the tip of a finger and brushing it lightly around the rim, a whole symphony would sing in their kitchen.

As Aislen's fingers circumnavigated the pendant, it played

its silvery lullaby. Not only did it give her a strong sense of security, but she felt as if it were speaking to her without words. She strained to hear what it had to say.

Her mother pulled into the hospital lot and parked near the ER entrance.

"If you don't mind, Mom, I'm just going to wait here in the car." As soon as the words passed across her lips, the charm let out a sour chord, falling out of tune. At the same time, a wave of nausea rolled through her. She winced, certain it meant she shouldn't argue with her mother.

"Oh, Aislen! Please come in with me. At least until I know Robert is all right. I don't want to face this alone."

Aislen was again surprised, as much by the intensity of her mother's emotion as she was by her calling the sergeant by his first name. She didn't understand why her mother seemed to care so much. The pendant in her fingers trembled and sang in tune again. A vision flashed through her mind—the memory of standing with her father surrounded by stars and galaxies.

"There will be other people there to help you, Aislen. I will make sure of that."

Her father's words were as crystal clear as a recording, embedded within the melody of the pendant. Could Sergeant Mathis really be someone he was talking about? The pendant pulsed against her fingers and fell silent. She took that as a yes.

"Okay," she told her mother, reluctantly releasing the pendant and getting out of the car to follow her into the hospital.

∞

SHE RECOGNIZED the man standing by the front desk right away. The detective was unshaven and looked like he was dressed in the same suit he had been wearing when she first met him at the A.R.C. two days ago. Her heart froze up a little, but the pendant remained still.

"I'm looking for Sergeant Mathis," her mother said to the nurse who was still making eyes at the detective.

"You must be Sabine," he said, turning toward her and extending his hand. "Detective Jackson. Bob has been asking for you non-stop since he was brought in—even tried to get one of us to go to your house and escort you two here."

"Sorry it took us so long," her mother said.

"Not a problem. Just glad you made it. It's a good thing you called dispatch and got him help as soon as you did. He may not have made it if we hadn't gotten to him on time. But it looks like he's going to be all right. Just a minor heart attack."

Detective Jackson turned his attention to Aislen. "Hello again, Miss Walker. Bob's been asking about you, too. He was hoping you'd get here before the medication knocked him out. He wanted to warn you about something."

"Warn me? About what?" This was not what she'd expected.

"Something happened to him tonight that shook him up pretty bad. At first, I thought it was the drugs talking. He kept babbling on and on about how the game is real and is convinced, of all things, that it was the video game that caused him to have a heart attack. It took a long time to get him to calm down."

"Yeah, he came to my house asking me about the game," Aislen said. "He told us he had gotten a copy of it and was playing it himself."

"Yeah, well," the detective said, rubbing his forehead as

though he wanted to erase something from his brain. "I'm not going to go into how he managed that. Let's just say Bob has done a lot for me over the years, and I'm gonna return the favor on this one.

"Bob kept saying the boy didn't know what he was doing when he shot his dad. Swore it wasn't really him. He wouldn't explain what he meant, just kept repeating it."

"That poor boy," her mom said.

"Yeah," Aislen said, remembering the confusion on the boy's face when he looked at her in the dream.

"Bob insisted you stay out of the game—and away from anyone tied to it."

She started to protest, but the pendant twitched against her skin, making her words falter.

"He says that you do. That you may not know them, but that they definitely know you."

The amulet tingled on her neck, then stilled itself again. She decided it was confirming the detective's words. Somehow, the game was connected to her dream. She didn't understand how that worked, but she knew it was true.

"Like I said," Jackson continued, "this could just be the meds talking. Lord knows, I hope it is. But he was dead serious about me passing on the message."

"Okay," Aislen said, somehow thankful that she had come into the hospital with her mother after all.

Detective Jackson straightened. "I gotta run—need to sign the release papers. They're transferring the boy to another facility tonight."

He started for the door just as the nurse came around to escort them back to Mathis, then stopped. "Oh shit—almost forgot." He glanced at Aislen. "I talked to your co-worker, Mr. Kellen. He said they could use your help tonight moving Blake."

Aislen felt the pendant snap to attention.

"He wants you to meet him at work. He said that he'll pick you up over there and you can drive with him to the A.R.C."

The necklace acted agitated, sparking against her skin. Aislen was confused. Was she or was she not supposed to go to the hospital? Was she or was she not supposed to meet Troy and help him move Blake? Her head was spinning with questions, and the pendant spun along with them.

Aislen looked at her mom, already holding the keys out. The gesture should have felt ordinary, but it landed with a weight she couldn't name. Maybe it was Mathis pulling her mom's focus—since when did she trust him this much? It hit Aislen that her mom had her own life, one Aislen clearly didn't know everything about.

And for a flicker of a heartbeat, taking the keys felt like more than borrowing the car—it felt like being handed the first step into something larger.

"Go ahead, Aislen. I'm good from here."

The pendant pulsed once—hard—then lay still, silent as stone. So it was okay to go? Her mom was safe with Sergeant Mathis?

"Are you sure?" Aislen asked about her mother and the pendant.

"I'm positive. You go help Mr. Kellen and that boy. They need you now, more than I do."

Then it surged again, faster, harder, almost dragging her toward the hospital doors. She swallowed against the pressure. Aislen finally understood what it was trying to tell her: her mom was safe, and it was okay for her to go to the hospital. She should get to Troy, she realized. Her father had told her there would be help, and she clung to that now. The pendant had to mean Troy—that he was the one she'd been promised.

She took the keys from her mom, gave her a quick kiss on

the cheek, and ran out the door toward Troy. The pendant left her no choice.

FORTY-FIVE

AISLEN DROVE like a demon through the city streets toward Chrysalis, the pendant wailing like a siren around her neck. "Hurry, hurry," she imagined it saying, but she was going as fast as she could.

She knew now how important Troy was. She understood. He was there to help her. It had been obvious all along, and she felt ridiculous for not realizing it sooner.

He had taken an interest in her from the beginning, had rescued her after she drank too much, but most importantly, he had listened. When her dreams left her shaken, he didn't laugh —he helped her make sense of them. That alone made him feel like a guardian angel. Like her dad, but actually here.

The charm at her throat screamed again.

"I'm going as fast as I can!" She yelled back, pushing the pedal to the floor and whipping down the street toward the facility. Her head was spinning, her stomach felt ill, and the closer she got to the building, the worse the vertigo became.

"I'm almost there," she told the pendant, wishing it would ease up on her.

She drove into the lot, scanning it for Troy's Mustang, but it wasn't there. The necklace fell silent, and she immediately felt calm and safe. She was in the right place. She was positive about that.

"I'll just go inside and wait for him," she told the pendant, and it responded by pricking her throat.

"Calm down! He'll be here soon. It's warmer inside."

She got out of the car and let herself into the back door of the facility with her key card. If Troy was going to come get her, he would look for her in the geriatric ward, so she made her way down the maze of long hallways, letting herself in through each of the locked doors. The pendant zapped her again, and her stomach lurched.

That was it! She had listened to the necklace and had done what it had told her. She was here now! It had to leave her alone before it made her vomit! She yanked it off her neck and slipped it into her jeans pocket. The howling stopped, and she immediately felt better. She sighed with relief.

She went to the nurse's station, but no one was there. They must be doing their midnight rounds, Aislen thought, and continued to wander around the ward.

The lighting had been lowered so the residents could sleep better. The hallways were dusky, the walls a ghastly shade of gray. Her path was lit by the blue night-lights that lined the walls, and her silhouette cast long and high behind her like a grim shadow puppet.

Heavy sighs and muffled snores of sleeping patients whispered from the rooms as she passed. Even in her sleep, Mrs. Crowley could be heard incoherently arguing with the voices in her head. A grunt issued from Mr. Spencer as he tried to get comfortable in his bed.

Aislen peeked into the dark rooms, looking for any sign of a charge nurse or an aide who could tell her if they had heard anything from Troy.

"Aaaaash-lyyynnnn." She heard the crooked voice call softly from room number 11.

It was Mr. Lange. How did he know she was out here? She peeked into his room. He was not in bed as he should be. He was still sitting in his wheelchair next to the window. The moonlight made the white of his hair glow in the dark.

"Aaaash-lyyyynnn, come here, my little poppet."

The old man was looking down at his hands, watching them intently as he computed his strange arithmetic, tapping his fingers against each other in a rapid, repetitive sequence. She stepped through the doorway. She felt the necklace awaken in her pocket.

"Ah, there you are," he said without looking up, the gravel of eons rasping in his throat. "I've been waiting for you."

"Uh, Mr. Lange, you shouldn't be awake at this hour. You should probably be in bed by now, don't you think?"

Mr. Lange looked up from his hands and focused his rheumy blue eyes on her.

"Come to Papa, Ashlyn, so I can get a better look at you."

The hackles rose up on her back, and she scoffed at her silliness. Sure, Mr. Lange was creepy as hell, but he was old and feeble. He couldn't hurt her.

The pendant trembled.

"I'm sorry, Mr. Lange. I think you are confused," she said as she made her way toward him. "My name is Aislen, and I am not your daughter."

"I am not confused, dear one," he squinted up at her. "*You* are."

Poor ol' guy, she thought to herself. She would hate to end up like this, with a brain so addled by dementia you couldn't keep your own memories straight.

"I'm sorry, Mr. Lange. But I think you really should be in bed now, getting some sleep. Do you need some help getting into bed?" She moved to the wheelchair to help him to his bed.

"I don't need sleep to dream, sweet girl." His fingers stopped twitching. "I only need you." He reached a frail, wrinkled hand up and grabbed hold of her wrist.

Startled, Aislen tried to pull her arm away, but his grip was strong, too strong for his age. His yellowing fingernails bit into her skin.

"Now come here like I asked," the old man screeched. He struck her across the ear, hard enough to make it ring, then twisted his gnarled fingers into her hair, wrenching her head down.

"I don't take no for an answer," he growled. "Your daddy and your granddaddy may have gotten away with it, but I'll be goddamned if you are."

Aislen tried to scream, but her neck was bent at too harsh an angle. She could only emit a weak gurgle. She could feel the pendant burning hot against her hip.

"I will have you, little girl." His words came out on a wet breath, his spittle splattered on her neck. "You will be the one to take me to the places I need to go, you hear? You will be the one to free me from this rotting body. Do you understand?"

Aislen choked on another scream and tried to wriggle herself free, but he pinned her to him in a tight embrace.

"Reelaaax," he wheezed. "You want to help your bloodline, now don't you?" He jerked her face toward his, pressing his forehead against her brow. She could smell his rancid breath. "Of course you do. Now, *let me in*."

An icy surge of energy prodded Aislen between her eyes, scratching to get into her skull. Cold tendrils worked their way into her brain, and her body went weak. It was as if the old man was trying to climb inside her head.

A violent shudder of revulsion racked her body, and with a sudden burst of strength, Aislen jerked away, pulling him out of the wheelchair. He yanked a chunk of her hair from her scalp as they both fell to the floor—she on her back, Mr. Lange on top of her. She scrambled, clawing at the slick linoleum until she was able to wrench free and get her feet underneath her. She stumbled for the door and out into the hall.

Mr. Lange made a weak attempt to crawl after her, slithering on his belly with his legs dead weight behind him.

"You can run, but you can't hide." His voice cackled in stereo, more inside of her head than it did from the room.

She ran as fast as her shaky legs would let her, down the halls and back through all the doorways she'd come through. She passed a bay of windows that looked out on the parking lot and saw the white headlights of Troy's Mustang pulling into the driveway.

"Thank God!" she heard herself say.

The pendant in her pocket electrified again, and her legs faltered. She fought the paralysis and pushed through the back doors of the hospital. The cold, winter air hit her like a wall. She tried to push through it, but it was thick and sludgy, and her feet felt slow. It was like being in a nightmare, unable to run. She fought with all of her might to move forward, but could only treadmill in one place. Her mind raged with anger and confusion. Troy was right there, her friend, her guardian angel, the reason the pendant had led her here. Why was it fighting her now?

Aislen saw the pulsing, red glow of Troy's brake lights on the far side of the lot and was invigorated. With renewed stamina, she broke free, trying to sprint for him. But as soon as she leapt forward, two arms seized her from behind and yanked her backwards. A hand clamped down hard across her mouth, sealing it with a wide band of sticky tape, forcing her to swallow another scream. Tight arms encircled her waist, pinned her arms to her sides, and lifted her off the ground. She was jerked in the opposite direction of where Troy was parked.

Aislen watched as Troy got out of the car. For one breathless second, relief flared so bright it hurt—Troy was here, he would see her, save her. But the joy curdled into despair as she felt herself yanked backward, his figure shrinking instead of drawing closer.

She let out a guttural moan for help, but he was too far away to hear. As she was pulled around the far corner of the building, he vanished from her sight, and the pendant in her pocket went deathly cold.

The shock of the amulet's sudden silence was even more terrifying than what was happening to her. Even as she was lifted and spun around like she weighed nothing at all, then shoved into the leather seat of a car so hard it knocked the wind out of her, all Aislen could think about was the pendant.

It had led her here. She was supposed to be here, but then it kept her from Troy, and now it was mute. Had she been wrong all along? Every signal, every sting and whisper—she thought she was following a path, but maybe she'd only been fooling herself. Maybe she couldn't trust her own instincts at all.

There was another flurry of movement as she was restrained in the seat, unable to move, barely able to breathe. Then his face appeared, so close all she could see were the glacier ice blue of his eyes and a shock of raven-black hair. He looked so deeply into her eyes that Aislen felt her soul freeze. She knew that face—the soldier from her nightmare.

"You're coming with me," he said.

The amulet remained silent.

She watched as the soldier slid into the driver's seat and started the car's engine. As she struggled to move just one finger of her shrink-wrapped body in an attempt to free herself, another feeling overwhelmed her, a horrible sinking realization.

This was not a dream.

EPILOGUE

HE LAY face down on the cold, hospital tile, the odors of pine and urine stinging in his nostrils, his cheek in a smear of drool, the front of his pants damp with shame. He had used every last ounce of his strength to pounce on the girl.

He hoped it had been enough.

The muted click of hard rubber tapped its way down the hall. He was ready to be lifted off the floor, but it didn't sound like the squishy footfall of the night charge nurse. The tapping continued until it reached his door, then it entered the room.

"Well, well, well. What do we have here?"

A chill passed over him where the man's shadow fell across his crippled body, and a sharp toe jabbed his shoulder several times.

"Looks like you really are the slug they always said you were."

Two rough hands dug into his shoulders, picked him off the floor, and tossed him into his wheelchair. It rolled backwards into the wall, bounced off, and inched forward again.

The hospital therapist, and Sigmund's personal prison

guard, pressed his foot against the wheel to stop the chair. Troy Kellen bent over and got into his face.

"Mr. Lange, do not think for one second that I do not know what you have been up to. Just what is it you are trying to accomplish? Are you trying to escape? You really think that is going to work? You're pathetic."

Troy reached out and grabbed Sigmund by the throat, squeezing his Adam's apple until Sigmund thought it would pop.

"My only job is keeping you on a leash. Don't test me. You'd better get it through that numb skull The 8 hollowed out for you—you are no longer Number One. You hear me, *Ichiban*? You'd better, or I will happily extinguish what life you have left.

Troy shoved Sigmund back into the wall, straightened, and cracked his neck.

"Now to find that girl you want so bad. And figure out why."

Troy turned on his heel and resumed his clicking back down the hall.

"Well, hello there!" Sigmund heard Troy say with a voice as sensuous as silk. "You're Leslie, right? You wouldn't have happened to see Aislen Walker around here tonight by any chance, would you?"

Sigmund scurried his thoughts back into a far recess of his brain and went back to tapping mudras on his fingers.

He hoped he'd gotten a good enough grip on Aislen. He was ready to escape his broken body—ready to let it die. But he needed to inhabit Aislen's body first. Blake was not a reliable host. But Aislen? She was perfect—young, vital, and a genetic match. The 8 would never see her coming.

In her blood, he would reclaim his throne.

SIGNATURE FREQUENCIES

"Music is a basic tool for activating the brain centers, especially the lobes that house memory and recognition."

We use music as a gateway to our memories and to our emotions. Below, I have provided links to music that helped me tap into the Signature Frequencies of the characters and relationships in Dream Walker. Feel free to practice "tapping in" through Spotify.

Enter at your own risk.

https://open.spotify.com/playlist/7toc9w9CoMBCqrBt
HxDaYR?si=642a224e1b974515

<u>AISLEN</u>

Starry Eyed ~ Ellie Golding

Glittering Clouds (Locusts) ~ Imogen Heap

In the Waiting Line ~ Zero 7

Don't Wake Me Up ~ The Hush Sound

<u>RAZE</u>

The Game ~ Disturbed

Narcissistic Cannibal ∼ Korn
Become the Bull ∼ Atreyu
Monster ∼ Skillet
No One Knows ∼ Queens of the Stone Age
Let Me In ∼ The Unseen Guest

MATHIS

My Heart Is Lost To You ∼ Brooks and Dunn
You Don't Know How It Feels ∼ Tom Petty
The Waiting ∼ Tom Petty & The Heartbreakers
Caught Up in You ∼ 38 Special

BLAKE

What I've Done ∼ Linkin Park
Devil On My Shoulder ∼ Billy Talent

TROY

Sky ∼ Joshua Radin
I Put A Spell On You ∼ Creedence Clearwater Revival

PRESTON & SABINE

Sway ∼ The Perishers
Trouble Sleeping ∼ The Perishers
My Heart ∼ The Perishers

AISLEN & PRESTON

Never Alone ∼ Barlow Girl

Q3

Video Game ∼ Lana Del Rey
Knights of Cydonia ∼ String Tribute

DEMESNE - The Game

Ghosts N Stuff ~ Deadmau5
Scary Monsters and Nice Sprites ~ Skrillex
Kill EVERYBODY ~ Skrillex
Killer (William Orbit Mix) ~ Seal

IN THE CLUB

Bubblin' In The Cut ~ Boreta
The Matrix ~ Bassnectar
Teleport Massive ~ Bassnectar

THE WOMB

FUSE ~ Hudson Mohawke

YOUR TURN NOW

SLEEP TO DREAM

Dream Weaver ~ Gary Wright
Breathe ~ Telepopmusik

THE DREAM REALITY

Enjoy the Silence ~ Depeche Mode
Across The Universe ~ Rufus Wainwright
Hymn for the Weekend ~ Cold Play
Where Is My Mind? ~ Pixies
4th Dimensional Transition ~ MGMT
Drive ~ Incubus

Dear Dream Walker,

Thank you so much for stepping into the beginning of this journey with me. I hope *Dream Walker* pulled you into Aislen's, Raziel's, and Mathis' worlds and left you eager for more.

The story continues in **Episode 2: *Time Walker*** — available now.

And I'm thrilled to share that the next two volumes, ***The Book of Raziel* and *World Walker,*** will both be released in **January 2025**.

If you'd like to be the first to know about new releases, sneak peeks, and free offers, please visit:

www.ShannanSinclair.com

Your support means everything. If you enjoyed *Dream Walker*, leaving even a short review helps new readers discover the series — and I truly love hearing your thoughts.

With gratitude,

Shannan Sinclair

ACKNOWLEDGMENTS

The writing of a book can be lonely work, but its crafting takes a team. I am indebted to the following individuals:

Dad & Diana ~ for believing in me as a writer and a messenger and for hounding me to get back to writing this book after I set it aside for too long.

Kelsea and Mattéa Overstreet ~ the two most kick-ass kids a mother could ask for.

Renea Dawes ~ your laughter and enjoyment of my first drafts encouraged me to continue.

www.ingramcontent.com/pod-product-compliance
Lightning Source LLC
Chambersburg PA
CBHW030517120726
47904CB00005B/1507